A GALAXY UNKNOWN

AGAINST ALL ODDS

Book 7

BY

THOMAS DEPRIMA

Vinnia Publishing - U.S.A.

Against All Odds

A Galaxy Unknown series – Book 7
Copyright ©2005, 2012 by Thomas J. DePrima

ISBN-10 : **1619310147**

ISBN-13 : **978-1-61931-014-8**

1st Edition

Amazon Distribution

Cover art by: Martin J. Cannon

Appendices containing political and technical data highly pertinent to this series are included at the back of this book.

To contact the author, or see information about his other novels, visit:

http://www.deprima.com

Acknowledgements

Creating a series like this would be impossible without support from many people. Encouragement from my good friend Ted King kept me writing new episodes during the years when I sought an agent or publisher, while his technical expertise kept me focused on making the science sound believable even when it was simply a product of my imagination. Invaluable suggestions and proofreading by Michael A. Norcutt greatly facilitated my efforts to keep elements of the story consistent with Navy ship design and military protocols. Beta readers James Richardson and Adam Shelley have helped keep the details straight and in concert with previous books while improving the grammar of the final draft. Finally, much of the grammatical accuracy is owed to Myra Shelley for her outstanding copy editing work. Thank you all.

This series of novels includes:

A Galaxy Unknown...

A Galaxy Unknown
Valor at Vauzlee
The Clones of Mawcett
Trader Vyx
Milor!
Castle Vroman
Against All Odds
Return to Dakistee

Other series and novels by the author:

AGU: Border Patrol...

Citizen X

When The Spirit...

When The Spirit Moves You
When The Spirit Calls

A World Without Secrets

Table of Contents

Chapter One
~ September 12th, 2281 ~

"Suicide!" Minister of Intelligence Vertap Aloyandro said fervently after viewing the vid message received from the Uthlaro Prime Minster. Because it was rare for him to display personal emotion in front of his King, he then closed his eyes and shook his head sadly, both because he had let his emotion show and because he had witnessed something that might destroy them all.

"Suicide?" King Jamolendre, the monarch of all Hudeera, echoed in surprise. "I asked for your most *positive* assessment, Vertap."

"And I have given it to you, my King. Our recent military actions have allowed us to regain significant territory lost to the Milori over time. No longer are we restricted to travel within our own solar system. But this endeavor, rooted in avarice, will certainly result in our ruination. This proposed pact will be our undoing; it is tantamount to— suicide."

"Lord Melendret and the noblemen loyal to him favor the pact. They hold great influence among the other nobles."

"Your Highness, we both know they are drunk with power. They saw our massed military attacks on sparsely populated and lightly defended Milori outposts as great victories, although they were nothing more than lightning raids against an enemy whose reduced resources were stretched far too thin to properly protect its vast territory. When the Milori withdrew their forces, deserting all forward positions along our border, it was to marshal those units in defense of their home world against attacks by Galactic Alliance warships. The nobles foolishly looked upon the withdrawal as a magnificent triumph by *our* forces. Our nobles have deluded themselves into believing we somehow *drove* the Milori out."

The king stood, stretched his six-foot, ten-inch frame, and stepped from behind his desk. As he silently circled the enormous office in his royal palace, his scaly, mottled, greenish-brown skin shone brightly, absorbing welcome warmth from the bright daylight streaming in through the windows. With the three fingers and opposing thumb of his left hand tightly gripping his right hand behind his back, his glance never left the embellished, hand-woven carpet beneath his feet as he passed elaborate sculptures and the magnificent paintings that lined the walls. On the third pass, he stopped near the seating that surrounded a large circular fireplace occupying the center of the room and dropped heavily into his favorite chair. The massive, thickly padded piece of furniture covered in a red, velvet-like fabric had been made to his specifications and body contours and included the normal rear cutout for the short reptilian tail all Hudeera males had. He often light-heartedly referred to this chair as his *seat of power* and always enjoyed its wonderful comfort while he presided over the frequent, informal meetings with the rich and powerful noblemen of the ruling class.

"If signed by all parties," Jamolendre said, "this pact would combine the military might of four interstellar powers. We know the Galactic Alliance is more powerful than our own meager forces, but surely even *they* can't stand against the combined might of all four nations."

The Minister of Intelligence moved nearer his Sovereign but didn't presume to occupy any of the empty chairs without an invitation to sit. "My King, I'm not prepared to agree with that assessment. Admiral Carver has a deserved reputation for defeating enemies who underestimate her abilities and resources. As the senior-ranking officer of Space Command in the former Milori territory, which they now refer to as Region Two of the Galactic Alliance, she would be the one to direct the action against any incursion. We would be pitting our

2

forces against hers. I can't imagine a more dangerous opponent."

"The Galactic Alliance apparently believes they're entitled to annex all of the territory formerly claimed by the Empire simply because they conquered the Milori. How can they possibly control an area that large when they didn't have enough warships to cover Galactic Alliance territory *before* it was tripled in size?"

"It has long been an accepted reality of war that to the victor belong the spoils, my King."

"I don't deny that the Milori, bent on conquest of the galaxy, invaded Galactic Alliance territory on two separate occasions, but our noblemen don't feel that one small fact entitles the Galactic Alliance to *all* the territory of the former Empire. We suffered at the hands of the Milori for generations, and we are entitled to a share of the conquered territory."

"That the Milori twice invaded the Galactic Alliance is not what concerns me, Sire. It's the fact that Space Command twice defeated the Milori invaders handily. And they *did* promptly return the former Gondusan and Hudeera territories taken by the Milori during our decades of hostilities, as was agreed before we commenced our raids against the Empire's border positions. They promised nothing else."

"*We* took our former territories back ourselves, Vertap— although the actions of Space Command against the Milori certainly helped make it possible by drawing off the forces protecting the border."

"My King, this proposed pact calls for the entire area annexed by the Galactic Alliance to be divided equally among the four signatories; that's considerably more than a *share* of the conquered territory. The Galactic Alliance isn't being asked to share; they're being ordered to get out. They won't leave without a fight."

"Their presence is no longer needed here, or wanted. With the Milori defeated and beyond any hope of ever resurrecting their forces, this part of the galaxy rightfully belongs to those who suffered for so long."

3

"The Uthlaro and Tsgardi never suffered under the Milori, your Majesty; they were active trading partners at all times and benefited greatly from their association. Do you feel this entitles them to half of the conquered empire?"

"They're included in the pact because we need their ships," Jamolendre said angrily. "Like the Gondusan territory and ours, their realms border the former Milori Empire and neither has any particular love for the Galactic Alliance."

"And what of the Ruwalch Confederacy? They share a significant common border with the former Milori Empire as well."

"The Ruwalchu are too far away to be of consequence. Their border with the Milori Empire territory is over two hundred parsecs from their home systems, and they rarely travel this far out. I've always been amazed the Milori didn't lay claim to part of their territory decades ago."

"The distance might have had something to do with it— and the Milori *were* preoccupied with us and the Gondusans. But perhaps the real reason is the Milori feared them. My agents have reported that the technology of the Ruwalchu is far superior to our own, or that of their other neighbors."

"We asked them for assistance when the Milori were driving us from our territory, but they refused to become involved unless the Milori invaded their space. I'll be damned if I'll see them benefit in any way from this accord!"

"Yes, my King. Have I understood correctly that this pact was first proposed by the Uthlaro?"

"That's right. They have the longest common border with the newly annexed Galactic Alliance territory, and they fear their Dominion will be targeted next if the GA isn't stopped and pushed back inside their former borders."

"That's a preposterous position. The Galactic Alliance has never exhibited unprovoked aggression towards any of its neighbors. For many decades it has shared common borders with three nations— three nations far less capable of defending themselves than the Milori— but it never coveted its neighbor's space. It only responded to an invasion of its territory by the Milori. And it even went so far as to allow a battered Milori invasion fleet to leave GA space after being defeated the first time. If the Milori hadn't invaded a second time, the Galactic Alliance would not have had to attack the Milori home system. Annexation became a necessity after the second defeat to ensure the Milori threat was gone forever. The Uthlaro are using fear of invasion as an excuse to expand their own territory and want to use us to help them accomplish their goals."

"Perhaps, but our own nobles won't be restrained from moving into the annexed territory to acquire new systems, and they believe the might of our combined forces will leave Space Command with no option but to quit the space."

"We've twice witnessed how Space Command responds to invasion fleets that threaten their territory, my King. I fear that any incursion will bring a dire calamity unforeseen by Lord Melendret and his supporters. I rather doubt Space Command will be as generous with us as they were with the Milori. After all, the Milori were declared adversaries all along, while we were allies. Are we prepared to have all our territory annexed by the Galactic Alliance should we declare war and be defeated?"

The king remained quiet for several moments and then responded, "We shall have to make sure it doesn't come to that."

"There's one more consideration, my King. The Uthlaro claim they wish our participation so we appear to have a united front. They no doubt appeal on that issue because our small fleet will add little to the combined forces arraying against the Galactic Alliance. Should our forces be destroyed in this campaign, who is to protect us from invasion by our Uthlaro 'allies?'"

The king was silent for several minutes and the Minister of Intelligence began to wonder if he should quietly depart. He was about to declare his departure when the king suddenly said in a more subdued and weary voice, "Vertap, I share your concerns, but I'm caught up in something I'm powerless to control. I don't wish to join this pact with the Uthlaro, but the nobles led by Lord Melendret have sufficient support to ensure we will. If I oppose too strongly, my power base will be so eroded that I'll be nothing more than a figurehead— a figurehead ripe for removal. It's an open secret that Melendret covets my crown. I can't let that fool depose me. I *must* sanction the Uthlaro plan."

"I understand my King," the Minister of Intelligence said solemnly.

* * *

"And we are meant to believe this union will somehow benefit the kingdom?" First Warlord Kalisnacos asked angrily as he stood in front of his chair in the large circular building that was home to the Tsgardi War Council.

A warlike alien race that bore a striking resemblance to tall, upright Terran baboons, the Tsgardi were only space travelers by virtue of having enslaved an expedition of peaceful travelers to their planet. They forced their visitors to bring them to Flordara, where they brutally and quickly subjugated the entire race. Under threat of death, the Flordaryns began making spaceships for the Tsgardi, a species whose lack of intellectual acuity ensured they would never be capable of producing their own.

"Our ships are no match for those of Space Command," Kalisnacos continued, his short, thick grey fur bristling. "Their ships are faster and their hull plating far superior. Our Flordaryn slaves have made no improvements in our technology since we conquered them, while Space Command continues to improve their fleet with every new class of ships. Is our role in this endeavor to be nothing more than to act as cannon fodder?"

"The Uthlaro are promising to share their technology with us if we become signatories," Premier Warlord Qerdesqa said. "Our participation will bring Light-375 speed to every ship in our fleet."

"That's a lie," Kalisnacos said. "The Uthlaro have never exceeded Light-262. They promise what they can't deliver."

"Light-262 capability was the most they would allow their shipyards to sell to anyone other than their own military," Qerdesqa said. "Their own ships have had Light-375 capability for some years. They also promise to help us improve our hull plating by providing Tritanium, for a price."

"Light-375 will make us faster than most of the ships in Space Command," First Warlord Ramdesci said, standing to deliver his comment. "And if we could strengthen our hulls, we would at last be able to face them on an equal footing."

"And when are these marvelous improvements to be made?" Kalisnacos asked. "The Uthlaro want to start this offensive immediately. It will take many years to replace the outer hull plating on every one of our three hundred warships, and perhaps just as long to improve our engine speed once we have the knowledge."

"As soon as Space Command is driven out of the new territory, the Uthlaro will help us begin to upgrade our ships," First Warlord Ramdesci said. "It will be worth the wait to become the equal of Space Command."

"We believed the Milori to be far superior to Space Command," Kalisnacos said, "and we've seen what happened to them. Space Command destroyed their fleet with ease and then laid waste to their home world when Maxxiloth still refused to surrender. The same could happen to us."

"The Milori invaded Galactic Alliance space," Ramdesci said.

"And how would our actions be any different?" Kalisnacos asked rhetorically. "The Galactic Alliance laid claim to all of the territory belonging to the Milori at the time the Milori surrendered to them unconditionally, although they allowed the Gondusans and Hudeera to reclaim the space taken by the Milori since Maxxiloth's great-grandfather first began to expand their borders into the domains of other nations."

"With the combined might of the four members of this pact," Ramdesci said, "Space Command won't stand a chance. Most of their ships are hundreds of light-years away, while ours are already gathered at key defensive outposts along our border. They can be made ready to cross into Region Two within a week. The Uthlaro have promised more than six hundred ships to this effort. We have three hundred ourselves. The Gondusans would add more than seventy and the Hudeera have more than thirty. That's a thousand ships. Space Command has only about four hundred warships total, and most of them would have to remain behind to defend their original territory."

"The Uthlaro don't have six hundred warships," Kalisnacos said loudly. "Our spies report they have only about three hundred, at most. They have a few dozen battleships and cruisers, an equal number of frigates, and the rest are destroyers. It's an impressive fleet to be sure when compared to the Gondusan or Hudeera forces but not so impressive when compared to that of Space Command."

"The Uthlaro had three hundred decommissioned ships when the Milori first began their invasion of the Galactic Alliance. They immediately began to retrofit those ships and move them to the Milori border lest Maxxiloth's aspirations include plans to absorb Uthlaro space as well. Although the older ships are a little slower and have less hull protection than their current fleet, they represent a formidable force. We estimate that Space Command can't commit more than two hundred ships at most," Qerdesqa said. "We'll have them outnumbered by five to one."

"Carver destroyed a Milori fleet of a hundred three warships with just fifteen SC ships," Kalisnacos said, "and then destroyed almost four hundred more of Milori's newest and most powerful warships with her fleet of a hundred sixty-two, all without losing a single ship of her own in either engagement. She's the new military commander of the annexed territory."

"Ah, but the Milori foolishly attacked Carver's ships in one large armada, twice," Ramdesci said. "The Uthlaro plan will have us spread out along the borders, simultaneously absorbing the territory as we move towards a central point. Carver will have to split her forces into numerous small battle groups to confront all of ours. Since she can't be in dozens of places at the same time, she won't be able to direct the actions of her ships in battle. We'll have destroyed most of her forces before she even learns of the attacks."

"I ask that the matter be put to a vote," Premier Warlord Qerdesqa said to the council. "All who agree that we accept the terms of the pact, stand up as your name is called."

As the roll was called, the member either rose to stand or remained seated. Only First Warlord Kalisnacos and two others of the eighty-six members were still sitting when the vote was over.

"The matter is settled," Premier Warlord Qerdesqa said. "We shall join the Uthlaro in driving out the invaders of the former Milori Empire. We shall deploy our forces and seize all systems in our path until we meet our allies coming from the opposite direction. Long live the Tsgardi Kingdom."

* * *

"How can this body even *consider* making war against such a powerful neighbor?" Senator Prime Curlekurt Emmeticus asked, addressing the Gondusan planetary senate. "We were unable to beat the Milori in a single battle, yet the Galactic Alliance destroyed their massive invasion fleets without losing a single ship."

"We have only their word for that," Senator Neodeet Literamus said loudly. "For all we know they might have lost hundreds."

Externally one of the most human-looking alien species yet encountered, the Gondusan's most obvious difference was their nose. Two pieces of cartilage covered by skin extended down each side of a single nostril, rather than a single piece of cartilage in the center of two

9

nostrils. The Gondusans always carried their fashion to excess, and the more powerful the person, the more excessive the fashion. Their garish costumes and use of gaudy makeup made them look like an overdressed Mardi Gras celebrant on Earth.

"The Galactic Alliance is an open society," Senator Prime Curlekurt Emmeticus retorted. "They allow anyone to travel freely in their space, even Tsgardi, as long as the travelers respect their laws. They have gone so far as to allow news reporters in a free press to travel on warships during military operations. Our intelligence service tells us the news reports were completely accurate. They were outnumbered seven to one in their initial encounter with the Milori fleet during the first invasion, and all ships were required to make substantial repairs afterwards. But following the second invasion where they were outnumbered only three to one, virtually every ship at Stewart Space Command Base was back in service within a few days of having destroyed a Milori invasion fleet of more than four hundred warships. We closely examined a video file broadcast by news services following the battle at Stewart. Our experts certify that it was un-doctored. Two ships, the most seriously damaged, were back in service within a month. Does my esteemed colleague honestly believe we can hope to defeat a powerful military like that?"

"We don't have to defeat them," Literamus said. "We merely have to drive them out of the former Milori territories and then pursue a peace agreement. The Uthlaro promise that the combined forces allied against Space Command will be comprised of over a thousand ships. Space Command will never even engage our ships. They'll be too busy running back to their old border."

"I believe you underestimate their resolve, Senator. They laid formal claim to the Milori Empire when the Milori surrendered, so this act would now be treated as an invasion of *their* territory. Everything we know about them indicates they will not run. They will stay and fight, to the last ship, to the last crewman if necessary. They are every bit as tenacious as the Milori and, when crossed, far more dangerous."

"The most powerful ships in their fleet are still at Stewart Space Command Base, more than two thousand light-years from our borders. A large force can't be assembled and moved here in fewer than eight of their years. This war will be over long before then and we will have a large share of the newly commandeered territory. The arriving Space Command ships will find they have no bases in the new territory from which to launch a campaign. Now is the time to strike, before they have time to expand into the new territory."

"The ships that destroyed the Milori had no bases in the Empire, yet it didn't stop them from laying waste to the Milori home world."

"After the Milori invasion fleet was destroyed, the home world was left practically defenseless. Maxxiloth was a fool to send his entire home world protection force to the borders to fight us and the Hudeera."

"That was Admiral Carver's plan. She used us to draw off his remaining forces, giving her an opportunity to destroy his infrastructure."

"Yes, that's exactly my point! Without us, she would not have been able to destroy the Milori! And how does she repay us? She declared possession of the entire Empire in the name of the Galactic Alliance and didn't allocate even a single system to us."

"Not true. It might have made her task more onerous, but I'm sure she would have prevailed even without our help. And though it seems to have escaped my esteemed colleague's attention, for our participation we regained all the territory the Milori had systematically stolen from us over decades of war. That was all Carver promised in exchange for staging a few lightning raids against border outposts. We lost no ships and quadrupled our territory."

"We were only taking back what was ours to begin with."

The battle of words raged on between the two senators for some time, with neither willing to concede to the other's point. The other senators listened attentively and quietly until the two tired of the verbal fencing.

* * *

"It is all arranged," Uthlaro Prime Minster Taomolu Barguado said to the Council of Ministers. "The Tsgardi, Gondusans, and Hudeera will join us in this endeavor."

Barely anthropomorphous in appearance, the Uthlaro had a very distinctive appearance. Their heads, shaped like the letter 'T,' were reminiscent of a Terran hammerhead shark because the eyes were located at the ends of the crosspiece. This gave them the ability to see more than three hundred degrees around their body without moving their heads. The mouth, located at the bottom of the head, was only used for eating and speaking. They breathed though pores in their skin.

"I never had any doubt about the Tsgardi's willingness to join," Minister Ambello Neddowo said, "but I'm surprised the Hudeera and Gondusans joined so quickly. I expected them to debate the issue endlessly. After all, they have only recently reacquired territory lost to them for decades. I thought they might hold some misguided appreciation towards Space Command."

"The vote in each case was close," Barguado said. "The Hudeera had fifty-eight percent in favor of the pact, while the Gondusans had just fifty-two percent in favor. Apparently there *was* some gratitude. That, or they fear the Galactic Alliance. We shall have to watch them both closely. They may try to withdraw from the pact after losing a few ships. We must be prepared to take over their forces if their leaders falter."

"You mean before we intentionally move against them and seize their entire territory?" Neddowo said, smiling.

"Of course," Barguado said. "The fleet we've been building since we first decided to annex the Milori Empire many annuals ago is now ready to begin operations. The special battle groups we've secreted throughout the former Milori Empire will join the Gondusan and Hudeera forces as they move forward, but our battle plan will always place our *allies* in the most dangerous battle

positions. By the time Space Command pulls back to their borders, our *allies* will have no fighting forces left, so there will be no resistance when we also annex *their* territory. The Hudeera, Gondusans, and Tsgardi are truly witless to think we need them to defeat the Galactic Alliance or that we would share the conquered territory with them."

Chapter Two
~ October 23rd, 2281 ~

Jenetta Carver sauntered down the shuttle ramp, her eyes carefully appraising the terrain of this new base. As much as she loved her time in space, it was always a thrill to step onto a planet with a breathable atmosphere.

The Marine posted near the bottom of the ramp braced to attention as she placed a foot onto the soil of the planet Quesann for the first time. Nearby, crewmembers from the ship stole surreptitious glances as they carried out their assigned tasks.

Even in the muted black uniform of a Space Command officer, Jenetta never failed to turn heads. Her enhanced DNA gave her the face and body of a mythological Greek goddess and would keep her looking as young as a recent Academy graduate for most of a greatly extended life. The four gold stars on each shoulder ensured that no one in Space Command would ever forget themselves and attempt to accost the tall blonde. Although capable of defending her own honor, the two large cats that accompanied her off the ship would gladly handle anyone who moved too close without an invitation.

With fur as black as space and weighing just a hundred sixty pounds each, Taurentlus-Thur Jumakas were smaller than Terran Jaguars, but they were just as deadly. The female cats appeared identical except for the tiny tuft of white fur on one's right foreleg where a laser shot from an assassin had grazed her. That assassin had learned about Jumakas the hard way. The cats were on him before he'd had a chance to fire a third shot at Jenetta. While one used its powerful jaws to break the arm holding the laser pistol, the other clamped equally powerful jaws around his throat. He died within minutes, his life's blood turning the space station deck crimson as it pumped out through

opened carotid arteries. There was some debate among the morgue staff as to whether the drugged-up assassin had died from blood loss or suffocation. In private, the cats were docile, even playful, but when protecting their mistress they were bundles of pure fury wrapped in muscle, teeth, and claws.

Even without her two pets, Jenetta had proven that it was unwise to attack her. During her career, she had permanently dispatched more than one enemy using the kickboxing skills she practiced religiously. Powerful people make powerful enemies, and Jenetta always had to be on guard against attacks. However, as the only sentient life on this previously uninhabited planet was her crew, she could relax slightly and enjoy being out in the sunshine for the first time after more than a year in space.

Located roughly thirteen hundred light-years from Earth and three hundred eight light-years from Milor, the planet Quesann was unquestionably Earth Class. In fact, it was the most Earth-like planet Jenetta had visited, coming closer to her home world than Nordakia, Obotymot, Siena, and Pelomious. Earth Class planets must have a breathable oxygen-nitrogen atmosphere with a roughly 20/80 mix and no more than two percent of non-deadly trace gases. They must have a mean temperature between 5 and 25 degrees Celsius, a mass between 0.7 and 1.3 times that of Earth, and a radius not less than 0.8 or more than 1.2 times that of Earth.

With a mass of 1.01 and a radius 1.06 times that of Earth, Quesann orbited a Type G2 Yellow MMK class V (dwarf) star once each three hundred seventy-one Earth days. The planet made one full revolution each twenty-four hours and eighteen minutes, Galactic System time. Hundreds of massive islands dotted the surface of the planet, making the calculated land-to-water ratio appear inaccurate, but even with the three main continents, land only accounted for thirty-three percent of the surface. The largest uninterrupted body of water was about half the size of the Atlantic Ocean on Earth. The planet had two polar caps and a molten core with tectonic plate move-

ment similar to Earth's. Fifteen percent of the islands contained active or dormant volcanoes. For now, the entire planet was declared 'off limits' to all but Space Command and Marine personnel. How long it remained that way was yet to be decided, but Jenetta intended to reserve just as much of the planet as possible for military use.

For the Space Command Headquarters of Region Two, Jenetta selected an island where the Milori had begun construction of a new military base a few annuals before the first invasion of Galactic Alliance space. When the new Milori commanding officer for the sector had visited the site, he decided it was far too cold to suit him. They then abandoned the base near the outer border of their empire to search for a planet or moon where the mean temperature was a more comfortable forty degrees Celsius, leaving the buildings in various states of completion.

At eighteen degrees above the planet's equator, the island was roughly the size of New Zealand on Earth. It encompassed some 264,000 square kilometers. The usable land mass would be adequate for most of Space Command's present and future needs. Since the nearest neighboring island was over two hundred kilometers away, security should never be a problem, although the distance could be covered in minutes by a shuttle. With an average daily temperature of twenty-three degrees Celsius that never varied by more than seven degrees, the crew rightly referred to it as a tropical paradise. Jenetta was adamant that the entire island be reserved in perpetuity for military use only, so no civilian areas were included on the maps.

Initial tests showed the base location to be biologically safe for all known sentient species, so in-depth studies had begun. Bots with biological survey modules were currently combing the island in ever widening circles as they cataloged all life forms, both micro and macroscopic, while checking the flora and fauna for any danger to recorded species. Bots with construction modules were

working with engineers to document the previous construction and develop plans for the layout of the new base.

"Good morning, Admiral," Lieutenant Carstairs of the *Colorado's* engineering section said as she stepped up to Jenetta and saluted.

"Good morning, Lieutenant," Jenetta said after returning the salute. "How are the surveys going?"

"Excellent, ma'am. So far, everything indicates this will be a superb location for the base. The ground is firm, the soil rich, the air clean, and the water potable, and the indigenous life forms so far appear to be biologically safe for hominal life. I wouldn't suggest anyone go swimming until we've had an opportunity to do underwater surveys, but this part of the island seems safe for human habitation."

"Very good, Lieutenant. That concurs with the Milori surveys. I'll look forward to viewing your final report."

"Aye, ma'am," Lt. Carstairs said before saluting again and turning to leave.

Jenetta had little to do at the moment so she took her time wandering around the site, enjoying the fresh air and the sun on her face. The ship had been in orbit for several days and would remain here for the immediate future while the planet was completely surveyed. The *Colorado's* sister ship, the *Yangtze*, was also in orbit, performing the surface mapping work.

* * *

A week later, Jenetta conducted a meeting in the bridge-deck conference room aboard the *Colorado*. Captain Fannon of the *Yangtze* and the senior officers of both scout-destroyer ships were present.

"Good morning," Jenetta said as she opened the meeting. "The purpose of this meeting is to discuss the findings of the survey work. Captain Fannon, why don't you begin?"

"Aye, Admiral. My people have completed the geological mapping of the planet and prepared annualized meteorological projections. The *Yangtze's* computer estimates 2.7 significant hurricanes could potentially pass over this part of the planet each summer. My engineers recommend all buildings be constructed to withstand hurricane-force winds of four hundred kilometers per hour, although on average the winds should never exceed one hundred seventy kilometers per hour."

"That shouldn't be a problem," Jenetta said. "Even our portable shelters, once properly anchored, are designed to withstand two-hundred-kilometer-per-hour winds. What season are we currently in?"

"We've established this as mid-winter, so we should have six months before the summer hurricane season begins."

Jenetta nodded. "The Milori were obviously aware of the potential winds because the buildings they were constructing would easily survive four-hundred-kilometer winds. The tunnel network that connects all surface buildings to the underground complex must have been intended for use during periods of severe meteorological instability or attack by outside forces. Thank you, Captain Fannon. Anything else?"

"Once the planet has been deemed safe, I'd like to request that off-duty personnel be allowed to travel down to the surface for a little R&R time."

"Of course. We'll have to do it on a rotating basis though so at least one ship is always fully staffed and ready to safeguard the new base and the people on the surface. The ship enjoying liberty must always have a sixty percent crew complement aboard. This is still a dangerous part of space, and we must be prepared to repel an attack at all times. Lieutenant Carstairs, I've read your complete report, but why don't you summarize it for the rest of the senior staff."

"Aye, Admiral," she said, nodding. "The island where the new base is being located does meet the criteria we use as a definition of a tropical paradise. It's very much like some of the islands in the South Pacific back home on Earth. In fact, except for the distribution of surface landmasses, the entire planet is as much like Earth as any other planet we have in the computer database. Once

Terrans start coming to this part of GA space, I'm sure this planet will become a favorite destination and possibly a second home to many if SHQ wishes to share the planet with civilians.

"Our survey of the island has turned up a few poisonous species of vegetation that must be avoided until they can be eradicated in habitable areas. There are small lizards and snakelike creatures, but none are venomous. They will inflict a painful bite, however, and contact should be avoided. They run at the sight of Terrans, so the only danger is if we pursue them. We've found one species of burrowing insect that has a sufficiently venomous bite to make a human extremely ill for several days, but it hasn't been found within three kilometers of the shoreline. People who enjoy making sand sculptures on the beach will be perfectly safe. A study regarding possible damage to the ecosystem from eradication of the dangerous insect is underway. Fresh water flow from the peaks to the north is available in great quantities, so no restrictions on use are necessary. We have noted the presence of potentially dangerous marine life in the ocean, so swimming should be prohibited until more extensive research is conducted. At the very least, I recommend installation of a barrier net a half-kilometer offshore and then a sweep of the enclosed area for predators or harmful marine vegetation and aquatic life forms.

"I'm amazed the Milori simply abandoned this base. They concentrated on completing an extensive underground complex first, so it's virtually ready to move into except for equipment. We'll need power generation, life support systems, computer systems, and furnishings, but the belowground complex is clean and dry. After cutting it from solid bedrock, they lined it with a meter of pre-stressed plasticrete. It's a hundred meters below ground level so it'll provide a safe haven from almost any aerial attack or bombardment. Above ground, there are three completed buildings and eighteen buildings in various stages of construction. One of the completed buildings was intended as a power station, but the equipment was never installed. We can install portable units for the short term to provide power to the entire site through the existing power grid conduits and wiring left by the Milori. We have neither the materials nor the equipment necessary to continue construction, so what we have now is all we're likely to have until supply ships begin to arrive."

"Thank you, Lieutenant," Jenetta said. "Good work." To the entire staff she said, "Good work everyone. Here's our current situation: The dozen ships we've revisited for supplies since we left Stewart SCB won't reach this location for almost eight more months. The other fifty M-designate ships we captured from the Milori and converted for Space Command use have been assigned to the Region Two fleet. They've been loaded from bulkhead to bulkhead with ordnance, supplies, and people, but they won't arrive here for fourteen months.

"The good news is that all three of the new *Prometheus*-class battleships are on their way here. Like all future warships and transports, they're sheathed in Dakinium and capable of achieving Light-9790. They won't be here for several more weeks, but they'll bring our first headquarters personnel, along with adequate supplies to obviate the need for return to our supply ships. They'll also be conveying thousands of personnel destined for placement at newly established bases in this territory. Several new Quartermaster transports capable of Light-9790 are nearing completion at the Mars shipbuilding yards. The supply depots are already assembling cargo deliveries for us. The new ships may arrive here even before the slow ships that departed Stewart more than a year ago. At Light-9790, we're only fifty-two days from Mars or Earth.

"I've been promised this command will receive twenty of the twenty-five new warships produced each year for the next decade. The reason we'll be receiving such a disproportionate share of the new ships is because we have the greatest need for their speed capability and hull integrity. But for the immediate future, we still face the problem of controlling a territory that's 2000 light-years across with just a handful of ships. The Admiralty Board fully expects this territory to sink into complete anarchy for perhaps as long a decade because it will be that long before we have sufficient ships to give us basic patrol coverage. I'm sure you realize that the deeper it sinks the more difficult it will be to resurrect it, so our task now is to minimize the turmoil until we can get this territory under control."

"Will the *Colorado* be remaining in Region Two, Admiral?" Lt. Commander Gallagher, that ship's first officer asked.

"Of course; this is where we're needed most."

"I only wondered if we'd be reassigned to the *Prometheus* now that three new battleships will be arriving to take our place. We were only intended as an adjunct to a battleship, after all."

"The *Prometheus* and *Chiron* will be receiving new scout-destroyers to replace the *Colorado* and *Yangtze* very soon, so these two small ships will remain here to bolster our forces until the Second Fleet becomes a reality. We'll need every ship we can get for a while, even if those ships weren't intended to perform as independent warships. The scout-destroyers will serve as the protection group for this base until the first dozen M-designate ships arrive."

"Where do we even start, Admiral?" Lt. Commander Ashraf, the *Colorado's* second officer and Jenetta's aide, asked. "We have a territory almost double the size of Galactic Alliance space before the annexation, virtually no ships, no supplies, and no bureaucracy, and we face complete ignorance of Galactic Alliance law throughout this new region."

Jenetta took a deep breath and exhaled it slowly. "It's a daunting task to be sure, Commander. We've been operating in war mode until now, able to simply destroy anybody or anything offering resistance, but now we have to switch back to crime prevention and protection activities. I've prepared a message for transmission to all planets that were part of the former Milori Empire. Thanks to the files we were able to download from captured Milori ships, we have contact information for every system. By now most have probably learned that the Milori have surrendered and we've annexed the territory, but this should clarify the situation for them.

"The message will be broadcast in Amer and the principal languages of this and the surrounding territories, including: Weutrak, the language of the Milori; Vewcalu, the language of the Uthlaro; Gucceral, the language of the Tsgardi; Fryvylous, the language of the Gondusans; and Lacynyc, the language of the Hudeera. Anyone capable of interstellar flight, or anyone who was subjugated by the Milori, will surely be familiar with at least one of these languages. We'll be appending a complete copy of the Simplified Galactic Alliance Law Text. Beyond that, there's little we can do except let the word spread as we enforce Galactic Alliance law."

"Where do you foresee the greatest problem, Admiral?" Fannon asked.

"Within their territory, the Milori effectively suppressed any civilizations with aspirations of achieving interstellar flight, so I expect most of the trouble will come from outside the territory. Tsgardi and Uthlaro smugglers and pirates will probably be the greatest threats, but we mustn't forget our old enemy, the Raiders. We knocked them off their feet in Galactic Alliance space before the annexation, but they'll probably see Region Two as fertile ground where they can establish themselves before we can bring law and order.

"We know the Raiders were in league with the Milori, but we don't know how extensive their power base was. We suspect they had a major falling out just before the second Milori invasion attempt. I'm basing that on the destruction of a Raider base by Milori warships just before they attacked Stewart, but the Raiders might still be firmly entrenched in this space. A fourth possibility might be independent Milori pirates. Part of the Milori invasion plan for Galactic Alliance space was to allow pirates and privateers to roam freely until their government was both ready and strong enough to assume complete domination. We've never encountered Milori privateers, but I imagine they exist. I don't expect the Milori government to sanction them openly, so we'll just respond to them as we would pirates. There may even be former military units that have found themselves without an organization and who turn to piracy for survival.

"But for the time being we're powerless to implement *any* control in this territory, so we'll stand down until the new battleships get here. I'll create a ship schedule for rest and relaxation. Dismissed."

* * *

In the weeks following, the crews of the *Colorado* and the *Yangtze* would have a rare opportunity to soak up the sun while lying on pristine beaches or enjoying other recreational pleasures. The ocean remained off limits, and the crews knew better than to violate such a directive on an alien planet, even if it did seem so much like home.

* * *

Twenty-two days later, as Jenetta sat in her command chair on the bridge reading a report, the com chief said, "Admiral, we're receiving a call from the *Themis*."

"Put it on the front viewscreen, Chief," Jenetta said.

"Aye, Admiral."

Jenetta watched as the image dissolved from a view of space to one of an SC captain on the bridge of a *Prometheus*-class battleship named after the mythological Greek goddess of justice. The message bar across the top of the screen identified him as Captain Sandor Erikson of the GSC Battleship *Themis*.

"Welcome to Region Two, Captain," Jenetta said.

"Thank you, Admiral. It's an honor for the *Themis*, *Boreas*, and *Hyperion* to join your command. May I offer my personal congratulations for your incredible successes against the Milori?"

"Thank you, Captain. How was your trip?"

"Very quick, Admiral; we're still all drunk with excitement at having traveled so far so fast. I can imagine your exhilaration when you pioneered this new technology."

Jenetta smiled. "It was quite a shock when we learned just how fast we had traveled. When do you expect to reach Quesann?"

"We'll be entering the system in a few minutes, Admiral. You should already have us on your sensors."

The officer manning the tactical station looked up and nodded as Jenetta glanced over. "We do, Captain. Link up with us using your bow airlocks when you arrive. I'm looking forward to meeting you, the other captains, and your senior VIPs."

"Aye, Admiral. May I suggest you join us aboard the *Themis*? I'm sure you'd like to see the new ship, and even with the overabundance of supplies and personnel, we still should have a lot more room here than aboard the *Colorado*."

"Fine, Captain. I would enjoy having a look around your ship after our conference. *Colorado* out."

"*Themis* out."

Forty minutes later, Captain Erikson and his first officer, Commander Kimberly Riccio, welcomed Jenetta and her senior officers aboard the *Themis*. They proceeded together to a large conference room for the meeting. The internal color scheme of the ship was slightly different from that of the *Prometheus* and *Chiron*, but the basic layout was the same. For Jenetta, it brought back memories of her first time aboard the original battleship of this class.

Everyone in the conference room stood up as the doors opened and Jenetta entered. The officers in the room immediately walked to where Jenetta had stopped. First in line were the three admirals, naturally. All Rear Admirals, Upper Half, they would each be assigned a StratCom-One base in the new Region.

"Admiral Carver, permit me to introduce Admiral Vincent Sprague," Captain Erikson said as a seventy-three-year-old officer saluted. Jenetta returned his salute and then extended her hand.

"It's a pleasure to meet you at last, Admiral," Admiral Sprague said as he shook the proffered hand, "and an honor to be part of your command. I was delighted when the Admiralty Board selected me to come here. Things had gotten a bit *uneventful* at Edwards Space Command Base in recent years."

"It's a pleasure to meet you, Admiral, and I'm equally delighted you were chosen to join us here." Smiling, she added, "I think I can promise you won't find the next few years *uneventful*. Welcome to Region Two."

"This is Admiral Rebecca Colsey," Captain Erikson said as Admiral Sprague moved aside and a woman in her late sixties saluted Jenetta.

"An honor, Admiral," Admiral Colsey said.

"It's an honor to have you in Region Two, Admiral. Brian Holt has mentioned that you and he are old friends."

"Yes, ma'am. Brian was the second officer on the destroyer to which I was assigned immediately following graduation from the Academy. I was the helmsman on his watch for my first three years aboard the old *Kiev*."

"You'll have to tell me about your adventures together sometime. Welcome to Region Two."

"Thank you, Admiral."

As Admiral Colsey stepped aside, Captain Erikson introduced the youngest of the three flag officers. Jenetta knew he was sixty-six, but his outward appearance was that of a fifty-year-old.

"And this is Admiral Jorge Mendez."

"I'm honored to meet you, Admiral," he said, "I've been looking forward to this meeting since I was informed I'd be serving in your command. It's a real pleasure."

"Welcome to Region Two, Admiral. I'm pleased to meet you and happy to have you with us."

After Captain Erikson had introduced Captain Neil Elder of the *Boreas*, Captain Lynda Stager of the *Hyperion*, and their first officers, Commander Diana

Durland and Commander Scott Hyland, Jenetta introduced Commander Fannon and Lt. Commander Soren Mojica of the *Yangtze*, and Lt. Commander Gallagher and Lt. Commander Ashraf of the *Colorado*. With the introductions out of the way, the group took their seats, and two mess attendants served coffee or tea to the group.

As the mess attendants left the room and the doors closed behind them, Jenetta said, "Ladies and Gentlemen, I'm very pleased you've arrived. We've felt a little lonely and isolated out here by ourselves since the Milori surrendered. Our first supply ships won't be arriving for months."

"Yes," Admiral Sprague said, "we passed them on the way here. They send their regards and report they're still proceeding at top speed. I wish we could have hooked up and dragged them along."

"The equipment, supplies, and personnel you've brought will allow us to begin operations here and save us from having to make another trip back to the ships for resupply."

"We'll be glad to be rid of it," Captain Erikson said, smiling. "We have equipment, people, and ordnance stuffed into every available square inch of space. I barely have enough room in my quarters to get to my bathroom.

"I know how you feel," Jenetta said, returning his smile. "When we launched our attack against the Milori, our two small ships were stuffed in a similar manner. It was a relief when I could finally walk around my quarters, but I later wished we could have brought even more."

"We'll probably feel that way once we start organizing the new bases," Admiral Colsey said, "and realize how many things we were unable to bring. At least we can look forward to more timely deliveries by the new Quartermaster transports. They're the largest single-hull transports ever built, and they'll be packing them from bulkhead to bulkhead for each of their trips."

"If the Mars timetable is accurate," Jenetta said, "the new transports will be here to resupply us even before the ships I dispatched while I was still the base commander at Stewart."

"Light-9790 has given us a considerable advantage over our neighbors," Admiral Mendez said. "I wonder how much longer the speed will remain a secret."

"I'm sure many have already heard the rumors," Jenetta said. "You can't expect to keep anything this monumental under wraps for long. I imagine foreign agents are already hard at work trying to learn the secret of Light-9790 speed. But as important as the speed is, the new hull material that makes us impervious to laser array fire is more valuable. We might not have been able to so easily destroy the Milori shipyards without it. The yards were ringed with laser weapon satellites. We must have taken a thousand hits to each scout-destroyer. We were able to completely ignore the satellites because we knew they couldn't harm us."

"It would be nice if the weapons folks could come up with a material impervious to torpedoes as well," Captain Stager said.

"Speed and total invulnerability may not be possible. The Dakinium is responsible for the speed improvement. If they change the formula to make it more indestructible, we might be pushed back to Light-450 again. It would be difficult trying to decide between near invincibility or Light-9790."

"I'll keep the speed," Captain Elder said. "The Phalanx system you developed while at Stewart will take care of most torpedoes. The speed will enable us to stop anyone from eluding us while enabling us to get away from any pursuers if the odds against us are too great."

"Captain DeWitt and her people in Weapons Research & Development did an incredible job in developing our Phalanx system. The last time I communicated with her, she told me her section was still working to improve the program code for the weapons computer module. She says they won't stop until she can guarantee one hundred percent effectiveness destroying incoming torpedoes. That would be wonderful, but I think it's an elusive dream. If faced with a dozen warships all firing torpedoes as fast as they can reload, they'll probably overwhelm any system we could develop."

"That's where the speed really comes in handy," Captain Elder said, smiling.

"Yes, there are times when you must stand your ground and fight to the bitter end, but there are also times when, as Shakespeare wrote, 'The better part of valor is discretion.'"

"With the Milori defeated," Admiral Colsey said, "there will be few instances where a Space Command vessel will have to retreat."

"Hopefully," Jenetta said. "But until we bring peace and stability to Region Two, we may find ourselves occasionally outnumbered by Raiders or pirates."

"Have you determined where we'll establish the first bases in this Region?" Admiral Sprague asked.

"Yes, I have. Prior to the second expansion in Region One, our bases were located roughly one hundred light-years apart. Following the expansion, bases were being established two hundred light-years apart. Stewart was the exception because we commandeered a Raider base that was ready to occupy. It was four hundred light-years from its nearest neighbor. Given our new speed capability, I've decided we'll initially establish a network of bases with each being as far distant as one thousand light-years from its nearest neighbor. As more bases are occupied, we'll fill in the gaps, with the eventual goal being to have all bases no more than two hundred light-years from a neighbor. Help will be less than eight days away for vessels with Light-9790. The Milori were maintaining eighty-six bases prior to their last expansion towards the Galactic Alliance outer border. Twelve of those bases were in territory returned to the Hudeera and Gondusans, leaving us seventy-two occupied bases."

"Occupied?" Admiral Colsey questioned.

"Yes. One of the Milori surrender terms requires them to keep a security force at each base to prevent scavengers from moving in to strip weapons or generally trash the place. The Milori forces are responsible for seeing that the base remains intact and in good condition until they can be relieved by our forces."

"Do you think they'll honor that agreement?" Admiral Sprague asked. "They didn't honor the first peace treaty we signed with them."

"I can't know for sure, but I'm hoping they will. I've tried to impress upon them that we'll treat them fairly if they cooperate. They already know what we're capable of if they betray our trust again."

"It'll take years for us to occupy seventy-two bases," Admiral Mendez said.

"Yes, so for our first operations I've identified three existing space station bases where our presence should have the greatest impact. I estimate we'll need twenty-two additional StratCom-One bases, with the remainder of the bases being designated as either StratCom-Two or StratCom-Three. That plan includes a number of new bases in the five hundred light-years of territory between the Region One outer border and the original Milori border. The Milori hadn't yet established any bases there, so those will have to be built from scratch unless we push some of the existing space stations for which we don't have an anticipated need to new locations. At Light-75, it would take years for the space tugs to position them but probably not as long as it would take to construct new stations."

"Even the initial twenty-five bases may take a long time to properly staff," Admiral Colsey said.

"True," Jenetta said, "and the onerous task of holding everything together out here has fallen squarely on our shoulders. We believe that the greatest threats to peace and stability will come from the Tsgardi and Uthlaro borders. The Gondusans and Hudeera were our allies in the fight against the Milori and they've been weakened by decades of war with the Milori, so I'm not expecting many problems from that direction. The border with the Ruwalch Confederacy should be fairly quiet because we believe that they, like us, just want peace. Reportedly,

29

their technology is adequate to ensure they have little to worry about from their immediate neighbors. The Uthlaro border is by far the longest of the five border areas we must safeguard and we know they have very close ties with the Raiders, so I've identified two bases in that part of Region Two for immediate occupancy. Each is roughly a hundred light-years from the border. A base located one hundred light-years from the Tsgardi border will be our third StratCom-One base. All three are within a thousand light-years of Quesann."

"It will be difficult to protect forward bases with just one warship at each," Captain Stager said.

"Actually, you'll each have two warships. When you arrive at the base, launch the scout-destroyer you each carry and allow it to operate as an independent ship, just as the *Colorado* and *Yangtze* operate now. I'd rather have one of these small ships at my disposal than an M-designate battleship.

"And speaking of M-designate ships, as soon as the first twelve arrive in seven months we'll unload them and three will immediately be dispatched to each base. Unfortunately, it will take them more than twenty-five months to reach your bases. When the rest of the force presently on its way to Region Two arrives next year, current plans call for each base to receive an additional nine ships. Those ships will proceed directly there rather than having to come here first. We'll also be ready to open several more bases at that time."

"It's so incredible that we'll reach the new bases in less than forty days," Admiral Sprague said, "but it'll take years for the older ships to get there. As I said earlier, I wish we could just hook them up and drag them along with us as we do with the scout-destroyers."

"That would be wonderful," Jenetta said, "but the scout-destroyers are DS, or Dakinium-sheathed, like the main ship, so it's possible to include them in the temporal envelopes. What I'm about to tell you is top-secret. Light-9790 only became possible because the Dakinium hull plating begins to resonate as the envelopes are created.

The resonance is entirely responsible for causing the formation of a second temporal envelope around the first. By instantly creating the resonance in the hull, both temporal envelopes can develop simultaneously. So you can't tow another ship at Light-9790 unless the hull of the towed vessel is also sheathed in Dakinium."

"I see," Admiral Sprague said. "Then it would be impossible for anyone else to develop Light-9790 unless they got the formulae for Dakinium?"

"Presently— and that's why it's the most closely guarded secret in Space Command these days. The Raiders have known of the discovery of Dakinium since their Tsgardi mercenaries tried to recover the cloning equipment on Mawcett, but I don't know if they're aware that the Dakinium allowed us to shatter the theoretical speed limit. Of course, as alien scientists learn that dual-envelope theory has not only been proven but, in fact, put into everyday use, they'll begin looking for ways and materials to duplicate what we've accomplished. Unlike the DATFA technology that allowed us to travel faster than light, we won't be sharing the formula for Dakinium with commercial users. That should prevent unscrupulous businesspersons from selling the process to our enemies as happened with temporal field generation. I estimate we should have at least ten years of speed advantage before anyone can develop their own materials. We must have Region Two completely secured by then."

* * *

Over the next several days, the people, equipment, and supplies destined for the headquarters base were off-loaded and transported down to the surface. A completed building on the planet was designated as a makeshift dormitory until the first of the planned housing units was completed. The other completed buildings were used as warehouses.

After the unloading, the crews of the battleships and the personnel destined for the new bases were allowed a few days R&R on the tropical island. The base complement immediately swelled to over ten thousand, causing special problems with food and sleeping accommodations. Many chose to simply sleep on the beach rather than shuttling back up to the ships. The weather cooperated by providing bright sunny days and clear evenings. The temperatures varied from a warm twenty degrees Celsius at night to a balmy twenty-six during the day. Large beach barbeques quickly arranged by food service personnel fed the thousands of vacationing crewmembers. Marines patrolled along the shoreline continuously to ensure no newcomers forgot the ban on entering the briny water.

Jenetta had dinner with the three admirals every evening and spent time in meetings with them each day until they were prepared for their new assignments. A week after their arrival, the three battleships departed for the thirty-one to thirty-nine-day journey to their new bases. Occupation of Region Two was underway.

Chapter Three
~ January 21st, 2282 ~

"Happy New Year Ladies and Gentlemen, from Region Two Space Command Headquarters – Quesann," Admiral Carver said to the members of the Admiralty Board. Her image filled the large, full-wall monitor in the meeting hall always used for their sessions. All ten members of the Board were at the large horseshoe-shaped table at Supreme Headquarters on Earth to view the message sent almost three weeks earlier. The gallery was empty today, but a couple of dozen aides and senior officers occupied chairs behind their admirals. Petty officer clerks, ready to rush off and take care of important matters if called upon by one of the admirals, sat behind the officers.

"Admirals Sprague, Colsey, and Mendez have arrived at their assigned bases and accepted responsibility for the stations from the Milori security forces left behind to safeguard the facilities. Each new commanding officer reports the base is in good condition. The Milori forces will be transported to Milor at the first opportunity. For the present, their orders from the Milori Viceroy call for them to wait on the station but remain apart from our personnel as much as possible. The admirals have each designated housing and recreation areas for the Milori and placed those sections off limits to Space Command personnel.

"The engineers immediately began working to adapt the space stations to our physical requirements and needs. Changing the signage to Amer is a simple matter and should be complete by the time you receive this, but it will require quite a bit more time to properly adapt equipment designed to be operated with gripper claws and tentacles so it can be operated comfortably by human hands.

"All the equipment, supplies, and ordnance have been offloaded from the battleships and placed into storage areas and armories aboard the stations. A Distant DeTect Network has been established at each station to provide an early warning of approaching ships. I've ordered that the scout-destroyers be treated as separate warships until reinforcements arrive and that neither ship departs the immediate vicinity of the station without R2HQ permission. It means we're unable to carry out normal Space Command functions, but given the hostile nature of the territory, protection of the base must take priority. When the first of the M-designate ships arrive in two to three years, the stations will be ready to begin limited patrol operations.

"Jenetta A. Carver, Admiral, Region Two Space Command Headquarters, Quesann. Message complete."

"Her report sounds very positive," Admiral Moore said. "Let's hope things continue to go so well in the future."

"We've heard some disturbing rumors of possible problems in the Uthlaro Dominion," Admiral Bradlee, the Director of Intelligence Services said.

"What sort of problems, Roger?" Admiral Platt asked.

"We have nothing definitive yet, just snatches of a conversation overheard in a bar. A junior Raider officer was talking about an upcoming operation against a Milori base."

"A Milori base?" Admiral Burke asked.

"Yes, but technically there are no Milori bases— only Space Command bases still occupied by Milori Security Forces. If they move against any bases in Region Two, they're moving against us."

"It must be a raid to steal weapons and ordnance before we take control," Admiral Ahmed said. "Admiral Carver has foreseen that possibility and ordered the Milori to man the bases until we arrive to prevent them from being stripped by thieves."

"I hope that's all it is. I've sent word that all agents should keep their ears especially open for any word about operations in Region Two and immediately relay the information to us, regardless of how insignificant they think it might be."

"Is there any chance this is sanctioned by the Uthlaro?" Admiral Hillaire asked.

"The Uthlaro have been closely allied with the Raiders for as long as I can remember. The captives of the Raiders have always been sent to the Uthlaro Dominion because human slavery is legal there."

"Do we have anyone inside the Uthlaro military?" Admiral Plimley asked.

"No. We haven't been able to turn any Uthlaro, and given our physical differences, there's no chance of sneaking in a non-Uthlaro. At least the Uthlaro don't resent the presence of Terrans and other species, as the Milori did, so we're able to see and overhear things occasionally."

* * *

Jenetta had paced around her briefing room for almost a half hour. She was bored. Until the new base actually began operations, she had very little to do. She had already been down to the planet that morning to observe the construction efforts, and she had read and responded to all the reports in her mail queue. She had even replied to all her personal mail from family and friends.

The computer annunciation system said to her, "Commander Fannon requests admittance."

"Come," Jenetta said, and the doors to her briefing room opened.

"Good afternoon, Admiral," the Captain of the *Yangtze* said cheerfully as he entered the room. "You wanted to see me?"

"Hi, Frank. Beverage?"

"No thank you, Admiral."

"Have a seat," Jenetta said, as she moved behind her desk and plopped into her own chair. She stared blankly at Commander Fannon without saying a word until he started to fidget under her gaze.

"Is there a problem, Admiral?" he asked, when she shifted her gaze away.

Jenetta took a deep breath and then let it out slowly. "No problem with you, Frank. You've done, and are doing, a great job. I'm very pleased you chose to join us on this venture."

Commander Fannon relaxed slightly and smiled. "Thank you. It's been my pleasure, Admiral. I mean that. I wanted some payback for what the Milori did to me and the crew of the *Lisbon* when they stranded us on that hostile planet, not to mention payback for the Space Command people we lost in the two invasion attempts. We've kicked ass out here, and I've loved every minute of it."

Jenetta smiled and nodded, then grew serious again. "I'm thinking about taking a little vacation."

"I know you haven't taken any time off since we left Stewart a year ago. Quesann is a great place to kick back for a few days and forget about the job. It would be nice if we had a five-star hotel here, but that'll come later. We can handle things while you rest up."

"I'm thinking about a longer vacation than that. I was thinking more along the lines of four months."

"Four months?"

"Yes, a trip to Earth will take fifty-two days each way."

"Earth?"

"I haven't been home in twelve years and right now I have little to do. It appears likely that once we're staffed here and we begin to exercise control in this region I won't be able to take sufficient time off for a trip to Earth for a number of years. The first of the M-designate ships won't be here for another five months. If I left now, I'd be back before they arrive. There's really very little that requires my personal attention in the meantime. We've installed the planetary defense laser arrays delivered by the battleships, so the base is well protected from orbital attack. If you can handle the space defense, our new headquarters security officer, Lt. Colonel Barletto and his Marines, should be able to handle everything dirt-side."

"The *Yangtze* can handle most anything that's likely to come our way, Admiral," Commander Fannon said confidently.

"I know, Frank, but I'd feel a lot better about it if we had a few more ships here. I keep thinking about the time the Raiders tried to retake Stewart and sent twenty-six warships at us. That was just a month after I had dispatched the *Thor* on a special mission that took it far enough away so it couldn't play a part in our protection. The three new battleships are more than a month away from here."

"As I recall, you repelled that attack."

"Yes, but the Stewart base is housed inside a giant asteroid, and we had four warships when the actual fight commenced."

"But none of them was impervious to laser fire, Admiral. That makes the *Yangtze* as good as five titanium-hulled ships because we only have to worry about torpedoes."

"I'd put our ships up against any Milori vessel, or even any five of them, but I wouldn't want to take on more than that because the number of incoming torpedoes might be too much for the Phalanx system."

"Then there should be nothing to stop you from taking a trip home while you can," he said, smiling. "The war is over, the Milori are finished, and we only have to worry about an occasional pirate or smuggler now."

"You're probably right. I've been agonizing over this decision for a week. I really want to do it now while I can."

"Then go, Admiral. I promise you we'll hold things together here. I won't tell you not to worry about us because I know you will, but we'll be alright."

* * *

Tapping the record button on the com unit in her briefing room aboard the *Colorado*, Jenetta faced the screen and said, "Message to Admiral Thaddeus Vroman,

Stewart Space Command Base, from Admiral Jenetta Carver aboard the GSC *Colorado*.

"Hi Thad, I hope everything's going well there and that you're fully recovered from your terrible ordeal at the hands of the Milori. I'm presently on my way to Stewart and we expect to dock there in about thirty days.

"I'm going to ask a big favor. As of the last messages I received from my sisters, Christa's ship was at the base and Eliza's ship was on patrol about five light-years out. If you could arrange it, I'd like you to transfer both of them to the *Colorado* for a quick trip to Earth. I think it would thrill my mom to see all of us together, and since they're only junior officers, their absence shouldn't adversely affect operations aboard their ships. The round trip from Stewart should take about two and a half months.

"Thanks, Thad. I'll see you soon.

"Jenetta A. Carver, Admiral, aboard the GSC *Colorado*. Message complete."

Jenetta leaned back in her chair and smiled. As excited as she was to be going home for a visit, she knew that taking Christa and Eliza would make the trip even better. None of them had been to Earth since the cloning process had produced the two identical *siblings* twelve years earlier. She knew her mother would be beside herself with joy once she learned of the impending visit, but she had already decided to keep the trip a secret from her until they arrived at Earth so mom wouldn't be a nervous wreck by the time they actually arrived.

*　*　*

Twenty days later Jenetta received a reply from Stewart. She raised the cover of her com unit and the face of Admiral Vroman filled the screen.

"Hi Jen, it was great to hear from you. Everything is going well here, and I've fully recovered from the ordeal on Siena.

"As to your request to take your sisters for two months— how could I refuse you anything? I owe you so much that I'm delighted to extend this very small courtesy. I've asked Captain Hyden of the *Bellona* to proceed to a rendezvous point of your choosing where Lt. Eliza Carver can be transferred aboard for temporary duty. He'll be contacting you directly to arrange the RP.

"I'm looking forward to seeing you again.

"Thaddeus Vroman, Admiral, Upper Half, Commander of Stewart Space Command Base. Message complete."

Jenetta didn't have long to wait for Captain Hyden to contact her. His message arrived a few hours later.

"Hi, Admiral," a smiling Edward Hyden said. "It's about time you arranged a little R&R for yourself. Eliza is excited about traveling to Earth and can't wait to board the *Colorado*. My navigator will append our current location coordinates and a suggested RP, assuming you're taking the most direct route from Quesann to Stewart. If you prefer a different RP, let us know as quickly as possible. See you soon.

"Edward Hyden, Captain of the *Bellona*. Message complete."

* * *

The GSC Battleship *Bellona* was waiting at the RP when the *Colorado* arrived. After supervising the linkup from the bridge, Jenetta hurried down to the bow airlock to greet her sister. Captain Hyden was standing with Eliza inside the *Colorado* when Jenetta arrived. Both officers came to attention when Jenetta approached and then saluted when she reached them.

After returning the salute, Jenetta extended her hand to both and said, "Welcome aboard, Captain. Welcome aboard, Lieutenant."

"Welcome back to Region One, Admiral," Captain Hyden said. "I'd like to offer my personal congratulations for your success against the Milori. I never would have believed that two tiny ships could bring the Empire to its knees, but those of us who know you knew you'd at least leave them smarting more than they could imagine."

"We had luck on our side," Jenetta said. "That and the fact the Milori never expected us to be able to hit back so quickly."

"Will you join me for dinner tonight in my dining room, Admiral?" Captain Hyden asked.

Jenetta would have preferred to continue her trip immediately, but it was late afternoon already and a few more hours wouldn't make enough of a difference for her to slight an officer who had just extended a courtesy. "Thank you, Captain. I'd be delighted to have dinner with you. 1700?" Jenetta knew most captains ate dinner around 1800 hours, but she couldn't help advancing the time by an hour. She would be able to depart at least an hour earlier than if she had allowed Captain Hyden to set the time.

"Fine, Admiral, 1700 it is. I'll see you then."

After Captain Hyden returned to his ship, Jenetta and Eliza walked to Jenetta's quarters. Once behind closed doors, they embraced like the close siblings they were.

"You're becoming decorously rigid, sis," Eliza said, smiling as they separated, "calling me Lieutenant in front of the Captain when he knows we haven't seen one another for over a year."

"I'm a four-star now, El, and people expect a certain behavior from senior admirals."

"Senior admirals only act that way because most of them are old, grumpy, and stuffy to begin with. You're none of those."

"I admit that my impulse was to embrace you and hug you with all my strength, but I have to set an example now and it's not proper for admirals to hug lieutenants."

Eliza grimaced momentarily, made a sniffing noise, and then quickly smiled again. "Where are the kitties?"

"What was that?"

"What was what?"

"That sniffing noise. I don't do that, do I?"

"I guess it's a mannerism I've picked up. We do have separate lives now, different experiences, and different social circles. So where are the kitties?"

"In my briefing room. I know that Captain Hyden has felt a little uncomfortable around them in the past. He tries not to show it, but I can always feel his discomfort."

"He's more of a *dog* man. He has a toy beagle now."

Jenetta giggled. "When Heather Gulvil first reported to Stewart, she told me she had a toy cocker spaniel. She said my cats could probably swallow her dog in one gulp. Of course I explained that Cayla and Tayna only eat meat that's well-cooked and wouldn't eat anything they didn't find in their food bowls, but I've often wondered how many people have felt their pets were in danger."

"Since regulations require that they keep them in their quarters, they probably felt safe enough."

"You're right, they probably did." Looking up at the wall chronometer, Jenetta said, "I have to get back to the bridge now. I'll see you later. Want to come to dinner with the Captain and me?"

"No, you go ahead. I wasn't really invited and I see him every day anyway. I'll grab something in the officer's mess later."

Returning to her quarters after her watch, Jenetta had plenty of time to wash up, change her clothes, and feed her cats. She reached Captain Hyden's private dining room a minute before 1700. The captain was already there and waiting. He jumped up as she entered.

"Relax, Ed. I'm still just Jen Carver when we're alone and don't have to maintain proper military protocol in front of other people."

He smiled. "Okay, Jen."

"How have you been?"

"Fine. Things have been pretty quiet since you left the sector. We've just been running our normal patrol routes. You put so many Raiders behind bars while you were the base commander at Stewart that it's been almost as quiet here as it is around Dixon."

"That's good to hear. I can say the same about Region Two right now, but I think it's just the calm before the storm. Our problems there haven't even begun yet. The Milori crushed anyone who got out of line, but by now the pirates have learned the Milori have had their teeth pulled. I expect them to start trying to build their own little empires in the absence of a heavy governmental hand. The worst part is there's absolutely nothing we can do about it. Not unless we suddenly find eight hundred fully crewed warships."

"That's a tall order. How many ships have been assigned to the second fleet so far?"

"Seventy-seven, but most of them haven't even crossed into Region Two yet. It will take years just to get them to their bases so they can start patrolling. I received all three of the new battleships that were recently commissioned, and that helps a great deal because they're capable of Light-9790. I have eight ships with the new speed capability now, if I count all the scout-destroyers as warships."

"You've certainly shown everyone what those small scout-destroyers can do. It makes me wonder if we need battleships any more. How will you be dividing up your forces?"

"I've identified twenty-five locations for StratCom-One bases, and each base should have at least fifteen warships assigned to it. To properly cover the entire region there should be an additional seventy-five lesser bases estab-lished, and I'd like to have an additional four hundred twenty-five ships to divide among them, but it's going to take a long time to come up with those eight hundred ships. The Mars facility is trying to ramp up production to a point where they produce twenty-five ships a year, but Region One is still severely short of their five-hundred-ship quota. What we need is a shipbuilding facility like Maxxiloth had. When we destroyed his shipyard, he had about a thousand warships in various stages of construction."

"Good God, the docks must have stretched on forever."

"It sure seemed that way. We left a hell of mess behind when we were done."

"All I know about your operation is that you accomplished it with just two small ships. Is it classified, or can you talk about it?"

Jenetta had known before she arrived that he'd want to hear about her incursion into the former Milori Empire, so she didn't disappoint him. She explained in detail the various steps she had taken to destroy the Milori military and civilian infrastructure, leaving the enemy no choice but to plead for a cessation of hostilities.

The *Colorado* separated from the *Bellona* just after 2100 hours. Jenetta had thanked Captain Hyden for accommodating her request and promised to have Eliza back in about two and half months.

* * *

The *Colorado* arrived in the vicinity of Stewart Space Command Base at 0400 hours. Anticipating the late arrival hour, Jenetta had decided to have the ship wait outside the port until morning and went to bed at her usual time. The *Colorado* would complete its docking when Jenetta arrived on the bridge in the morning. When she learned of the estimated arrival time, she chastised herself for not checking before linking with the *Bellona*. She could have enjoyed a more leisurely meal with Captain Hyden and not felt compelled to advance his normal evening meal hour.

Although Jenetta was sure Lt. Commander Ashraf was experienced enough to handle the approach and docking maneuvers without her supervision, the SC Handbook *strongly* recommended the captain's presence on the bridge during all docking and undocking operations. It would set a poor example if she ignored it.

The Colorado moved inside the base as soon as Jen arrived on the bridge in the morning. Lt. Commander Ashraf had no difficulty with the docking procedure and turned over command of the bridge as soon as the dock master certified the airlock seal and she had reported the status of the ship to Jenetta. After accepting command of the bridge, Jenetta checked her message queue and then prepared to disembark the ship. Lt. Maria Cruz, Jenetta's third officer, would have the bridge watch while Jenetta was off ship.

Lt. Commander Ashraf, temporarily resuming her role as an admiral's aide, joined Jenetta as she walked to the airlock.

"Did you get breakfast?" Jenetta asked.

"Yes ma'am. I had a chance to wash up, change, and grab a bite."

"Good. I'll try to make this visit with Admiral Vroman brief so you can get some sleep."

A large crowd was waiting as they stepped onto the docking platform that ran the length of the habitat. A line of Marines had prevented them from pressing close to the ship's pier, but when someone spotted her and shouted something, the crowd began to yell and applaud with a deafening din. The station's public relations officer stepped forward with Admiral Vroman. Both came to attention and saluted. Jenetta responded as military protocol dictated and then tried to say hello over the noise. Admiral Vroman wisely gestured to a low platform that had been set up. Jenetta understood immediately, nodded, and climbed up onto the makeshift stage. Admiral Vroman followed her, then walked to the podium and raised his hands to quiet the crowd. It took several attempts.

"Good morning. I hadn't realized when we informed the press Admiral Carver was arriving today that the word would spread so quickly. I suppose that's a testament to the grapevine we have here on Stewart. I won't keep you waiting, since you've obviously come here to see Admiral Carver and not me, so here she is."

Admiral Vroman stepped out of the way and gestured for Jenetta to speak.

"Good morning," Jenetta said as she stepped up to the microphone. "It's great to be back here at Stewart, which I've come to think of as my second home. I see a great many familiar faces in the crowd and I'm happy to say you're all a little safer now than when I left. The Milori will never invade our territory again." Jenetta had to pause as the crowd erupted in applause and cheering. When it died down she said, "Some of you may have heard I've been given the job of bringing peace to the annexed territory. That's true, and it will be as difficult an undertaking as the one I faced bringing stability and the rule of law to Stewart's assigned area of the Frontier Zone."

Jenetta paused and looked at Admiral Vroman for a second. "I guess we're going to have to find a new term for that area. It's hardly a frontier anymore since it sits almost squarely in the center of Galactic Alliance territory." Looking back at the crowd, she continued, "The Galactic Alliance now stretches 2000 light-years further out than it did last year. Taming the new territory is going to take years of effort. Not just mine, and not just that of my officers and crews, but all of ours. I'm talking about miners, freight-haulers, traders, farmers, merchants, and everyone else who makes their living out here. There are opportunities for everybody as long as you obey the law. The Raiders will find *their* opportunities as limited there as they've become here." Jenetta paused as laughter rippled through the crowd.

"Thank you for coming out to welcome me back. It's nice to know I haven't been forgotten." Another laugh rippled through the crowd. No one could conceive of anyone on Stewart not knowing of, or forgetting, Jenetta Carver. "Thank you," she repeated, waving to the crowd, and a thunderous applause rocked the dock area.

Jenetta turned to Admiral Vroman as the crowd started to dissipate. "I thought I was going to have a quiet walk to your office," she said, smiling.

"I'm afraid I mentioned to a couple of people that you were coming and the word got to the press. When they pressed me for confirmation, I admitted that you were coming for a very brief visit. They're still waiting for you to talk to them now that most of the crowd has left."

Jenetta turned and saw that the Marines were now letting the press approach the stage. She sighed and re-turned to the podium where she answered questions for about half an hour. A couple of reporters asked repeatedly when the official vid logs of the Milori actions were going to be declassified, and she kept referring them to Supreme HQ on Earth. When she decided they'd pretty well covered everything, she took one last question, thanked them for coming to greet her, and then waved to them as she walked off the stage. The reporters reluctantly turned to face their own 'oh-gee' cameras and wrap up their stories as Jenetta, Admiral Vroman, and Lt. Commander Ashraf walked to the base commander's office.

As they entered the Admiral's office, Jenetta was surprised to find it already occupied by eight warship captains. The entire group came to attention and saluted.

Jenetta returned their salute and said, "As you were."

"Everyone who was in port wanted to welcome you back, and I felt it would be better to meet in here instead of doing it in front of the press."

"I agree," Jenetta said just before she circled the room, stopping to say hello, shake hands, and exchange a few pleasantries with each officer.

As with Captain Hyden, everyone wanted to hear about Jenetta's tactics against the Milori, and she spent about two hours telling the officers about the campaign. The captains would have liked to stay for hours and discuss every aspect as they used to do over dinner in Jenetta's dining room, but Jenetta hinted she was anxious to get underway. Everyone understood and, almost as a group, took their leave, giving Jenetta a little time with Admiral Vroman.

"That was a remarkable feat, Jen," he said.

"We never could have done it without the *Colorado* and *Yangtze*. I love those little ships. I wish I had a dozen more of them."

"Have the Milori on the space stations given you any problems?"

"Not yet. The Viceroy told them to comply and they're complying. A Milori warrior would never disobey an order. They will happily fall upon their own sword if ordered to do so by their commander."

"What's going to happen to their world now?"

"They're working to rebuild their infrastructure. I'm afraid I made quite a mess. I regretted doing it, but Maxxiloth's refusal to surrender made it necessary."

"It had to be done. We couldn't have them attacking us again in five or ten years after they'd had a chance to rebuild their warship fleet."

"We'll keep an eye on them and make sure they never threaten their neighbors again." Standing up, Jenetta said, "I guess I'd better get going. Steve Powers told me he ordered Christa to report to the *Colorado* by 0900 hours, so she should be aboard by now."

"I was hoping you'd stay for lunch."

"I'd love to, but I don't have the time today. On my return trip I promise I'll stay for dinner, if I'm invited."

"You have a standing invitation for dinner anytime you're in the area."

"Thanks, Thad. And thanks for arranging for my sisters to be available for the trip."

"My pleasure, Jen. Have a safe trip."

* * *

Christa was conversing with Eliza in Jenetta's quarters when Jenetta returned to the ship.

"Christa!" Jenetta said excitedly as she entered her sitting room. The two women hugged warmly for a few seconds before pulling back to arm's length and looking at one another. "You look good."

"So do you, except your shoulders are drooping a little."

"Yeah, the four stars are a little heavy— a bit ostentatious, aren't they?"

"On you, they look good. I was surprised when I heard the news. I wondered if you'd accept them."

"I gave the matter a lot of thought after I received the message from Admiral Moore. It's going to be five more years before my ship is ready to be commissioned, and I have to be working somewhere, so it might as well be in Region Two."

"You don't seriously believe you're going to get a ship now, do you?"

47

"They promised me one. I'm going to hold them to it."

"But that was when you were a brevetted two-star. Now you're a permanent four-star, by confirmation of the Galactic Alliance Council."

"Then I guess I'll be the first four-star to captain a battleship. They promised me and I intend to hold them to it. But right now I have to get to the bridge and get us underway. Next stop, ladies, is Earth."

Chapter Four
~ February 24th, 2282 ~

"I've received a message from Admiral Carver," Admiral Moore said to the Admiralty Board members during their regular session. "She's on her way to Earth."

"To Earth? Why?" Admiral Platt asked.

"She says she hasn't been home for twelve years and hasn't even taken any personal leave since becoming the base commander of Stewart eight years ago. She feels that now is the best time to leave the new headquarters base because there's little to do until the ships assigned to the Second Fleet actually begin to arrive and construction can begin."

"This is dereliction of duty," Admiral Hubera said. "I told you all that putting her in command of Region Two was a mistake, but you insisted she was the best person for the job."

"Oh, Donald, not again," Admiral Hillaire said. "Her fleet has virtually no people and no ships yet. She's wisely taking a break now before she's really needed. How do you see that as dereliction of duty?"

"Roger's section has information about a pending Raider attack. She should be at her headquarters, ready to direct the defensive efforts."

"How can she possibly mount a defensive effort when she has no ships or people?" Admiral Platt asked. "Roger, have you identified the target?"

"No, we haven't," Admiral Bradlee said. "We haven't gotten any new information since our agent overheard that one scrap of conversation."

"Have you relayed that information to Admiral Carver?" Admiral Ahmed asked.

"No, I haven't. I was hoping to have something a little more tangible before raising her concerns. The Milori had almost ninety bases, and for all we know, the base being discussed might be in the returned Gondusan or Hudeera territory."

"But what if they were talking about mounting an attack on the new Headquarters base?" Admiral Woo asked.

"That's extremely unlikely, Lon. The Milori had deserted the base, which was only partially completed at the time. There would be little to gain until the first supply ships get there and I don't have to remind you that the twelve ships with supplies are the newest, fastest, and best protected warships from the M-designate fleet."

"Whatever their target, Carver shouldn't have left her post without prior authorization," Admiral Hubera said.

"We made her the supreme military authority in Region Two, Donald," Admiral Burke said. "Just who was she supposed to get permission from?"

"I'm not saying she couldn't take a few days off," Admiral Hubera said, "but that doesn't include leaving her command for four months."

"A few days off," Admiral Hillaire echoed. "That's generous of you, Donald. Perhaps you'll consent to giving her a few additional days in another eight years."

"Admiral Carver is the best one to decide when and for how long she can afford to be away from her command," Admiral Moore said. "Since she hasn't been made aware of the intelligence from the Uthlaro Dominion, she can't be faulted for thinking this was the opportune time to enjoy a very well-deserved vacation."

"Will she be appearing here, Richard?" Admiral Platt asked.

"She has made a request for a meeting with the Board while she's on Earth."

"She's probably going to ask for more ships and people," Admiral Hubera said.

"She knows we're giving her everything we possibly can," Admiral Ressler said.

"And it isn't nearly enough," Admiral Moore said. "We've given her a problem comparable to emptying

Lake Superior with a ten-liter bucket. If we had anything else to give, she'd get it, but we must retain most of our present fleet to patrol and protect Region One. As it is we're a hundred fifty ships short of the approved ship strength for this region alone."

* * *

"Excuse me, Viceroy," Exalted Lord Space Marshall Berquyth's aide said, "I'm most sorry to disturb your meditation, but we've received a message from the governor of Ekoqulith. He says that dozens of ships have encircled the planet and shuttles have landed in the capital. They're rounding up government employees and demanding the complete surrender of all citizens. Anyone who resists is slain."

Berquyth was stretched out on the carpeted floor of his office in the palace to perform the daily Milori prayer and meditation ritual of Danisu. "I've issued orders that all Milori military, militias, and citizens are to comply with Space Command fully," he said. "Our empire is gone, Flinuq. The Galactic Alliance controls this part of space now and they can land wherever they want. I'm surprised to hear that Space Command is killing people though. I didn't think they were like that, even with people who resisted."

"But they're not Space Command, Viceroy, they're Tsgardi."

Berquyth opened his eyes wide. "Tsgardi? What are Tsgardi doing there? Ekoqulith is fifty light-annuals inside our border. Uh, I mean the Galactic Alliance border."

"We didn't get any more than what I've told you. The transmission suddenly went silent."

"Silent?"

"Yes, Viceroy. It cut off in mid word, as if the equipment suddenly malfunctioned or the signal was suddenly jammed."

Lord Space Marshall Berquyth closed his eyes again. His aide waited for several minutes, unsure if he was dismissed.

"Should I do anything, Viceroy?" the aide finally asked.

Berquyth opened his eyes again. "No. I will send a message to Admiral Carver. Space Command must deal with this. We've been forbidden to take any aggressive action outside our solar system. We can only protect our home planet. Help me up."

* * *

"That fool Wesyesku didn't activate the jamming satellite before the attack began, Captain," Warrior Colonel Ekulosque said in the attack review meeting days after the fall of Ekoqulith. "We didn't realize it until our com operator detected an encrypted outgoing message."

"What?" the Tsgardi captain said. "That idiot! You're sure the message was encrypted?"

"Yes, my Captain."

"Then it wasn't just a general cry for help. If it was encrypted, it was directed to someone of importance. The sender no doubt informed them of the takeover. Warrior Major Wesyesku has cost us the element of surprise in future engagements. Many Tsgardi will die because of his carelessness. When I see him he'll learn personally what a lattice projectile to the chest can do. Where is he?"

"I've already seen to his punishment, my Captain. He won't be making any more such mistakes. I promoted his immediate subordinate into his vacated position."

"Very well. What's done is done. It's time to continue on to our next objective."

* * *

"We've received an encrypted message for Admiral Carver from the Viceroy of Milor, Colonel," the com operator said to Lt. Colonel Barletto, the senior security officer at Space Command Headquarters – Quesann. "They've used a discontinued code for the encryption, but it's still in the system."

"Place it in her queue," Lt. Colonel Barletto said to the image on his com unit. "She'll handle it when she returns from vacation."

"But it's marked 'most urgent,' sir."

52

"Most urgent, eh? I suppose I should look at it then. Forward a copy to my com station."

When the copy appeared in his queue, Lt. Colonel Barletto selected it from the list and tapped the play button. The image of Exalted Lord Space Marshall Berquyth filled his screen.

"Admiral Carver, we've received a most distressing message from the governor of Ekoqulith. The planet was under attack by a large Tsgardi taskforce. After dozens of ships ringed the planet, shuttles began landing in the capital. The Tsgardi started rounding up our people and slaying anyone who resisted. The transmission went dead at that point as if the sender was interrupted or the signal was jammed.

"As the planet lies within Galactic Alliance Region Two space, Ekoqulith is entitled to protection from outside aggression. I humbly request that you immediately dispatch a taskforce to retake Ekoqulith, return its government to its people, and punish the aggressors.

"Exalted Lord Space Marshall Berquyth, Viceroy of Milor. Message complete."

Lt. Colonel Barletto knew that this problem could only be handled by the Admiral. He leaned back in his chair as he performed a quick mental calculation and exhaled the breath he had been holding since the message began. At three light-years per hour, it would take eighteen days for the message to reach Earth. Admiral Carver had left on January 23rd, so she would already have been on Earth for a week before the message reached the *Colorado*. Barletto sighed and issued the command to reroute a copy of the message, re-encrypted with a current code. He hated to interrupt the Admiral's long overdue vacation, but he knew she'd have his head if he didn't forward the message immediately.

* * *

"Six more days," Jenetta said to her sisters as they sat on the carpeted deck in her sitting room. They had eaten dinner and were now playing with the cats as they talked.

Jenetta was brushing Cayla's thick coat of fur, while Eliza and Christa were petting Tayna a few feet away.

"When are you going to call mom?" Eliza asked.

"When we enter Earth's solar system. If I call before then, she'll be in a complete frenzy until we get there. This way she'll only have to wait a few hours to see us."

"Are we stopping to pick up Hugh?"

"No," Jenetta said sadly, "not this trip."

"Why not?" Christa asked. "You two have a fight?"

"No, nothing like that. The second officer of the *Bonn* has just been promoted off the ship and the third officer is away at some training conference. They're out on patrol and Captain Simpson can't spare her first officer right now. And I wouldn't ask her to."

"It's too bad we couldn't bring Billy with us. His first, second, and third officers are all aboard ship and he was only ten light-years from Stewart."

"But he's a ship's captain now. He wouldn't want to be separated from his command for two months."

"Why not?" Christa said. "You're separated from yours for four months."

"That's different. I was just sitting around on my hands waiting for my ships to arrive. As it is, I'll still be back before they get there. Besides, I've wanted to address the Admiralty Board in person ever since they began pinning all these stars on me."

"What are you going to tell them?"

"I don't know yet. I'd like to resign, but I really think I can make a difference in Region Two once some ships begin to arrive. I just want to get the region straightened out and then turn it over to someone else."

"Have you thought what it's going to be like, stepping down after being one of the most powerful people in Space Command for so long?" Eliza asked.

"El, you know I've never sought the power. And being responsible for trillions of lives doesn't exactly help one sleep at night. I'll be content to merely be responsible for a few thousand lives aboard ship again. You'll understand better when you attain the rank yourselves. You were born before I had risen very high, so you don't share these memories."

"We have the memories of you being the second officer on the *Prometheus* and the Captain of the *Song*. I miss those days. All we do now is steer the ship wherever we're ordered."

"You're just one step away from becoming Lt. Commanders. With your next promotions your duties and responsibilities will increase tremendously. For one thing, you'll have the watch for a part of each day, even if it's only during the first watch when the captain is off the bridge."

"It can't come soon enough," Eliza said. "People expect Christa and me to be just like the great Jenetta Carver. It's difficult trying to measure up to yourself. Here we are, still just lieutenants after more than nine years of service."

Jenetta smiled and said, "Oh, come on now, El, show me one other twelve-year-old who's come as far and fast as you and Christa have? You know that on average, officers don't reach Lt. Commander until they've had between fourteen and eighteen years of service."

"But you're a four-star already."

"I'm also going to be forty-six in a couple of months."

"If we hadn't been cloned from you, we'd be thirty-two now based on eleven years from Academy graduation."

"Be patient a little longer. Space Command is desperate to increase the size of our fleets now that we've tripled our territory. Promotion rates are going to speed up tremendously as new positions are created. Within a couple of years' time you might very well have that extra half-stripe."

* * *

Six days later the *Colorado* docked at Earth Station Three. Most of the crew was from Earth and Jenetta had established a schedule so everyone aboard would get at least one full week of leave.

Fearing she might have problems if she was recognized aboard a shuttle in the mass transit system— and there was little doubt she would be— she exercised her prerogative as captain of the ship and a flag officer in Space Command to use one of the *Colorado's* shuttles. Jenetta delighted in taking the helm for the first time in years. She was a little rusty but got the feel of the tiny ship quickly enough.

The shuttle had to sit in a holding queue until it received clearance down to the Potomac Space Command Base, but once authorized, they made the trip to the surface in just eighteen minutes. The short flight had given Jenetta enough of a feel for the small craft that she was able to touch it down with the gentle touch of a feather falling to the ground.

"That was wonderful!" Jenetta exclaimed as she shut everything down. "It's been a long time since I actually took the helm controls."

"Now that you've had your fun, it's time to pay the piper," Eliza said.

"What are you talking about?"

"Look at the bow monitor."

Jenetta raised her eyes to look at the monitor. Dozens of people were streaming in through the entranceway in the shuttle-pad blast walls now that the engines had shut down. A few were carrying hastily constructed signs that read, 'Welcome home Jenetta.'

"Oh, no! How do you suppose they heard about me coming?"

"Are you kidding?" Christa asked. "The entire planet probably knows by now. The reporters at Stewart probably sent off their stories before we even left port."

"But I never announced that my destination was Earth."

"Somebody must have leaked it then," Eliza said, grinning. "Admiral, your audience awaits."

"I think we'll need a squad of Marines first," Jenetta said jokingly.

"Oh, come on," Christa said, "this is a Space Command base and these people are members of the SC family. They aren't going to attack you. Besides, El and I are here to run interference for you if you need it. Just ratchet up the speech-writing center of your brain and make them feel delighted they came out in the cold weather to greet you."

Jenetta smiled. "The speech-writing center of my brain, eh? Okay, but you'd better stay in here with Cayla and Tayna. My girls might get confused by all the shouting."

"Don't worry," Eliza said. "You couldn't get us out there on a bet. Go placate your fans."

A cheer went up as the shuttle hatch opened. A squad of Marines had arrived and was keeping people back. The base's senior officers came to attention near the bottom of the ramp and saluted as Jenetta stepped out of the ship. She wondered if her wait in the holding queue above Earth had been to give the command time to organize. Jenetta returned their salute and then waved to the crowd, causing the cheering to grow louder. Standing at the top of the ramp, she waited until the uproar started to die down a little and then raised her hands for silence.

"Good evening. This is my first trip home in twelve years and it's so nice to see I haven't been forgotten." She received the laughter she was hoping for and paused while it persisted. "A lot has happened since my last visit and I'm happy to inform you that everyone who works in space, or travels through it, is far safer today than at any other time in the past twelve years." Another cheer went up and Jenetta again paused, waiting until the din subsided.

"But freedom is never free and many of our Marines and Space Command personnel have, as always, paid for it with their blood, and sometimes with their lives. Despite my best efforts to keep our people safe during our encounters with the enemy, I've lost far too many comrades, but I'm overjoyed that peace is finally on the horizon. We've kicked the Raiders so hard they've dropped out of sight. And the Milori will never again threaten any of their peaceful neighbors in this galaxy." Jenetta had to pause again as another cheer went up.

"The task ahead of us now is to take control of the newly annexed territory and make it as peaceful as this Region has become. I'll need your help and support, but together we can do it. There's not a doubt in my mind about that. I promise you I'll continue to devote every fiber of my being to protecting you, your families, and your loved ones. Thank you for coming out tonight to welcome me home and God bless you all."

Another thunderous cheer arose on the pad. Jenetta took a few seconds to scan the faces in the crowd and then slowly walked down the ramp. The base commander and his senior staff officially greeted her as she stepped onto the base. After the introductions were over, Jenetta moved towards a crowd still being restrained by the Marines. The Marines moved aside as she motioned them to part and people pressed in around her to shake her hand or simply just touch her. At five-eleven, she was taller than most of the women in the crowd and most of the men as well. She worked the crowd like a politician running for office as she smiled widely and glad-handed her admirers. Slowly the shuttle pad area began to clear, and Jenetta's petite mother was finally able to reach her daughter.

"Hi, Momma," Jenetta said as they embraced.

Tears were streaming down her mother's face and she was too choked up to say anything. The tender scene seemed to embarrass some of the remaining people in the crowd, and they quieted down considerably.

"Where are Christa and Eliza?" her mother was finally able to ask.

"They're still inside the shuttle with my pets. We felt it was better they stay there for now. Once the crowd thins a little more, they'll come out."

Annette Carver finally relaxed her grip on her daughter and stood back. "I'm forgetting my friends, dear." Turning, she gestured towards several women behind her. "This is Dorothy Nelson. Her daughter Beverly was in your command when you were at Stewart. She's on board the *Lima*. This is Linda Reilly. Her son is on the cruiser *Plantaganet*. He was also in your command when you were at Stewart. And this is Diana Michelle. Her son Jonathon is on the *Pholus*, one of the battleships that have been sent to your fleet in Region Two. He's a Lieutenant."

Jenetta smiled and nodded at each of the women as they were introduced. "I'm pleased to meet you, ladies. While I don't believe I've met your children personally, I'm sure each one is a credit to his or her ship. If I happen to be aboard any of their ships in the future, I'll be sure to look them up."

The three women stepped closer, all trying to talk at once. Jenetta smiled and tried to listen to the three conversations as the women talked about their progeny and how proud they were to be part of Jenetta's command.

The crowd had thinned considerably by then, but a lot of people had remained behind, not willing to leave until they had gotten close to Jenetta and had an opportunity to tell her about their children, spouses, or other relatives who were serving, or had served, in her commands. There were even a couple of people who waited around to thank Jenetta for her kind vidMail after their spouse or child had died in battle with the Milori. She again offered her condolences and spent some time explaining the circumstances of the deaths once she learned to which ship they'd been posted.

Finally, the shuttle pad was almost empty except for a few stragglers and the platoon of Marines. Christa and Eliza emerged from the shuttle with Cayla and Tanya, who immediately bounded to Jenetta's side. Jenetta looked on as her mother embraced each of the daughters she had never met in person. The people who still remained in the area had moved back a couple of steps when the large black cats emerged from the small ship.

Jenetta used a handheld remote to close and lock the shuttle hatch while her mother and sisters began to move towards the pad's entranceway. A driverless vehicle waited outside the blast walls to take them to the house, and a squad of Marines followed along in two vehicles, serving as a protection detail while she was there.

The house had changed little since Jenetta's last trip home. Her sisters knew it as well as she did because they shared her memories of growing up there. Jenetta's cats immediately recognized her faint scent in the house despite the years that had passed since her last visit and treated the home as their own. They began exploring as soon as they entered the house.

One of the few differences was the wall of photos in the dining room. The gallery now included images of Christa and Eliza as lieutenants, the medal ceremony where Jenetta received her first Medal of Honor, the images taken of the three girls when they were on Nordakia, and the ceremony on Stewart where Admiral Jenetta Carver had pinned captain's bars on her brother Billy. There was also a shot of Jenetta with the four gold stars that showed her rank to be that of a senior Admiral. It replaced the earlier image of her as a Lieutenant Commander that had been on the wall when she was last home.

"Where did you get that image, Momma?" Jenetta asked. "I don't remember posing for a picture like that since I was last promoted."

"A friend of mine had her son alter a picture of you with two stars. He's a computer whiz. Kind of like you when you were young."

Looking at the image very closely, Jenetta said, "He's good. Now that I look at it carefully, I can see a little fuzziness around the edges of the stars, but it's barely noticeable."

"My favorite picture is the one of you girls together on Nordakia. You look like princesses in your long gowns, hair extending almost to the floor. With your cats at your feet, it really adds a look of royalty to the picture."

"As an azula on Nordakia, Jen *is* royalty now, Momma," Christa said. "All members of the family Carver are recognized as noble born. You're the Azula Mum on the province of Gavistee on Obotymot."

"The Azula Mum?"

"Of course," Jenetta said. "I guess I didn't explain it as thoroughly as I should have when I told you about it. If you'd like to take a trip, you can live at the family palace for as long as you wish. There's a staff of twenty-five there with no one to serve. You'll have the run of the estate. I understand the weather is improving each year as more of the dust clears that was kicked into the upper atmosphere by the meteor. My chamberlain hopes to resume limited agricultural production in a few years."

"Would I have to dress in one of those long gowns if I go there?"

"Not anymore," Christa said. "The clothing requirements have changed for the better. We're glad you like the image, but we all hope we never have to dress like that again. You have no idea how uncomfortable those gowns were."

Annette smiled. "You girls never could stand to wear anything feminine."

"It wasn't that it was feminine," Eliza said. "The palace dressmakers had made the gowns too small and we had to wear corsets just to squeeze into them. We're not fat, so compressing the muscle around our midsections was almost unbearable."

"You'd never know it from looking at the picture. You all look so relaxed and comfortable. And I still can't believe you're all here together. This was the best gift you could give me."

Jenetta didn't mention it might be another six years before she would be home again. She didn't want to diminish her mother's joy at having them home, even if it was just for a short time.

Chapter Five
~ March 24th, 2282 ~

Over the next week, the four women spent most of their time together. Jenetta explained about the cloning process and the initial emotions she'd had to work through when she learned she'd been cloned. Christa and Eliza talked about their efforts to separate their lives from Jenetta's past and establish a new identity for themselves. After that, all three women took turns telling their mom about the things they had experienced since Jenetta had last been on Earth.

Jenetta had hoped to meet Richie's wife during her first trip home since the marriage, but her sister-in-law Marisa was off-planet visiting her own parents at the Sebastian colony.

On the morning Jenetta was to report to the Admiralty Board, Christa and Eliza made plans to go shopping with their mom. Jenetta had always avoided shopping trips when she was young, and they knew a day at the mall with her daughters would delight Annette. Two of the female Marines from the protection detail would accompany them since many people would assume that either Christa or Eliza was Jenetta, or because some people might want to get a close-up look at clones.

* * *

Jenetta used her shuttle to fly alone to the Space Command Headquarters Base in Nebraska. She had debated whether to bring the cats and then decided to take them along. They had almost become a part of her identity, after all, and they always had a certain calming effect on overzealous newsies and curious civilians.

As she climbed the wide stone steps to the impressive Admiralty building, she rehearsed in her mind what she was going to say. Lt. Commander Ashraf was waiting for her in the rotunda, just inside the entrance doors.

"Good morning, Admiral."

"Good morning, Lori."

"Have you been enjoying your time at home, ma'am?"

"Very much, thank you. My mother is beside herself with joy that we've come for the visit I've been promising for so long. Our assignments kept taking us farther and farther out. I'm happy to have finally made it. This is only my second trip home in twenty-five years. The last time was when we brought the *Song* home for repairs after the Battle for Higgins. How's your family?"

"It's wonderful seeing them all again. It's been as long since my last visit— twelve years— as it has been for you. When you turned command of the *Song* over to Captain Yung, we were sent to the sectors near Dixon for patrol duties. We moved into the former Frontier Zone when the borders were expanded. At least my brothers and sisters are all on Earth, so my folks have some comfort there."

"A life in space is tough on family life, romances, and friendships. Hopefully, the new speed improvement will help everyone cope just a little better. Instead of taking three months to get here from Higgins, the trip is only four days."

The few minutes of peace they had enjoyed were interrupted by newsies as they converged on Jenetta from all sides. Her cats kept them at a respectable distance as Jenetta repeated that she had no statements to make right now, but the more obnoxious newsies continued to shout questions at her until she reached the Board's outer chamber. Correspondents weren't permitted into the chambers except by special invitation.

A clerk greeted Jenetta and her aide and asked them to have a seat until the Board was ready to convene. They sat in silence as Jenetta again slipped into meditation about the meeting.

At 0945, the clerk invited Jenetta and her aide to enter the meeting hall but added that pets weren't permitted.

Jenetta looked at the two cats and said, "Cayla, Tayna, wait out here for me."

The two cats had stood when she did but now sank back down to prone positions. They watched intently, the flicking ends of their tails their only movement as she walked to the doors and disappeared into the meeting hall. The clerk walked nervously back to his desk— nervous because the attention of the cats had shifted to him once Jenetta was out of sight. They seemed to understand he was responsible for separating them from their mistress.

Inside the hall, a clerk escorted Jenetta to one of the seats reserved for visiting admirals at the horseshoe-shaped table. A holographic display at the front edge of the table identified her to the other flag officers who would attend the meeting. It hardly seemed necessary, so Jenetta assumed that it was mainly for archival recording purposes. Lori took a seat directly behind Jenetta.

The Board Admirals, along with their aides and clerks, began to enter the chamber from an entrance opposite that of the outer chamber a few minutes before 1000 hours. Jenetta stood and shook hands with each of the admirals, then exchanged pleasantries until it was time for the meeting to begin. She had met all but one at the ceremony when she received the Medal of Honor years earlier. Admiral Hubera hadn't attended that day, but she knew him from her days at the Academy when he had been a professor there. He seemed pleasant enough today, but distant.

"This meeting of the Admiralty Board is now open," Admiral Moore said. "We welcome Admiral Jenetta Carver as a visiting flag officer to this session."

The Board discussed old business first, which included nothing that concerned Jenetta or Region Two, then moved to new business.

"Admiral Carver, you've requested time to address the Board," Admiral Moore said. "You may make your presentation now."

"Thank you, Admiral. I was quite astounded when this Board chose to place me in command of Region Two, but if that is your wish, I shall do the job to the best of my abilities. I know you are well aware of the problems confronting me as I carry out the duties of my position. Region Two is twice as vast as Region One, and establishing proper patrol coverage will take many resources and much time. Prior to their last expansion effort, the Milori had six hundred ships in the fleets tasked to maintain control over an empire just two-thirds our size. I have eight ships in my fleet at present. When all of the M-designate ships and the twelve Mars-built ships arrive a year from now, I'll have one sixth of the Milori strength, but it will be an additional five years before they can reach the remotest sectors of the Region.

"I know that most of the output from the Mars shipyard for the next ten years has been pledged to Region Two, and I will not ask for a more generous share of Space Command's assets than that already promised. I propose instead that the output from the yard be modified."

"Modified in what way?" Admiral Plimley asked. As the Director of Weapons Research & Development, she headed the committee that directed ship construction at the yard, although the full Board decided the quantity and class of the ships.

"It takes six or more years to build a new battleship. Each *Prometheus*-class battleship is one thousand, nine hundred seventy meters in length and has a crew complement of three thousand, five hundred."

"We know that already," Admiral Hubera said testily, "get to the point."

Jenetta stared silently at the curmudgeon for several seconds while he stared back. She had never intentionally done anything to incur his wrath and his attitude surprised her, but she didn't flinch as she returned his glare with a steady stare of her own. He had just spoken to her as he had when she was a cadet in his class. But she wasn't a cadet any longer; she was a flag officer, just as he was. In fact, she out ranked him— a fact that was eating away at him as he watched a superior officer who appeared to be about twenty-one years of age. Jenetta could see the bitterness in his eyes.

"On the other hand," Jenetta said, continuing, "a *Colorado*-class scout-destroyer is one-twentieth the size of a battleship, requires one-twentieth the construction resources, could be completed in one-twelfth the time, and only requires a crew one-twentieth that of a battleship. I would gladly accept twenty scout-destroyers in place of one battleship. More precisely, I would prefer to have sixty new scout-destroyers instead of the next three battleships earmarked for Region Two. The resources required to produce and crew the ships would be about equal."

The members of the Board looked at one another as they thought about her statements. Admiral Platt was the first to speak.

"A scout-destroyer can't do the things a battleship can do. A point you might be overlooking is that a battleship has twenty times the firing capacity and carries a battalion of Marines."

"I would pit any DS scout-destroyer against any non-DS-hulled battleship. I need warships capable of Light-9790, and I need them in quantity as soon as possible. I realize everyone may be thinking of these small ships simply as adjuncts to battleships, but they are much more than that. I was able to crush the Milori resolve to continue the war with just two such vessels."

"But you didn't have to fight any ship-to-ship engagements with them," Admiral Burke said.

"While true that I didn't fight any prolonged warship-to-warship battles with them, I know their capability. We were struck thousands of times by laser pulses when we destroyed Milor's shipyard. We were able to completely ignore the ring of laser weapon satellites because we knew they couldn't harm us. It would be no different in a ship battle. We would only have to worry about torpedo strikes. And don't forget, I took and held Stewart for months with just one crippled scout-destroyer."

"What about the lack of Marine fighter craft?" Admiral Woo asked. "And scout-destroyers wouldn't allow you to have the number of Marines normally found even on a destroyer, nor their landing craft and armored assault vehicles. Wouldn't you be better off having twelve new DS destroyers instead of sixty scout-destroyers?"

"Right now I need quantity more than overall ship capability. I don't anticipate any planet-side actions until we first get basic control of space. I'm not saying battleships, cruisers, frigates, or destroyers wouldn't be much more utilitarian in an area of space where we have already established a degree of control, or that I wouldn't *love* to have a fleet of them. I would, most definitely. But I need as many warships as possible right now and I think the best solution is to mass-produce the scout-destroyers. These small ships can zip to the furthest reaches of Region Two in a matter of weeks, giving us a presence there *years* before our older ships can arrive. Any criminals who attempt to establish a power base in remote areas where governmental vacuums presently exist will find us stalking them long before they anticipate our arrival."

"We have five scout-destroyers nearing completion now," Admiral Hillaire said. "They're intended for the *Prometheus*, *Chiron*, *Atlas*, *Hercules*, and *Epimetheus*. Would they make such a difference if we could send them to you when they're completed?"

"An immense difference. You can't think of these small ships as merely scouting vessels. I would use every one as a full-fledged warship until they could be replaced by destroyers, frigates, cruisers, or battleships. While it's true they can't carry the armament or supplies of a full-sized destroyer or the fighters and personnel of the larger ships and must return for resupply more often, five more ships would almost double my current fleet size. I could either allow two of our three bases to begin making limited patrols, or I could open two more bases."

"You believe two ships are adequate to protect a base?" Admiral Hubera asked.

"I'd much prefer to have a minimum of five full-size warships protecting every base, but as was the case with Stewart when it became a base, we simply don't have that luxury. I'm forced to stretch my resources as much as possible and hope I'm not risking lives any more than necessary. Ladies and gentlemen, right now we have an incredible edge over every other military in this quadrant of the galaxy. We all know that won't last, because once intelligent beings see what's possible, they find a way to accomplish it themselves. The possibility of attaining Light-9790 is not idle speculation anymore. I'm sure every nation's military has intelligence agents trying to learn how we've done it, if they don't already know. Once they do know how it's accomplished, they'll be working to duplicate it. We know one way, but it may not be the *only* way. We have to take advantage of our technological superiority while we have it to secure Region Two. In future years, the scout-destroyers will be less adequate for the job we must do, but right now each is more useful than an older battleship for the task at hand, and one-twentieth the cost."

"Thank you for your suggestion, Admiral," Admiral Moore said. "We'll study the shipyard construction schedule and see if the changes you request are possible. Is there anything else you wish to bring up for discussion?"

"No, Admiral. My weekly reports contain everything that concerns the Board."

"In that case, Admiral Bradlee has some information for you. Roger?"

"Admiral Carver, we've received information that Raiders may be planning an attack against a former Milori base in Region Two. The information comes from part of a conversation overheard in a bar in the Uthlaro Dominion. We have no specifics, and for all we know the base being discussed could be in Hudeera or Gondusan space now. Truthfully, it could be anywhere because the Milori were spreading out in their goal to rule the galaxy. But we felt you should be made aware of the information."

"When did you learn of this?"

"The information arrived here two months ago, but the conversation took place three months ago."

"Three months? The Raiders could have traveled more than sixty light-years since then."

"We didn't want to alarm you unnecessarily. We've been trying to get more precise information since then."

"I see. I appreciate your desire to have substantive information before reporting something overheard in a conversation, but in the future, it would be helpful to learn about such reports immediately, even if it's only a rumor or partial information."

"Of course."

Jenetta sat quietly while other business was discussed. She appeared to be listening intently to the business of the Board, but she was in reality only half-listening, most of her brain being used to consider the information about a base attack. The meeting was adjourned just before 1200.

"Admiral Carver," Admiral Moore said as the flag officers rose from their seats, "would you join us for lunch?"

Although not a command, Jenetta realized from the way it was worded that it was more than an invitation. She had intended to return directly home, but instead said, "Thank you, sir, I'd love to. May I bring my pets?"

Admiral Moore hesitated for a second and then said, "I wasn't aware they were here. Of course you may."

"Thank you, sir."

"Call me Richard, or Rich. May I call you Jenetta?"

"It's Jen to my friends, Rich."

Admiral Moore smiled. "Where are your pets, Jen?"

"In the outer chamber. I was told they couldn't be admitted to the meeting hall."

"That doesn't apply to the pets of flag officers, as long as they don't interrupt the meeting."

Jenetta walked to the door and opened it. "Cayla, Tayna, come with me."

The two large cats jumped up and sprang for the open doorway while the clerk who said they couldn't enter looked on in horror. With her pets at her side and Lt. Commander Ashraf following, Jenetta walked to the private entrance on the opposite side of the meeting hall where Admiral Moore was waiting. The door opened into a wide corridor with doors on either side.

"I've read about these *pets* of yours, Jen," Admiral Moore said as they walked towards the end of the hallway, "but I'd never seen a picture of them. They're larger than I imagined."

"They're an average size for Taurentlus-Thur Jumakas. They make excellent companions for a senior officer in a command situation where he or she has little contact with peers."

"How long did it take to train them?"

"They were already trained to provide security for a gemstone shop on Taurentlus-Thur when I received them. I never had to provide any additional training."

"But they responded when you spoke to them in Amer."

"I can't explain that. From the beginning I've only spoken to them in Amer, and they've always seemed to implicitly understand what I say. With a Terran animal, you have to repeat commands precisely the same way every time. I speak to my cats the way I would speak to another person."

"I've heard they were intelligent animals. You're saying now that they understand spoken language?"

"All I can say is that they understand *me*. And they understand when someone is threatening me. When that assassin at Dixon Space Command Base tried to kill me, they attacked him without any verbal command from me in a shopping area filled with people. They knew who presented the danger before I was aware of him and took action to stop him. They saved my life."

As they reached the end of the corridor, the doors there slid silently open. Since their implanted CTs permitted access to secure areas, any flag officer listed in the Space Command central computer could open the doors to the private dining room simply by approaching them.

The other admirals were already seated in the room when Admiral Moore and Jenetta entered. Two large circular tables in the center of the large room, each capable of seating a dozen people, were set for dining. The Admirals occupied one and their aides the other.

Once seated, Admiral Moore said, "Jen, in here we're always on a first-name basis." Gesturing to each of the flag officers, he gave their first names, then said to the others, "Admiral Carver prefers that her friends call her Jen."

"Jen," Admiral Platt said, "we've all read the reports and seen the vid logs of your campaign in Milori space, but I'd like to hear some of the things that aren't typically included in reports. For example, what were you feeling when you laid waste to the Milori home world?"

Jenetta breathed deeply before responding. "I was filled with many different emotions. I was upset that so many Milori citizens would be injured or killed, but I knew the attack was the only way to bring Maxxiloth down. Since he was the motivating force behind the invasions where so many of our people died, I eagerly anticipated his downfall. I was thankful Milor wouldn't be able to wage war against us again for a long time and I was hopeful the action would end the killing. Ultimately, it did."

"I'm sorry you're only going to be here for one more week, Jen," Admiral Hillaire said, "it would be great if you could visit the two Space Command Academies on Earth and address the corps of cadets."

"I've already promised these two weeks to my mother. I can't break my word now."

"Perhaps Jen can extend her trip to Earth," Admiral Platt suggested. "After all she's traveled such a great distance to get here and another week shouldn't make much difference. Even with an extension of her stay, the ships she's expecting at Region Two headquarters won't have arrived when she returns."

"That would be wonderful," Admiral Hillaire said. "I know the students at NHSA and SHSA would love the opportunity to hear you speak, Jen."

Unable to come up with a good reason why she couldn't extend her time on Earth by another week, Jenetta smiled and said, "I suppose another week here won't impact operations in Region Two."

"Great," Admiral Hillaire said, smiling as if he had just pulled off a coup, "I'll speak to the commandants at the academies this afternoon and have them make arrangements for your visits next week."

Over the next several hours, Jenetta answered a steady barrage of questions about her exploits. It was like all the dinners she had hosted while a base commander. One could watch vid logs and simulations for a year and never get the full flavor of a battle until viewed through the eyes of someone who was there, especially when that someone had developed the battle plan and directed the action.

* * *

Jenetta was halfway home when she received a message from the *Colorado* that Quesann had forwarded an important communication. In the privacy of the *Colorado's* cockpit, she grimaced as she viewed the message from Exalted Lord Space Marshall Berquyth. It was already more than three weeks old. The contents of the message, combined with the conversation overheard in the Uthlaro Dominion, gave Jenetta a sickening feeling. The Raiders had a history of employing Tsgardi mercenaries, but in the Viceroy's message he spoke of dozens of ships surrounding Ekoqulith. 'Dozens of ships' would seem to indicate the Tsgardi Kingdom was behind the invasion in Region Two. They might be trying to expand their territory while Space Command was still substantially under-strength there.

With just eight ships at her disposal, Jenetta wasn't in any position to rush to the defense of Ekoqulith. The Milori had maintained control over the planets in its territory by forbidding weapons that could be used against their masters at a future time, so most of the planets in

Region Two were defenseless. The Tsgardi ships were no match for Space Command ships, but she couldn't send one or two ships against dozens of warships, even if she had them. The problem might already have become one of digging out an enemy who'd become entrenched on a planet. Such an operation would take companies of Marines she didn't have.

The odd piece in the puzzle was the Raider conversation. Were they waiting for the Tsgardi to draw Space Command away so they could attack bases along the Uthlaro border without fear of intervention? If so, they had definitely gotten stuck with the dirty end of the stick because, unlike the planets, the bases were far from defenseless. They would fall to an overwhelming force, but they would draw a lot of Raider blood before that happened.

Jenetta leaned forward and tapped the record button on the com panel.

"Message to Exalted Lord Space Marshall Berquyth, Viceroy of Milor, Palace of the Emperor, Milor, with a copy to the Admiralty Board.

"Viceroy, I've just received your message regarding Ekoqulith. Unfortunately, this attack has come at a time when I've just returned to Earth for a brief visit. I shall be back at my new Region Two headquarters at Quesann in two Terran months and I'll address the situation at that time. I'm sorry I can't react sooner, but the distances involved preclude any earlier action. Since the transmission appeared to have been jammed during the attack, might I suggest you attempt to make contact with all your people and forces still off-world and warn them of potential problems. If you fail to receive answers, we might be better able to determine the level of threat to your people.

Jenetta Carver, Admiral, Space Command ship *Colorado* in Earth orbit. Message complete."

"Computer, new message. To all base commanders in Region Two. Copies to the Space Command Admiralty Board and all ship captains in Region Two."

"I've just received word that a large Tsgardi taskforce has attacked and seized the planet Ekoqulith. According to a message from the Viceroy of Milor, the planet was encircled by dozens of warships just prior to the attack. Communication with the planet was lost soon after the Tsgardi began to land on the surface. An attack on a planet so far inside our border with such a large force means we must consider this a full-scale invasion. At this time we have no other information, so you should be prepared for anything, including evacuation of your base if an overwhelming enemy force approaches. It might be a wise precaution on the part of space station commanding officers to move all ordnance stored in the station armory back into your battleship to prevent it from falling into the hands of an enemy should an emergency evacuation become necessary. Two ships are certainly not adequate to defend a station against a massed assault, even with the station's defensive armament in support.

"I've also been apprised of a Raider conversation overheard in the Uthlaro Dominion where an attack on a Milori base was mentioned. Since ownership of all Milori bases was ceded to us as a result of the annexation, this might also portend a coordinated attack on our resources from the opposite side of Region Two. Again, be prepared for anything. It appears that forces from outside GA space intend to attack us while our position in Region Two is still very weak.

"Jenetta Alicia Carver, Admiral, from the GSC *Colorado* at Earth.

"Computer, append a copy of the Viceroy's message to the prior Admiralty Board message."

Jenetta pressed the button that would send the messages to the *Colorado* for retransmission to Milor, Region Two, and the Admiralty Board. She had less than a week left of her original vacation, but the new situation would weigh heavily on her mind from then on.

* * *

Fully expecting to be recalled to appear at the Admiralty Board once they received her message, Jenetta wasn't surprised when the summons came just one day later. As before, she met Lt. Commander Ashraf at the entrance to the hall.

"Not much of a vacation, Admiral," Lori said, "when you have to appear twice at the Board and spend a day at each of the academies."

Jenetta smiled. "It could be worse, Lori. They could have scheduled a medal ceremony or required me to make an appearance before the Galactic Alliance Council where I'd have to listen to speeches for hours instead of merely giving a couple of short ones to a group of bored cadets."

"Since you didn't make it back for your class's twenty-fifth reunion, it may be nice to see your old alma mater again."

"Yes, I have to admit it'll be nice returning for a brief visit."

"And even nicer to come back as a huge success?"

"There's that too," Jenetta said, grinning.

Having reached the outer chamber of the meeting hall, Lt. Commander Ashraf waved her hand at the sensor, causing the doors to open. The same clerk from the previous visit asked them to have a seat until the session was ready to begin.

At 0945 the clerk invited them to enter the hall and take their seats. He once again reminded Jenetta that pets were not permitted in the hall.

"My cats will accompany me this time, Chief," Jenetta said as she walked towards the doors.

The clerk didn't argue or raise any objection whatsoever. Chief Petty Officers who argued with senior admirals could suddenly find themselves reassigned to positions considerably less pleasant and prestigious than working for the Admiralty Board.

Jenetta didn't take her seat immediately this time. As a stream of aides and clerks began to enter the meeting hall, she walked towards the entrance that led to the office side of the building. When the admirals came from their offices, she greeted them as friends, rather than merely as fellow officers. The meal they had enjoyed together in the private dining room had already instilled a sense of camaraderie that hadn't been there prior to her first appearance. Admiral Hubera was the only one who had been quiet and aloof, and he remained distant again on this day. A minute before 1000 hours, everyone took their seats.

"This special session of the Admiralty Board is now convened," Admiral Moore said. "We shall dispense with the reading of minutes and move immediately to the topic at hand, namely the new threat from outside our borders. Admiral Carver's presence has been requested so she might personally offer her assessment of the situation. Jen, give us your appraisal."

"As you've learned from the message received from the Viceroy of Milor," Jenetta said, "the Tsgardi have apparently entered GA space with the intention of seizing at least one planet. It would be too optimistic to assume they intend to stop there. For them to begin an action of this sort has to mean they intend to seize a portion of our territory and annex it to their own empire while our hold on that part of space is still tenuous. Our intelligence on the capabilities of their warships is that they are limited to a top speed of Light-225, so it will take them quite a while to conquer even a small area. Once the Milori have had a chance to query their off-world contacts, we'll have a better idea of the scale of their invasion."

"How do you think the Raiders fit into the equation?" Admiral Bradlee asked.

"We know the Raiders have often employed Tsgardi in their operations," Jenetta said, "but this is different. This may be a situation of the Tsgardi employing the Raiders to create diversions. Neither the Tsgardi nor the Raiders should know the true size of our forces in Region Two, so it may be an attempt to divide our fleet by pulling half of it to the other side of the territory."

"Or the Raiders may be looking to establish their own territory where their bases will finally be safe from Space Command," Admiral Ahmed offered.

"Trying to seize part of our territory would be a foolish way to create their own region of space," Admiral Plimley said. "They have to know we won't stand for it."

"I suppose our dream of enjoying a few decades of relative peace was too much to hope for," Admiral Ressler stated sadly.

"Is Region Two even worth another war?" Admiral Woo asked. "We're only there to keep the Milori from attacking us again. The Tsgardi would probably keep them in check for us."

"It's too late to back out now," Admiral Moore said. "If we simply cede the territory it would send a dangerous signal. We can't have our neighbors think we're afraid of the Tsgardi, or that we won't fight for what we've already laid claim to."

"An even worse situation," Jenetta said, "would be if the Tsgardi got their baboon paws on Milori ship-building technology. They'd be able to double their speed, improve the strength of their hulls, and give us a rougher time with every encounter. Right now, a Tsgardi warship doesn't stand an even chance against one of our oldest warships still in service. That would change very quickly if they seized the Milori shipyard and enslaved their scientists, engineers and technicians, as they did with the Flordaryns."

"We know the Tsgardi warships don't match up with our own," Admiral Burke said, "but how much of a threat are they really? What I'm getting at is: What will it take to push the Tsgardi back behind their own borders?"

"I suppose that depends on how many ships the Tsgardi have devoted to this effort and what ships I have for the counterattack," Jenetta said. "Our new scout-destroyers are easily the equivalent of three of their best destroyers, and our new battleships are probably equivalent to ten or more of our scout-destroyers simply because the hull plating on the battleships is denser, their Phalanx defense provides better coverage than the small ships, and they can fire torpedoes much more rapidly."

"Our best estimate is the Tsgardi have at least three hundred warships," Admiral Bradlee said.

"Then I'd need either a hundred scout-destroyers or ten new DS Battleships to repel a massed invasion force if I'm to feel completely confident we'd win the day."

"What if you must fight with just the ships already assigned to Region Two?" Admiral Plimley asked.

"The M-designate ships we captured in battle are among the best built by the Milori," Jenetta said. "Once they were repaired, and converted for our own use, we installed the new Phalanx defense system. Each should be more than a match for any two Tsgardi warships of equal size. Combined with the dozen older ships built at the Mars facility that are on their way to Region Two, I'm sure we would win the day if we only had to take on a hundred fifty Tsgardi ships. With my seventy-four-ship fleet against three hundred Tsgardi warships, the outcome is naturally less certain, but we would do our best."

"I asked you at our last meeting if the five scout-destroyers currently nearing completion at Mars would make such a difference, and you said they would," Admiral Hillaire said. "Following receipt of this new information, we've decided to assign them to Region Two as soon as they're launched. The battleships will have to wait for their scout-destroyers until we handle this new situation."

"Thank you," Jenetta said. "Their addition to my fleet will make a considerable difference."

"We've also reviewed the construction schedule at the yard," Admiral Plimley said. "We've decided it would be unwise to halt construction at any of the docks so new scout-destroyers could be constructed. The ships currently under construction are needed just as urgently. But we've almost completed construction of new docks intended for the retrofit of older ships so their speeds can be improved. Rather than begin those retrofit operations when project-ed, those docks will be used for the construction of scout-destroyers. We estimate that once we're in full production mode we can produce ten scout-destroyers every six months. Within a year's time you'll have an additional twenty scout-destroyers. Combined with the five new ships you'll receive now and the eight already assigned to your fleet, you'll have a force of thirty-three DS ships capable of Light-9790."

"Although it's not even half what you say you need to decisively defeat the Tsgardi," Admiral Platt commented, "it might be enough to halt their fleet's progression until additional ships can be completed and delivered."

"I think I can safely say," Jenetta said, "that the thirty-three ships will allow me to harass the Tsgardi enough to make them rethink their position. We know very little about their battle tactics, since the Milori kept them bottled up in their own territory, but we've had enough contact with Tsgardi mercenaries to suspect they prefer a massed assault. If I can get them to divide into smaller battle groups, we can take them on a group at a time and reduce their numbers significantly. Three hundred Tsgardi warships is not an insurmountable force once I have the ships you're promising."

"We've also moved ahead with staffing plans for Region Two Headquarters," Admiral Moore said. "Admiral Poole of Griffiths Space Command Base has been designated as the base commander of Quesann. Admiral Kanes will assume command of Intelligence in Region Two and Admiral Buckner will head up your Supply & Logistics Section. Poole, Buckner, and additional Region Two headquarters senior personnel will arrive with the first new transports. Admiral Kanes is ready immediately and you may pick him up from Higgins on your return trip."

"In light of this new development, would you prefer I postpone my visits to the two Academies?" Jenetta asked of the Board rather than anyone specifically.

Admiral Hillaire, as Director of the Academies, was the first to respond. "Since you don't yet have the resources to commence action against the Tsgardi, I don't think an extra week is going to make any difference. Does anyone disagree?"

"I don't," Admiral Bradlee said. "Even if the ships currently underway to Region Two had already arrived, there would be little Admiral Carver could do to prepare for the confrontation. And it will take most of the ships assigned to Region Two almost two years to reach the Tsgardi border from Quesann."

"I expect the Tsgardi to be halfway to Quesann by then," Jenetta said, "if they continue their move into Region Two. We're the only force that can stop, or even slow, their progress. I have to wonder if they've been planning this ever since the Milori first invaded us. They may have been just biding their time until the Milori were too weakened to resist their attacks."

"I think you're giving them too much credit, Jen," Admiral Platt said. "By all assessments, their intelligence is limited. Having such a long-range plan would seem inconsistent with the norm."

"Then they either came up with this plan when they realized the Milori wouldn't be able to stop them," Admiral Bradlee said, "or someone else has instigated this invasion."

"To what end, Roger?" Admiral Plimley asked.

"Possibly to distract us from our patrol activities, which might indicate the Raiders are behind it after all, or perhaps someone else who has designs on our territory and wants us to move most of our resources towards the Tsgardi border?"

"I can believe the Raiders having a hand in this," Admiral Burke said, "but it doesn't seem likely anyone else would be involved."

"Why not?" Admiral Woo asked.

"We just destroyed one of the most powerful militaries in this quadrant, and thanks to the brilliant tactics and leadership of Admiral Carver, our forces are completely intact. In fact, we're far stronger militarily than we've ever been. Who would be so foolish as to attack us now?"

"It would have to be someone who doesn't fear our military capability," Admiral Ahmed said. "We know little of the Ruwalch Confederacy, except for the rumors of their technological ability. Since their nation is located on the far border of Region Two, we've never had direct contact with them."

"Our new speed capability offers us the opportunity to travel farther for diplomatic missions than we ever considered feasible before," Admiral Ressler said. "Once this matter with the Tsgardi is settled, we must consider establishing formal diplomatic relations with our new neighbors."

"The Uthlaro might very well be involved," Admiral Burke offered. "We know they're very closely aligned with the Raiders. Perhaps they're in this together and are using the Tsgardi as pawns to distract us."

"And we can't forget our neighbors here in Region One," Admiral Platt said. "Just because they've never threatened our borders before doesn't mean they're not involved. New threats in Region Two would have us concentrating more of our resources that way instead of behind us."

"The Clidepp Empire is in total disarray," Admiral Bradlee said. "Their central government is crumbling under its own weight. They're ripe for a coup d'état by rebels and are hardly in a position to attack us to gain territory. And the Aguspod aren't organized well enough to even consider such an attack. Their forces have all been devoted to fighting the Raiders, just as ours were until the Milori attacked us."

"Yes, but look how we responded to the attack from the Milori," Admiral Hillaire said. "Our forces were immediately re-tasked from police functions to war response. The Aguspod could just as easily change the focus of their forces."

"We seem to be in agreement that the Tsgardi would not have entered into this action by themselves," Admiral Moore said. "Therefore our Intelligence Service has their work cut out for them. Roger, find out who's behind this operation so we can adequately prepare for the next phase of their plan."

Chapter Six

~ March 31st, 2282 ~

Jenetta was able to relax and enjoy the remainder of her two-week vacation after her second meeting with the Admiralty Board, although it was difficult to keep her mind free from thoughts about her command, knowing an invasion was currently taking place in Region Two.

For the first time in years, she actually appeared in public wearing something other than a uniform when she consented to wear a dress purchased by Eliza and Christa during their first shopping trip. It delighted Annette, who had despaired of ever again personally seeing her oldest daughter in anything but a military uniform. The sisters looked like three average, vivacious young women out for a shopping trip with an older woman who might be their grandmother. But if they'd hoped they'd be less conspicuous if Jenetta wasn't wearing the four stars on her shoulders, they were disappointed.

It had already been widely reported in the media that she was staying on the Potomac base, and newsies, hoping to get an exclusive interview, followed her around whenever she appeared in public. Her pets kept them a dozen meters away, and then it was simply a matter of tuning them out until they understood they were being ignored and stood zero chance of baiting her into giving them a response. But they continued to follow her while shooting a never-ending stream of pictures and videos. An advertising company got the phone number at the house and continued to call, requesting that Jenetta appear in a series of commercials for a client's products. Media show production people also kept pestering her to appear on their shows. Jenetta finally had all calls screened through the base communications center.

* * *

At the beginning of her third week on Earth, Jenetta piloted the *Colorado's* shuttle to the Northern Hemisphere Space Academy for the visit Admiral Hillaire had arranged. Accompanied only by Lt. Commander Ashraf and her cats, she was enjoying the flight so much that she was tempted to prolong it by making a quick side trip somewhere— anywhere. But people were waiting, so she put her personal desires aside and touched down on the assigned pad at the designated time.

The school superintendent and many of the Academy's senior officers met Jenetta at the shuttle pad and they came stiffly to attention as she descended the ramp. A full-dress band played loudly in the background, making it difficult to hear the names of the officers as they were introduced. Like many officers who had never met Admiral Carver, Rear Admiral (Lower) Josef Ponte held some resentment towards her rapid climb to the third— some say the second— most powerful position in Space Command, and he felt a little awkward greeting a senior officer who looked as young as his students. His own climb had been steady but hardly meteoric. At times, it had seemed agonizingly slow as he advanced on the career path he had plotted for himself. At sixty-eight years of age, he had lately begun to wonder if he would ever get a second star, but he hid his uneasiness behind an amiable smile.

"Admiral Carver," he said after the introductions and brief ceremony was over, "I can't tell you how honored we are to have you visit NHSA to address the cadet corps."

"It's my pleasure, Admiral. It's my first trip back since I graduated in '56, and I've been looking forward to it."

"It's hard to believe you graduated almost twenty-six years ago, Admiral. If you changed your uniform, you wouldn't look out of place mingling with the corps of cadets."

"Yes," she said, smiling agreeably, "but I assure you I did graduate in '56. Admiral Stinson was the superintendent back then."

"I remember him well. He was an instructor when I attended NHSA from '28 to '32."

"Where were you posted after graduation?"

"To Supreme Headquarters. Unlike yourself, I didn't make the cut for the group that went into space. I worked on Admiral Bendzet's staff until he retired, then managed to get a teaching position here at the school. I taught Alien Anatomy from '60 until '68, when I was appointed Assistant Superintendent. I became Superintendent three years ago."

"Congratulations on your appointment, Admiral. Only Space Command's finest are charged with shaping the minds of our future generations of officers. And only the finest of that group become superintendents of our academies."

Admiral Ponte blushed slightly at receiving such praise from an officer whom he regarded with jealousy. "Thank you, Admiral." Looking down at Jenetta's pets, he said, "These must be the cats I've heard so much about."

"They've been with me for a little over eleven years now. They've become an integral part of my life, almost like children."

Admiral Ponte nodded, thinking back to the stories he'd heard about the animals and how they were always instantly ready to protect their mistress. 'Children' wasn't the term he would use to describe a pair of animals ready to kill in a fraction of a second. "Would you care for a quick tour of the school, Admiral? I'm sure there have been many changes since you were here last."

"I'd love a tour."

As part of the Academy's expansion program, new dormitories had replaced the smaller buildings and additional classroom buildings had been constructed. Wherever they went, cadets jumped rigidly to attention until they had passed. On a five-meter raised balcony in the center of the student dining facility, Jenetta enjoyed lunch with Admiral Ponte and the school's senior officers while a couple of thousand cadets ate their meal beneath the always watchful eyes of the school administration. Afterward, the tour continued until it was time for the assembly.

Jenetta sat on the stage while Admiral Ponte introduced her, although no introduction was really necessary. She received a standing ovation as she walked to the podium, so she just smiled until the students finished their greeting and retook their seats.

"Good afternoon," Jenetta began, "I'm pleased to have this opportunity to speak to you today, and I promise I won't keep you too long. I'm sure you're all anxious to get back to your classes in Quantum Mechanics, Spatial Binomials, and Astronavigation." Like students everywhere, the cadets always appreciated an occasional short break in the afternoon from the rigors of intense academic instruction, and a chuckle passed quickly around the hall.

"You're extremely lucky to have been born when you were. The galaxy is opening up to us like never before and you have a unique opportunity to share in the exploration activities and adventures that still lie ahead of us. With the sudden demise of the Milori Empire..." Jenetta had to pause as the entire cadet corps rose to their feet, applauding and cheering for almost thirty seconds.

As the cheering died down and the students returned to their seats, she smiled and said, "I agree with that sentiment completely." Returning to her prepared speech, she continued. "With the sudden demise of the Milori Empire and the Galactic Alliance Council's decision to annex their former territories, we face numerous challenges and hurdles, the extent of which we're only beginning to realize. It will take us years just to get our ships in place to begin patrolling the new territory and perhaps decades to merge the inhabited planets there with the Galactic Alliance family of member worlds.

"The Admiralty Board has this past week approved a request from me to substantially increase the Second Fleet's quota of scout-destroyer ships. Resources are being allocated immediately to begin stepped-up production at the Mars facility. Although the actual speed capability is classified, I'm sure most of you have heard the rumors. Let me just say our new ships are faster than anything envisioned just a decade ago. I know you'll be as thrilled as I've been to be a part of this emerging technology. In the months ahead, many of you will receive an introduction to the battle tactics developed for this new class of warship.

"When I leave Earth in a few days, I'll be starting my trip back to Region Two where I'll continue overseeing the establishment of our new Headquarters base on the planet Quesann. From that location, we'll work to bring peace and stability to a part of the galaxy which has for a century known little but war and violence. Because Terrans weren't tolerated in the former Milori Empire, we have little first-hand knowledge of the worlds in Region Two, so we'll be relying on the file data we recovered in captured Milori vessels as we feel our way along.

"In a few months' time, as my graduating class prepares to assemble in celebration of our twenty-sixth reunion, you members of the class of '82 will be graduating. A greater number of graduates than ever before will be assigned shipboard duty because of both the larger class sizes at the Academy and the increased quotas of new officers accepted for duty in space. The GSC Warship Command Institute has likewise greatly expanded its class sizes. Space Command needs every one of you to do your best, both now while you're preparing for the day when you get your orders to report to your ship and later when you actually assume your duties. I'll need hundreds of new ships in the coming decade and the crews to man them, so many of you will be joining me in Region Two. But should you be assigned patrol duties in one of the less active areas of Region One, don't ever think your role isn't just as important as those of your fellow officers assigned to Region Two. Only by keeping things quiet and under control in your sector will others be free to focus their full attention on keeping things quiet and under control elsewhere. With each of us doing the job assigned to us, no matter how unimportant or tedious you may feel the job is at times— and I've had my share of those— we are working together to ensure our families and friends remain safe and free.

"We must never again allow the Raider organization or any other crime syndicate to attain such a strong foothold in our territory that they threaten the lives and prosperity of our citizens. I've done my best to wipe out that threat...." Jenetta had to pause again while the entire assembly rose to their feet and drowned out her words with cheers and applause. She smiled and took a quick gulp of water from the glass on the podium while the students expressed their feelings.

"...but the job of further reducing that organization's piracy, murder, slavery, illegal drug smuggling, illegal weapons sales, and other illicit activities will now fall on your shoulders and those of your fellow officers. As is the case with most line officers who have advanced to flag officer rank, my duties continue to move me further and further from the action. And perhaps that's as it should be. As this old warhorse takes a step back to make room for you new stallions, and stallion-ettes, remember that my heart will always be with you at the forefront of our battle lines. I envy you the experiences and adventures that await you.

"Thank you for sitting through my long-winded speech. Good luck with your studies, and remember that everything you learn here will be useful one day. Pay close attention to the material your instructors are cramming into your head. God bless you all. I'll look forward to seeing you in Region Two."

As Jenetta stepped back from the podium, the entire student body stood and applauded for all they were worth. The building seemed to shake from the thunderous applause and stamping feet. Jenetta smiled and waved as Admiral Ponte stood and moved to the podium. He waited patiently, dividing his attention between Jenetta and the students as the entire cadet corps seemed unwilling to stop cheering. Finally, he put up his hands in a gesture that told the cadets to ease off and the din began to subside.

When it had quieted down, he said, "Admiral Carver, I doubt you'll find anyone on this campus, or anywhere else for that matter, who views you as an old warhorse."

The student body erupted in genuine laughter.

"I'm equally sure that anyone at the Academy would deem themselves very fortunate indeed to be assigned to a ship or base in your command when they've completed their studies. And you can be sure that anyone joining you in Region Two is ready for the challenge after receiving the best education Space Command can offer. With you in command of Region Two, we know the new territory is in the best possible hands."

Jenetta smiled and said, "Thank you, Admiral."

Turning back to the corps of cadets, Admiral Ponte said, "And now it's time to return to your studies. This assembly is dismissed."

After saying goodbye to the senior officers present, Jenetta and Lt. Commander Ashraf returned to the shuttle pad.

Admiral Ponte remained with them until they entered the shuttle and then watched as the small ship lifted off. A part of him wished he, too, could be making the trip to Region Two.

* * *

Two days later, Jenetta and Lt. Commander Ashraf visited the Southern Hemisphere Space Academy where Jenetta received just as enthusiastic a reception as she had received at NHSA. After a tour of the school and lunch with the senior officers, she addressed the corps of cadets in an assembly, giving a very similar speech. As at NHSA, the corps of cadets expressed their admiration and respect for the things she had accomplished during her years as a Space Command Officer.

* * *

After returning to the Potomac Base, Jenetta was able to spend two more days with her mother before it was time for her tearful goodbye. Her departure was less eventful than her arrival, but a number of close friends of her mother, as well as the base's commanding officer and senior staff, turned out for her liftoff.

Back aboard the *Colorado*, preparations for departure had already been completed, and the ship left Earth orbit within an hour of Jenetta's arrival with her two sisters. They would reach Higgins in less than four days.

The conversations in Jenetta's quarters during those four days centered mainly around the trip to Earth, although thoughts of what was transpiring in Region Two were never very far from their minds. She had briefed them on the situation as soon as they were away from Earth. She hadn't told them earlier because she hadn't wanted to diminish their delight in being home while they were still with Mom.

Jenetta had had enough of bands and cheering throngs for a while so she specifically requested the reception be a quiet one when she sent a communication to Admiral Holt, the commanding officer at Higgins, informing him that she would be arriving in several days. Her main reason for stopping there was to pick up Admiral Kanes, although she owed Admiral Holt a visit. Still, she hoped to make the stop a quick one and planned to arrive just before dinner because she knew she would be invited to attend at least one meal.

Jenetta was sitting in her chair on the bridge when the space station came into view and the image was projected onto the large front monitor. The sight of Higgins never failed to bring a smile to Jenetta's face. She remembered the first time she had seen the massive space station floating in synchronous orbit above the capital city on the planet far below.

Jenetta requested and received special clearance for a straight-in, high-speed approach. Normally they would spend the better part of a day approaching the station once they reached the outer marker.

After the docking maneuvers were complete and the airlock integrity tested, the hatch of the *Colorado* was opened. Jenetta stepped out of the ship with her cats and walked down the pier to the dock platform. A security officer with a platoon of Marines waited there. Nearby workers and onlookers, merely curious about the presence of the Marines until that time, recognized Jenetta immediately and began to crowd around. The Marines immediately went to work keeping everyone a few meters away, while the security officer snapped to attention and saluted Jenetta.

"Marine Captain Reggerio, Admiral. I have a car waiting to take us to the Admiral's dining facility."

"Lead on, Captain," Jenetta said as she returned his salute.

As the officer turned to lead the way, Jenetta glanced at the crowd that was massing. She smiled and waved to them. Her acknowledgement brought quick applause, and a few people began to shout the two syllables of her last name in a sort of chant that grew in intensity as she walked towards the car.

The two Marines who had been guarding the car jumped into the front seats after Jenetta, her cats, and the captain had climbed into the rear of the large limousine-like vehicle. As the 'oh-gee' limo moved away, the Marines who had kept the small crowd at bay were able to relax and walk to their own vehicles.

At the entrance to the administration section of the base, the car was waved through immediately. There should be relatively few civilians around from that point on, and there were none visible as the car braked near the entrance to the dining halls. Marine Captain Reggerio, still nervous after sharing the rear of the vehicle with two enormous and deadly cats, not to mention one of the most senior officers in Space Command, jumped out of the limo almost before it had stopped moving and stood by the vehicle.

As Jenetta stepped out, the two Marines at the entrance doors, already at attention, stiffened even more, and one activated a tiny device on the forefinger of his left glove to open the doors. Jenetta walked through the doorway with her cats and followed the corridors to Admiral Holt's private dining facility with Marine Captain Reggerio and the two Marine security people as an entourage. Space Command personnel in the corridors moved out of Jenetta's way as she approached, coming to attention with their backs against the walls until she had passed.

Her entourage halted outside the Admiral's dining room as Jenetta entered, and the three people talking near the center of the room turned to greet her.

"Welcome to Higgins, Admiral," Admiral Holt said in his booming voice. The six-foot, two-inch-tall officer was approaching eighty-five now but still appeared very fit.

Jenetta walked directly to him and reproached him jokingly. "Admiral? It was always Jen before, and we've known each other since I was a mere ensign."

"You were an ensign by virtue of graduating from NHSA, but you were never *mere*. I recognized that from the time you first arrived at Higgins, ma'am."

Jenetta smiled. "Stop it. It'll always be Jen for you, sir."

"Sir?" he said smiling. "Now who's being formal?"

"Sorry, force of habit. How have you been, *Brian*?"

"Great, Jen. It's wonderful to see you again."

Admiral Holt extended his hand, but Jen sidestepped it and moved in close to give him the type of hug usually reserved for a favorite uncle. He responded by chuckling, then wrapping his arms around her and hugging her for a couple of seconds.

As she stepped back, he said to her, "You haven't changed a bit. You're still the prettiest officer in Space Command. I could almost wish to have gone through that DNA recombinant procedure myself."

"I didn't appreciate the pain and suffering I went through when the Raider doctors performed the procedure, but I have to admit that now, as I move towards middle age, having the body of a young adult is not altogether unpleasant. At least it hasn't been the hindrance to my career that I once feared."

91

Nodding and then gesturing towards the officer on his left, Admiral Holt said, "You remember Admiral Margolan, don't you?"

Turning towards Rear Admiral, Upper Half, Margolan, Jenetta said, smiling, "Of course I do; besides presiding at my court-martial, he pinned on one of my insignia when I was promoted to Lt. Commander." Extending her hand to the thin JAG officer who was closer to the mandatory space retirement age than he cared to think about, she said, "How are you, Chester?"

"Just fine, Admiral," he said, his shock of white hair shaking slightly as he nodded his head. "And I prefer Chet."

"Okay, Chet. It's Jen. Congratulations on receiving your second star."

"Thanks, Jen."

"And of course you remember Admiral Kanes," Admiral Holt said.

"Of course. We're old friends," she said, looking at the five-foot, eleven-inch intelligence officer. His brown hair was starting to gray slightly at the temples, but his steel-gray eyes were just as piercing as ever. "How are you, Keith? Congratulations on your promotion to flag rank." Jenetta extended her right hand and when he took it, she covered the handgrip with her left hand.

"Thank you, Jen. I'm delighted to have been assigned to your staff in Region Two."

"And I'm delighted to have you with us. We have a monster of a task ahead of us, and your knowledge and insight will be invaluable."

"Shall we sit down?" Admiral Holt invited. "I'm sure the meal is almost ready."

Jenetta nodded and took her seat at the table as the others did. As the mess stewards began serving the meal, the quartet engaged in small talk.

When the stewards were finished and had left the room, Admiral Holt asked, "What's the latest in Region Two, Jen?"

Looking at Admiral Margolan, she said, "I'm sure Brian and Keith are aware of this, but I don't know if you've been apprised of the situation in Region Two, Chet. This information is classified secret and should not be mentioned outside this room." Taking a breath, she said, "We have unsubstantiated information that the Tsgardi have invaded Region Two with the apparent intent of seizing part of our new territory."

"Unsubstantiated?" Admiral Margolan repeated in a questioning voice.

"The report comes from the Viceroy of Milor. He claims to have received an urgent plea for help from someone on the planet Ekoqulith. As yet we do not have any confirmation through Space Command official channels that the Tsgardi Kingdom is involved, nor even confirmation by Space Command personnel that the planet was attacked. This action, if there was an action, might have even been initiated by the Raiders using Tsgardi mercenaries in the guise of Tsgardi military troops. At this time we just don't know the full situation."

"Given the distance to Region Two," Admiral Holt said, "there appears to be little likelihood we'll be dramatically affected here."

"Perhaps not dramatically, but a new invasion threat may pull some of your patrol forces away. And if Region Two heats up substantially, you may find it a little more difficult to get new supplies and personnel. A war any-where in our territory will affect everyone in Space Command."

"How do you intend to proceed, Jen?" Admiral Kanes asked.

"At the earliest opportunity, we'll have to send a ship to Ekoqulith and determine for ourselves just what has happened there, unless the Tsgardi Kingdom issues a declaration of war before then or something else occurs to confirm their invasion."

"There's been no declaration of hostilities?" Admiral Margolan asked.

"None, which might cause some to construe that the Tsgardi government isn't behind it. I don't share that opinion, but in the absence of a formal declaration we can treat all attacks as piracy."

"Because the treatment of pirates can be different than the treatment of prisoners of war?" Admiral Holt asked.

"Exactly. We can use a slightly heavier hand when interrogating pirates because our conduct isn't governed by a myriad of past military treaties."

"You'll still have to observe Galactic Alliance law," Admiral Margolan warned.

"Of course, but Region Two is still under Martial Law. As Military Governor, I have a slightly freer hand than I would otherwise have. I won't break the laws, but I might have to bend a few if we're to nip this thing before it gets out of hand, assuming it isn't already out of hand."

"What can I do to help you, Jen?" Admiral Holt asked.

"You've already done it by giving us Keith and the people he's selected to bring along."

"I wish I was going with you," Admiral Holt said. "It would be a grand way to finish out my career. Chet and I are both nearing the point where we'll be recalled to Earth to serve our remaining years in the service."

"I'd love to have you with us, Brian. As the new head-quarters develops, I know the same pseudo-political bureaucratic infrastructure found in headquarters every-where since militaries were first formed will develop. I've managed to avoid much of it until now because I've always been posted at the remotest regions of Galactic Alliance space in situations with a high turnover in personnel, but I know those days are over. I'm going to find myself right in the center of something I'm ill-prepared to handle. I don't fear the Tsgardi half as much as I fear becoming embroiled in politics. Your years of fighting in the political trenches would be invaluable."

"I thought you might want me for my good looks and keen sense of humor," Admiral Holt said, chuckling.

"That's naturally an important part of it," Jenetta retorted with a smile.

"What about the rumors of other possible involved parties, Jen?" Admiral Kanes asked. "Anything new?"

"Everything we know has been included in your briefings. The general feeling is the Tsgardi are far too obtuse to organize something like this. They were afraid of Milori might, and it makes sense they should be afraid of us for the same reason. If they have really invaded our territory, somebody has to be prodding them. Your job will be to determine exactly who is holding the stick so we can prepare to meet them. Upon reaching Quesann and assuming your new position, all agents and contacts in Region Two will report to your section so we won't have to wait for intel to be collected at Earth and filtered back to us. But we don't have anywhere near the number of information-gatherers we need. We may not be sure who's involved until they're knocking at the front door."

The discussion turned to lighter matters after that, with discussions of past battles and tactics. They had finished their desserts and were enjoying their coffee when Admiral Holt's aide entered and whispered something to him.

After the aide had delivered the message and left, Admiral Holt said, "All of Keith's people are aboard the *Colorado*, as are his spacechests. You can leave whenever you're ready, Jen."

"Thank you, Brian," Jenetta said as she stood up. "As much as I hate to eat and run, I am a bit anxious to get underway."

The other officers rose as she did.

"I understand completely," Admiral Holt said. "I'd be just as concerned if trouble started while I was away from my command. I'm glad you could join us for dinner tonight, and I hope you'll be able to avoid a new conflict. We'd all like to see a period of peace and stability now that the Milori have been dealt with."

"Yes, but I believe another very serious fight is coming our way. We weren't prepared to take immediate control of an area anywhere near as large as Region Two, and everyone knows it. I suppose it was just wishful thinking that everyone would behave until we could establish our full presence there. Let's hope a little saber-rattling will send the Tsgardi scurrying back across their border."

"Just before the Battle for Higgins," Admiral Holt said, "Larry Gavin predicted that one day we would clash violently with the Uthlaro. Keep one eye on that border, Jen. That may be where the real trouble is brewing."

* * *

The *Colorado* arrived at Stewart Space Command Base some sixteen days later. Neither the *Bellona* nor the *Chiron* where in port, so Jenetta's sisters would either have to wait at Stewart until the ships returned or transportation to them could be arranged. If not for the urgency of the situation, Jenetta would take them directly to their ships, but she didn't want to waste the extra day— or days— necessary to locate both ships and deliver the two officers. She wished now she hadn't promised Thad she would stay for dinner when she returned, but a promise was a promise, and she knew the captains in port were anxious to hear firsthand about the final days of the Milori Empire.

Attendance at the dinner was limited to officers holding the rank of Captain or above, and still the dining room was filled to capacity. The continuing expansion of Stewart had resulted in a greater number of senior officers than had been posted there when Jenetta was the Base Commander. Not all the captains present for the meal held ship commands, but even the officers who only piloted a desk each day were anxious to hear Jenetta give her accounts of the attacks on the Milori home world, ship docks, and outposts. The dinner also gave Jenetta an opportunity to renew friendships with some of the officers who had served under her during her years at Stewart.

Being four hundred fifty light-years closer to Quesann and still not having received any calamitous news from Region Two had taken the edge off Jenetta's worries sufficiently for her to relax somewhat and enjoy her evening with old friends and fellow officers. She had already shared parting goodbyes with her sisters. Frequent messages in the months ahead would sustain them until they met again.

Just after midnight, the *Colorado* backed slowly away from the airlock, turned ninety degrees to larboard, then started gliding slowly forward. Once clear of the hollowed-out asteroid that housed the base, the course to Quesann was laid in and the ship accelerated away so quickly that it seemed to vanish. Speeding through the cosmos at Light-9790, the ship would travel slightly more than twenty-five light-years each Earth day, reaching Quesann in just thirty-two days.

* * *

Seven days out of Stewart, Jenetta summoned Admiral Kanes to her briefing room.

"You wanted to see me Jen?" he said as the door closed behind him.

"Yes, Keith. I've received a message from Admiral Sprague that I think you should hear right away. I posted Vince to a former Milori space station we've designated as Coleman Space Command base. It's located approximately a hundred light-years from our border with the Tsgardi Kingdom. Care for a cup of coffee first?"

"I'm fine," he said taking a seat.

Jenetta pressed the play button and the message displayed on the wall monitor. An image of an agitated Admiral Sprague filled the screen.

"Jen, we've completed the evacuation of Coleman and are proceeding at Light-9790 to Quesann. Our Distant DeTect network picked up a large force of ships heading towards the base at Light-225, so we assumed them to be Tsgardi warships and evacuated as per your orders. All ordnance had already been moved back aboard the *Themis*, and our last act was to disable key systems in ways not easy to find even by Space Command engineers. The Tsgardi may occupy this base, but it'll take them a lifetime to get it functional. When we retake it, it will only require a few days to re-enable the systems we've incapacitated.

"I'll brief you fully when I see you at Quesann.

97

"Vincent Sprague, Rear Admiral, Upper, Base Commander of Coleman Space Command Base, aboard the *Themis*."

"Here's my reply," Jenetta said, tapping another key on her com console.

The image on the screen changed to one of Jenetta, and her voice could be heard saying, "Hi, Vince, you've taken the correct action. Two ships are inadequate to repel a large Tsgardi force determined to take or destroy a station.

"I regret we were unable to support you better at this time and I promise we'll restore your command as soon as an acceptable risk level is achieved.

"The *Colorado* is just days from the border with Region Two and we expect to arrive at Quesann in twenty-five days. I'll see you then. I'm relieved that everyone in your command is safe.

"Jenetta Carver, Admiral, Commander of the Second Fleet and Military Governor of Region Two, aboard the *Colorado*. Message complete."

"The message from Vince is fourteen days old," Jenetta said to Keith. "It was routed through Quesann. I've also sent messages to Admirals Mendez and Colsey to evacuate their bases and proceed to Quesann with all haste, assuming they haven't already done so. We know the Tsgardi aren't in this alone, so there's no telling where the next attack will occur."

Jenetta took a sip from her coffee mug while Keith Kanes thought. It was he who broke the silence with, "I can't see where you had any other option. Until we know what's going on or we get reinforcements, you had to consolidate your forces for the protection of Head-quarters. You certainly couldn't have pulled the ships away from the space stations while they were still occu-pied by our people."

"I may have been a bit premature when I rushed to occupy the bases without adequate warship protection."

"We all expected this region to sink into a quagmire of lawlessness until a strong military presence could be reestablished. We thought that for the foreseeable future our only worry was piracy. You were taking the proper steps to reassert control. No one expected an invasion by forces from outside the region."

"I should have anticipated it," Jenetta said.

"You're Jenetta Carver, not Jesus Christ, even if you do share the same initials. Don't beat yourself up over this, Jen. Save it for the enemy."

Chapter Seven

~ May 26th, 2282 ~

Jenetta was on the bridge of the *Colorado* twenty-five days later as it entered orbit around Quesann. The battleship *Themis*, with the scout-destroyer *Amazon* securely nestled beneath it in the special docking collar, was in orbit, as was the scout-destroyer *Yangtze*. Both bases along the Uthlaro border had been evacuated without incident and the *Boreas* and the *Hyperion* were expected to arrive within days.

"Admiral, you're receiving a com message from Admiral Sprague," the com operator said.

"Forward it to my briefing room," Jenetta said as she rose from her chair and walked to her office on the larboard side of the bridge.

"Aye, Admiral," the chief petty officer at the com station said before she disappeared into the briefing room.

Jenetta raised the com panel screen as she sat down at her desk, and a head-and-shoulders image of Admiral Vincent Sprague appeared.

"Good morning and welcome back to Quesann, Jen," Admiral Sprague said.

"Good morning, Vince," Jenetta said.

"I hope you had a pleasant vacation."

"It was very pleasant— until I received word about the attack on Ekoqulith." Scowling slightly, she said, "I'm going to vent my displeasure for interrupting my first vacation in twelve years when we find out who was responsible for that attack."

"I understand. I'm equally upset about having to evacuate my command."

"Have your people settled in, Vince?"

"We've finished shuttling everyone down, but they're still moving into their temporary quarters on the base. We haven't yet had time to remove all of the supplies, equipment, and ordnance the *Themis* transported back here. The Tsgardi may occupy the station temporarily, but they won't be dining on Space Command food or using Milori ordnance against us when we arrive to reclaim it."

"Excellent. If the military arm of the Tsgardi Kingdom is as bad as their merchant forces, you can expect quite a mess when you get back. But you will get back, and you'll have all the resources I can free up to help you get the station back in order."

"Thank you, Jen. I'm looking forward to returning. I didn't like deserting our position. I've never run from a fight before."

"You didn't run, Vince. It was an orderly strategic withdrawal in the face of overwhelming numbers. Our pullback was necessary while we marshal our forces for the fight ahead. We couldn't afford to lose you and your people needlessly, and there was nothing to be gained by delaying the Tsgardi at that point. Where are the Milori, by the way?"

"We've established a section in the housing compound for them here on the base. It's large enough to accommodate them and whatever number of Milori will be arriving from the other two bases." Changing his expression slightly, he added, "It's interesting, but their attitude seems to have changed considerably. When we first arrived at the station, it was as if they suspected that we planned to kill them, although they cooperated completely. Then after a few weeks, they began to understand we meant them no harm and they simply became— distant, remaining in the sections of the station assigned to them. When I notified them that we were evacuating the station and that they should prepare to leave, they offered to assist us in moving the supplies and ordnance. They were quite helpful. On the trip here they became almost cordial. Perhaps they appreciated the fact that we weren't going to simply leave them to face whatever enemy invader was on its way to the station. The Milori know they aren't loved either inside or outside of this territory, especially by the races they've subjugated with practices of extreme prejudice."

"It would be unusual to love your conqueror, which is why we face such an uphill battle to win their trust. I wouldn't bet a single credit on my chances of surviving on Milor for a full day since I was the one who ordered the virtual destruction of their military/industrial complexes. We only targeted factories, power plants, and armories, but a lot of Milori had to have been killed in collateral damage. That we were only striking back after two attempts to invade our territory may not count for much. It may be generations before any Milori can think of me without their mind becoming clouded by a killing rage."

"At least the Milori culture is so disciplined to following the dictates of their authority figures that most won't succumb to their baser instincts."

"I hope so," Jenetta said. "The idea of establishing a compound for Milori assassins on the base isn't a comforting one."

"I doubt you have anything to fear from these groups. They're all professional warriors who will follow their code of conduct to the point of dying unnecessarily if so ordered by their commander. I suppose your position as military governor of this part of space makes you their commander now."

"That's an interesting speculation. I admit I hadn't considered it until now."

"Their planetary government has ordered them to obey all orders from Space Command, so it's reasonable to assume they'll consider you their commander-in-chief."

"Hmm, that would make things much easier in the days ahead," Jenetta said, thoughtfully. "We'll have to think of a suitable test."

"I've heard that when Milori commanders are suspicious of a warrior's loyalty, they give him a weapon and order him to kill himself. If he does, they know he was loyal all along."

"That would definitely establish a warrior's loyalty, but it's a bit more extreme than I was thinking, and it does end a warrior's usefulness."

"I believe the Milori reasoning is that warriors share common loyalties to command. If the most obviously doubtful of the group will comply, then it's assumed all are loyal."

"It's a bit tough on the chosen individual," Jenetta said, grinning.

"Yes," Admiral Sprague said, chuckling, "it's hardly something we'd ever adopt as SOP in Space Command. Will you be coming down soon?"

"I'm going to contact Captain Erikson and have him separate his scout-destroyer from the *Themis* so we can dock with him using the docking collar. The *Colorado* is loaded from bow to stern with supplies, and given the lack of an orbiting station here, it will be easiest to offload supplies to the *Themis* so they can be loaded into full-sized shipping containers for transport to the surface along with whatever you brought back from the station. While at Earth, it made sense to fill every available niche aboard ship before we returned. My quarters are so crowded I can barely get to my bathroom."

"I understand. That's the way it was aboard the *Themis* for our trip both to the station and back. Let me know before you come down and I'll arrange for a suitable greeting assembly."

Jenetta smiled. "Thanks, Vince, but I've had enough of marching bands and large greeting assemblies for a while. I realize that protocol demands an assembly to greet a returning commanding officer and I wouldn't want to upset tradition, but let's keep it small. I'll have you notified before I come down so we can get the formalities out of the way."

Admiral Sprague smiled. "I agree with that sentiment most of the time, but protocol must be observed. We *are* welcoming Admiral Kanes as well as yourself, after all. I'll keep the assembly as small as possible."

Once most of the supplies had been offloaded from the *Colorado* and Jenetta felt comfortable establishing a time for her arrival on the planet, she had Admiral Sprague's aide notified. She then traveled to the surface with Lt. Ashraf while Admiral Kanes traveled down in a separate shuttle with his aide and the senior members of his staff. Protocol dictated that senior officers arrive in separate transports. She thought it was a holdover from the days when travel down to a planet's surface wasn't as safe as it had become, and an accident could mean the loss of multiple flag officers.

The *small* assembly Admiral Sprague arranged involved two hundred Space Command officers, NCOs, and crewmen, but at least there was no marching band. Since the base was now home to more than three thousand, mostly station personnel temporarily relocated from Coleman, Jenetta supposed that two hundred could be considered a small assembly.

Despite the absence of a band, the ceremony of greeting a returning four-star admiral followed formal SC protocol procedures, with Admiral Sprague and the base's senior officers lining up to welcome Jenetta back and greet Admiral Kanes. At least Jenetta didn't have to make any speeches, and the crewmen were dismissed as soon as the six 'oh-gee' vehicles filled with officers pulled away from the landing zones.

The progress made in transforming the partially completed base into the headquarters for Space Command in Region Two was no less than amazing. Construction bots were hard at work everywhere, making good use of the materials delivered with the initial arrival of the battleships. A complete road system had been laid out as soon as the plans for the base had been finished. Necessary only to structure the flow of traffic, roads were no longer miles of concrete or macadam. Opposed-gravity vehicles didn't need paved surfaces. Instead, once the location was decided and the soil prepared, a groundcover of special grass was planted. It never needed mowing and retained its special color year-round. The color represented the roadway's intended use. Buried transmitters limited speeds and flying altitude, provided location coordinates, and notified the operator of other vehicles or obstructions ahead of the vehicle. Since the silent 'oh-gee' vehicles flew at five- or ten-meter altitudes, depending upon their direction, there was no danger to pedestrian traffic.

Once the roads and sidewalks were completed, lawns and general landscaping quickly followed. The base was quickly taking on the appearance of any base on Earth, and Jenetta was so preoccupied with observing the changes that she didn't realize where they were when the driverless vehicle slowed, sank close to the ground, and stopped at a gated compound. Two Marines saluted as twin gates rolled back to permit the vehicles to enter. It may seem sort of silly to have a gate, as the 'oh-gee' vehicle could have simply flown up and over the obstruction, but once the compound was complete, such behavior would see the vehicle shot down in flames before it had gotten twenty meters inside the compound.

"What's this, Vince?" Jenetta asked of Admiral Sprague.

"Your quarters, Admiral. The base engineers have been working around the clock to get it ready before you returned."

"My quarters?"

"The Military Governor of Region Two needs a home that befits the status of her position."

As the vehicle entered the grounds, a three-story-tall, trapezoidal-shaped building that reminded Jenetta of the Royal Palace on Nordakia came into view. It appeared to encompass some three dozen acres. Half the windows on the top floor had large cantilevered balconies with roofs. A cascading waterfall fell from the roof at the front center of the building. Jen immediately realized that the compound walls projected a holo-dome image to hide the building from anyone outside the grounds. Important structures were often disguised this way, either to reduce their susceptibility to attack, increase privacy, or simply to provide a more pleasant view in a crowded urban environment. From inside the grounds, it appeared the residence was the only building for hundreds of square kilometers. From outside, the grounds appeared to be nothing more than an empty park with numerous fountains and beautiful landscaping.

"A home?" Jenetta echoed. "It looks like a palace."

"It is exactly that. It was modeled after your own royal palace on Obotymot. Remember that this planet will become the focus of governmental activity for thousands of light-years, just as Earth is the focus in Region One. You are the leader of this arm of the government, and that means you need a home that will impress visitors, while allowing you to entertain planetary leaders, dignitaries, and other important persons. The Governor's Palace will serve that purpose splendidly. The palace is far from complete, but your private quarters are ready to occupy. The rest of the building is still under construction, and the two outdoor swimming pools that will be located in the center courtyard and garden area of the building are still nothing but large excavations right now. The exterior landscaping work is coming along nicely though, and your gardens will be magnificent once the flowers begin to bloom."

Jenetta sighed silently to herself. Performing as Military Governor was the part of the job she dreaded most. As a Nordakian Azula, and a Lady of the Royal House, she had been schooled in palace protocols, but that didn't mean she enjoyed engaging in such behavior. She was most comfortable on the bridge of a ship and longed for nothing more than a command position on a battle-ship. As she looked at the palace, she could almost feel her dream slipping away from her. Each additional mantle of office seemed to erect new barriers between her and the bridge of the once promised battleship.

Over the next hour, Captain Neveho, the commanding officer of the base's engineering section who had come to Quesann with the initial arrival of the battleships, led the small party on a tour of the partially finished palace. The tour was naturally restricted to those parts that were safe to enter. Jenetta's personal quarters occupied the entire top floor of one wing and were easily large enough to house a hundred crewmembers. Her bathtub looked more like a swimming pool than a normal bathtub and yet was dwarfed in a bathroom that seemed large enough to hanger a shuttle. No fewer than ten housekeeping bots were permanently assigned to just her quarters. They would ensure her laundry was picked up promptly and properly stowed upon return, that she had clean towels and fresh bed linens daily, and that not even a speck of dust could be found anywhere in her apartment. Of course, to keep them from getting underfoot, sensors in the apartment used her CT to track her movements so the bots always knew where she was. As soon as she left a room, the doors on their storage closets would pop open and they would rush out to perform necessary duties, re-entering their storage locations before she returned.

"Whose idea was it to build this palace?" Jenetta asked when the tour was over.

"It was part of the original plans for the base, as provided by Supreme Headquarters on Earth, Admiral," Captain Neveho said. "They took the layout of the base construction begun by the Milori and drew new plans for the entire base to be constructed in three phases around the existing, incomplete structures. The engineers had already begun preparing this site by sinking the shaft to tie in with the underground complex and laying the foundation for the palace before you left. I guess you had so much on your mind that you didn't question the construction activity out here, and with the holo-dome in place since work began, you wouldn't have noticed anything unless you had come to the site to investigate why perimeter walls had been erected. The dozen M-designate ships headed this way contain most of the materials needed to complete phase one, and future deliveries by Quartermaster ships will deliver the remainder of the supplies we'll need— such as the marble facing— over the next several years. The engineers have also built a private residence for the new base commander, Admiral Poole, on Admiral's Way, although nothing so grandiose as the Governor's Palace. Admiral Sprague is occupying the house until Admiral Poole arrives to assume his role as base commander. Temporary VIP quarters have been prepared on the second floor of the palace for Admiral Kanes and for Admirals Colsey and Mendez when they arrive. All resident admirals will, of course, have their own residence on Admiral's Way when phase one is complete. In phase two, residences for visiting admirals and dignitaries will be constructed. Phase three will see residences for officers and their families built, and phase four will provide private housing for NCOs, crewmen, and their families."

"Thank you, Captain. You've done an outstanding job in my absence."

Captain Neveho beamed proudly and said, "Thank you, Admiral."

"Ladies and gentlemen," Jenetta said to her entourage, "thank you for the warm reception. It's time to take my leave of you now because I need to meet privately with Admirals Sprague and Kanes. Only our aides will be joining us, so you may return to your duties."

With Jenetta leading the way, the officers walked to a conference room that adjoined her quarters on the third floor. As they approached the room, Lt. Commander Ashraf hurried ahead to make sure the cleaning bots were back in their storage closets before the admirals and their aides entered.

Jenetta walked past the large table and straight to a beverage synthesizer where she ordered a mug of Colombian, black, after placing a mug from a rack into the machine. When nothing happened in several seconds, she repeated her request. When still nothing happened, she said, "Display diagnostic routine," but the machine remained unresponsive. Turning to her aide she said, "Lori, call the palace mess steward and order a pot of Colombian for me and whatever everyone else wants."

After taking the beverage orders, Lt. Commander Ashraf used the com on the table to call the newly opened palace kitchen. She ordered the beverages and then told the mess steward to place a call to engineering so someone would be sent to repair the conference room's beverage synthesizer.

Jenetta settled into an 'oh-gee' chair at the head of the table but held off beginning the meeting until the beverage cart arrived and everyone was served. They made small talk until the mess steward had left. Admirals Kanes and Sprague took seats on her immediate left and right, leaving most of the table empty because their aides took seats in the chairs around the walls. Jenetta took a sip of coffee and approved of the taste. She then opened the meeting, asking Admiral Sprague to brief her fully on the evacuation of the station and relate any impressions he might have regarding the vessels detected approaching the station. He couldn't really offer anything revealing, but they spent an hour discussing the topic before Jenetta filled him in on everything she and Keith Kanes had speculated upon during the voyage back to Region Two. By the end of the meeting, all three admirals were in agreement that little could be done until the M-designate ships arrived at Quesann.

* * *

In the weeks following, the battleships carrying the station personnel from the evacuated Kanngari and Pellman bases arrived at Quesann and disgorged their passengers and cargo. As with Coleman, all ordnance, foodstuff, and equipment that could be removed had been loaded into the battleships. The loads were hardly noticeable in the enormous new warehouses built on the base, but the ships had practically been bulging at the seams for the month-long voyages. The two admirals, used to enjoying spacious living quarters, commented that there were so many crates, boxes, and shipping containers in their sitting rooms and bedrooms that they had to turn sideways to get to their bathrooms.

* * *

When the dozen M-designate ships arrived after two years of travel, the personnel were anxious to celebrate their arrival, but Jenetta insisted their supplies be unloaded before anyone received liberty. The possibility of an attack by outside hostile forces meant that essential business must be completed before pleasure commenced. Although Jenetta had defeated the Milori in battle, the M-designate ships were among the fastest in the SC fleet until the DS ships had gone into production at the Mars' shipyard. With twenty first-line SC warships now in orbit around the planet, personnel on the surface could finally feel secure.

* * *

After allowing the crews of the M-designate ships to enjoy two weeks of liberty, Jenetta began a series of daily meetings with the other four admirals and the captains of the vessels. The main topic was naturally how best to repel the invaders and assert their control over the territory now that support was arriving from Region One.

"Our number one priority is intel," Jenetta said as the daily meeting started. "Although we have our suspicions, we still don't really *know* who is behind the invasion and attack on Ekoqulith. We've been unable to make contact with planetary officials since we first received the message about the attack from the Milori Viceroy. Now that the first ships have arrived from Stewart, I intend to lead a taskforce to Coleman to find out exactly what we're facing. The M-designate ships will remain here in defense of the base, while the DS ships accompany the *Colorado*."

"All eight DS ships will be leaving Quesann then?" Admiral Mendez asked.

"Yes, I may need the firepower a lot more than the base does. The twelve ships remaining behind should be adequate for your defense. We have another fifty M-designate ships headed this way, scheduled to arrive within six months. Half were initially headed directly towards the occupied stations, but they've all been rerouted to Quesann. They'll be here long before any Tsgardi taskforce could arrive. The recently launched quartermaster ships are currently being loaded and will be departing the Earth solar system soon. With their new engines and Dakinium hulls, they're as fast as the new battleships. They should arrive within two months. How's that for unique— a transport as fast as a battleship?"

"Do you feel it's prudent to lead this taskforce personally, Admiral?" Admiral Colsey asked. "Perhaps it would be wiser to direct the taskforce from here."

Jenetta shook her head slightly before saying, "I have to be out where the action is. The taskforce can't wait three weeks to get instructions from me once they locate the enemy. Admiral Poole will be arriving aboard one of the Quartermaster ships in two months to take over as base commander of Quesann and Admiral Sprague will fill in for me here until I return."

"But the taskforce may find themselves involved in a serious battle," Admiral Mendez said. "We can't afford to lose you unnecessarily."

"I was named as military governor because of my success in battle, not because of my experience as a bureaucrat. The bridge of a ship is where I can best serve Region Two at this time." Smiling, Jenetta added, "Besides, I want to go. Once we engage this Tsgardi taskforce, I may not have an opportunity to get off Quesann for years."

* * *

A month later, the taskforce from Quesann was just twenty-two light-years from Coleman, with an ETA of less than a day. Jenetta, in command of the *Colorado*, had taken the point, with the remainder of the taskforce just fifteen minutes behind.

It was just past noon, GST, when the tactical officer said urgently to Jenetta, "Admiral, we've just passed a number of ships headed in the opposite direction."

"All stop," Jenetta said. Twisting slightly in her bridge chair she added, "Com, notify the taskforce to stop where they are and hold position."

"All stop," the helmsman repeated as he touched his console to stop the drive from generating new envelopes.

He didn't cancel the existing envelope, but the ship immediately came to a dead stop in space.

"Aye, Admiral," the chief petty officer on the com said, her fingers already activating the pre-established encryption scheme and readying frequencies for transmission. "Message sent, Admiral," she said after speaking the message.

"Tactical, can you identify the ships?" Jenetta asked.

"The computer has identified them all as being of Tsgardi design. According to the Milori ship configuration database, all thirteen ships are *Vekemacos* class destroyers."

"Helm," Jenetta said, "turn us around and pursue, but hold us four-point-one billion kilometers off their sterns."

"Aye, Admiral," the helmsman said.

"Tactical, signal general quarters."

As the alert began to sound throughout the ship, the tactical officer said, "GQ alert sounded."

"Com, establish a vid link with each ship in the taskforce. Put them up on the front screen."

"Aye, Admiral."

A few seconds later, vid images of the captain of each ship began to appear on the monitor. As soon as they had received the order to stop, the captain of each ship had moved to his or her command chair on the bridge, if not already seated there. When every ship was represented, Jenetta addressed her officers.

"We've just passed what appears to be a Tsgardi taskforce of thirteen ships. We've reversed course and are pursuing just beyond their DeTect sensor range. When we move up, I expect them to stop and confront us. Separate the scout-destroyers and be prepared to move in on my command. Our goal is intel, so we want some of them alive, if possible. Don't risk your ships, but cease firing on any enemy ship that has been put out of action. Helm, take us to five hundred thousand kilometers off their stern at Light-450."

The crews of the scout-destroyers had been living aboard the ships, even though they were docked in the special bay beneath their battleship. Upon receiving the message to halt, they'd prepared to deploy and were already separated from the mother-ship by the time Jenetta began to move in on the Tsgardi taskforce.

"Admiral, the enemy ships have stopped and spread out in a V-formation," the tactical officer said.

"All stop," Jenetta said to the helmsman. "Are the ships on the flanks closer to us or away?" she asked the tactical officer.

"Away, ma'am."

As the *Colorado* stopped generating new envelopes, the ship again came to a stop. Since the SC ships had been traveling at Light-9790, the rest of the taskforce was still some two trillion kilometers beyond the point where the Tsgardi had stopped to turn and face Jenetta's ship.

"Com, hail the Tsgardi ships," Jenetta said.

A few moments later, the baboon-like image of a Tsgardi warrior appeared on the front monitor. He was older than most Jenetta had seen, no doubt a senior officer in the Tsgardi military.

"I'm Admiral Carver of the Galactic Alliance Space Command. You're trespassing in GA space. Please explain your presence here."

The Tsgardi waited until the translator had finished relaying the entire message before responding. "I'm Admiral Kelacnius of the Tsgardi High Command. It is you who are trespassing. You had no right to claim this space."

"This territory was part of the Milori Empire and was ceded to the Galactic Alliance as part of the Milori surrender. We have announced our official annexation, as I'm sure you're well aware. You *are* trespassing. You never had any claim to this part of space and were lucky the Milori tolerated your presence as a neighbor and respected your borders. Now, do you turn around and leave our space voluntarily, or are you going to force me to take action?"

"Take whatever action you feel capable of," he said contemptuously. "That tiny ship of yours can't stand up to

113

even one of my destroyers. I suggest you return immediately to the territory the Galactic Alliance controlled before the Milori attacked you, or you won't live to see another day. Go now— or stay and die."

"Exactly my advice to you, Admiral," Jenetta said. "Tsgardi warships don't stand a chance against Space Command warships, even the smallest."

The Tsgardi admiral bristled at the comment. "Enough talk!" the Tsgardi officer shouted. "All ships, move in and silence this young fool permanently!"

The image on the *Colorado's* large bridge monitor changed to one of space in front of the ship. Jen gave the com operator the signal to cut the outbound signal.

"Com, notify all ships we're moving to engage the enemy," Jenetta said. "Invite them to join us. Tactical, deploy an IDS jamming satellite."

"Aye, Admiral."

"Tactical, notify all gunners to fire as soon as they have target lock. Helm, attack plan Delta-Three, Sub-Light-Five."

The plan would have the *Colorado* engage the enemy ships and pass directly through their front lines, then remain in their midst so the enemy had to be careful when firing lest they destroy their comrades.

"Message sent, Admiral," the com chief said.

"Jamming satellite deployed, Admiral," the tactical officer said.

"Activate the satellite," Jenetta said.

"All IDS frequencies are jammed," the com chief said. "Normal RFs are open and available for broadcast or reception."

"Helm, engage."

At Sub-Light-Five, it took just ten seconds to close the distance between the *Colorado* and the Tsgardi ships. The *Colorado's* gunners opened fire as soon as they locked on their targets and filled space with laser fire while the Tsgardi fired with abandon at the *Colorado*. Passing close to the lead Tsgardi ship, the *Colorado* commenced a circling path inside the v-shaped formation. As expected, initially there was a noticeable lack of torpedoes fired at the *Colorado*. The Tsgardi probably didn't give the tiny SC ship a chance of surviving the initial onslaught of laser fire.

By the time the Tsgardi realized the small *Colorado* was continuing to fight on at full strength despite being hit by hundreds or perhaps thousands of laser pulses, their own taskforce was reacting to the damage inflicted by the *Colorado*. Great and small rents in their hulls were allowing the atmosphere in every ship to escape unabated. Huge areas of their ships were depressurizing. The Tsgardi finally switched to firing torpedoes and attempted to compensate for the earlier dearth by firing as quickly as possible with complete disregard for hitting their fellow ships. The *Colorado's* Phalanx weapon system was forced to commandeer a greater and greater share of the laser arrays as it strove to stop the incoming torpedoes, leaving the *Colorado's* torpedo gunners to make up the shortfall in offensive weapons fire. The bow's ten tubes, along with the four stern tubes and dual tubes on both the larboard and starboard sides, were belching torpedoes as quickly as they could be loaded.

The fire coming from the Tsgardi ships had already diminished considerably when the *Colorado* was jarred by a torpedo detonation.

Almost before the ship had stopped vibrating, the helmsman was announcing, "Admiral, we've lost the starboard sub-light engine."

"Can you compensate with thrusters?"

"Not with the type of maneuvers required."

"Are the stern engines intact?"

"Aye, Admiral, so far."

"Tactical, where's the taskforce?"

"They'll reach us in— eighteen seconds."

"Helm, get us out of here. Head towards the taskforce."

"Aye, Admiral," the helmsman said as he keyed in the information and engaged the engines.

Almost immediately the *Colorado* was speeding away from the fight as they accelerated towards the taskforce at Sub-Light-100. Seconds later, the taskforce, heading towards the Tsgardi ships at Light-9790, passed them by so quickly that they were just a blur on the sensors.

"Helm, all stop." Via her CT, Jenetta said, "Engineering, I want a damage assessment on the star-board sub-light engine immediately. Just the bad news, not a thorough assessment."

"Aye, Admiral," she heard, "Give us twenty minutes."

"You have five. There's still a battle being waged back there."

"Aye, Admiral, we'll have a preliminary report for you in five minutes."

"Carver out."

"Engineering out."

Jenetta sat in her bridge chair staring at an image of space on the large monitor while she waited. To an observer she was icily clam, but inside she was in turmoil. She hated being sidelined while her ships were engaged in battle, but she forced herself to appear calm for the benefit of her crew. In four minutes and forty-eight seconds, she received a message from Lt. Patricia Gorci, her chief engineer.

"We took a direct hit to the starboard nacelle, Admiral. The torpedo tried to fly up through the exhaust. It's pretty ugly, but it's still out there. If it had been a standard tritanium nacelle, it would have been ripped away, along with a good portion of the hull in that section, but the nacelle contained the force of the blast and the ship's hull is intact."

"Is the engine usable at all?"

"Negative. We'll have to break it down to see if anything is salvageable, but our preliminary look using a vid bot indicates it's had it."

"Thank you, Patricia. Are we all buttoned up again?"

"Affirmative, Admiral."

"Okay, we're heading back to the battle site then. Carver out."

"Engineering out."

"Helm," Jenetta said, "Take us back as quickly as poss-ible, but stay wide of the site until we know what the situ-ation is."

"Aye, Admiral."

In seconds, the ship had come to a stop a thousand kilometers from the battle scene. It only took one glance to determine the battle was over and the SC taskforce had been victorious. The outcome had never been in question, but Jenetta was relieved to have her expectations proven.

"Message coming in from Captain Erikson, Admiral," the com operator said. "Now the other captains are hailing us as well."

"Put them all up on the front monitor," she replied.

Almost immediately an image of Captain Sandor Erikson of the *Themis* appeared, followed by images of the other captains.

"Is everything alright, Admiral?" Captain Erikson asked as the eight-way conference setup was complete.

"We took a torpedo hit to our starboard sub-light engine," Jenetta replied, "so I felt it best to get out of the way before you arrived. We couldn't continue to fight without it because it restricted our ability to carry out the necessary maneuvers in sub-light."

"Was anyone injured?"

"No, the hull remained sealed, but we'll need some repair time before we can fight again. How about all of you? Any casualties?"

"We're fine," Captain Erikson said, a sentiment echoed by the captains of the other ships.

"Good."

Actually, you didn't leave much for us, Admiral," Captain Sandor Erikson of the battleship *Themis* said jokingly. "They were all either partially or totally out of commission when we arrived."

"There were only thirteen of them, Sandor," Jenetta said in the same lighthearted vein. "We'll try to find you a larger group next time." Then, turning serious again, she added, "From the way Admiral Kelacnius spoke, I'm assuming this is a full-scale invasion by the entire Tsgardi military. Our intel is that they have over three hundred ships, and while their ships are inferior to our own, they have a decided numerical superiority, so I don't expect them to turn around and head for the border. We'll have to drive them back or wipe them completely out."

"This is going to be a turkey shoot," Captain Neil Elder of the battleship *Boreas* said.

"Let's not get overconfident, Neil," Jenetta said. "As the damage to the *Colorado* shows, we still have to be very wary of torpedoes. Now that the shooting is over, let's do the grisly work. Send out your search-and-rescue parties to see if anyone is left alive aboard those hulks. Don't take any chances. If they don't want to be rescued, leave them, but make sure the ship is permanently disabled and unable to send any messages back to their headquarters after we leave."

"Aye, Admiral," the ship captains answered before beginning to organize search parties composed of Marines and Engineering personnel. The Marines provided the force to capture prisoners and the engineers provided the expertise to rescue trapped Tsgardi from airtight compartments.

Once the Tsgardi ships were searched and cleared of any enemy warriors found alive, the dead were photo-graphed and had their elbow prints recorded before being stored in empty shipping containers. While the grisly work progressed, engineers were busy uploading the contents of each Tsgardi ship's computer to the *Themis'* system where Admiral Kanes and a few of his intelligence people waited to begin their work. When the uploads had been completed, engineers began permanently disabling the ships' systems and anchoring the broken hulls together so the ships could be moved to Coleman Space Command Base once the station was again in Space Command hands. For the time being they would be left in space with a warning buoy about the navigational hazard and a warning not to board the ships. The warning probably wouldn't stop scavengers from trying to salvage the ships, but if caught aboard the ships or with scavenged parts in their possession, the charges against them would be compounded because they had chosen to disregard the trespassing warnings from Space Command.

Admiral Kanes and his people spent days interrogating the Tsgardi prisoners and combing through the computer files. Thousands of written documents and tens of thousands of vid messages had to be viewed, translated, and fit into the picture the intelligence people were trying to construct. The combination of efforts enabled Admiral Kanes to develop a clear understanding of the problem in front of them.

Aboard the *Colorado*, Jenetta raised the com screen in her briefing room when informed Admiral Kanes was calling.

"Hi, Keith. How goes the effort?"

"We're only partway through the documents and vid messages, but I've got a pretty good idea of what we're facing, Jen. The situation is far worse than we expected. Are you available for a face to face?"

"Sure, Keith, come on over."

"I'll be there in twenty minutes."

Jenetta pushed the screen down and thought about Admiral Kanes' words. She almost wished she had made him tell her on the com what he had found, but she knew it must be so serious he didn't want to risk anyone overhearing him or somehow intercepting his encrypted transmission. His ominous words, "The situation is far worse than we expected," would echo in her mind until he arrived.

Chapter Eight

~ August 29th, 2282 ~

Kanes entered Jenetta's briefing room when invited and sat in one of the two available chairs facing her desk. He sighed deeply while staring at the floor, making Jenetta think the news was so bad he didn't know where to start.

"I'm listening," Jenetta said.

Looking up he said, "It appears we are currently at war with the Tsgardi, the Uthlaro, the Gondusans, and the Hudeera. They've signed a mutual aggression pact in which they vow to expel us from Region Two and divide this territory up among themselves."

Jenetta stared at him for a few seconds before responding. "I understand now why you were reluctant to say that over an open line, even one with standard ship-to-ship encryption. Are you sure of your facts?"

"Yes. I got the story first from some of the Tsgardi we interviewed. They wanted to brag that we didn't stand a chance even if we had surprised their battle group with a new ship that could absorb hundreds of laser pulses and still manage to fight on. But I didn't totally believe it until we reviewed plans we found in their computers and viewed some of the recorded vid messages."

Jenetta said somberly, "I can accept the Tsgardi and the Uthlaro, but the Gondusan and Hudeera connection doesn't make sense. Their forces are limited. They can't make much more than a token contribution to such an effort."

"That's true, but the Tsgardi say the Uthlaro insisted they be involved to make the pact more acceptable."

"Acceptable?"

"I suppose they meant *acceptable* to the various alien races in Region Two. They apparently want to portray us as marauding conquerors and themselves as beneficent liberators. Of course, the planets in the territory will have to swear allegiance to the new government as soon as they're annexed and they have no choice about belonging to the new government."

"You're absolutely sure of all these facts?" Jenetta asked. "The Uthlaro, Gondusan, and Hudeera are definitely involved?"

"To the extent that the documents can be trusted." Handing Jenetta a data ring, he said, "Here's a transcribed copy of the plans we found, plus all other pertinent documents and messages we've decrypted so far. The ring also contains several of the more revealing interviews with Tsgardi prisoners. The Tsgardi have pledged three hundred ships, the Hudeera thirty, the Gondusans seventy, and the Uthlaro have pledged more than six hundred."

"*More* than six hundred?"

"Yes, *more* than six hundred."

"But I thought the Uthlaro only had half that many."

"Apparently they have far more than we ever suspected."

Leaning back in her chair to look up at the ceiling, Jenetta said, "That means we're facing about a thousand ships."

"Nine hundred eighty-seven, as of now."

"Just a tiny drop in a very large bucket. Captain Elder said this was going to be a turkey shoot, but if they come at us in force, we're going to be the turkeys. If the intel is correct, the Uthlaro Military warships are not only far faster and better protected than Tsgardi ships, but also faster and better protected than what they've been willing to sell the Raiders."

"The Uthlaro have promised that in exchange for their participation in this pact, the Tsgardi will get the help and materials they need to make their ships as powerful as ours. New developments have been non-existent in Tsgardi warship construction since their program began, and they fall further behind everyone else each decade. The promise of new technology had to be the motivation behind the Tsgardi decision to take on an adversary far stronger than themselves."

"Have the Uthlaro discovered the secrets of Dakinium or Light-9790?" Jenetta asked, sitting up again.

"We don't believe so. One of the Tsgardi bragged that soon they will have tritanium hull plating and Light-375 speed capability that rivals ours."

"That's something of a relief," Jenetta said.

"Even when the rest of our M-designate ships arrive, we're going to be outnumbered almost fifteen to one, facing enemy warships with tritanium hulls and at least Light-375 speed. As you said, if they come at us in force like the Milori did, we're going to be the turkeys."

"I still have trouble believing the Hudeera and Gondusans are involved in this. We just helped them recover territory the Milori had seized during decades of confrontations."

"Apparently, the promise of a new, greatly expanded territory was too strong a motivation to ignore."

"It also doesn't make sense the Uthlaro would give a share to the Hudeera, who would only be contributing thirty ships."

"That is rather odd," Keith agreed.

"What's the plan? When did they intend to announce they had declared war on us and when do the Uthlaro plan to attack?"

"They don't plan to tell us about the war until they deliver the ultimatum in person at Quesann. They believe we'll have no choice but to sue for peace and agree to leave *their* space. The Tsgardi say the Uthlaro have also begun their part of the campaign. They're moving across the border and driving through our territory, absorbing space stations and treating our border like a collapsing balloon. They've also sent hundreds of ships to the Gondusan and Hudeera border areas to beef up the groups crossing the border there."

"If they already have forces positioned near the Gondusan and Hudeera borders, they've been planning this for some time— definitely before we defeated the

Milori. Unless our intel is wrong and they've overcome the single-envelope speed barrier."

"I think we would have heard something if they had. I believe your first assessment is correct— they've been planning this for a very long time. Our war with the Milori must have upset their original plans and they're simply adjusting to fight a different force."

"If that's true, then they must have felt confident they can defeat the M-designate ships in a toe-to-toe."

"That's true. Oh, and I learned how you were able to learn of the invasion before they planned. A Tsgardi officer failed to activate the jamming equipment in time at Ekoqulith. He paid for the mistake with his life."

"If not for that message, we might still be completely ignorant of this *undeclared* war."

"Forewarned is forearmed, but I'm not sure it's going to make much of a difference. How can we defeat an armada of a thousand ships?"

"Nine hundred eighty-seven," Jenetta said, correcting him.

"*You* said it was just a tiny drop in a very large bucket."

"From now on I'm going to keep very close track of every single drop. Despite our edge in hull strength, we can't beat a force that outnumbers us fifteen to one, so we certainly can't wait until they reach Quesann. Our best chance is to search them out now while they're attempting to move through our territory from border crossing points in small groups and whittle down their forces a bit at a time. They've been using jamming techniques to suppress news of their attacks and we'll do the same. I jammed the IDS bands during this engagement to hamper their ship-to-ship communications, but it also served to keep them from transmitting a message home once they saw they had underestimated the durability of the *Colorado*. We must keep the enemy from learning about the strength of our new hulls for as long as possible. From now on we jam all IDS communications whenever we engage any THUGs."

"Thugs?"

"Tsgardi, Hudeera, Uthlaro, and Gondusans. Good thing the Ruwalchu aren't involved," Jenetta said smiling, "I would have had trouble working them into a suitable acronym."

"I'm glad you can still joke about it," Keith said.

"The news is grave, but there's always a silver lining."

"You see a silver lining?"

"Yes," she said, smiling again, "I'm going to be away from Quesann a *lot* longer than I anticipated."

Keith shook his head a little, then chuckled in spite of his intention to remain perfectly serious.

"If you're ready," she said, "we should get underway for Coleman. We have a great deal of work ahead of us."

"Just give me twenty minutes to get back to the *Themis*," he said, standing up.

"Keith," Jenetta said, "good job. I'm glad you're here."

Smiling, he said, "As am I. I've always known we'd make a good team."

As Admiral Kanes left the room, Jenetta raised the screen on her com unit and began reviewing the contents of the data ring.

* * *

The SC taskforce reached Coleman Space Command Base in twenty-two hours. Jenetta would have preferred to bring the destroyed Tsgardi ships with them to secure them under the guns of the station, but it was impossible because the top speed they could be towed was Light-75. When the time came to move them, it would take tugs more than seventy-six days to drag them there.

The enormous space station, in orbit around an F5 Blue/White Class IV Sub-giant without any inhabitable planets, was dark. Only basic navigation lights were illuminated, but that didn't mean the station was uninhabited. Jenetta ordered the taskforce to remain twenty-five thousand kilometers away while several squadrons of Marine fighters went in to investigate. When no fire was forthcoming, several shuttles containing Marines and engineers were sent in.

It took hours for the Marines to search the station, but they came up empty. Marine Captain Haines reported in as soon as they had completed their initial sweep.

"No Tsgardi, Admiral, but we've seen lots of signs they've been here. They probably couldn't get anything operational so they moved on. We'll do another, more complete sweep as soon as we have more forces."

"Thank you, Major. We'll begin docking procedures immediately. Carver out."

"Haines, out."

*　*　*

For the very first space stations put into orbit around Earth, functionality was everything. The incredible cost of putting materials into orbit meant nothing unnecessary was sent up. Most of those first stations were cramped and uninviting. By the time the Galactic Alliance had been formed, the situation had reversed. Putting enormous payloads into space had become dirt-cheap when compared to costs before the development of opposed-gravity engines. Designed by different teams of architects, each eager to leave their stamp on the universe, the new stations sacrificed functionality to accomplish distinctive-ness. Most stations were so unique in appearance that they could be identified by their silhouette. The three stations currently orbiting Earth were jokingly referred to as giant Christmas tree ornaments. There were three only because of their lack of usable space. With the first station, myopic designers and administrators didn't plan for sufficient docking piers to accommodate the eventual volume of traffic and number of ships that would want to moor at the station. A second station, not much larger than the first, was discovered to be inadequate before it was even finished, necessitating construction of a third station. Plans were currently in the works to replace the three stations with one enormous station. The three small stations would be dragged by space tugs to inhabited planets with less traffic where a smaller station would suffice.

In recent decades, most new stations had taken on an appearance like that of Higgins— at least until Jenetta had started converting former Raider stations for Galactic Alliance use. Housed inside an enormous asteroid, the former Raider stations were the ultimate in functionality, with little thought given to external esthetics. Ideally suited for locations in hostile space, serious consideration had lately been given to having all new bases follow a similar model. There certainly wasn't any lack of giant asteroids in Galactic Alliance space.

The station facing the small taskforce now was another unique form. It had the appearance of a gargantuan ice cube. It was boxy, with slightly rounded corners. Docking piers jutted out around the entire station, although only on the bottommost level, and appeared almost like small rivulets of ice melt that had begun to flow away from the main body.

A second sweep of the station using ten platoons still failed to turn up any Tsgardi. All ships docked without incident and the engineers immediately began to work on re-enabling the systems and reversing the efforts of the SC engineers when the station had been evacuated. Most systems were restored in hours, but it took two days to get everything back on line. The laser arrays were once more operable and a number of Milori torpedoes carried back to Quesann when the station was evacuated were unloaded from the *Themis* and stored in the station's armories where they could be accessed by the station's automatic loading systems in an instant. Minor damage caused by frustrated Tsgardis far too ignorant to get the systems working again was repaired quickly.

As soon as the *Colorado* docked, its engineers began work on the starboard sub-light engine. There were no enclosed docks, so the engineers had to work in full EVA suits. Senior engineers from the other ships joined the repair effort, as much for the learning experience as the desire to assist. This would be the first attempt at making emergency exterior repairs to a DS ship since it had left

Mars. After three days, Lt. Patricia Gorci presented her report at a conference of the ship's senior officers aboard the *Colorado*.

"Bad news, Admiral; we can't repair the starboard engine. It needs to be replaced."

"Then replace it, Lieutenant."

"The nearest replacement engine is at Quesann, Admiral."

"Quesann?"

"Yes, Admiral, I'm afraid so."

"Any suggestions?"

"I'm afraid not, Admiral. Between the scout-destroyers and the battleships, we stock all parts likely to malfunction in our sub-light engines, but we never counted on having to replace an entire engine."

"I guess we have no choice then. The ship can't fight without its starboard engine. It will have to travel back to Quesann and be repaired. Make your preparations for the trip, ladies and gentlemen. I'll be remaining with the taskforce, so Lt. Commander Ashraf and I will transfer to the *Themis* until the *Colorado* rejoins us."

Lt. Commander Peter Gallagher and Lieutenant Maria Cruz, the ship's first and third officers, would act as captain and first officer for the trip back to the base and then again for the trip to rejoin the taskforce. Jenetta watched the ship leave from the station's docking ring before walking to the *Themis*. Her cats and luggage had already been moved into her new quarters that morning.

* * *

"This will make the task ahead more difficult, Keith," Jenetta said to Admiral Kanes when he joined her in the office attached to her VIP quarters.

"Losing a ship for two months when we're already so shorthanded is a severe blow. Let's hope it's the last."

"We'll be getting five more scout-destroyers very soon," Jenetta said. "They'll help substantially."

"What will we do now?"

"Now? Now we go hunting for more groups like the one we found out here."

"We shouldn't have to look very hard," Kanes said. "The documents found in Admiral Kelacnius' safe identify the point on the border where every Tsgardi battle group crossed and its approximate route. The fool should have destroyed them."

"I think we took him too much by surprise. He probably never would have dreamt in a thousand years that one tiny ship could be responsible for the destruction of his battle group."

"According to the documents we found, this battle group was number three of twenty-two. The higher numbers extend towards the Gondusan border, with the lower numbers assigned to two groups back towards Region One. Each group is composed of between eleven and sixteen ships, depending upon the tasks established for each group."

"Assuming this intel is correct and they're maintaining a reasonably straight front on this *collapsing balloon*, as you called it, we'll remain somewhat parallel to the border as we head deeper into the territory, moving slowly towards the center of Region Two to keep pace with their advance. Now that we know their plans and we know where to look for more, our speed will allow us to cover forty times as much territory as they can while we search the designated areas looking for battle groups."

"What about the Uthlaro?"

"We should focus on fighting one enemy at a time, Keith. We know we can kick the stuffing out of any Tsgardi ship on a one-to-one basis."

"But shouldn't we concentrate on the Uthlaro while we're strong? They are definitely the most dangerous of the four pact members. If the Tsgardi get luckier with their torpedoes than this group did, they might knock out one or more of our ships."

Jenetta stood up and walked around her office as she thought. Finally she said, "No, let's stick with the Tsgardi. Even with Light-9790, it would take us months to cross to the other border and we'd lose the benefit of the great intelligence data you've accumulated if we don't act on it now. I think our best move will be to destroy as many of the Tsgardi battle groups as possible before they realize we're out here. Of course, the Tsgardi could get lucky and hurt us as you've said, but if they don't, we'll be almost twice as strong when the five new scout-destroyers arrive. Our number will jump from eight to thirteen. After we've knocked the Tsgardi completely out of this game, we'll destroy the Gondusan force and then that of the Hudeera. The Uthlaro will suddenly find themselves all alone in this 'undeclared war' and we'll only have one enemy on which to concentrate all our attention."

"We'll probably find Uthlaro ships with the Gondusans and Hudeera. And Tsgardi battle group twenty-two is very near the Gondusan border."

Jenetta nodded then shook her head. "I'm probably more angry about the Gondusan and Hudeera invasions than about the invasion by the Tsgardi or Uthlaro. They were our allies, albeit to a small degree, against the Milori."

"They were only acting in their own interests, as they're doing now. They owe us no loyalty. For us, the distraction to the Milori was worth returning their former territory to them. I don't think they owe us anything, *nor we them*."

"You're probably right."

* * *

The taskforce left Coleman the next day. Two platoons of Marines and a dozen engineers remained behind to occupy the station. Since the Tsgardi battle group assigned to take the station had already passed by and then been destroyed, there seemed little chance any invader would again attempt to take the station. The Tsgardi prisoners were immured in the station's brig. With the torpedoes returned to the armories and the laser weapons functioning, the station could defend itself from attacks by a small force.

A thousand ships make an impressive armada until spread out to cover three sides of a territory that stretches across fifteen hundred light-years. Then it becomes difficult to find any of those ships when they aren't trying to be found. The seven-ship SC taskforce spent three days crisscrossing space once they arrived in the area where they expected to find the next Tsgardi battle group before finally locating it.

This time they weren't seeking information from the Tsgardi, so Jenetta placed no restrictions on the force the ships in her taskforce could use to defeat the enemy. It was more important they not lose any more ships. The scout-destroyer *Amazon* had taken point, and when it spotted the enemy ships it immediately sent a message to the taskforce. There was no need for talk this time, so the *Amazon* announced it was attacking then jammed the IDS band communications. When the rest of the taskforce arrived, they found the *Amazon* engaged with sixteen Tsgardi ships. Several had already been destroyed by torpedoes and most of the others were damaged in varying degrees. The arriving ships immediately joined the fray and made quick work of the remaining ships.

Although not willing to put her ships at greater risk to collect what information the prisoners could provide, Jenetta was perfectly willing to accept the gift of additional intel when it was available. While Marines photographed the dead and recorded their elbow prints after completing their search for any live Tsgardi, she authorized the engineers to upload the contents of the shipboard computers to the *Themis*. The dead were stored in shipping containers for later disposal.

"Twenty-nine down and just nine hundred seventy-one to go," Jenetta said to the captains of the taskforce on a seven-ship conference vid-link from her office aboard the *Themis* just before the taskforce was due to leave the battle site. "Good job, *Amazon*."

"Thank you, Admiral," Commander Kimberly Riccio, the *Amazon's* captain, said.

"When reviewing the logs of the first two encounters, one thing became apparent," Jenetta said. "There was a three-minute period when the Tsgardi fired almost no torpedoes at our ships. It was only after they realized their laser weapons were having little or no effect that they began sending torpedoes our way as quickly as possible. Therefore, I'm amending our battle plan. Upon identifying a Tsgardi battle group and notifying the rest of the ships in the taskforce, the scout destroyer will wait twelve minutes before beginning its attack run. That will allow us to arrive just about the time the Tsgardi are ramping up their use of torpedoes. With so many more targets, there's less chance of a single ship becoming as overwhelmed with torpedoes as the *Colorado* and *Amazon* were during their attacks. Does everyone understand?"

The captains all responded, either audibly or by nodding.

"Good. The *Yangtze* will take the point next. Good hunting, Captain Fannon."

"Thank you, Admiral. The crew of the *Yangtze* will do their best to locate another battle group quickly."

* * *

After just two days of crisscrossing the next area identified by Admiral Kanes' intelligence staff, the ship commanded by Commander Fannon discovered Tsgardi Battle Group Five, composed of eleven destroyers and one cruiser. As with the *Amazon* and the *Colorado* before her, they signaled the taskforce they were preparing to attack and jammed IDS communications. Fannon waited the mandated twelve minutes before they moved in, then used attack plan Delta-Three. The Tsgardi responded by spreading out into their standard 'V' battle formation as the *Yangtze* approached at Sub-Light-Five. Without information about the success of the SC attack plan against other Tsgardi battle groups, the enemy ships responded according to their training and the *Yangtze* was fully involved when the main taskforce arrived. The enemy cruiser took a lot more killing than the destroyers, but it, too, succumbed quickly when the seven other SC ships arrived and began filling it with laser fire. The Tsgardi battle group managed to fire more than two hundred torpedoes total, but all were destroyed before they got close enough to any of the DS ships to do any damage.

"This has been too easy," Captain Neil Elder of the battleship *Boreas* said from the privacy of his briefing room when the site had been cleaned up and Jenetta had set up a seven-ship vid-link conference with all captains. "I don't want to appear overconfident, but what gave these Tsgardi the idea they could defeat us? They only have titanium hulls on their warships, for God's sake."

"At the time they entered into their pact, they were probably unaware of our development of Dakinium," Jenetta said. "If we were fighting with older ships having tritanium hull plating, the outcome of these engagements would be a lot less certain."

"Our attack plan wouldn't be so bold, that's for sure," Commander Diana Durland, Captain of the *Boreas'* scout-destroyer *Danube* said. "Having a hull impervious to laser fire is a great comfort when the point ship begins its attack on the group."

"What now, Admiral?" Captain Lynda Stager of the battleship *Hyperion* asked. "Do we continue along the Tsgardi front wiping out battle groups?"

"For as long as we can. At some point they'll either learn of our tactics and adjust, or we'll run out of Tsgardi ships and have to rethink our attack plan against our other enemies. "I don't expect the Uthlaro to be so rigid in their response to the sudden appearance of one small scout-destroyer."

"Will the battleships get a first crack at any of the Tsgardi battle groups, Admiral?" Captain Sandor Erikson of the *Themis* asked.

"Not while attack plan Delta-Three is working so well, Captain. The Tsgardi don't consider the small ship much of a threat, so they don't scatter. By the time they learn differently, their ships are damaged almost to the point of being incapable of interstellar travel. Let's stick with this format until we have to change. The *Danube* will take the point next. Good hunting, Commander Durland."

"Thank you, Admiral," Commander Diana Durland, the Captain of the *Danube* said. "We'll bring home the bacon— or, in this case, the monkey-meat," she added, smiling.

"After the *Danube*, the *Hudson* will take the point, then it will fall to the *Amazon* again. If there's nothing else to be said, let's go bag our limit of baboons."

* * *

"Good Evening, and thank you for responding so quickly to my call for this emergency meeting of the Admiralty Board," Admiral Moore said as he took his seat in the large hall the Board used for its regular meetings. As was normally the case for emergency sessions, the gallery was empty, but a dozen or more aides and senior officers occupied chairs behind their admirals. "This message," the admiral said, gesturing towards the still dark, large, full-wall monitor occupying one end of the room, "received two hours ago was transmitted more than three weeks ago by Admiral Carver from Coleman Space Command Base." Turning towards one of his aides, he said, "Play the message."

The monitor was illuminated with a head-and-shoulders image of Admiral Jenetta Carver sitting in the office adjoining her VIP quarters in Coleman. As the message began to play, Jenetta was heard to say, "A taskforce, composed solely of the eight DS ships assigned to the Second Fleet, have met and engaged a Tsgardi battle group of thirteen destroyers approximately one hundred twenty-five light-years inside our borders. I know now that this battle group was assigned the task of commandeering Coleman by whatever means necessary. Upon their arrival, they found the station dark and empty. They were unable to restore the systems disabled by our engineers during the evacuation and so moved on quickly.

"After several days of investigation, Admiral Kanes and his staff have concluded beyond any shadow of doubt that Region Two has been simultaneously invaded by four interstellar powers working in concert to expel the Galactic Alliance. The four powers are the Tsgardi, the

Hudeera, the Uthlaro, and the Gondusans. We've learned that they've signed a mutual aggression pact that will see our territory divided up among the four powers once we have been defeated and expelled.

"Documents found in the safe of the Tsgardi battle group leader outline the plan, giving the specifics of their involvement. One thousand ships, most of them Uthlaro, have begun crossing our borders on three sides. The plan is to squeeze us out slowly, with all enemy ships converging at Quesann. There was never any intention of declaring war until they arrived at the Region Two Headquarters, where they would issue their ultimatum. An error on the part of a Tsgardi officer, executed for his mistake, was responsible for us being alerted to the invasion prematurely. We have learned of the plans early enough to make a substantial difference, but my forces are greatly outnumbered. The first fight with the Tsgardi went well. Only the *Colorado*, which led the assault, was damaged in the engagement. I hope our luck holds as we can't afford to lose any more ships. The *Colorado* has returned to Quesann for replacement of its starboard maneuvering engine damaged by an enemy torpedo during the battle and hopefully will rejoin us in two months. We desperately need its firepower in this massive endeavor.

"It's my intention to seek out the Tsgardi battle groups and engage them as soon as they're located. Since war hasn't been declared, I'm treating all invading ships as pirate vessels. At each encounter we will jam the IDS band so word of the engagements can't get back to the Tsgardi home world until it's too late for them to act. With luck, we can destroy much of the Tsgardi fleet before they even know what we're about. Our intel, derived from maps and plans found in enemy ships, tells us the Gondusan and Hudeera fleets have been strengthened by ships from the Uthlaro fleet, so defeating them will present much greater challenges. The documents found by Admiral Kanes' people state that the Uthlaro have brought over six hundred ships into our territory. This is almost double the number we believed they had available. It's indicative of a plan hatched long before we defeated the Milori. I believe they had intended to invade the Milori Empire and annex its territory when Maxxiloth had been sufficiently weakened by his attacks on the Galactic Alliance, so our annexation following the Milori surrender must have come as a great shock. I also believe that their announced intention to share this prize with three other powers is a lie. If they could unseat us, they would no doubt turn on their allies and eject them from the territory. They might even be planning to annex the territory of their so-called allies.

"The battle plan, and other relevant data, is appended to this vid message. Admiral Kanes will shortly be relaying a complete report to Admiral Bradlee's office.

"It's imperative the Board expedite, to whatever extent possible, the development of the DS ships promised to the Second Fleet. The speed and strengthened hull of the new ships provides our only chance of defeating such a large and powerful enemy armada. By the time any older ships not already underway could arrive, most of Region Two could already be in the hands of the THUG pact. We leave now in pursuit of more Tsgardi battle groups. I'm sure we have your approval and blessing in this endeavor.

"Jenetta Carver, Admiral, Commander of the Second Fleet and Military Governor of Region Two, aboard the *Themis*. Message complete."

After the accompanying documents, messages, and vid images of the prisoner interviews were played, there was complete silence in the Board's meeting hall.

The silence was finally broken after several minutes by Admiral Hillaire. "We thought the situation with the Milori invasion to be impossible, but this is far worse. How could the Uthlaro have implemented such a campaign without our agents picking up the slightest shred of information about their plans or the construction and staffing of so many ships? For them to send more than six hundred must mean they have several hundred or more still protecting their territory."

"Unless they sent everything they have," Admiral Plimley said. "They know we beat the Milori and might see us as a far greater threat, motivating them to send their entire fleet."

"They wouldn't be that stupid," Admiral Burke said. "Would they?"

"This might be an all-or-nothing scenario with them," Admiral Ahmed said. "If they fear we have expansionist ideas that include their territory, they might feel this will be their only opportunity to halt our progress before we're knocking on their door."

"No, this was planned a long time ago," Admiral Bradlee said. "You don't build and staff six hundred, or nine hundred, ships without expansionist goals of your own. Their territory is about the size of Region One. We've always felt that five hundred ships was more than adequate for our defense."

"Until the Milori invaded us," Admiral Woo said. "Perhaps the Uthlaro feared they would be Maxxiloth's next target and wanted to be prepared."

"Regardless of their past intentions, they've invaded our territory now and we have to stop them," Admiral Platt said. "We must send Admiral Carver every ship we can. What's the current situation at the Mars Shipbuilding Facility?"

"The five scout-destroyers we promised Admiral Carver during her visit will be ready to launch within the next few weeks," Admiral Plimley said. "We can possibly speed that up and launch them within a week. We have nine new battleships under construction. The *Prometheus* class will end with completion of the next three. The six after that are all of the new *Ares* class. In line with our plans to step up production to twenty-five new DS warships every year, we also have fifty destroyers, twenty-one frigates, and fifteen cruisers under construction."

"What's the status of the refit docks where we intended to produce more scout-destroyers?" Admiral Ressler asked.

"We've laid the hulls for ten more scout-destroyers, but it'll be about five months before they're ready to launch."

"Any way that can be sped up?" Admiral Hillaire asked.

"I'll get together with the yard manager and his assistants and see what we can do. May I brief them of the reason for the urgency?"

"Yes," Admiral Moore said, "but make sure they understand it's still classified top-secret. We can't allow any newsies to learn of this until after the Tsgardi know we've discovered their plans and are targeting their battle groups."

"So in seven or eight months, Admiral Carver will have fifteen additional scout-destroyer ships to add to her taskforce," Admiral Burke said. "If her assessment of the fighting ability of these little ships is accurate, that should help her immensely."

"Twenty-three ships against a thousand still leaves Admiral Carver ill-prepared to protect her region," Admiral Ahmed said, "but at least she won't lack for supplies and ordnance. We've dispatched the two new quartermaster transports that were recently completed. They'll arrive at Quesann in thirty-five days. Two more transports will be launched in a couple of months, and we can immediately send them off with more ordnance and supplies. Since it will only take four months for the round trip, my four new ships can make three runs every year until Quesann has everything it needs."

"I just wish we could send her a couple of hundred ships today," Admiral Moore said, "but, as she said, older ships not already underway cannot get there in time to help. However, a fleet of ships aligned along the border of Region One will ensure that the Uthlaro stop at the former border if the they get past Admiral Carver. Let's prepare a list of the ships that can be sent."

"Our plan to produce twenty-five new ships each year was established back when we only had to provide patrol coverage for Region One," Admiral Plimley said. "Now that our territory has been enlarged to four times that size, our need for four times as many ships is obvious. We must have more docks. I'm not saying we need anywhere near the thousands Maxxiloth had, but an increase is clearly called for. I propose we make plans to quadruple the number of ship docks at the Mars' yard from one hundred to four hundred."

"Quadruple?" Admiral Hubera said.

"Yes, Donald. Quadrupling the yard will give us one hundred new ships each year. That will be barely enough if we're going to patrol a territory that stretches three thousand light-years."

"Obviously," Admiral Moore said, "our appropriation from the GAC isn't nearly adequate for our current needs. I'll prepare a presentation for the next committee meeting and see if I can convince *them* of the need."

* * *

"We're unable to make contact with eight of our battle groups, sir," Premier Warlord Qerdesqa's aide said upon returning from a special meeting with the First Director of War Room Communications.

"What? No contact at all?"

"None, sir. Reports from all eight groups are overdue."

"Which groups haven't reported in?"

"The center of the line from Group Three that overran Coleman SCB to Group Ten, who crossed the border almost halfway to the Gondusan border."

"How many ships?"

"One hundred nine warships, including three cruisers and one battleship."

"Which battleship?"

"The *Slepeakus*, sir."

"The *Slepeakus* is our newest battleship."

"Yes, sir. It was placed in the center of the groupings so it could respond to any resistance along the line."

"Have there been any reports of contact with Space Command?"

"No, sir. We've received no messages at all following their previous reports that all was normal and that they were proceeding on schedule."

"If our ships had been engaged in battle, they would have reported in before attacking."

"Yes, sir. They should have."

"Can this be attributed to some sort of space anomaly? Something to do with a pattern shift in the dimensional displacement frequencies or something?"

"It's unlikely that eight different battle groups could be affected."

"Then what could be the reason?"

"Uh— uh— I can't imagine anything except Space Command, sir," the aide said.

Premier Warlord Qerdesqa stared at his aide intently. "How could it be Space Command? We know that Carver has very few ships in the former Milori Empire."

"Our operatives on Stewart have told us that sixty-two of Milor's newest and fastest ships, the ones Carver rebuilt after she defeated them, have been transferred to her command."

"It would take annuals for those ships to reach the areas where our battle groups were last reported."

"Carver also received the three new battleships launched last year."

"It'll be annuals before they even reach Stewart. No, it must be something else. I wonder if the Uthlaro are up to something by destroying our ships under the guise of enemy action."

"They wouldn't intentionally weaken our combat effectiveness before Space Command is driven out. Would they?"

"No, you're probably right; it has to be Carver. Perhaps First Warlord Kalisnacos was right when he warned us about her."

"But our last reports have her on Earth. We received news broadcasts she was touring their military academies about the same time we crossed the border. She can't be involved. She's annuals away from Region Two."

"What else can possibly be responsible for eight missing battle groups?"

"We're at a loss to explain it, sir."

"Was Carver directly involved in the attack on the Milori home world?"

"According to all reports, she commanded one of the ships."

"How did she get back to Earth so quickly?"

"Uh, unknown, sir."

"There's more here than meets the eye."

"How should we proceed?"

"Have every other battle group meet up with the group on their starboard quarter so the strength of each group is doubled. And order them to report *any* sightings of ships, Space Command or otherwise, as soon as they're detected."

"But we won't be able to cover as much territory if the groups combine."

"How much will we cover if we continue to lose ships? Eight groups represent more than a third of our invasion fleet. Have the newly combined groups cover the most important targets each of the two smaller groups would have visited."

"Yes, sir."

Chapter Nine
~ November 14th, 2282 ~

"This group is substantially larger than any we've encountered previously, Admiral," Commander Diana Durland, Captain of the *Danube*, said, "and it's a considerable distance from where we expected to find a battle group. The strength of the signal from the DeTect scans leaves no doubt it's either a battle group or a convoy. The twenty-five ships are about the size of warships. Should we move in using attack plan Delta-Three and then abort if it's a convoy?"

"No, hold up, Captain," Jenetta said from the *Themis* conference room she had taken over for an office. "It looks like the Tsgardi have either adjusted to our attacks or combined forces for some other purpose. What targets lie along their current path?"

Commander Durland posed the question to her tactical officer, then turned back to the screen. "Nothing special for a hundred six light-years, then they'll encounter the Louswalma system, Admiral. According to the files, the fourth planet has been an important agricultural producer for the Milori."

"That's about six months' distance for a Tsgardi warship," Jenetta said, thinking out loud. "They wouldn't combine groups this far out in preparation for an attack on that system. If this is a battle group, the size has to be related to not being able to contact the battle groups we've destroyed. Well, we were expecting it to happen at some point. Captain, stand by. When I give the word to engage, activate your IDS jamming, but wait a full fifteen minutes before moving in so we all arrive at about the same time. One ship would be very overmatched by a group this size."

"Aye, Admiral."

Tapping a button on her com console, she said, "Com, establish a vid-link conference with all captains."

In less than ten seconds, the image of every ship's captain was visible on the large monitor on the wall in Jenetta's office.

"The *Danube* has detected the presence of some twenty-five vessels believed to be Tsgardi warships. It appears they've combined two smaller battle groups into one larger force, probably because so many of their battle groups aren't responding to hails. We're going to jam the IDS bands and then move in. The scout-destroyers will use attack plan Delta-Three and the battleships will use attack plan Echo-One. It's unlikely we can guarantee containment of all ships once they see our strength, so the scout-destroyers will pursue any that try to escape, targeting their temporal field generators to prevent them from escaping in FTL, while jamming any IDS broadcasts. We're not trying to take prisoners here, so just blast them to space dust as soon as you have a shot. They have us outnumbered three to one, so be careful and good luck. Prepare to engage. Everyone ready?" Jenetta saw every captain nod. "Engage."

The ships had stopped in space but not cancelled their double envelopes. The *Themis* surged ahead as the helmsman activated the Light-9790 setting. Jenetta stood up and walked with Lt. Commander Ashraf to the ship's bridge. The location, course, and speed of the Tsgardi taskforce had been keyed into the computer and transmitted to every ship during Jenetta's conference call. Disappearing from their former locations in a blur of light, the SC ships appeared just a million kilometers in front of the advancing Tsgardi ships fourteen minutes and twenty-six seconds later.

As the small SC fleet was recorded on the forward scanning systems, the Tsgardi collision avoidance systems immediately halted their advance. They hadn't paid attention to the signal generated when the *Danube* passed them because of its Light-9790 speed and because it was on the outer fringe of their DeTect range. Gone in a fraction of a second, the Tsgardi tactical officers had all assumed it was an anomaly, but they couldn't mistake the sudden appearance of six SC ships directly in front of them.

The Tsgardi were still trying to contact one another to coordinate their action when the three scout-destroyers from the main force passed through their outer perimeter of ships and began circling inside, laser arrays blazing. The SC battleships moved to circle outside the Tsgardi battle group in a counter- clockwise pattern, their laser arrays blazing as well. Torpedoes from both scout-destroyers and battleships began to decimate the Tsgardi ships while the Tsgardi gunners were still running for their battle stations.

When the *Danube* arrived seconds later, it joined the fray inside the Tsgardi group of ships. Already, a number of Tsgardi vessels had stopped firing, but the larger size of the force meant the battle would rage on longer than previous battles and the Tsgardi ships were able to fire hundreds of torpedoes at the circling SC ships.

It seemed inconceivable, but no Tsgardi ship broke for open space. They stayed in their formation position and continued firing until they couldn't fire any more. No Tsgardi torpedo struck an SC ship, but a couple came close before the ship's Phalanx system destroyed them. Eighteen minutes after the *Danube* flashed through the Tsgardi outer perimeter, the battle was over and the Tsgardi ships were silent. None would ever again slice through space at greater-than-light speeds unless they were being towed.

* * *

"Still feel it's a turkey shoot, Captain?" Jenetta asked Captain Neil Elder of the *Boreas* during a seven-ship conference linkup of the commanding officers following the cleanup efforts.

"Not so much, ma'am. A couple of their torpedoes got just a *little* too close for comfort. I'm glad they only had a three-to-one superiority in numbers."

"I told the Admiralty Board I would feel good about our chances up to five to one, but that I wouldn't like to fight against greater odds. Too much can go wrong when multiple ships are all firing their weapons at you."

"Should we alter our tactics if we come across another group as large as this one, Admiral?" Commander Durland asked.

"Do you have a revised plan to offer?"

"I've read the reports on the tactics you employed against the Milori. The use of WOLaR torpedoes here might enable us to reduce the size of the battle groups before we fully commit to the attack. We could position ourselves in front of their path and fire the torpedoes before we appear on their sensors. They'd actually run into our weapons. The stealth coating on the torpedoes, coupled with their small size, would probably keep them from being identified by their DeTect system. Our weapons specialists could remotely guide the torpedoes to a point in the center of the Tsgardi formation and detonate them."

"That's an interesting proposal, Commander, but when we used the WOLaR against the Milori, we had them in very tight clusters. The Tsgardi are moving in a V-formation, but they're spread out quite a bit. The WOLaR torpedoes would be considerably less effective."

"Yes, Admiral, but the hull integrity of the Tsgardi ships isn't nearly as great as that of the Milori ships since the Tsgardi use titanium instead of tritanium. It doesn't require nearly as much force to puncture them."

"That's true. Of course, there's the matter of Light-225 speed to consider also. Unless timed to the nanosecond, the WOLaR weapons would be useless. We'd have to slow the Tsgardi to sub-light, or stop them."

"We do have electronic debris field generators on board that would fool their collision avoidance systems into shutting down their light-speed engines," Captain Lynda Stager suggested.

"Yes," Commander Durland said. "If we could accurately determine their course and speed, we could set up an ambush the way the Raiders used to stop commercial vessels. We could then guide the torpedoes towards where we expect them to stop. Once they'd stopped, the torpedoes would be bearing down on their location."

"How does everyone else feel about this idea?" Jenetta asked.

"It has some merit," Captain Sandor Erikson of the battleship *Themis* said, "but we won't really be able to judge its effectiveness until we try it because we don't know what the reaction of the Tsgardi will be when they encounter the debris field. They might change their formation to search for the problem. And rather than simply detonating our torpedoes in the center of their formation where most of the force would be wasted, I would fire WOLaR weapons at specific points along their V-formation, hoping to take out all the ships in that zone. Even if the damage was minimal, the confusion it'd cause should help us tremendously."

"That's our plan then," Jenetta said. "If it's successful, we'll use it until we find something better or the Tsgardi change their tactics again. If that's all, we have lots of work to do and limited time. Let's prepare to get underway to the next area where we'll conduct a search for a Tsgardi battle group. Good hunting, *Hudson*."

"Thank you, Admiral," Commander Scott Hyland, Captain of the *Hudson*, said.

* * *

"Sir, I have bad news," Premier Warlord Qerdesqa's aide said to him. "We're unable to make contact with three of the combined battle groups."

The baboon-like creature turned to stare at the younger officer. "Which groups?"

"The groups combined from battle squadrons eleven through sixteen, sir."

"And we haven't received anything since their last weekly reports? No reported sightings of ships or suspicious phenomena?"

"Nothing, sir. When their reports became overdue, the First Director of War Room Communications attempted to contact them personally to learn the reason for the delay, but there has been no response to his communication. All groups were permitted adequate time for response, and we should have heard hours ago."

"What of the groups made from seventeen through twenty-two and the first two groups?"

"All four groups report everything is normal. They haven't spotted any other ships and are proceeding according to their orders."

"This doesn't make sense!" Premier Warlord Qerdesqa suddenly shouted. "Why aren't they reporting in? What has happened to them? If they encountered enemy ships, why didn't they report?"

Qerdesqa's aide just stood looking at the floor somberly.

"Notify the War Council Secretary that he must call a meeting immediately to discuss this."

* * *

The taskforce welcomed the return of the repaired *Colorado*, which increased the force to eight ships again. The engineers had worked around the clock at Quesann to get the engine replaced as quickly as possible. An entire hold aboard ship housed another spare maneuvering engine in case it was needed, with the other holds filled to overflowing with replacement torpedoes. Tethered beneath the small ship was a spare sub-light engine half as large as the ship itself. Jenetta had decided the taskforce should have a *Prometheus*-class battleship-maneuvering engine on hand also. Sheathed in Dakinium, it presented no problem when the small ship engaged its Light-9790 speed to catch up with the taskforce. A massive hold aboard the *Boreas* had been prepared for its regular storage.

"If the attack plans are correct," Admiral Kanes said from his office aboard the *Themis*, "we have either eight small groups or four larger groups left out there. We've destroyed one hundred eighty-nine Tsgardi warships and have three hundred twenty-one prisoners aboard the *Themis*."

"That's not very many prisoners," Jenetta said from her briefing room aboard the *Colorado*. "Those hundred eighty-nine ships must have been crewed by close to a hundred thousand warriors."

"We've recorded ninety-four thousand, eight hundred dead. Based on the crew complement files we've been able to upload, we estimate that as many as five hundred more may have been lost through holes in the hulls following torpedo strikes or simply disintegrated from the force of the blasts."

"It's too bad we couldn't have notified the Tsgardi after we destroyed their first battle group and convinced them to recall their ships and end this invasion."

"They wouldn't have done it, Jen. You practically have to beat a Tsgardi over the head with a hammer just to get his attention."

"We've certainly done that during the past few weeks. The loss of their ships has to be like a blow from a sledgehammer, so I'm sure we have their attention. I can't imagine why they haven't recalled their ships."

"Tsgardi may be fierce fighters, but they've never been known for their intelligence. Remember the incident Vyx reported where he was holding his laser pistol on two Tsgardis and they reached for their lattice pistols anyway?"

"Yes, I do. When we started this I said we'd have to drive them back or wipe them completely out. Since we're not driving them back, our only alternative is to wipe them out."

The image of Admiral Kanes was suddenly replaced with that of the *Colorado's* com chief, who said, "I'm sorry to cut in on your conversation, Admiral, but the *Amazon* is signaling they've found the next Tsgardi battle group."

"Thank you, chief. I'll be right out."

"Aye, Admiral."

As the image of Admiral Kanes reappeared, Jenetta said, "Sorry Keith, the *Amazon* has located our next battle group. It's time to go back to work."

147

"Aye, Admiral. Kanes out."

"Carver out."

* * *

"Admiral, you have a message from the GSC *Mississippi*," the com operator said to Jenetta through her CT as she showered after her morning workout.

Tapping her Space Command ring she said, "Thank you, chief. Is it a priority message?"

"Negative, ma'am."

"Okay, I'll view it when I arrive on the bridge. Carver out."

After a quick breakfast, Jenetta walked to the bridge with her two pets and proceeded directly to her briefing room after greeting the watch team, learning the status of the ship, and relieving Lt. Commander Ashraf. She made herself a mug of coffee while her cats settled into their usual places and then walked to her desk and sat down. Lifting the com panel, she highlighted the *Mississippi* message line in the queue and pressed the play button. As she sat back and sipped at her coffee, the image of a young officer appeared. The message line identified him as Commander John Cleviss.

"Hello, Admiral," the image said. "I've been functioning as group leader for the *Mississippi*, *Seine*, *Nile*, *Thames*, and *Tigris* on our trip to Region Two. We'll pass out of Region One in two days. Our current destination is Quesann, but before we left Mars we were briefed on the situation in Region Two, so we're ready to change course to join you if that is your wish. We're all thrilled at becoming part of your command and await your orders.

"Commander John Cleviss, Captain of the *Mississippi*. Message complete."

Jenetta leaned forward and tapped the record key on the com unit. "Message to Commander John Cleviss, Captain of the *Mississippi*.

"Welcome to Region Two, Captain. My taskforce is currently located deep in our territory, searching for the last of the Tsgardi groups in this part of space. There are still two groups remaining on our side of the border between Coleman and Region One, and we suspect they might have consolidated into one group. If they have, the group will most likely consist of between twenty-five and twenty-seven Tsgardi warships. My tactical officer will append the coordinates where we'd expect to find them, along with the routes and timetable they were supposed to follow originally. Your job is to hunt them down and trail them until we can join you. Separate and crisscross the area at Light-9790 until you locate them, then pull back after you determine their course. Under no circumstances are you to engage them, nor even alert them to your presence.

"Jenetta Carver, Admiral, Commander of the Second Fleet and Military Governor of Region Two, aboard the *Colorado*. Message complete."

* * *

"What is this?" Commander Stephan Cross said to the vid screen in his briefing room aboard the *Nile*. His image was just one of the five appearing on the large wall monitor showing all officers involved in the conference call. "We bust our backsides to get here and now we're just supposed to sit and wait until the great Jenetta Carver comes here to show us how to fight Tsgardi?"

"At ease, Commander," Commander Cleviss said from his briefing room aboard the *Mississippi*. "You're bordering on insubordination. Our orders are to find the Tsgardi warships, then wait until the taskforce arrives before we even alert them to our presence. The Admiral said that if the two groups have merged, the consolidated group will be composed of up to twenty-seven warships. Do you really want to take on twenty-seven warships with five small scout-destroyers for your first time in real battle?"

"We've all had simulator time for these ships, John. They're impervious to laser fire, and the Phalanx system will take care of the torpedoes. We're practically indestructible. If we have to wait for the Admiral to arrive every time before we engage the enemy, this war will last forever."

"We have our orders, Stephan, and we'll follow them to the letter. We were ordered not to engage the enemy under any circumstances and that's the way it will be. If you even alert the Tsgardi to our presence, I'll bring you up on charges myself. Understood?"

"Aye, Commander," he said sullenly. "Understood."

"Good. Okay, we've got our orders. We'll split up when we reach the area in a few days and begin searching for the Tsgardi battle group. Any other questions? No? Then goodnight. *Mississippi* out."

* * *

"Message from the *Mississippi*, Admiral," the com operator announced to Jenetta as she worked in her briefing room.

Raising the com panel, Jenetta selected the message from the queue and tapped the play button. The image of Commander Cleviss appeared and began speaking.

"Admiral, we've located the Tsgardi battle group and, as you speculated, they've consolidated into one group of twenty-seven vessels. Unfortunately, they were alerted to our presence when they encountered the *Nile*, the ship that located them. Commander Stephan Cross, the *Nile's* captain, says his ACS dropped his envelope when it detected the Tsgardi approaching on a reciprocal course and dropped him right in their midst despite our standing orders calling for us to disengage our ACS when traveling at Light-9790. There was a two-minute exchange of laser fire before the *Nile* was able to reconstitute its envelope and engage its Light-Speed drive.

"Admiral, I'm sorry we were unable to keep our presence a secret. We're currently following the Tsgardi outside of their sensor range. I'm appending coordinates of our present position and course information.

"Commander John Cleviss, Captain of the *Mississippi*. Message complete."

Jenetta tapped the record button and said, "Message to Commander John Cleviss, Captain of the *Mississippi*.

"The taskforce has destroyed the last of the groups except for the one you're trailing, and we're already on our way to your location. Continue to follow the Tsgardi until we meet up.

"Since all other Tsgardi battle groups have been dealt with, having the last Tsgardi battle group encounter one of our ships is no great loss and it was bound to happen during our searches. It's unfortunate the Tsgardi were witness to our Light Speed improvement though. I'm assuming the *Nile* used Light-9790 to escape the battle group. I would have liked to keep that secret for just a while longer.

"We should meet up with you in three days. Stay well back until then. The Tsgardi firepower from a group of twenty-seven ships could overwhelm your ships. We'll take them on as a single force.

"Jenetta Carver, Admiral, Commander of the Second Fleet and Military Governor of Region Two, aboard the *Colorado*. Message complete."

* * *

Premier Warlord Qerdesqa walked into his sitting room where his aide was waiting.

"I'm sorry to awaken you, sir, but we've had a communication from Admiral Zerkovhas aboard the battleship *Pstorirus*. He says he encountered a ship they believed to be Space Command. They exchanged fire and the ship appeared to disintegrate in front of them."

"Disintegrate?"

"Yes, sir. They were firing upon it with their laser weapons and torpedoes when it disappeared."

"Disappeared. Did it disappear or disintegrate?"

"The Admiral used both those words, sir, just as I have relayed them. He said that after the encounter the battle group continued on their course and there were no further incidents. He probably would have waited to report the incident with his regular weekly report, but you said you wanted to hear immediately of any encounters."

Qerdesqa began pacing back and forth without saying anything. His aide stood by silently.

"If the Space Command ship disappeared, then it might mean they've developed some kind of system for cloaking their presence, but if they disintegrated we have nothing to worry about. Send a message to Zerkovhas immediately. Ask him to describe exactly what he witnessed. It's important he be as descriptive as possible."

"Yes, sir. I'll take care of it immediately."

* * *

"Do you understand the plan, ladies and gentlemen?" Jenetta asked the captains of the scout-destroyers during a vid conference following the taskforce rendezvous with the new ships.

All five captains nodded.

"Good. We've used this method in our last six encounters with the Tsgardi, and it's worked out very well. The Tsgardi have been so disoriented when we arrive that the danger to our ships and crews has been greatly reduced as we engage them. If everyone is ready, let's go wrap up the Tsgardi part of this invasion."

An hour later, the Light Speed engines of the Tsgardi battle group were shut down as they encountered the electronic debris field. Within seconds, before they had even issued the call for all hands to go to battle stations, the WOLaR torpedoes were exploding in their midst. When the Space Command vessels arrived seconds later, the officers were screaming at their com operators as they tried to communicate with the remaining ships. The fight was over in ten minutes.

Later that day while the cleanup was under way, Jenetta had a visitor aboard the *Colorado*.

"Commander Cleviss is at the door," the door interface announced.

"Come," Jenetta said, pushing down the cover of the com unit.

As the officer entered, Jenetta said, "Welcome aboard, Commander."

"Thank you, Admiral."

"Have a seat."

"Yes ma'am."

"Your ship did well in the battle, Commander. I'm glad to have you with us."

"Thank you, Admiral. Your plan was brilliant. I was amazed at the lack of fire coming from the Tsgardi ships."

"The plan was developed by the captains of the ships in the taskforce. We all had a hand in it."

"Yes, ma'am."

Jenetta looked at the officer intently. He obviously had something on his mind, but he didn't know how to begin. She decided to wait until he found his tongue.

"Ma'am," he finally said, "I would be remiss in my duty if I didn't report something. Commander Stephan Cross of the *Nile* was clearly unhappy with having to wait until the taskforce arrived. I believe he might have deliberately arranged to confront the Tsgardi battle group, although I made your orders quite clear. I even told him that if he alerted the Tsgardi to our presence I'd bring him up on charges."

Jenetta leaned back in her chair and looked at the nervous officer without saying anything for almost a full half-minute. "That's a very serious charge, Commander."

"Yes, Ma'am. I know. I've known Stephan since the Academy, and he's always been a bit— bold."

"There's a very old saying from the early days of aviation on Earth that goes: 'There are old pilots and there are bold pilots, but there are very few old, bold pilots.' We want officers who aren't afraid to take the fight to the enemy when necessary, but we also want our officers to follow their orders explicitly unless they are out of touch with senior command or the conditions have changed dramatically. Do you have any proof he violated his orders?"

"No, ma'am, no specific proof. It's just a feeling, knowing how he felt and how impulsive he can be at times."

"Well, he's required to submit his bridge logs of any action, but it's possible he could have arranged a confrontation just before the start of the log period he sent. I could order he submit his bridge logs for the prior hour to see if he first encountered the Tsgardi from a distance and, after determining their speed and course, deliberately set a course that would have him confront them. Do you feel we should do that, Commander?"

"Uh, I don't know, Admiral."

Jenetta nodded. "An investigation like that can have an adverse effect on a crew. Right now we need everyone focused on the job at hand. The Tsgardi will know soon enough it was us behind all their missing ships, and we still have a tremendous job in front of us. What say we forget this discussion ever took place?"

"If that's what you want, Admiral."

"I think it's best. I will keep my eye on Commander Cross though, to make sure he toes the mark from now on. Thank you for bringing this to my attention, Commander. You've done the right thing."

"Yes, ma'am."

"Extend my appreciation and regards to your crew for a job well done, and I'm delighted to have you here as part of the Second Fleet."

"Yes, ma'am. Thank you, ma'am."

"Dismissed, Commander."

Commander Cleviss rose to his feet and came to attention, then turned and left the briefing room. Jenetta returned to her work on the com unit. She was preparing a speech to be sent to the Tsgardi War Council.

* * *

"My fellow Tsgardi," First Warlord Kalisnacos said to the other members of the Tsgardi War Council as he stood up in the large circular hall, "we meet here today to discuss the gravest of matters. Before I open the discussion, there's a message you should see." He nodded to an aide and then sat down. The image of Admiral Carver appeared on the large monitor and she began to speak. All of the members grabbed for the translation earphones hanging on the seat back in front of them.

"Tsgardi warlords, for those of you who don't know me, I'm Admiral Jenetta Carver, Commander of Space Command's Second Fleet and Military Governor of

Region Two. I'm speaking to you today as your conqueror.

"The forces of my Second Fleet have destroyed all three hundred of the ships you sent into Region Two as an invasion force. We have several hundred prisoners and they will be returned to you as soon as our business is settled. Let me be perfectly clear; I'm not *asking* you to do anything. I'm *telling* you what you will do.

"First, you will announce your unconditional surrender.

"Second, you will immediately free all Flordaryn captives and give them safe and reliable transport off your world so they may return to their own. If even one Flordaryn is retained on your world, Space Command will exact a terrible price.

"Third, you will immediately recall *all* Tsgardi military personnel outside your home solar system. That includes those on planets, moons, and space stations.

"Fourth, you will cease all construction of military interstellar space vessels immediately. You will have no further need of them.

"You have a decision to make today. You can surrender to the Galactic Alliance or you can remain resolute in your stand against the GA and see your world reduced to ruins around you if you survive the devastating holocaust that will come. Either way, the Tsgardi Empire is now history.

"I give you twenty-four Earth hours to give me your answer. Do you surrender and see your territory peacefully annexed by the Galactic Alliance, or do we reduce your world to ashes and annex your former territory afterwards? I'll leave the choice to you."

The image disappeared to be replaced by the Space Command logo. All of the warlords in the hall jumped up and started screaming at once. First Warlord Kalisnacos stood and held up his hands for quiet. It took ten minutes before the screaming stopped and he could be heard.

"Fellow Tsgardi, it's true. For weeks now our battle groups have, one by one, failed to respond to our messages. We haven't known until now what was happening to them. We knew before we began this ill-conceived invasion that it might have serious consequences, but even I never considered that Space Command could destroy our forces with such apparent ease, annex our empire, and isolate us in this solar system. We committed virtually all our ships to the invasion, so we have only the dozen or so that remain as part of the home guard, but if Space Command was able to destroy our entire fleet, they would have little trouble with the older ships left behind. I leave it to you to decide our fate. Do we live on or see our species die in flames and destruction? Do we surrender and accede to her demands or see our planet devastated as she did to the Milori? Perhaps worse. I leave it to you."

As Kalisnacos sat down, the hall erupted in screaming again. As warlords screamed accusations at other warlords, fistfights began to break out and guards scurried to contain the combatants. Kalisnacos watched apathetically, knowing that whatever the decision of this body, the Empire was finished. Space Command had been too strong an opponent for them. The only hope for the Tsgardi now was that the Uthlaro would be successful, and even that wasn't much of a consolation because he feared the Uthlaro almost as much as he had feared the Milori. Given half a chance, the Uthlaro would probably not hesitate to annex the Tsgardi Empire. The question might better be phrased: Is it better to be annexed by the Galactic Alliance or the Uthlaro Dominion?

* * *

When the reply came from the Tsgardi home world, Jenetta turned on the com immediately and selected the message from the queue. As she pressed the play button, the face of an aged Tsgardi filled the screen.

"Admiral Carver, I am First Warlord Kalisnacos. I have been asked to convey our response. I was opposed to this invasion because I knew Space Command was strong, but I admit that even I never realized how strong you are or that you could destroy our invasion fleet so easily. We are at your mercy.

"The War Council offers you our unconditional surrender. We do not wish to see our world reduced to ashes and we will comply with all of your demands. Arrangements are already being made to transport the Flordaryns safely to their own world, and all off-world military personnel have been notified to prepare for immediate return. Without our Flordaryn shipbuilders, there can be no construction of interstellar military vessels.

"We acknowledge your annexation of our former territory and will restrict our military to our own solar system and the protection of our home world.

"If there is anything else you require, forward your instructions directly to me. I have been named as Premier Warlord following the sudden death of Premier Warlord Qerdesqa, the leader of the invasion effort."

Jenetta smiled sadly. It was a shame so many Tsgardi had to die to satisfy the power greed of a few leaders, but that was the way of war. Still, she was glad this part of the invasion was over. With the Tsgardi's unconditional surrender a matter of record, she could send her planned messages to the Gondusans and Hudeera, and prepare for the battles to come. She estimated the Uthlaro couldn't consolidate their distributed forces into one battle group in less than a year's time, but she would have to work fast to take on as many groups as possible while they remained small. There was no doubt at all that the most difficult and deadly part of this campaign still lay ahead.

Chapter Ten

~ March 3rd, 2283 ~

"We have received an important message from Admiral Carver of the Galactic Alliance Space Command," Senator Prime Curlekurt Emmeticus said, addressing the Gondusan planetary senate. "It was addressed to my attention and I have already viewed it." To a clerk, he said, "Play the message."

The image of Jenetta appeared as senators reached for translation headsets. Most had gotten them settled on their heads before she began speaking.

"This message is intended for the Gondusan and Hudeerac Order leaders. Space Command is aware of your plan to overthrow our government in Region Two by engaging in an undeclared war, with intentions of dividing our territory among yourselves and your pirate allies. We will not stand for this treachery, and we will show you the strength of our resolve and the power you have recklessly chosen to ignore by your actions.

"Over the past months, we have systematically destroyed all three hundred ships the Tsgardi sent across our border in twenty-two groups. I have, this day, received the unconditional surrender of the Tsgardi Empire, and their entire territory has now been annexed by the Galactic Alliance. I now make the Gondusan and Hudeera leaders a most generous offer. Recall your ships at once and I will not destroy them. I will not destroy any ship proceeding back towards their home world, but I will destroy any military ships headed into Region Two without permission. As part of your unconditional surrender, you will cede to the Galactic Alliance all territory recovered after our war with the Milori. There is always a price for treachery, and this is the price I demand of you. Should you fail to surrender unconditionally, I will annex your entire territory after I destroy your fleets and lay waste to your home world. What I did to Milor will seem like a minor distraction compared to the destruction I will rain down upon your planet. We have terrible weapons, powerful enough to kill every man, woman, and child on a planet, or simply obliterate your planet from your solar system.

"The decision is yours. Surrender now, peacefully, or die horribly. Once I engage the first ship from your military, my offer to accept a peaceful surrender is withdrawn."

The message of surrender from the Tsgardi Prime Warlord Kalisnacos was appended to Jenetta's message and the senators scrambled to change the translators from Amer to Gucceral. The senate clerk restarted the appended message when everyone was ready.

The senators sat in stunned silence at the completion of the second message. Both had been a blow, but Jenetta's message had been intentionally harsh. She knew they would not surrender if she appeared the slightest bit weak. They had steeled themselves for a fight, and she knew they had to envision their planet in flaming ruins before they'd surrender without firing a shot. Since both the Gondusans and the Hudeera had retreated before the Milori, she didn't think she would have very much trouble with the forces from either planet. They'd both been relying on the Tsgardi and Uthlaro to do most of the fighting.

"She wouldn't dare!" Senator Neodeet Literamus screamed angrily as he jumped to his feet.

"She has already done it to Milor," Senator Prime Curlekurt Emmeticus said. "What makes you believe she would hesitate to destroy *our* planet? We invaded their territory with plans to steal it. Did you really expect they would simply sit back and allow us to push them out? I tried to tell you how powerful they are, but you didn't want to hear it. They destroyed the entire Tsgardi fleet of three hundred ships located along a border of some seven hundred light-years in a matter of months. Everyone keeps telling me Carver has no ships. Will someone please tell me how she destroyed the Tsgardi fleet?"

"It's a lie," Literamus said. "She couldn't have done what she claims."

"Do you not believe your own eyes and ears? You saw the surrender message from Kalisnacos."

"A clever contrivance. Let's send a copy to the Tsgardi. I bet they'll get a huge laugh out of it."

"Very well, let's do that," Emmeticus said. "Will the senate clerk please see that the message purported to be from the Tsgardi is verified immediately." Returning his attention to Literamus, he said, "It will take about fourteen days for a reply. I just hope Admiral Carver will wait that long. If it does prove to be correct, what then my learned friend?"

"I'm content to wait until we know for sure."

"You won't be satisfied until death is raining down on us from above."

"Our planetary guard will protect us against bombardment from outer space."

"And who's going to protect the planetary guard? Don't you realize what you've gotten us into? If we surrender now, we'll only lose the territory we finally got back after Space Command destroyed the Milori. If we delay, we'll lose everything, including our lives."

"Trust me. It's all a ruse. The Tsgardi haven't surrendered. Carver is famous for her chicanery."

* * *

"My King," Minister of Intelligence Vertap Aloyandro said quietly to King Jamolendre, the monarch of Hudeera, as he sat reading at his desk.

"What is it, Vertap?"

"I've received a message from Admiral Carver. I assume she sent it through me because I was her contact during their war with the Milori, but it's intended for you and the noblemen."

"What does she have to say? Is she at all aware of the invasion yet?"

"Most definitely, my King. I think you should view it immediately," he said, holding out a data ring with shaking hands.

The king took the ring and dropped it onto the data spindle in his media tray. His console automatically adjusted for the proper translation of Amer to Lacinyc and he sat back to view the message.

By the time the two messages had completed, all color had drained from the king's face. "What have we done?"

"We invaded the space of a friendly neighbor with whom we had developed a good relationship, with plans to deprive them of their territory."

"Send for Lord Melendret and the other noblemen immediately. They must see this without delay."

"Yes, my King. I'll summon them at once, but it may take some time for them to gather. Most are off-world surveying the worlds we recovered after the Milori were defeated."

* * *

"Ladies and Gentlemen, I have some good news for a change," the image of Admiral Carver said from the full-wall monitor in the Admiralty Board hall. "Following the complete destruction of the Tsgardi invasion fleet in Region Two, the Tsgardi have surrendered unconditionally. I have established a number of requirements, and they seem to be complying. One of the requirements was that they immediately free all Flordaryn slaves and provide them with transport to their home world. I'm going to be a bit too busy to ensure their compliance for a while, but I made them understand that failure to comply would carry grave consequences. Oh, and I annexed all the territory of the former Tsgardi Empire to the Galactic Alliance. I realize we have more than we can handle right now, but knowing the violent nature of the Tsgardi, I felt it was the only way to control their warlike ways in the future. Their military is now restricted to their home solar system as a home guard.

"I've sent messages to the Gondusan and Hudeera governments in an attempt to frighten them into surren-

161

dering as well. I felt that with the surrender of the Tsgardi, their resolve might be considerably weakened. We know that the strongest partner by far in this pact is the Uthlaro, and we shall see how much the Gondusan and Hudeera are willing to rely on them for protection.

"My taskforce of thirteen ships is currently underway to a sector where we expect to find Gondusan ships. If they're traveling back to their home world we'll leave them alone, but if they're still proceeding into Region Two we'll engage them. I told the Gondusans and Hudeera that once we confront any of their forces, the offer for a peaceful surrender is withdrawn.

"Thank you for the extra five scout-destroyers. Their added strength was welcome in our final engagement with the Tsgardi force, and I know they will be invaluable as we battle the Uthlaro.

"Wish us luck."

"Jenetta Carver, Admiral, Commander of the Second Fleet and Military Governor of Region Two, aboard the *Colorado*. Message complete."

"She seemed almost cheerful," Admiral Burke said.

"She was able to deliver good news for a change," Admiral Woo said, "The Tsgardi represented almost one third of the ships in the invasion armada. Even though their ships were far inferior to our own, they still represented a large threat."

"She's also where she wants most to be— on the bridge of a ship," Admiral Platt said.

"What are we going to do about Admiral Carver's annexation of territory without prior approval from the Galactic Alliance Council?" Admiral Bradlee asked.

"I'll bring the matter to the Council immediately," Admiral Moore said. "I doubt there'll be any repercussions once I explain the situation. Admiral Carver is correct that annexation is the only way we'll be able to control the Tsgardi in the future."

"What if she somehow finds a way to defeat the Uthlaro and then annexes *their* territory?" Admiral Hubera asked. "Their space is as large as Region One."

"That would be a problem," Admiral Moore said. "We're stretched too thin as it is. Thank heavens the new ships can travel as fast as they can. We'd never have a hope of controlling a territory as large as Region Two is becoming without Light-9790."

"Donald has raised a valid point," Admiral Hillaire said. "If Admiral Carver does manage to defeat the Uthlaro, can we just send them back to their own space? Won't they attack us again when they feel strong enough, as the Milori did?"

"The annexation of Uthlaro space is for the Galactic Alliance Council to decide," Admiral Moore said.

"Yes, but they're going to look to us for a recommendation," Admiral Platt said.

"For that matter, what if the Uthlaro defeat Carver?" Admiral Hubera asked. "Will we simply walk away from Region Two, or will we mass all our forces and go at them again?"

"A good question, Donald," Admiral Moore said. "But we won't know the answer to that until after Admiral Carver first engages the Uthlaro and has an opportunity to assess their ships and fighting ability."

* * *

"Admiral, our search has turned up two separate groups of ships," Commander Cleviss of the *Mississippi* said. "The first is composed of about five ships and the second group has about ten ships. Both are following the same course."

"What's the distance between them?"

"About four-point-five billion kilometers. Both are moving at the same speed of Light-337, so the second group isn't trying to close the gap."

"So anyone encountering the first group wouldn't even see the second group with their DeTect sensors," Jenetta said aloud.

"Yes, ma'am. What do you think it means?"

"I think it means we've found the Gondusans *and* the Uthlaro. The second group might be hanging back, waiting until someone attacks the first group so they can

163

rush in and surprise the attackers. Good work, Captain. Stay back out of sight for now."

"Aye, Admiral."

Jenetta established a vid-link conference with her captains and explained the situation. "What I'd like to do is employ a modification of what we did with the latter Tsgardi battle groups. We'll set up the electronic debris equipment, but we'll let the Gondusans through. As soon as the Uthlaro ships come into range, we'll jam the IDS, trigger the electronic debris field, and fire our WOLaR torpedoes. Then we'll race in and see if the Uthlaro are as tough as the rumors say they are."

"Sounds like a good plan to me," Captain Sandor Erikson said. "We know it worked well against the Tsgardi."

"Anyone got any suggestions for how it might be improved?" Jenetta asked. When no one offered anything, she said, "Okay, then it's time for the block party. Let's go greet the neighbors."

An hour later, the trap was laid and Space Command tactical officers watched their sensor displays showing data transmitted from a sensor buoy left near the ambush point. The Gondusan ships were allowed to pass, but when the second group of ships appeared on the sensors, IDS communications were jammed, the electronic debris field was triggered, and the WOLaR torpedoes seeded in the area were activated.

The Uthlaro ships continued on through the debris field as if it wasn't there but then dropped their temporal envelopes and accelerated at Sub-Light-5. Their failure to cancel FTL where expected had put them well beyond the range of the torpedoes.

"Tactical," Jenetta said, "Disable all seeded WOLaR torpedoes. All ships move in."

The command to engage the enemy was transmitted on the UHF frequency selected for the operation, and all ships began to move as one.

As the two forces closed to effective firing range, space was illuminated with pulses of coherent light. The

Space Command ships tried to implement an Echo-One attack pattern where they would encircle the enemy ships, but the Uthlaro refused to be contained and kept moving out of the circle of the Space Command vessels attacking them. They never provided a stationary target as the Tsgardi had done.

After ten minutes of heavy fighting while jockeying for position, severe damage to eight of the ten Uthlaro ships barely permitted them to carry on the fight, but their gunners continued firing until they breathed their last. With the SC ships concentrating on the two remaining Uthlaro ships, one tried to make a break for it. It began building its temporal envelope as it rocketed away at Sub-Light-100. The *Danube*, *Nile*, and *Thames* took out after it, trying to destroy its temporal generator, but failed. The Uthlaro ship could only attain Light-375, while the three scout-destroyers could attain Light-450 with a single envelope and stay close enough so the enemy ship never escaped their IDS jamming shroud.

Several times the *Danube* passed in front of the enemy ship, hoping to halt it by having the collision avoidance system shut down the Light Speed engines, but it appeared the Uthlaro ACS system had been taken off-line. Finally, the *Nile* attempted the envelope-merge maneuver where a pursuing ship moves close enough to merge temporal envelopes with the quarry, allowing laser fire to strike the temporal envelope generator of the pursued ship.

As the laser gunner watched the helmsman nervously, his finger poised above the fire button, the helmsman nodded. That signal meant the envelopes would merge in exactly five seconds. In six seconds the Light-Speed engine would be disengaged, so the gunner had just one chance. With older ships there had always been the chance the quarry would fire its laser cannons at just the right instant and the pulse would hit the pursuer, but that wasn't a problem on the DS ships.

At exactly five seconds, the gunner fired his laser weapons and the *Nile* dropped its temporal envelope. The helmsman immediately used the sub-light engines to put a little distance between the *Nile* and the Uthlaro vessel on the assumption that the maneuver had been successful.

The hit was perfect and the temporal envelope of the fleeing Uthlaro ship dissipated as the temporal generator disintegrated. The *Nile* suddenly found itself alone with the enemy ship as the *Danube* and *Thames* continued on at the original FTL speed of the Uthlaro ship.

As the Uthlaro vessel came to a sudden halt, the gunners still alive aboard the heavily battered ship once again opened fire. The gunners aboard the *Nile* reciprocated and the space between the two ships was filled with light pulses and torpedoes for several minutes. However, the crippled Uthlaro vessel was no longer a match for an undamaged scout-destroyer, and its weapons were silenced one by one. The Uthlaro ship ceased firing torpedoes after the first two minutes of fighting, and it appeared to the bridge crew of the *Nile* that they had destroyed all of the enemy's tubes with their fire. As they circled the now silent ship, the *Danube* and the *Thames* reappeared. It had taken several minutes to turn around and return to the place where the Uthlaro vessel had dropped from FTL.

Still using the UHF frequency, Commander Diana Durland, the senior officer among the three said, "Well done, *Nile*. My compliments to your helmsman and gunner on an excellent maneuver."

"Thank you, Captain Durland," Commander Stephan Cross said. "Shall we search for survivors in airtight compartments?"

"Negative. We don't have any Marines aboard."

"My people can handle it," Cross said.

"Negative, Captain. The Admiral has ordered that search and rescue operations only be conducted by Marines. Since we must continue to jam IDS communications until we're sure no one aboard can send a message, we'll have to return to the original site of the battle before we can arrange to take a couple of Marine platoons aboard. You wait here with your prize to ensure it doesn't suddenly come to life. Someone will be here as soon as possible."

"Aye, Captain Durland. We'll remain here."

The *Danube* and the *Thames* built their envelopes and departed so suddenly that they appeared to simply disappear. Cross sat in his bridge chair, fuming that he had to babysit a wreck and yet couldn't even search his prize and perhaps claim a small souvenir. Space Command looked the other way when officers took souvenirs such as a plastic nameplate or uniform patch. As long as they were not taken from prisoners, these items presented no hazard and the value was inconsequential. This battle group consisted of the first Uthlaro warships ever encountered by Space Command, and Cross was anxious to see what their military ships looked like inside.

* * *

The Space Command ships at the site of the original fight were standing well off from the Uthlaro vessels as the latter were searched for survivors by Marines from the three battleships.

Using the UHF frequency, Commander Durland contacted Jenetta as soon as they dropped out of Light-9790.

"We were able to prevent the escape of the Uthlaro ship, Admiral. The *Nile* is standing by to make sure they don't manage to get any IDS messages off in case anyone is left alive. Once it's been searched, it can be towed back here and secured with the others. It's got a lot of holes in it, but it's largely in one piece."

"Excellent work, Captain."

"It was the *Nile* that actually stopped her, Admiral, with an envelope merge-and-fire. She didn't respond to our crossing her bow. She either had her collision avoidance system turned off or the sensors had been damaged in the fight."

"I suspect the former," Jenetta said. "The main group never even slowed when they encountered the electronic debris field. Perhaps their sensors are able to identify the

167

electronic nature of the debris field and thus allow their ACS to ignore the signal. They probably deactivate the ACS after that so an enemy can't do what you attempted."

"Aye, ma'am. That's the way it seemed to us."

"Link up with the *Boreas* and take on a company of Marines, then return to where you left the *Nile*. Once the Marines search her for survivors, have your tug or the *Nile's* tug drag her back here."

"Aye, Admiral. We'll link up immediately."

"Good. *Colorado* out."

"*Danube* out."

* * *

An hour later the *Danube* returned to where the *Nile* had been left, but the two ships were no longer there. Durland immediately ordered the com operator to hail the *Nile* on the UHF band. She knew the Light Speed generator of the Uthlaro ship had been utterly destroyed, so it had either been towed away or was using the sub-light engines.

"We have a response from the *Nile*, ma'am," the chief at the com said.

"Put it on the front monitor."

An image of the *Nile's* bridge appeared a second later. The quality wasn't as good as an IDS band communication, but Durland immediately recognized that the officer in the command chair wasn't Commander Cross.

"Who's the senior line officer aboard the *Nile*?" she asked.

"I am, ma'am. I'm Lt. Commander Sammuthy."

"Where's the captain?"

"Uh, he's aboard the enemy ship, Captain."

"What's he doing— never mind. Where is the Uthlaro ship?"

"Just ahead of us, ma'am. We're maintaining close surveillance so they can't emerge from our jamming shroud."

"Send your coordinates and speed."

"Yes, ma'am."

A second later the com operator said, "I have them, Captain. Routing them to helm."

"Helm, get us there, now."

"Yes, ma'am. ETA, five seconds."

Seconds later the *Nile* and the crippled Uthlaro ship appeared on the view screen.

"*Nile*, what your situation?"

"Uh, the Captain went aboard the enemy ship with a small rescue party of six and was apparently taken prisoner. The Uthlaro sent us a message on normal RF saying that if we tried to stop them they'd kill the captain and the rescue party."

"Send me the com frequency they used."

"Yes, ma'am," the officer said, nodding to the com operator on his bridge. "Sending."

"I have it, Captain," the com chief on the *Danube* said.

"Hail the Uthlaro ship," Durland said to the com chief.

A second later the bloody image of an Uthlaro appeared. At least Durland assumed it was blood. It was blue and was dripping from several gashes on the Uthlaro's face.

"I've told you to leave us alone or we'll kill your people."

"This is Captain Durland of the GSC scout-destroyer *Danube*. Heave to immediately or we will open fire."

"What's 'heave to' mean?"

"It means stop where you are and prepare to accept boarders."

"If you attempt to stop us, we'll kill your people."

"If you kill even one of our people, we'll kill all of yours aboard your ship and all the prisoners we've rescued from the rest of your battle group."

"I don't believe you. Space Command doesn't kill prisoners."

"You don't know my Admiral. Admiral Carver isn't like other Space Command officers and neither am I. If you wish to test me, go ahead and kill the rescue party that boarded your ship. I'll immediately give orders to my

Marines that anyone found alive is to be killed in the slowest and most painful manner possible."

"You've already killed most of my crew."

"That was in battle. Once the battle is over, we try to rescue any survivors. That was the reason for the party that boarded your ship. They were there to search for survivors and help them if possible."

"Back away and allow me to send a message to my family on the IDS band— then I'll surrender."

"I'm sorry. Any messages from prisoners must be examined for possible encrypted messages before we can allow them to be sent."

"I'll kill your people if you don't allow me to send my message."

"I see. Then it *is* a message to your command under the guise of a family message."

The Uthlaro scowled at Commander Durland and then muttered something unintelligible. "This conversation is over."

"Tactical," Captain Durland said, "have our gunners take out their sub-light engines."

"Aye, Captain," the tactical officer said before activating his CT and speaking to the waiting gunners.

A second later, laser pulses flashed out from the *Danube's* arrays, striking the larboard and starboard nacelles on the Uthlaro ship, then the stern engines. The gunners didn't stop until the engines had been reduced to scrap. The *Danube* and *Nile* helmsmen cut power to their own sub-light engines and drifted along behind the Uthlaro ship as it lost propulsion and maneuvering capability.

Chapter Eleven
~ March 14th, 2283 ~

"Marine Company Four," Commander Durland said via her CT, "prepare to board the enemy ship. Be aware that there are definitely alien survivors. They are hostile and armed, and they have a rescue party from the *Nile* in captivity."

"Understood, Captain," Durland heard in her CT. "We're moving in. Nevers out."

A few seconds later, two shuttles could be seen traveling towards the enemy ship. The Marines chose to enter in a part of the ship that was definitely depressurized. They would already be inside before they were likely to meet any resistance. A patchwork of images from the helmet cams of the Marines filled the bridge's forward monitor on the *Danube*.

The Marines slowly made their way through the ship, briefly checking all bodies they found along the way. When they reached the center of the vessel, they encountered working airlock doors into a section with atmosphere. They took time to change out of their EVA suits and into their combat body armor while one squad watched both forward and rear approaches inside the pressurized area.

Moving out, they hadn't gone more than fifty meters when they discovered several dead crewmen from the *Nile*, their weapons still holstered.

The helmet cam on the Marine company leader, Lt. Nevers, recorded the identities of the crewmen as Nevers said, "These people are DOA. From the readings on their suit monitors, they've been dead for more than ninety minutes. Continuing on."

After walking another twenty meters while checking every room opening into the corridor and welding the door closed using a tube of special adhesive after the room had been searched, the Marine on point found three more Space Command personnel in a heap inside a storage closet. Nevers moved up to check the bodies for life signs.

"These people are deceased as well," he said. "Their suit monitors indicate they died less than five minutes after the others. Their weapons are missing, but there's no sign of damage in this corridor. It looks like they were herded here and then executed. Continuing on."

It was almost another hour before the Marines encountered a live Uthlaro crewmember. As they passed through a closed, airtight door, a laser pulse narrowly missed the Marine on point. He dropped to his stomach and returned fire. The hallway filled with light pulses for a few seconds as the Marines behind him likewise opened up. As the corridor returned to normal, the only evidence of the brief fight was the burn marks that covered the walls in the area where the shots had originated.

The point man got slowly to his knees, expecting another pulse from the end of the corridor, but nothing came. Bent low, he moved cautiously forward and found the body of an Uthlaro around a corner in the corridor. The body, riddled with still-smoking holes, was holding one of the Space Command laser pistols. The Marine breathed a sigh of relief and stood up straight just in time to receive a laser pulse dead center to the chest.

He stumbled and fell backwards to the deck as another light show ensued when the Marines behind him opened fire on the second shooter. A few seconds later, the body of the Uthlaro crewmember fell out of the doorway where he had been hiding. The Marines were using their weapons on narrow beam rather than wide, and the light beams had punctured the composite material of the doorway frame, then continued on through the assailant's body.

"Damn! This new body armor really does work," the Marine who had been on point said as a fellow Marine helped him to his feet.

"Of course it does," the other Marine said. "It's made of the same stuff as the new ships. As long as you take the hit where you're covered, you can't be hurt by either a wide pulse or narrow beam. The LT said Admiral Carver's command was the first to get it."

"If I make it back to my rack tonight, I'm gonna send the manufacturer a message of thanks."

"Send it to Admiral Carver. She's the one who discovered the stuff on Dakistee and then argued with the Admiralty Board until they finally agreed to use it for body armor and APCs. They didn't want to risk having any of it fall into enemy hands, but Carver argued that it wouldn't fall into enemy hands if the Marines wearing it, or riding in it, were still alive to fight."

"Where did you hear that?"

"My cousin clerks at the Admiralty Board. She gets to sit in on all the meetings so they can have her run errands if they need something. She can't talk about a lot of the stuff they discuss, but most of the regular weekly messages from Carver aren't classified. When I was post-ed to the Admiral's command, Sissy began sending me everything she could. I learned that when she was the base commander at Stewart, Carver must have requested a hundred times that her grunts get new armor made from the Dakinium. The board finally agreed to begin manufac-ture of the new armor after the Milori attacked Stewart. So send your message to the Admiral with a copy to the manufacturer instead of the other way around."

"Yeah," the Marine said. "I will."

"Logan, you okay?" Nevers asked after speaking with the captain of the *Danube*.

"Hundred percent, Lieutenant. The armor saved my ass."

"Good. Fall back to the saddle. Sanchez, you're on point. Let's move out, Marines. We have only one man left to find. The Captain of the *Nile* was leading the rescue party. All other members are accounted for."

"Damn! *The captain*?" Sgt. Sanchez said, "What the hell was he doing in here before we had a chance to clear this ship?"

"I'll let you ask him when we find him," Nevers said testily. "Now move out, Marine."

As the Marines moved towards the center of the ship, they encountered more and more armed Uthlaro crew-members. Every corridor became a firefight location. They must have been close to the bridge when they discovered the body of Commander Cross. According to his EVA suit monitor, he had been dead since before the *Danube* returned to find the *Nile* missing.

Picking up his body, the Marines began retreating to the corridor where they had entered the pressurized part of the ship. They took a few minutes to assemble a collapsible 'oh-gee' carry-all in a protected area, then placed his body on it, adding the others along the way while one squad guarded their retreat.

A half-hour later, they were back at the shuttle. An hour later, they were stripping off their EVA suits aboard the *Danube* as the shuttle settled to the deck of the shuttle bay. Nevers made his way to the bridge as soon as the bay was pressurized.

"They were all dead long before we caught up with the ship, Captain," he said to Durland. "It looked like they were executed because the three in the corridor still had their weapons holstered and the three in the storage closet were dumped there. All of them were shot at very close range, probably less than two feet. They were probably surprised and captured within minutes of entering the ship."

"And every Uthlaro you encountered fired at you?"

"Affirmative. They don't want to be rescued."

"Then we'll respect their wishes because we're not simply going to release them and let them go on their way." Walking to her bridge chair, she took her seat. "Com, hail the *Nile*."

"Lt. Commander Sammuthy is standing by," the com operator said.

"Put him up on the monitor." When his image appeared, she said, "Commander, it appears that all our people were executed within minutes of entering the ship."

"Yes, ma'am. We were watching the feed from the helmet cams."

"Since the Uthlaro don't wish to be rescued and we can't just leave them here, we're left with only one option."

"Yes, ma'am. I can definitely live with that."

"They were your fellow crewmembers. Would your gunners like to finish our business here?"

"I'm sure they would."

"Then have at it, Commander."

The *Nile's* laser gunners opened fire on the Uthlaro ship and didn't stop until there was no doubt every part of the ship had been depressurized. It was possible some Uthlaro could have survived in EVA suits, escape pods, stasis beds, or shuttles, but there were no pressurized corridors they could use to spring ambushes. The *Danube's* tug joined the *Nile's* tug for the trip back to the original site of the battle. The tugs would continue to jam the IDS band until the Uthlaro ship was searched again. The *Nile* and the *Danube* would return to the battle site at Light-9790, while the tugs would proceed there at their top speed of Light-75. It would take them almost an hour, while the scout-destroyers would be back in less than thirty seconds once their envelope was built.

* * *

The situation at the original battle site was progressing normally except that it appeared several Uthlaro ships were in considerably worse shape than when the *Danube* had left.

"How did you make out, Captain?" Jenetta asked when Commander Durland contacted her.

"I have bad news, Admiral. Commander Stephan Cross and six of his crew are dead."

"Dead? What happened? Did the Uthlaro ship come back to life and get off a torpedo?"

"No, ma'am. Commander Cross led a rescue party aboard the Uthlaro ship before we returned. It appears they were captured. The ship tried to escape using their sub-light engines while telling the *Nile's* First Officer they would kill the rescue party members if the *Nile* took any steps to further incapacitate their ship. When I caught up with them, I took it upon myself to destroy their sub-light engines. The Marines I sent in found the bodies of the missing rescue party. According to the reports filed by the platoon leader, the rescue team had been executed by laser pistols fired at close range. Their suit monitors indicate they were dead before we even left the *Boreas* with the Marines. The Marines encountered heavy resistance, so once they had recovered the bodies I ordered them out."

"And the Uthlaro ship?"

"We couldn't leave them and they refused rescue, so I allowed the crew of the *Nile* to finish our work there. Our tugs are hauling it back and it should be here within an hour, but there are no pressurized areas remaining in the ship."

Jenetta nodded. "Good work, Captain. We've had similar experiences here. Our search and rescue parties were also fired upon, and we had no choice but to end the careers of the Uthlaro warriors who refused to surrender. We also have no survivors to worry about."

"Do you suppose it will be like this with every Uthlaro battle group, Admiral?"

"I don't know, but it certainly looks that way. We'll be prepared now if that turns out to be the case. What was Commander Cross doing aboard the Uthlaro ship?"

"Commander Cross was a— bold officer, who sometimes failed to follow the strictest interpretation of the orders he was given. When he offered to have his people search the ship for survivors, I repeated your standing orders that only Marines conduct the search and rescue missions. I ordered him to wait there with his prize to ensure it didn't suddenly come to life. He did remain with the Uthlaro vessel as ordered, but he chose to conduct a rescue mission personally."

"And his boldness cost him his life and that of six of his crew."

"Yes, ma'am. I can't say what he was thinking when he undertook that mission."

"Thank you, Captain. Your crew can stand down for a while. We'll be here for at least several days, perhaps a week. I want our engineers to survey every part of the Uthlaro ships looking for weaknesses we can exploit the next time we encounter them, and they can't start their examination until our Marines have eradicated every last vestige of resistance."

"Aye, Admiral. *Danube* out."

"*Colorado* out."

As Jenetta returned to the report she was working on, she shook her head slightly and murmured to herself, "There are old pilots and there are bold pilots."

* * *

"The surrender of the Tsgardi Empire has been amply confirmed," Senator Prime Emmeticus said, addressing the Gondusan Planetary Senate in special session. "We have received a communication from Prime Warlord Kalisnacos himself. He admits he doesn't know how she could have destroyed his fleet so easily, but every word Admiral Carver spoke has been verified as accurate. We should assume her threats to destroy our planet and annex our entire territory will be likewise true unless we recall our ships and cede the recovered territory to her immediately. We don't know how much longer she will wait. I leave it to you, senators."

"Carver may have destroyed the Tsgardi fleet," Senator Neodeet Literamus said, "but that doesn't mean she can beat the Uthlaro. We know how powerful their ships are. They promised us their protection if we joined the pact."

"The Uthlaro are far away, trying to absorb Region Two. Carver can come here, do what she has threatened, and be gone before any of our ships can return or the

Uthlaro can arrive," Emmeticus said. "One of the battle groups sent by the Tsgardi was destroyed not far from our border. Carver could have come here already if she wished."

"You can't know that," Literamus said. "She might still be on Quesann, hundreds of light-years from here."

"And she might be a light-year away just waiting to hear our answer, or preparing to strike if we don't respond."

"We can't simply surrender unconditionally. Not without firing a single shot," Literamus said.

"We can and should," Emmeticus said. "Our involvement in this pact should never have happened, and the sooner we're out of it, the better off we'll be."

"But she insists we surrender all the territory we took back from the Milori. That was our territory to begin with."

"And that's the price we'll have to pay for starting this foolish venture. It's better than losing all our territory and witnessing the destruction of our world."

"I move we put it to a vote," Literamus said.

* * *

"Their military ships are an order of magnitude above the stuff they sell to others," Commander Davis Swarth, senior engineer aboard the *Themis* said, as he pointed to the large image of an Uthlaro destroyer hovering above the holo-table at the front of the room. The conference room was the largest available aboard the *Themis*, and it was crowded. Every officer at or above the rank of Lt. Commander was in attendance. Many were forced to stand around the outer walls of the room.

"Their hulls are composed of three layers of tritanium with self-sealing membrane, making even their destroyers as resilient as our pre-Dakinium-hulled *Prometheus*-class battleships. Each frame section is a separate airtight compartment. Additionally, no crucial functions are located outside the core of the ship, so punctures and torpedo strikes kill very few key personnel. We have to hope we hit vital areas that will incapacitate the ship because simply opening sections to the vacuum of space won't do it.

"We have identified several areas we should concentrate on during our battles. They're the most vulnerable points and will stop the Uthlaro ships faster than random strikes. Of course, targeting their engines will stop their movement, but it doesn't incapacitate their laser arrays or prevent them from firing torpedoes."

Swarth said, "Computer, change image to wire representation." The solid holo-image of the Uthlaro destroyer immediately changed to a wire view of the same ship. Using a pointer to indicate a spot on the image of the Uthlaro destroyer, he continued. "All gunners should concentrate their fire on this area amidship, just above and behind the maneuvering engine nacelles, and pour everything we've got into that point. The central computer for the ship is located there, and if they lose that, they lose all shipboard functions. It's well-shielded with tritanium, so we really have to clobber that spot. Other than that, target their temporal envelope generators so they can't escape and their torpedo tubes so they can't fire on us. We can pretty much ignore the laser arrays until the other points are neutralized because they have no effect on the Dakinium. That's all we have, Admiral. The Uthlaro have done an excellent job on the design of these ships."

"Thank you commander," Jenetta said. "In how many cases did we stop the Uthlaro by destroying the central computer during the most recent engagement?"

"In almost every case, Admiral. Although we weren't targeting it, we lucked out in eight out of ten ships. From examining the logs, we've learned that the ship that managed to reach Light Speed probably had the least damage in that part of the ship until the *Nile* peppered it following the recovery of our people."

"Is everyone clear on the points to target?" Jenetta asked.

Everyone in the room nodded or voiced their understanding.

179

"I've appointed Lt. Commander Soren Mojica of the *Yangtze* to replace Commander Stephan Cross as commanding officer of the *Nile*, and Lt. Adel Baran will advance to first officer of the *Yangtze*. All except the captains and their first officers are now dismissed."

Jenetta waited until most of the officers had left and the doors of the conference room were closed before continuing.

"As you all know, the electronic debris field didn't work with the Uthlaro, so we'll discontinue use of that procedure. We got that system from the Raiders, and the Raiders do a great deal of business with the Uthlaro, so the Uthlaro may have even developed that system originally. When we activated the sending units, the Uthlaro simply continued as if unaffected. I also expect that their helmsmen have been trained to override the ACS system as soon as they sense the debris field because the Uthlaro ship the *Nile* chased couldn't be stopped when a ship crossed its path. The ACS had to have been deactivated by that point. They must have stopped solely to engage us. If we assume other Uthlaro captains are as eager to engage, we'll simply use our presence to stop them.

"We've recovered the WOLaR torpedoes we fired, refueled them, and returned them to our armories. We'll discontinue their use in *stopping* the Uthlaro, but we shouldn't ignore their use in *fighting* the Uthlaro once we engage since we now know how difficult it is to destroy their ships and that they won't surrender while they have an ounce of strength left.

"Now that we've been briefed on the points our gunners should target, I'd like to have each of the scout-destroyer captains assign two of their best gunners, one each on the larboard and starboard sides, to concentrate solely on the temporal generator. If a shot at the generator is impossible due to the tangential track, those four gunners should concentrate solely on the torpedo tubes until a shot at the generator is possible. I'd like you battleship captains to assign half a dozen gunners on each side of your vessel to target the same points. Our first goal must be to stop the Uthlaro from escaping the battle site. The envelope-merge maneuver is too dangerous to make it a regular part of our plan. By stopping them from leaving the battle site or limiting them to sub-light speeds, we can simply pound them until they can't fight any-more."

"I know that in the past," Captain Sandor Erikson said, "we hesitated to use the WOLaR torpedoes on single ships because there wasn't very much left afterwards, but I think we should change that policy towards the Uthlaro, Admiral. We've seen they won't surrender while alive, so we know we have to utterly destroy them."

"Yes, you might be right. Admiral Kanes, have your people had any luck with the computer cores we recovered?"

"Not yet, Admiral. As Commander Swarth said, we stopped eight of the ten Uthlaro vessels by destroying their central computer. The cores were damaged in all eight. In the other two, the cores were damaged in the later destruction of the ship when the crews refused to surrender and continued to fight. We'll keep working on them, but we have very little intel so far, except for our knowledge of their ship construction and their ferocity. Based on what we know of the previous border-crossing points, we should pretty well be able to predict where we'll find the next Uthlaro/Gondusan battle groups."

"I wonder if the Gondusans we allowed to pass unmolested even know their shadow is gone." Jenetta mused.

"I suppose it depends on how closely they're working together," Kanes said. "Were the Uthlaro their coconspirators or their guards?"

"You think the Uthlaro were there to drive them on?"

"Perhaps that's the intent if they falter. The Uthlaro have to know the Gondusans aren't as aggressive as they are. I was surprised they were involved when I learned of the pact's signatories. The Uthlaro must have promised them protection from us."

"I've given them plenty of time to verify that the Tsgardi are out of the game," Jenetta said, "but they haven't responded yet. I hope they aren't relying on the Uthlaro to protect them because we're going to ensure the Uthlaro will be a bit busy protecting *themselves* for a while."

"Can we take the Uthlaro if they have numerical superiority in future engagements?" Kanes asked. "This ten-ship battle group gave our thirteen-ship taskforce a rough time for a while."

"We'll take them, as long as we don't have to fight too many at once. Based on what we've learned about them, we'll have a distinct advantage in any fight where our numbers are equal simply because their laser weapons can't harm us. Where they have numerical superiority, things will be a lot less certain. We know their ship construction now and where to target our weapons. If we can just keep them from alerting their command about the durability of our hulls, we'll continue to have a major advantage. They'll expend a great deal of time and effort trying to puncture us with their laser arrays, to no avail, instead of firing every torpedo possible at us. If a day comes when they don't fire a single laser pulse in our direction, we'll know our secret is out."

* * *

"My lords, you've seen the vid message from Admiral Carver," King Jamolendre said to the nobles assembled in the great hall of the palace, "I'm anxious to hear your thoughts."

"Has this claim about the Tsgardi surrender been verified?" Lord Melendret asked.

"Yes, it has, according to my Minister of Intelligence. The Tsgardi have acknowledged that their fleet was completely destroyed. They surrendered unconditionally rather than see their world reduced to rubble."

Lord Melendret breathed in deeply and let it out slowly, using the time to think of a reply. "Have we contacted the Uthlaro? They promised us this wouldn't happen. They promised us their protection from any retaliation if a Space Command vessel somehow got through the lines."

"We've sent numerous messages. They aren't responding."

Lord Melendret breathed deeply again, then put a hand to his forehead and looked down at the table in front of him.

"We must respond to Admiral Carver soon if we're going to surrender," the king said, "or we risk being attacked because she hasn't heard from us."

"We cannot surrender!" Melendret said vociferously. "We will not surrender the territory stolen from our fathers!"

"The admiral said she will destroy our world and seize all our territory if we don't surrender before she's forced to fight our ships!" the king said just as loudly.

"I heard the message!" Melendret screamed at the king. "I heard it!"

The nobles around the hall looked on in stunned silence. Lord Melendret definitely had his own agenda, but he had never before been openly disrespectful to the king.

"I'm sorry, your majesty," Melendret said apologetically. "I'm just so upset by this development that I forgot myself for a moment. I beg your forgiveness."

"I understand," King Jamolendre said calmly. "I openly opposed this pact, but your impassioned rhetoric convinced the other nobles it was a good idea, and you managed to garner enough support to make my voice inconsequential."

"I was only doing what I felt was best for our world," Melendret said.

The king, emboldened by his new power over Melendret, said, "You were doing what you felt would bring you greater riches, and possibly the crown someday. Now you have brought us to the brink of destruction."

Melendret bristled at the remarks. It didn't matter that they were true— the king had no right to state them openly.

183

"Now, it falls to my shoulders to save us from your avarice," the king added, specifically addressing the block of nobles that had pushed for the pact. "We shall have to surrender before our world is destroyed and hope that Admiral Carver will treat us decently in spite of the damage you have done to the good name of our kingdom. If anyone has a dissenting opinion or a suggestion for another way out of this impending disaster, I'm listening."

The hall was silent as the gathered noblemen stared down at the table in front of them. The king stood up in front of his chair and walked regally back to his office. Melendret would never again openly challenge the king's decisions, but that silence had come at too high a price. They would have to surrender all territory outside of their solar system.

* * *

"Admiral, a message has arrived for you from the Hudeerac Order," Jenetta heard on her CT as she groomed her cats in her stateroom.

Tapping her Space Command ring she said, "Forward it to my office, Chief."

"Aye, Admiral. You have it."

"Thank you. Carver out."

Walking into her office, she sat at the desk and lifted the com screen. When she selected the message from the queue, the image of King Jamolendre appeared. She leaned back in her chair as the translation came through the speakers. When it was over, she smiled and composed herself before tapping the record key.

"Your majesty, you've made a difficult but very wise decision. I would have hated to destroy your world, but I would have done it nevertheless if it remained the only way to end your involvement in this aggression. Recall your thirty ships at once, and then vacate all territory you occupied after our war with the Milori. I have all the maps, and I know where the borders were. Your remaining area will remain the sovereign territory of your world, and we will not trespass into it unless invited. The people on the worlds within Region Two are no longer your subjects. They may continue to live there and even trade openly with commercial enterprises in your kingdom, but you may neither exercise any control over them nor send any military vessels into that part of the Galactic Alliance without advance permission.

"My warships will not attack any military vessels headed back towards your territory but will attack any headed *into* Region Two, so I advise you to issue the orders with all due haste."

"Jenetta Carver, Admiral, Commander of the Second Fleet and Military Governor of Region Two, aboard the *Colorado*. Message complete."

With the message from the king, the Uthlaro were left as the sole aggressor in Region Two. The Gondusans had surrendered unconditionally and begged for mercy. As with the Hudeerac Order, Jenetta ordered them to recall their ships at once and vacate the territory regained after the Milori were defeated. She knew that surrendering the space was difficult and would cause hard feelings for some time to come, but they had to understand there were always consequences of participation in a war, especially when they were the aggressor.

*   *   *

"The Gondusans and Hudeerac Order have surrendered unconditionally to Space Command," Uthlaro Prime Minster Taomolu Barguado said somberly to the Council of Ministers, "both before even firing a single volley. The defeat of the Tsgardi was the blow that started the collapse. Carver frightened the cowards into surrendering with threats of annihilation that surpassed anything we'd offered them to remain resolute."

"Have we seized the ships of the Gondusans and Hudeerac Order as we planned so that our takeover of their territory will be easier later?" Minister Ambello Neddowo asked.

"No, we haven't. A number of the battle groups that were tailing the Gondusan groups have failed to respond to our calls."

"What? Why weren't we told?" Neddowo demanded.

"We have only known for a short time. Our technicians have been trying everything to reestablish contact."

"How many groups haven't reported in?"

"Seven. Seventy ships in all."

"Seventy?" Neddowo screamed. "Which groups?"

"The groups beginning with the one closest to the Tsgardi border, or rather what was the Tsgardi border before Carver annexed their territory."

"You lose contact with seven contiguous groups and don't feel it's important enough to inform us immediately? Have we put the wrong person in the Prime Minister's chair?"

"They're not that much overdue, except for the first."

"Don't you understand the significance of this, you fool? Space Command is working their way down from the Tsgardi border, taking our ships out as they encounter them."

"Space Command?" Barguado echoed. "You said Space Command didn't have any ships in that area and couldn't get them there for years. How could it be Space Command?"

"Space Command has destroyed the Tsgardi battle fleet. What else *could* it be you witless idiot?"

"A problem with the dimensional stability of space in that sector might cause such temporary problems, according to one of our engineers."

"I hope he's right, but I wouldn't count on it. Have you consulted with our military planners?"

"They steadfastly state that it would be impossible for *anyone* to defeat seventy of our vessels without at least one getting off a warning message."

"That sounds reasonable. To what do they attribute this silence then?"

"They're at a complete loss to explain it."

"What do they suggest?"

"They say we should keep trying to contact the ships until we receive a reply."

"More idiots!" Neddowo ranted.

"What do you think we should do, Minister?" Barguado asked.

"How should I know? I'm not a military planner or a communications engineer."

Barguado nodded. "Then we do nothing?"

"We should continue to monitor all communication frequencies and see if Space Command has increased their com traffic."

"How would we know what communications are from Space Command? All messages are encrypted."

"I told you I'm not a communications engineer or military planner."

"Obviously," Barguado said, still rankled that Neddowo had twice called him a fool.

"If any more ships fail to report in on time, I want to be notified immediately. And call me if this communications blackout should suddenly lift. Do you understand?"

"I understand."

"Good," Neddowo said before storming out of the Council chambers.

* * *

"It doesn't make sense, Jen. The Uthlaro have to know by now that some of their ships are missing," Admiral Kanes said to Jenetta as he sat across from her in her briefing room aboard the *Colorado*.

"You would think so, but they haven't altered their tactics yet. Their ships are still traveling in groups of ten along the same predictable routes towards a centralized position in Region Two. The only difference is we haven't seen any more Gondusan ships."

"The Gondusans must have recalled them to their own space as they promised to do when they surrendered."

"I hope so. Without them to confuse the situation, we only have to worry about one enemy."

"But it's an enemy who still has an estimated five-hundred ships— incredibly powerful ships— and who is bent on driving us out of the territory."

"If we can continue to take them on ten at a time, we have a good chance of beating them."

"But it can't last. They can't be that stupid. Can they? It doesn't make sense they became as powerful as they are if they really are that stupid."

"We've learned that their people are fanatically loyal, Keith. The only possible explanation for not changing tactics I can imagine is that their military is being run by businessmen without any military experience. Perhaps they think the sheer weight of numbers is enough. Perhaps they thought we'd just run away when we saw them coming at us with a thousand ships."

"Well," Kanes said, "as far as we know, their military has never actually fought an enemy. Their territory has never been invaded, probably because they posed little threat, and their products were needed by both their warlike neighbors and the Raiders. We know that Maxxiloth traded with them heavily, and probably his great-grandfather did as well."

"So why have they decided to go to war now? If they're primarily businessmen, why not just concentrate on their businesses?"

"Maybe they feared that Maxxiloth's great-grandfather would invade them, so they began to build up their military. It's possible that once they had a powerful military, it bothered them that it wasn't occupied in something productive."

"You think they started this war to give their military something to do?" Jenetta asked incredulously.

"Well, doubling or even tripling the size of their territory, as would have been the case if they'd seized the Tsgardi, Gondusan, and Hudeera territories once they had possession of Region Two, would give them vast new supplies of raw materials and a market they could control and keep to themselves."

"But they already have a territory that's the size of our Region One."

"Businessmen can become so greedy at times that they lose perspective."

"I suppose. But now that we've destroyed a hundred of their ships, you'd think they'd wake up and realize they shouldn't have started this war in the first place."

"That won't make a difference if their government is being run by businessmen. Businessmen are used to suffering a certain amount of loss; it's just numbers to them. An often-used solution is to simply throw more resources at it, like a gambler who, after losing a hand at blackjack, doubles his bet on the next hand and continues to double his bet every hand until he wins. The odds say that he has to win eventually and he'll recover all his losses immediately."

"That might work with credits, but once a ship and her crew are destroyed you don't simply win them back."

"That may not matter to them if they win an engagement and still have many more ships in reserve. Their goal is to acquire territory, not preserve their forces."

"You think they have more ships to put against us?"

"I don't know. I believed our intel and thought they only had half as many as they've committed so far. But they'd be pretty bad businessmen if they committed all their resources from the beginning without any reserves to call upon."

Jenetta nodded. "What do the brilliant minds in your intelligence section speculate the Uthlaro will do next?"

"Like you, we thought they would have already changed tactics. We think that eventually they'll do as the Tsgardi did and double up their groups. Perhaps they'll even triple them up. We don't think for a second they'll retreat because they know they still have a vast numerical superiority."

"If they double their battle group size, we'll have to rethink our attack methods. We've had our hands full just containing groups of ten ships. I doubt we can handle twenty without getting hurt."

"I believe we'll still win the engagements decisively if they double up, but we may not be able to prevent one or more ships from getting away and reporting back to their command about our hulls being impervious to laser blasts.

An Uthlaro ship almost broke free in both of the last two encounters."

"It's improbable we'll be able to keep the secret of our ships' resistance to laser fire much longer. Too many people know about Dakinium. The Raider commandant knew about it ten years ago when we seized Raider Eight and turned it into Stewart Space Command Base. The Milori witnessed our attack on their space docks when we destroyed all the ships in production so *they* have to know we're impervious to laser weapons. Someone in the Uthlaro Dominion must know about it. I can't understand why the information hasn't worked its way up to the high command already."

* * *

"Ten groups!" Minister Ambello Neddowo shouted. "We've lost contact with ten contiguous groups now! That's one hundred warships! Does anyone here still think the loss of contact is owed to the dimensional stability of space in their sectors?"

Uthlaro Prime Minster Taomolu Barguado and the Council of Ministers stared silently at Minister Neddowo. As one of the wealthiest Uthlaro citizens on their planet, Neddowo was accustomed to the silence of subordinates when he ranted.

"What are you doing about this, Barguado?"

"We're at a loss to explain it."

"Are you? Then let me explain it to you. Space Command is gobbling up our fleet, a bite at a time."

"Space Command could not possibly have gotten ships to the areas where our ships are disappearing— not this quickly. If they had dispatched an entire fleet immediately after the Milori surrendered, they would still be a light-year away from where our ships have gone missing."

"Gone missing? Gone missing? Is that how you are thinking of this, Barguado? No wonder we continue to lose ships. They're not being destroyed," he said mockingly, "they've simply— gone missing."

"If Space Command was responsible for our missing ships, we'd have heard something from our operatives on Stewart," Barguado said.

"Why do you believe our people on Stewart would know anything? They're not even in Region Two. Do you have anyone on Quesann?"

"Uh, no, not yet. The planet has so far been limited to Space Command personnel. Several of our operatives who have covers as legitimate journalists have applied for visas, but no transportation to Quesann has been available yet. And once they can go, it will take several years to get there."

"Then we must get to someone who already knows what's going on."

"We've tried for years, but Space Command people are too loyal. We haven't been able to turn anyone."

"If the Raiders can do it, then so can we. I'm authorizing a twofold increase for your information budget. You find someone and find them soon. *Someone* in the know will sell information if you wave a million credits under their greedy little Terran noses."

"Yes, Minister," Barguado said.

* * *

"Good morning," Admiral Moore said to the assembled admirals of the Admiralty Board as he took his seat in the large hall they used for their meetings. It was a closed session, so only the admirals, their aides, and a couple of dozen clerks were present. "As you know, Admiral Carver continues to make amazing progress in the situation she faces in Region Two. The Gondusans and Hudeera have surrendered unconditionally and ceded back that part of their territory Admiral Carver allowed them when we defeated the Milori. The armada now facing our forces has been halved, but the most difficult part of the fight, by a wide measure, still lies ahead of us.

"Admiral Carver has forwarded a recommendation that the seven-member rescue party who entered the Uthlaro ship each be awarded the Space Command Star. In a private communication, she informed me that the officer

191

who led the party, Commander Stephan Cross, did so in violation of her standing orders that Marines clear all enemy ships before Space Command personnel enter. However, before that incident he had been a good officer and a credit to the service. We'll never know what prompted him to enter the ship with such careless disregard for the safety of himself and his people, but that part of the record will remain sealed. All in favor of the posthumous award of seven Space Command Star medals signify by raising your hands." Looking around the horseshoe-shaped table, Admiral Moore said, "It's unanimous," to his clerk.

"Loretta, can you give us an update on the situation at the yard?" Admiral Moore asked of Admiral Plimley, referring to the shipbuilding facility in orbit around the planet Mars.

"As you know," Admiral Plimley said, "the senior people at the yard have all been briefed, privately, on the situation in Region Two and are continuing to put every resource possible into the construction of the scout-destroyers. They've hired more workers and are operating a full twenty-four-hour schedule on those docks. With our firm commitment to produce three hundred of the small ships over the next decade, additional economies of scale have been realized. They believe they'll be able to reduce the completion time on the small ships by as much as one third without adversely impacting the current delivery dates established for destroyers, frigates, cruisers, and battleships. The three new *Prometheus*-class battleships will be ready to launch in two and half months."

"Excellent. When do you anticipate the next group of scout-destroyers will be ready to launch?"

"If nothing unexpected happens to delay their completion, all ten should be ready in less than two and half months."

"Wonderful. And the next group will be ready four months following these ten?"

"If not sooner."

"Excellent. If Admiral Carver can reduce the size of a thousand-ship armada by half with just thirteen ships, the additional three battleships and twenty scout-destroyers has to help her halt the progress of the remaining ships aligned against her."

"With luck," Admiral Plimley said, "we should be able to get her four new DS destroyers and two new DS cruisers at about the same time the second group of ten scout-destroyers are ready for launch."

"You've been able to advance their construction schedules by that much?"

"The yard manager has pulled some of the crews off the warships that can't possibly be launched for more than two years and put them on the ships that are nearing completion. He says he has so many people working on them that, at times, the crews are falling over one another. He hasn't told them the reason, but they understand the urgency and are putting everything they have into getting these six ships completed early. They've seen the flurry of activity over at the docks where the scout-destroyers are being built and know something big is up."

"By now the Uthlaro know all about the surrenders of the Tsgardi, the Gondusans, and the Hudeera," Admiral Hillaire said, "so the importance of keeping everything a secret has disappeared. Perhaps it's time to hold a press conference about the *undeclared* war?"

"Keeping any specific information about Admiral Carver's operations a secret, of course," Admiral Bradlee said.

"Of course," Admiral Hillaire said. "I'm simply suggesting that the people of the Galactic Alliance should know a new threat exists, and while *they* are presently in no danger, they should be aware that we are doing our best to handle the situation. It might help military recruitment if our people know we have been invaded *again*. Recruitment levels have dropped since the Milori invasion failed and we annexed their territory."

"I'll have the information office draft a release," Admiral Moore said. "The GA Council has just approved my request to expand the Mars shipbuilding facility. They've approved the construction of three hundred additional docks. We haven't been allocated the funds to commence laying hulls just yet, but I believe that to simply be a matter of time. With the facility expansion, we should be able to produce one hundred new warships each year, or more if some of the slips are used to produce scout-destroyers.

"Our next topic is to appoint a new commanding officer to McCardin Space Command Base. You all have a copy of the list of eligible officers. Does anyone care to make a recommendation?"

Chapter Twelve
~ May 2nd, 2283 ~

"Nothing!" Commander Omega Kostopolis, Captain of the scout-destroyer *Seine* said in exasperation. "We've twice performed a Level One search of our assigned territory and haven't caught sight of a single ship, or even a residual ion trail!"

"Thank you, Captain," Jenetta said. "I'm sure your crew did its usual thorough job."

"Thank you, Admiral."

"*Colorado* out."

"*Seine* out."

"Another dry hole," Jenetta said to Admiral Kanes who was seated across from her in her briefing room aboard the *Colorado*. "That makes four in a row."

"I suppose we'll have to accept that the Uthlaro have changed their battle plan. Frankly, I'm surprised it took them as long as it did."

"Yes, but it would have been nice to pare their fleet down a little further. Still, they have a hundred forty fewer ships now than they did before. That's almost twice the number currently assigned to my Second Fleet."

"What now, Jen?"

"We'll return to Quesann to resupply. Our ordnance stocks have gotten precipitously low, but I was reluctant to stop while we were having so much success against the Uthlaro. We knew they'd change tactics eventually, and I wanted to confront as many groups as possible before that happened."

"How soon did you want to leave?"

"Now that the *Seine* has completed a second search of its grid section there's nothing to keep us here. We can head for the barn as soon as our ships have all returned. I've been considering a slight detour, though. Milor lies almost directly in our path, so perhaps we should stop there briefly so I can visit with the Viceroy."

"You're not planning on going dirt-side, are you?"

"Not hardly. After what I did to their planet, even their protection details would be trying to kill me. We'll remain in orbit and I'll invite the Viceroy to come up."

* * *

Seventeen days later, the thirteen-ship taskforce entered the Milor system. There were several dozen warships at defensive posts throughout the system, but when the Space Command taskforce announced their arrival and intentions, they were passed through without further challenge. Milor Approach Control immediately directed the ships to parking orbits above the planet.

"Greetings, Admiral Carver," Viceroy Berquyth said when communications were established. "Or should I call you Governor Carver?" He immediately waved an arm as if the matter was of no consequence, then said, "Regardless, welcome to Milor."

"Thank you, Viceroy. I'm delighted that an opportunity to visit with you has presented itself. We are on a return trip to our base at Quesann."

"And I am delighted you've taken time from your hectic schedule to stop. Would you like to come down, or shall I come up?"

"I think it would be better if you come up. I imagine there are many hard feelings toward me, and your protection details might find their task too onerous."

"Not at all, Admiral. Since the *unfortunate* and *premature* death of our late Emperor, Maxxiloth, we've been inculcating our people with the idea that Milor will be far better off under the rule of the Galactic Alliance than it ever was before. Schoolchildren now pledge their undying allegiance to both Milor and the Galactic Alliance before classes begin each day, and a daily stream of public service announcements praise the Galactic Alliance on all voice and vid channels. Everyone on the planet knows that Space Command was only trying to stop Maxxiloth from waging war further when it targeted installations with military value, and a great deal has been made of the fact that you did everything possible to avoid civilian locations. Your smiling image now looks down on our people, with that of my own, from every location where Maxxiloth's sinister face appeared before. You are regarded as a hero on our world for having saved us from future decades of war. We all knew Maxxiloth wanted to rule the galaxy. Our people never would have ceased dying in futile wars while he lived."

"But there surely must be hard feelings among those who lost loved ones in the battles with Space Command or for the destruction we caused when we attacked your planet."

"Their enmity has been turned towards Maxxiloth because it was he who started and perpetuated the aggression. He sent our people out to attack a peaceful neighbor and brought the destruction down upon our heads when you defended yourselves. Many of the social programs instituted to rebuild our planet bear your name."

"I have to admit to being quite stunned by this revelation, Viceroy."

Smiling, the Milora said, "I invite you to come down and see for yourself, Admiral. I believe you will be just as stunned by the open reception you receive."

Hesitating for only a second, Jenetta said, "Very well, Viceroy, what time would be convenient?"

"It's early morning here in the capital, Admiral. How about joining us for the midday meal we enjoy when the sun is at its zenith? I'm not sure what your people call that time."

"We call it noon."

"Very well, please join me at noon. Your shuttle will be cleared to land on the palace grounds."

"I'll see you at noon, Viceroy. Carver out."

"Viceroy Berquyth, out."

* * *

As Jenetta stepped from the shuttle, a military band began playing an odd Milori tune unfamiliar to Jenetta. A small crowd that had gathered behind a row of palace guards hooted and slapped their semi-soft gripper claws together. Jenetta smiled uncertainly and waved, wondering if the people were being paid to welcome her or if they were palace employees herded outside by their supervisors. She still couldn't believe she wasn't the most despised person on the planet. Her Marine guard parted as she reached the bottom of the ramp to allow her through as the Milori Viceroy stepped forward from a row of dignitaries. He bowed and welcomed her to the surface before turning and introducing the eleven other ministers from the Ruling Council. Jenetta in turn introduced Lt. Commander Ashraf.

"Admiral Carver, everyone is *delighted* to welcome you here," the Viceroy said as they walked towards the palace. "I wish to be the first Milori to congratulate you on your success against the Tsgardis, the Gondusans, and the Hudeera. I admit I had serious misgivings when I received the message from you in which you said you were on Earth. I should have known you'd already be aware of the invasion and working to repel the invaders."

"I wasn't aware of the invasion until I received your message, Viceroy. Thank you for informing me so quickly."

"Then you really were on Earth?"

Yes, I was. I went home for a visit before I became so bogged down in my duties here that I couldn't get away again for years."

"The rumors are true then. Space Command has made significant improvements in faster-than-light travel."

Jenetta looked at him in surprise. "I would have thought you knew all about our advances. You did have Admiral Vroman for some months before depositing him on Siena."

"The main information gleaned from Admiral Vroman was that you had tried to use a new indestructible material to cover your ships but that it interfered with the FTL drive system. There was no mention in our reports that the 'interference' was an incredible leap forward in FTL speeds. We only knew that, as a result of complications, the prototype had remained at your Mars facility for several years."

"It would seem that something was lost in translation. And yes, the 'interference,' as you call it, was the ability to travel significantly faster than the theoretical limits of FTL travel. The prototype remained at Mars while our people worked on finding ways to properly harness the incredible speed advancement so it could be used in all our new ships. Or perhaps Admiral Vroman had less information about the project than I thought. It was top-secret back then. It still is. But I doubt if it's really much of a secret anymore, especially since we started turning out new ships designed to use the speed in everyday travel. Surely your military planners must have wondered how we were able to bring the fight here so soon after your fleet attacked my command at Stewart."

"The consensus was that you had already sent ships after the first invasion attempt."

"No, we were perfectly serious about our hope to enjoy a period of peaceful coexistence when we sent your fleet home after signing the treaty. We didn't want your territory. The decision to annex it was made only because we knew Maxxiloth would continue to invade us every time he'd built his fleet to a point where he felt strong enough to take us on again."

"You were right, of course. Maxxiloth was quite mad. We would never have seen peace in his lifetime. When he announced he was going to share our metallurgical procedure for the production of tritanium with the Tsgardi, along with the secrets of achieving Light-450, the Council of Ministers knew we must act. We knew that once we lost our technological dominance, the Tsgardi would attempt to throw off the yoke Maxxiloth's great-grandfather had placed around their necks. The sharing of that information would have meant more decades of hostilities even if the Galactic Alliance hadn't annexed the empire. And I do apologize for marooning the *Lisbon* crew on Siena. The ship's database didn't contain information regarding the existence of such hostile indigenous wildlife as they faced.

"Our world is far better off now. I must admit to enjoying life a great deal more without the constant pressure of waging war."

"I would love to experience that myself for a while," Jenetta said.

"Now that you've repelled the invaders, perhaps you can."

"We've only stopped three of the four signatories to the pact that would see us driven from this territory so it could be divided up among the aggressors. The Uthlaro are still in play."

"Really? They haven't attacked any planets or former bases in the Region for many weeks."

"How do you know that?"

"After receiving your suggestion that we make contact with all our people still off-world to warn them of potential problems, we asked them to send us a coded message once each day while they remained unmolested. We've been able to track the progress of the aggressors across the region by knowing which planets, outposts, or space stations continued to send. There have been no changes in weeks."

"I see. Have you been able to make contact with any who had previously gone silent?"

"The planets occupied by the Tsgardi have all resumed communications. The occupying forces have been picked up by transports and the planetary governments are reestablished, although most of the senior leadership was slain in the takeovers. From those locations that fell to the Uthlaro, we've heard nothing, but we continue to try once each day."

"The Uthlaro invaders might have left jamming satellites in orbit at each location when they moved on. I hope they haven't done worse. We haven't had a chance to look into the situation yet. We've been a bit busy."

"As I can imagine."

"Viceroy, I was a bit surprised to see your shipyards so active as we passed the planets they orbit." Jenetta had waited until she felt the Viceroy was somewhat off-guard before informing him of her observation.

"Of course, Admiral, of course. Oh! I hope you don't think we're attempting to build a fleet to oppose the Galactic Alliance."

"The thought did cross my mind."

"You can put your mind at rest because it's nothing of the sort. You have to remember that our economy was focused almost *entirely* on the business of war. After you attacked us, the planet was in ruins. In the solars after the attack, our entire economic infrastructure began to collapse in on itself. I decided that we had to get people back to work immediately, both earning a living and paying taxes. Since so very many of our people had only worked in the shipyards for their entire lives and had no other training, I ordered them to start repairing the damaged ships. Our engineers had told us the repairs would take substantially more effort than starting from scratch, so it was the ideal solution. The workers would have jobs for twice as long as if we had simply started building new ships while we slowly retrained our work-force and moved our manufacturing base to consumer products our people could buy. Our public works projects kept people busy while factories were retooled. The program was hugely successful, and it's helped get our economy back on track. We haven't built even one *new* warship, and as workers complete a ship, we transition a percentage of them to permanent jobs in other industries, such as the production of home appliances and private vehicles."

"I see. Have you been able to rebuild your power grid and telecommunications systems?"

"We still have many projects in progress, but most basic services have been restored. In those communities where repairs to permanent power systems haven't been completed, we have portable generators that provide power for half of each day. Within an annual, the entire power grid will be restored and better than ever because it had been neglected annual after annual while Maxxiloth continued to shift budgeted funds to military projects. The lives of our people are better already because new household appliances are available again from factories that had been converted to produce only military goods and munitions."

As they neared the palace's main dining room, two attendants pulled open the doors so the party could enter. The sumptuous dining hall was quiet, but one table near the center of the room had been prepared for dining. Once they had taken their seats, a small army of waiters swarmed in carrying platters of foods. The Terrans received foods appropriate for Terran palates while the Milori received foods appropriate for their physiology. Jenetta had never been adverse to new dining experiences, but she preferred that her food at least be dead when she ate it. The Milori, on the other hand, preferred that it still be wiggling as it passed down their gullet. They used an eating utensil that reminded Jenetta of chop sticks. It attached to their gripper claws so they could pick up the food without damaging it before they ate it. The Terrans were given forks.

"I'm delighted you've been able to make such wonderful progress in overcoming the damage from the war," Jenetta said. "The attitudes of your people will hasten the day when Milor will be welcomed as a full voting member in the Galactic Alliance Senate and Council."

"Having a voice on the august body that oversees the quality of life in so much of this quadrant of the galaxy is something we would welcome," the Viceroy said. "We *are* a part of the Galactic Alliance now and look forward to the day when we become a fully participating member."

"Has your planet experienced any shortages of vital necessities such as food or medicine?"

"Some supplies are low, and we've been making do without some food items from off-world that we had become accustomed to, but things are improving. Our freighters are resuming work now that they know they won't be attacked by Space Command vessels."

"We have never attacked unarmed freighters, even in time of war. Even armed freighters aren't attacked as long as we believe their weapons are only for protection and they submit willingly to inspection when ordered to heave to."

"I know, Admiral, but under Maxxiloth our warships had orders to attack and destroy any ships of an enemy nation, including passenger liners. Our freighter captains were frightened after your last visit here. It's taken awhile for them to acknowledge they're in no danger from you."

"Yes, it will take awhile for our people to know each other and become comfortable in each other's company."

"Exactly."

"The Galactic Alliance's policy is basically live and let live, although we do restrict the transport of certain dangerous materials and substances, forbid the development of certain dangerous technologies, and have no tolerance for the abhorrent practice of slavery."

"What will you do now against the Uthlaro?"

"I'm not sure about our near-term activity. We've upset their original plan, and as you know, they've stopped attacking targets in Region Two. We've lost track of them, but if their goal remains one of confronting us at Quesann, I estimate they could be there in just under two Terran years. We'll be there to meet them when they arrive."

"I wish you luck, Admiral. I mean that sincerely. I would not like to find my world under the thumb of mercenary Uthlaro masters."

* * *

Following lunch, Viceroy Berquyth invited Jenetta to take a tour of the city with him. Although she tried to decline politely, he practically pleaded with her to come along, and she finally, reluctantly, agreed. They stopped at several historical sites in the city and concluded the tour at a new hospital that bore her name. The Admiral Jenetta Carver Hospital specialized in serious injury cases and emergency care. There were far too many places where her name appeared on wall signage, ID badges, and uniforms for them to have been created since she first arrived for the unscheduled visit. The cornerstone of the new building also bore her name, engraved deeply into its surface. Everywhere she went, she was applauded in the Milori tradition of slapping their gripper claws together.

The SC taskforce left planetary orbit as the day was ending at the Palace of the Viceroy. Jenetta had finally become convinced that the remarkable attitude expressed towards her was genuine. She knew, of course, that the Milori Council of Ministers wanted a voice in the Galactic Alliance Senate and that the fastest way to get that was by convincing the GAC they were deserving of a seat. It was amazing what a planet-wide propaganda campaign could do. They had suffered incredible hardship when Jenetta carried the war back to their solar system, but they would be better off in the future, and even the ministers had benefited from Maxxiloth's death. Being in the inner circle of a tyrant didn't ensure that one lived either a long or happy life.

* * *

The return trip to Quesann took twelve days at Light-9790. As soon as they entered the solar system, they knew they were approaching a well-protected base. The fifty M-designate ships assigned to the Second Fleet had arrived several months earlier, joining the dozen that had arrived in June of the previous year. The twelve Mars-built, pre-DS ships assigned to the fleet were slower and so had only arrived a week earlier, just one day before the new group of ten S/D's and three new DS *Prometheus*-class battleships. With the arrival of these warships, the size of the Second Fleet had grown to ninety-nine, when the scout-destroyers were counted as separate warships. It was a far cry from the size of the expected Uthlaro armada, estimated at roughly five hundred, but it couldn't fail to impress anyone approaching the planet.

This time Jenetta was unable to avoid the formal greeting afforded a victorious officer of her exalted rank.

The unconditional surrender of the Tsgardi, the Hudeera, and the Gondusans, the freeing of the Flordaryn people, and the annexation of a massive amount of new territory demanded a hero's welcome even though the fight was far from over. Jenetta would have preferred saving any celebrations until after the war, but she bowed to protocol and accepted the tribute. She hoped there would be reason to celebrate after the Uthlaro arrived because she knew that most of the fighting and dying was still ahead of them. The enemy would not foolishly divide their forces again. When they came, they would be coming en masse.

Although all vessels are required to always have sixty percent of the ship's company on board during times of war, the sheer number of off-duty crewmen had swelled the base's population to unexpected proportions. Most required accommodations during their R&R time, and the base housing officer had shoehorned them into all available surface housing before starting to fill the under-ground complexes. There was more than adequate space underground for everyone on the base, but who wanted to spend their time in windowless environments when they could be in surface quarters? Being housed underground was like being back aboard ship.

From the size of the crowds, it appeared to Jenetta that everyone who was off duty had come to participate in, or simply observe, the welcoming ceremony. Jenetta quickly formulated a speech in her head as she exited the shuttle and the band began to play. She was greeted first by Admiral Poole, the new commander of the base, and spent a couple of minutes trying to hear and be heard above the sounds from the nearby band before being introduced to Admiral Buckner, her new Supply & Logistics Director. Admirals Sprague, Colsey, and Mendez were there, as well as the senior officers on the base. When the introductions and greetings were completed, Admiral Poole gestured towards the podium. Jenetta stepped up to the lectern as the band finished the marching tune it was playing.

"Good morning. Thank you for this wonderful greeting. It's great to be back on Quesann and feel the sun on my face. I'm delighted to have met Admiral Poole, our new base commander, and Admiral Buckner. And it's wonderful to see my old friends, Admiral Sprague, Admiral Colsey, and Admiral Mendez. Admiral Kanes has, of course, been with me while we've been off *kicking* Tsgardi and Uthlaro butt."

Jenetta had to pause as the crowd erupted in applause and yelling.

"It's wonderful to see Captains Barletto and Neveho again, who have both done an excellent job during my time away from Quesann. I'm especially impressed by the progress our engineering folks have made. It's hard to believe this is the same place I visited a couple of years ago when we were scouting for a headquarters location. This planet is as much like Earth as any I've seen or heard about, and our people have turned this into more than just a base— it's become a home to many of us." Jenetta paused for effect and changed the focus of the speech. "But now, treacherous outsiders have invaded our territory with plans to evict us from our new home. The Uthlaro believe they are powerful enough to make us run back to Region One. Well, my answer to that is that Space Command doesn't run from *anyone*."

Jenetta paused again when a tumultuous cry of assent issued from the crowd.

"It's we who will do the evicting. We'll evict the Uthlaro from our territory and inflict such losses that the survivors will never even consider coming back here again."

Jenetta waited until a new outburst from the crowd died down.

"Those of you who are on leave should enjoy yourselves and get your systems recharged, because when you return to your ships, you should be prepared to spend as much time as possible preparing for the arrival of the Uthlaro. Know your way to your battle station so well you can get there while blindfolded and spend as much time in

206

the simulators as you can afford because when we confront the enemy we have to be perfect. Every minute you devote to practice now will pay off when the Uthlaro arrive. The Uthlaro are a dangerous adversary, but together we're going to send most of them to *Hell!* God bless you all!"

Her last few words were almost drowned out by the reaction from the crowd to her words about the Uthlaro and then by the thunderous applause and yelling that followed. She waved to the crowds while she walked to a waiting vehicle and continued to wave until she was away from the area. Admiral Poole, Admiral Kanes, and Lt. Commander Ashraf accompanied her in the driverless vehicle.

Admiral Poole conducted a drive-by tour of the base, and Jenetta marveled at the dramatic changes. At the conclusion of the tour, the vehicle returned to the shuttle so Jenetta could get her pets and then brought Jenetta and her aide to the palace. Admiral Poole was dropped off at his office and Admiral Kanes was dropped off at his new residence on Admiral's Way.

"It's a little intimidating, isn't it?" Jenetta said to her aide as the two Marine guards came to attention at the front door. "I mean, all this space for so few people."

"After the cozy quarters on the Colorado, it does seem spacious. But I'm sure it will seem like home after a while. And you'll never be lonely. At any one time there's an entire company of armed security people on duty, discretely hidden in security rooms for the most part, and I'm sure you'll always be able to find a mess steward or two."

"Admiral Poole said the palace has been completed. Would you like to take a tour with me?"

"Of course, Admiral."

"I just hope they have the beverage synthesizers working by now," Jenetta quipped as they began their tour of the first floor.

Two hours later they wrapped up their tour at Jenetta's enormous third floor apartment.

"If the intention of the designers was to impress, they've succeeded. *I'm* certainly impressed. It's a lot like the palace on Nordakia, but at least I won't have to wear those tight, floor-length dresses here."

"I understood that the practice had ended there."

"It's not mandatory anymore, but I'd wager there are still some older women stubbornly clinging to the old ways. There are always people who refuse to alter their behavior when sweeping changes come about. Please schedule a meeting of the base's most senior officers for tomorrow morning and then go relax for the rest of the day."

"Aye, Admiral. I'll be in my new quarters in the east wing if you need me."

"Okay, Lori."

* * *

The next morning when Jenetta entered the large meeting room in the recently completed Headquarters Building with her pets, it was like walking into an Admiralty Board meeting. The building had, in fact, been patterned after the Admiralty Board hall on Earth. Seated around the horseshoe-shaped table were all six of the other admirals currently in residence on the planet— Admiral Poole, the new base commander, Admiral Buckner, the new Supply & Logistics Director for Region Two, Admirals Sprague, Colsey, and Mendez, the base commanders forced to evacuate their commands, and Admiral Kanes, the head of Intelligence. Arrayed behind the admirals were their aides and clerks.

"As you were," Jenetta said in response to the movement to stand up by the officers and personnel in the room, and everyone resettled themselves into their chairs. A clerk attempted to bring Jenetta a steaming mug of Colombian coffee as soon as she sat down but had to wait until the cats sniffed him before they'd allow him close enough to hand it over. Jenetta took a sip before starting.

"Good morning. Thank you for the warm reception yesterday. I hope we have equal cause for celebration in the years ahead. As most of you know, we've lost contact with the Uthlaro armada. We believe they're on their way here to confront us and demand we leave this territory. Our intelligence information indicates their fleet is five times the size of our Second Fleet so this encounter will be a defining moment in this war. If we're not victorious, we'll sure make them know they've chewed on something they should have left alone, and I guarantee few of them will be returning home."

"Are we just going to stay here and wait for them to come at us?" Admiral Colsey asked.

"If we knew where they were, we'd go out to meet them," Jenetta said. "But without such information, we can't leave the planet unprotected while we scour the entire territory. They've stopped trying to gobble up planets, so we can't track them by knowing who is still able to communicate with us. I imagine they've established a rendezvous point somewhere and all their small battle groups are proceeding there at their top speed. Five hundred ships make an incredible armada, but Region Two is so vast that a thousand such armadas could easily be hidden in it. Given that we have no patrols out there and that freighter operations are only now resuming, we can't rely on receiving any reported sightings. If we assume they'll want all their ships to participate in the attack on Quesann, then we know they can't be here before the end of next year at the earliest. It would take that long for the ships we were attempting to locate just after they changed their tactics to arrive here if they came straight in."

"Couldn't we send out the newest ships to search for them?" Admiral Mendez asked.

"Now that the base has been so well supplied, I've issued orders that a Distant DeTect network of sensors be placed out as far as a hundred billion kilometers from the planet. We'll have sufficient warning of their imminent arrival to prepare a suitable greeting. Additionally, scout-destroyers will constantly patrol out as far as twelve light-years from the base. They can return here in less than half a day if they sight any of the enemy ships approaching, giving us ten full days to prepare for the attack. The DS ships will provide our first line of defense, so I hesitate to send any of them out any further than that. It could prove to be an impossible task to find the armada in Region Two without information about their location. It sometimes took us days to locate the battle groups when we knew their approximate location and course."

"What's your assessment of the Uthlaro ships and the fighting ability of their personnel?" Admiral Sprague asked.

"Their ships are extremely well-built for the purpose of waging war, with hulls as strong as our pre-Dakinium *Prometheus*-class battleships. Their crews are fierce and fight to the death rather than surrender. Once we engage them, the battle will only end when one or the other of us is no longer able to fire a weapon."

"Whew! I'm almost sorry I asked."

"Although we outnumbered them in each of our encounters, the Uthlaro fought smart and with all their being. They only tried to break ranks when the outcome of the battle was decided. And I suspect that then it was only so they could relay information of the fight back to their command. We blocked all IDS bands so they couldn't let anyone know what had happened."

"Would you have defeated them if you'd been outnumbered?" Admiral Poole asked.

"It would probably have depended upon the size of the battle group."

"Say five to one."

"Like the odds we're facing now? I doubt it. I'd naturally like to think we'd have been victorious, but realistically I believe we would have been badly damaged in such an encounter. The number of torpedoes coming at us would have meant that at least some of them would have gotten through."

"So you're saying we don't stand a chance of beating them if they arrive as one armada?" Admiral Buckner asked.

"No, I'm not saying that at all. I'm just trying to make you understand it won't be easy. It won't be like fighting the Tsgardi. Perhaps we'll come up with something to even things up a bit. We have more than eighteen months to consider every possibility. I'm also expecting the arrival of at least sixteen additional DS ships before the end of this year. The Admiralty Board has said we'll receive ten more scout-destroyers, four destroyers, and two cruisers. If we receive no other ships before the Uthlaro arrive, the forty-one DS ships we will have should be able to take out over two hundred of the Uthlaro ships on their own, leaving the rest of the fleet outnumbered by only three to one."

"*Only* three to one?" Admiral Mendez echoed. "Three to one with an enemy whose ships are more solid and well-built than most of our own?"

"I'm trying to put as positive a slant as possible on the situation. I'm confident we'll prevail. I won't accept that the Uthlaro can invade our territory and absorb it while I live."

"What can we do to help, Jen?" Admiral Colsey asked.

"I'm afraid there's little any of us can do right now except wait. We mustn't allow ourselves to become too complacent if nothing happens for a while because I can assure you the Uthlaro are definitely coming."

* * *

"I see that no more of our ships have— gone missing," Minister Ambello Neddowo said to Uthlaro Prime Minster Taomolu Barguado.

"Not since we ordered them to abort their previous orders and rendezvous at the new staging area," Barguado replied.

"And we still haven't heard from any of the ships we lost contact with?"

"No, no contact."

"Then it had to be Space Command. Carver somehow managed to get a taskforce into every location where we had sent ships."

"We still haven't been able to learn anything about her operations. Either no one knows, or no one is talking. It's frustrating that our bribes aren't finding any takers. Don't these Galactic Alliance people understand the value of a credit?"

"They're a strange breed. When the Raiders were plundering their shipping, they cared more about the people that were lost than about the cargo. Will all the ships rendezvous on schedule?"

"The two hundred forty-six reserve force ships we were holding back for defense of our border will arrive later than originally projected. A few problems with power systems delayed their embarkation by six solars, but they'll still arrive at the rendezvous point three solars before the scheduled departure for Quesann."

"I don't like the idea of leaving ourselves completely defenseless," Minister Ulalahu Valhallo said. "I wish you would rethink your position, Ambello."

"We need every ship we can muster for this final push," Minister Neddowo said. "The reserve ships will have to make up for the ones that *went missing* and the ships we were counting on from the Tsgardi, Gondusans, and Hudeera. As it is, we'll only have seven hundred sixteen instead of the one thousand we had planned on."

"But if Carver has fewer than a hundred ships, she can't possibly stand against even the original four hundred sixty ships. She'll have to sign the accord giving us possession of the territory and then remove her forces from Region Two."

"Carver is more like *us* than other Terrans because she'll do anything to win. All of our intelligence reports show she's not afraid to risk the lives of every crewman who serves her if it'll buy her an advantage. I can understand someone like that. She took a small taskforce into battle against a Milori fleet five times her number and won, then bluffed her way out of a situation where she was outnumbered twelve to one. She's clever and gutsy. We'll have to *prove* to her that we have the power to drive her out. When she sees our entire fleet approaching Quesann, she'll know she's lost."

"And what if she's stronger than you think?"

"She's not. I can name every warship assigned to her and its class. She doesn't stand a chance against our fleet— but she might die trying."

* * *

Jenetta had endured the frustration of waiting for an enemy to arrive on other occasions. When the first Milori invasion fleet was discovered in Galactic Alliance space, she'd had more than eight months to prepare for their arrival at the place she'd selected to make a stand. She'd had an equally long waiting time when the Milori invaded Galactic Alliance space the second time. But waiting almost two years for an invading armada to appear was almost too long. She knew the time was appreciated by shipyard personnel struggling to complete ships for the battle, but it gave the people charged with fighting the battle too much time to think about the dangers and dire consequences of the meeting.

The days seemed interminably long as the base waited for the arrival of the Uthlaro fleet. Jenetta was often observed late at night wandering the empty corridors on the third floor of the palace, deep in thought. Security patrols in the palace, alerted to her approach by the people monitoring the halls on a closed loop vid circuit, had sufficient time to duck into security rooms until she was out of sight.

Having done everything she could to prepare, Jenetta knew she had to turn her attention elsewhere. When a quartermaster ship arrived with the entire Marine staff for a new base, Jenetta threw herself into the effort. Working with Major General Hiram Grant and his staff, Jenetta and her planners selected an appropriate island that would allow the Marine Corps all the space they would ever need for their base. Located nearly a quarter of the way around the planet, the Marines had a hundred thousand square miles of beaches, lakes, swamps, desert, plains, forest, and mountains for military maneuvers, gunnery ranges, and fighter practice.

For several weeks Jenetta had the distraction of the new base to occupy her mind. Her greatest enjoyment during this time came from traveling to the new Marine base in a fighter she had commandeered for her private use. She loved to hug the landscape, flying so low over the water and islands that her protection detail, following in a shuttle at a safer altitude, were sure she was going to kill herself one day.

Although instrumental during the initial phases of the base creation, her role was steadily supplanted by others as the construction progressed. It was, after all, General Grant's base. She had to allow him a free hand in its design and construction. After a few weeks there was little for her to do except make periodic inspections to view the progress.

Chapter Thirteen
~ September 4th, 2283 ~

~ September 4th, 2283 ~

"Admiral," Lt. Commander Ashraf said to her com unit in Jenetta's outer office, "you have a message marked *most urgent.*"

The com unit on Jenetta's desk buzzed lightly as Jenetta was reading a report. "Com audio on," she said and listened to Lori's words before calling up her message queue and identifying the new message. The sender was listed as 'Vertap.' She knew immediately the sender was Vertap Aloyandro, the Minister of Intelligence for the Hudeerac Order. Since their first communication, all messages had been encrypted, so she knew she'd need the data ring containing the encryption codes if she was to view the message.

Walking to her wall safe, she keyed the proper code, then pressed her entire hand against the front plate for a second. A second later the safe door swung open. Removing a small box of data rings, she pushed them around with her finger until she found the correct one, then replaced the box, closed the safe and returned to her seat. After touching the ring to the spindle in her media drawer, she tapped the play tab on the com unit. She was required to lean in towards the com unit for retinal confirmation before the message would play. The face of Minister Aloyandro assembled on her screen as the encryption software decoded the message.

"Good day, Admiral. If you're seeing this message then you still have the data ring I sent you. With the permission of my Sovereign, I would like to propose that a new relationship be forged between our people. Those of us who know of your abilities and reputation were totally opposed to the Hudeera alliance with the Uthlaro; however, Lord Melendret managed to win the support of enough powerful nobles that the voice of my Sovereign, spoken in opposition to the pact, became lost in the torrent of words from those whose unbridled greed, or desire for retaliation against the Milori, dictated their actions. By a vote of fifty-eight percent to forty-two percent, we found ourselves following a path many knew would lead to ruin. When you destroyed the Tsgardi, saner voices were once again heard in the chambers. Lord Melendret and his followers have fallen into disgrace, and my Sovereign is again the undisputed leader of our people.

"Although the Tsgardi, Gondusans, and Hudeera have withdrawn from the pact, the Uthlaro continue to press on and fully intend to drive you from Region Two. This is not something I would like to see because I have feared all along that they will seek our small territory next. I expect your intelligence sources are still a bit limited in the Uthlaro Dominion, but we've had an extensive array of agents there for some time, including deep-cover agents in the government itself. We know, for example, exactly where the Uthlaro fleet is assembling in preparation for their assault on Quesann and the schedule established for their departure. If such information would be useful to you, perhaps we can shape a new relationship between our people.

"In exchange for the return of the territory recently ceded to the Galactic Alliance, I offer you the complete cooperation of my Intelligence Section in all matters related to the Uthlaro. This territory is miniscule and inconsequential when compared to that of the Galactic Alliance, but it is very important to us. Should you be defeated by the Uthlaro, our territory would be of no consequence, and should you win, you would be able to claim a territory fifty times its size from the Uthlaro.

"As time is critical, I'm sure you won't delay in responding.

"Minister Vertap Aloyandro. End of message."

Jenetta leaned back in her chair to stare at the ceiling while she thought. If the information the Hudeerac minister could provide was accurate, it would be invaluable. The small section of space they desired was, as the minister said, inconsequential. Jenetta had only demanded it because she had to impose *some* levy on them for participating in the pact. She sat back up in her chair, composed herself, and tapped the record button.

"To Minister Vertap Aloyandro of the Hudeerac Order from Jenetta Carver, Admiral, Commander of the Space Command Second Fleet and Military Governor of Region Two.

"Minister, such information as you offer would be very useful. I'm pleased to hear that King Jamolendre once again firmly holds the reins of power in your government. If the information you offer is genuine and accurate, I will agree to the establishment of a new relationship which will include the return of all territory taken from your people by the Milori emperors and recently ceded to the Galactic Alliance. Naturally, we would expect the improved relationship between our governments to include a provision that we have continued access to such information that you collect about the Uthlaro. The Galactic Alliance desires only friendly relationships with all its neighbors who desire the same.

"Jenetta Carver, Admiral, Commander of the Space Command Second Fleet and Military Governor of Region Two. End of message."

After sending the message, Jenetta returned to her report. It would take almost three weeks for the message to reach Aloyandro and then three weeks for his reply.

* * *

When the reply arrived from Minister Aloyandro, Jenetta played it immediately. There had been no reported sightings of the Uthlaro fleet in eight months and only expected ship traffic had been reported via the newly activated Distant DeTect sensor net. Ten scout-destroyers had arrived in June, bringing the total of Dakinium-sheathed ships to twenty-three. The base was ready for whatever came. Touching the encryption ring to the media spindle, the image of Minister Aloyandro appeared.

"Good day, Admiral. I'm pleased to once again be working with the Galactic Alliance for the betterment of both our people. I'm appending a full report that includes everything we have on the Uthlaro Campaign. It includes all of their earlier plans, as well as everything we know up to the minute I send this message. I will immediately forward all new information in the usual way. The return of the ceded territory will ensure my Sovereign remains in power for his lifetime. We anxiously await your announcement of the turnover.

"Minister Vertap Aloyandro. End of message."

Jenetta immediately copied the attached document to a secure file and then reviewed it. The routes of the battle groups her taskforce had destroyed were there, and the schedule was accurate. The plans also showed the routes of all other battle groups prior to the change in plans. Up to that point everything looked one hundred percent accurate. It was enough for Jenetta to immediately send for Admiral Kanes.

When Kanes arrived, Jenetta was still pouring over the documents. "Come in Keith. I've received the information I told you about from the Hudeerac Order."

"Does it look genuine?"

"The part I can verify is one hundred percent accurate. It's as if this came directly from the Uthlaro Military Ministry. Here, I'll put it up on the wall monitor."

Jenetta tapped a button and the images she had been reviewing on her com screen also appeared on the large wall monitor in her office.

"This is the revised plan, developed after they realized they had lost contact with a dozen of their battle groups. It shows their rendezvous location and their projected time-table."

"Do you think we can trust the data?" Keith asked.

"I'm sure the Hudeerac Order would like to have their territory back, and I sincerely believe my contact doesn't wish to see the Uthlaro in control of this space. He fears they will be gobbled up next."

218

"But if we go running off to confront the Uthlaro at this location and they show up here while we're gone, the base might be lost."

Jenetta sighed. "I know the dangers. However, if we can hit them where they're not expecting us to be, we can get in a few good licks and still be able to race back here to greet the survivors properly. If I only take the twenty scout-destroyers for this mission, the base will have the protection of the six DS battleships and seventy-four older ships."

"It's your call, Jen."

"I can't afford to pass up an opportunity to strike them once more before they get here. According to these documents, the Uthlaro armada currently stands at seven hundred sixteen."

"Seven hundred sixteen? We were estimating no more than five hundred."

"They've pulled in their entire reserve fleet of ships to replace those of other pact members, as well as the Uthlaro warships lost to us. If we attempt to defeat that many in a toe-to-toe slugfest, we'll lose too many ships. I keep thinking back to the first battle with the Milori. We were barely able to contain the group that escaped from our encircling minefield. I *have* to take the chance. The next group of DS ships will arrive in eight days, so the base will have the protection of ten additional scout-destroyers, four destroyers, and two cruisers. I just have to hope the intel is accurate and that the Uthlaro don't arrive during the eight-day gap."

"Can you reach the rendezvous point before they deploy?"

"If we leave immediately, we should just make it. Want to take a ride?"

"I wouldn't miss it for anything."

"Alright, pack your spacechest."

* * *

The twenty small ships left orbit before midnight. Jenetta wished with all her heart the ten additional scout-destroyers under way to Quesann had already arrived so

219

she could bring them with her, but the twenty would have to suffice.

It took nineteen days to reach the assembly point the Uthlaro had reportedly chosen. Two of the scout-destroyers were on point and passed the Uthlaro fleet on either side at the very fringe of their extended sensor range. To the Uthlaro it would seem like a momentary anomaly, if they even noticed it, but it was enough for the SC ships to produce an accurate graphic representation of the stationary armada. When they called to make their reports, Jenetta set up a twenty-ship vid link conference.

"They're just where you said they'd be, Admiral, linked together in large clusters," Commander Diana Durland of the *Danube* reported, "but our computers only detected four hundred sixty in the scans, not the expected seven hundred sixteen."

"That tally agrees with our computer information, Admiral," Commander Omega Kostopolis of the *Seine* said.

"The reserve ships coming from the Dominion must have been delayed," Jenetta said. "We'll wait for a while before we attack. Let's give them a chance to get here."

"But what if the fleet moves out?" Commander Scott Hyland of the *Hudson* said. "We could lose the opportunity."

"That's true, but our intel is that the other ships will be coming, and I want to have as many targets as possible before we attack. Commander Romonova?"

"Yes, Admiral?"

"Take the *Thames* to a point where you can observe the approach to this location from Uthlaro space without being detected and report any movement of ships."

"Aye, Admiral."

"The rest of us will remain here and wait."

Four days later, the *Thames* reported the imminent arrival of two hundred fifty-six ships." They should join the Uthlaro fleet at the RP in two hours, Admiral,"

Commander Romonova said when a taskforce conference link had been set up.

"Very good, Commander. All ships should prepare for battle. We'll give them a chance to get settled in before we strike. The *Tigris* will do a flyby in six hours to record their positions. All tubes should be loaded with WOLaR torpedoes. That will put three hundred sixty torpedoes on target. Once we have the plot information from the *Tigris*, we'll establish vectors for approach and departure and target points for each ship."

Jenetta had time for two mugs of coffee and a trip to the head before the *Tigris* relayed its sensor data. The information was shared with the other ships, and the attack plan was finalized. Each of the three hundred sixty torpedoes was assigned a specific target point where it would do the maximum damage. The twenty small ships then moved to their deployment locations so they could approach the armada at Light-9790.

"We'll commence this operation at exactly 0320. Each of you will arrive one thousand kilometers from the armada and fire a full volley of torpedoes at your designated targets. Drop a sensor buoy, then accelerate to maximum sub-light speed while building your departure envelopes. Your navigators all have your assigned vector for Light-9790 speed. We'll be fifty billion kilometers away before any of the torpedoes reach their targets. From there we'll head for the established rendezvous point and wait for the data from the buoys. Any questions?"

"Is 0320 significant?" Commander Dillon Wilder, the commanding officer aboard the *Tigris*, asked. "Is it their sack time or something?"

"No. As far as we can determine, the Uthlaro don't observe any particular time for rest. There's always a fourth of the crew on duty. They have four seven-point-three-hour watches each day. Anything else?"

"Isn't this the maneuver you used at Milor?"

"Yes, it is. It worked very well once. Let's hope it works again. Some of the Uthlaro ships have been here for many months waiting for the others to arrive, so they might have grown complacent in their tight clusters. By approaching at Light-9790, we'll be inside their alert perimeter before their sensors even report our presence. If your torpedo gunners are fast and accurate, we'll do some serious damage today. Anything else?" When no one spoke, Jenetta said, "Okay, let's go kick some Uthlaro butt so hard it lodges up between their eye sockets."

The mood on the bridge of the *Colorado* was tense, as it was on the other ships. Jenetta sat coolly in her bridge chair, sipping coffee as if she had nothing more on her mind than deciding what to have for breakfast. The plans had been set, the course laid in, the double envelopes built, and there was little for her to do except give the word to engage the Light-9790 drive.

At 0320 Jenetta said simply, "Engage." The ship moved quickly and arrived where it was supposed to be, on time. After firing all bow tubes, the tactical officer immediately launched a sensor buoy. The helmsman began rebuilding the double temporal envelopes while torpedo guidance specialists were still directing their torpedoes for maximum effect. In most cases the target point wasn't a spot on a hull, so the specialists were using coordinates in space for the point of detonation. They locked their settings as the helmsman announced the envelopes were built. The *Colorado* disappeared at Light-9790 before a single shot had even come its way. Over the next twenty seconds, the rest of the taskforce appeared around the *Colorado* at the RP.

"Everyone complete their mission without a problem?" Jenetta asked when a conference call had been set up.

The other captains, all smiles now that they were fifty-billion kilometers from the enemy ships, either nodded or verbally confirmed that they had.

"Very good. We should have data from the sensors any time."

"Coming in now, Admiral," The tactical officer said.

"Put it up on the front screen, Lieutenant."

An enhanced view of the armada they had just attacked, provided by coordinating the signals from the sensors deployed at the RP, appeared on the large monitor at the front of the bridge. Suddenly, a tremendous explosion that almost white'd out the screen erupted among a group of clustered Uthlaro ships, then another and another and another. For most of the next thirty seconds, the front monitor was a blank screen of blinding white as multiple explosions filled the space being observed by the twenty sensors.

As the explosions ended, blackness descended over the area once again. The sensor buoys compensated for the changed light level and immediately relayed an enhanced image of the area as the bridge crews of the SC ships stood transfixed by the spectacle. Where the most formidable armada ever seen in space had been just seconds before, there was now death and destruction on an unprecedented scale. The Uthlaro fleet had been ripped asunder by the three hundred sixty WOLaR torpedoes. The destruction had taken less than a minute. Sections of broken ships tumbled off into the blackness of space as minor explosions continued to ripple through the former fleet. Bodies and parts of bodies, most blackened by explosions or fire, floated everywhere.

At first glance it seemed that the entire fleet must surely have been destroyed, but then a few ships began to move, most dragging broken sections of other ships that dangled from docking points.

"Wow!" Commander John Cleviss of the scout-destroyer *Mississippi* said.

"I think this should slow their advance down a bit," Jenetta said, seeming almost apathetic.

"They can't possibly recover from this," Lt. Commander Soren Mojica, the Captain of the *Nile*, said. "They'll have to turn around and head home."

"It wouldn't stop us," Jenetta said. "And from what we've seen of their dedication to duty, they'll keep coming at us until they're dead. We'll hang around and watch for a while to see what happens. According to my intel, they weren't scheduled to leave here for a few more days."

"Shouldn't we attack them now while they're still in shock and finish the job, Admiral?" Commander Kimberly Riccio of the *Amazon* asked.

"Look at the telemetry," Jenetta said. "Ships are already moving away from one another. It appears that a quarter of their ships are under power. We hurt them, but there's still a very large and dangerous force there. And right now everyone still alive aboard those ships is awake, angry, and looking for enemy targets. Let's give them some time to get tired and stand down before we send our regards again."

A day later, a number of the Uthlaro ships had moved off a short distance to a staging area apart from the site of the destruction, but they didn't link up. They maintained at least a ten-kilometer distance from one another. According to data from the sensor buoys, two hundred three ships had left the original area and five hundred thirteen remained behind. Over the next two days, three more ships moved out of what Jenetta had begun calling the 'Junkyard.'

At 1417, the two hundred six Uthlaro ships got underway towards Quesann.

"Aren't we going to pursue, Admiral?" Commander Frank Fannon of the *Yangtze* asked.

"No, we know exactly where they're going and when they'll get there. I'm more interested in the Junkyard right now."

"The ships in the Junkyard are in no condition to attack Quesann, Admiral," Commander Omega Kostopolis of the *Seine* said.

"No, not as they are, but they're trying to get their ships repaired. If they do, they'll either join the others or attack the base on their own if we've been able to destroy the others. We've already learned how tenacious these warriors are. They will not turn back while they live. They'll just keep coming at us until they cease to breathe.

I want to make *sure* none of the ships in the Junkyard can follow their original orders."

"So do we attack them again?" Commander Scott Hyland of the *Hudson* asked.

"Yes, at 1630. The Uthlaro fleet will be two hours away and unable to return in time to be helpful. Everyone prepare their ship. We'll commence action in two hours."

Jenetta had time to send reports to Quesann and the Admiralty Board and take care of a lot of little details before she was needed back on the bridge.

At 1630 the twenty ships engaged their engines and returned to the Junkyard, immediately jamming the IDS bands with deployed satellites. Many of the five hundred ten ships were beyond repair, but Uthlaro crewmen in EVA suits and bots were everywhere, working on the less damaged ships. As the SC ships arrived, they immediately began pouring laser fire into the central area of the damaged ships where the computers were located. Some ships began to return fire and a few managed to get torpedoes off, but as the devastating fire from the taskforce of tiny ships ripped the guts out of any enemy ship not already ripped apart, the resistance died quickly. Knowing that the Uthlaro would never surrender while they lived, the taskforce continued to pour fire into the ships until every ship was permanently out of action. It may have seemed like overkill, but the small SC force didn't let up until there was no doubt every ship was dead. When they ceased fire, none of the five hundred ten ships would ever be useful for anything except scrap metal. The Junkyard was truly a junkyard when the taskforce pulled back to a safe distance as a security precaution.

"Now I'm *sure* we'll never have to face any of those ships in battle," Jenetta said. "I suppose we should change the name from Junkyard to Graveyard."

"There are still two hundred six warships headed towards Quesann, Admiral." Commander Diana Durland of the *Danube* said. "How do we stop *them*?"

"It's four hundred ninety-one light-years to Quesann, and it will take them more than sixteen months to get there at Light-375, so we have plenty of time to prepare our greeting. If anyone has any ideas, please share them. We certainly can't pursue and use the envelope-merge tactic to stop them, and we already know the electronic-debris tactic won't work on them."

"The only thing I can think of is to confront them," Commander Frank Fannon of the *Yangtze* said. "Perhaps they're angry enough to stop and destroy a taskforce of small SC ships."

"I'm not entirely sure we'd be successful in a fight where we're outnumbered ten to one, Frank. We might be better off waiting until we meet at Quesann. I like the odds of two to one a whole lot better."

"Okay, Admiral," Commander Fannon said, smiling. "What you say makes sense."

* * *

"I have distressing news," Uthlaro Prime Minster Taomolu Barguado said to the Council of Ministers. "Admiral Krakosso has sent word that just hours after the reserve forces joined them, while they were in war conference, the fleet was attacked at the rendezvous point.

"Attacked?" Minister Ambello Neddowo said, jumping up from his seat. "Attacked by whom? Who would attack a seven-hundred-sixteen-ship armada?"

"I can think of only one answer to that— Space Command."

"How many of their ships did we destroy?"

"According to the report from Admiral Krakosso, the enemy ships appeared suddenly, attacked in a lightning raid, then disappeared within minutes of their arrival."

"Did we destroy any?"

"No, none. The damage was apparently all one-sided."

"Damage? Did we lose ships?"

"Yes."

"In a lightning raid?"

"Admiral Krakosso reports that five hundred ten ships were damaged too badly to continue on schedule. They will attempt to make repairs and catch up."

"What?" Minister Neddowo said, sagging back into his chair in shock. "Five hundred ten ships damaged too badly to continue immediately?"

"Yes, that's the number given by Admiral Krakosso."

Sitting up straighter again, Neddowo said, "That's impossible. Either he was drunk when he said it or you were drunk when you listened to his message."

"I've had the clerk prepare it for playback, if you'd care to listen for yourself."

"I certainly would."

Barguado nodded to the clerk and the image of Admiral Krakosso appeared on the large monitor. "Sir, it's my sad duty to report that we have been attacked most viciously. Twenty small ships appeared from nowhere, without warning, fired weapons of incredible power, and then disappeared again. It happened too quickly for us to respond while they were about us, and we cannot pursue them because we don't know where they went. Two hundred six ships will continue on to the objective, and while most of us have sustained damage to some degree, all are space-worthy. The five hundred ten we leave behind have varying degrees of damage, but many are beyond repair. Our engineers will attempt to return as many as possible to service using the destroyed ships for replacement parts. We estimate no more than one hundred fifty can be restored to service before we engage the enemy. They will try to catch up or else join us at our new base at Quesann.

"Admiral Krakosso. End of transmission."

Minister Neddowo sat silently in his chair, staring at the table in front of him with glassy eyes. His mouth was working but nothing could be heard by those around him.

"What is your pleasure, Gentlemen?" Barguado asked. "Shall I recall the fleet while we still have at least two hundred six space-worthy ships marginally capable of defending our borders?"

"No!" Neddowo suddenly screamed. Jumping up, he screamed, "No, no, no! Not when we're so close!"

"Close to what?" Barguado asked. "Annihilation of our fleet?"

"If Carver had a quarter of her fleet patrolling five hundred light-years from Quesann, then it reasons other parts of her fleet are patrolling other areas. When our fleet arrives at Quesann, we'll be virtually unopposed. We'll destroy her base and cut off their links with Region One. They'll be too far away from their supply line and they'll have to leave the Region."

"We've lost six hundred seventy ships to Carver," Minister Ulalahu Valhallo said. "We can't afford to lose any more."

"We don't know we lost those first ships to Carver. Barguado said we've only lost contact with them."

"After this latest defeat, I think we can safely assume we lost them to Carver," Barguado said.

"We must continue. We have two hundred more ships in various phases of construction, so we can easily replace the lost ships. Many of the ones we sent were older ships anyway."

"Older or not, they represented a substantial investment," Valhallo said.

"This initiative will work."

"And if it doesn't?"

"If it doesn't, I'll personally reimburse the treasury. That's how sure I am of its success."

"Very well, Ambello," Valhallo said. "We'll continue on your personal assurance this venture will be profitable, *or* you'll reimburse the treasury for all losses."

* * *

"My King, I've received another message from Admiral Carver," Hudeerac Minister Vertap Aloyandro said after entering the King's sumptuous office and walking to where His Majesty was relaxing in his favorite chair with a good book.

Closing the tome and looking up, King Jamolendre sat up and said, "What does she have to say, Vertap?"

"She thanks us for the information we sent regarding the location of the Uthlaro fleet. She states her twenty-ship taskforce was able to engage the Uthlaro there and that she successfully destroyed five hundred ten of their warships, most of which were destroyers. Two hundred six damaged vessels managed to get away, but she's confident they'll locate them again."

The king's shock was reflected on his face. "She destroyed five hundred ten Uthlaro warships in one engagement with just twenty ships?" the king asked.

"That's what she claims, my King."

The king slumped against the back of his chair. "Space Command must be far more powerful than I ever could have imagined." Shaking his head, the king said, "How could we ever have allowed ourselves to become associated with the Uthlaro?"

"The damage has been largely undone, my King. Admiral Carver says she will notify the Admiralty Board of her decision to return the ceded territory to us. She'll make the official announcement at a suitable time after the Uthlaro have been dealt with, but she won't interfere with any of our ships traveling through the territory. We're free to continue our trade with any planets located there and defend the territory as before."

"Wonderful. Thank you, Vertap. The kingdom owes you a huge debt of gratitude."

"I'm happy to have been of service, my King. Uh, Admiral Carver has also requested any information we have on the Uthlaro warship production facilities."

"She wants to know the location of their shipyards?"

"Yes, my King."

"She means to destroy them I suppose, as she did with the Milori shipyards."

"That would be a reasonable assumption."

"Send her anything we have, Vertap. We want to stay in the good graces of Admiral Carver and the Galactic Alliance. And if she does destroy the Uthlaro ability to produce warships, we'll have one fewer powerful neighbor on our borders to worry about."

"Yes, your majesty."

* * *

"I apologize for the short notice," Uthlaro Prime Minster Taomolu Barguado said to the Council of Ministers, "but we've received a message from Admiral Carver and I felt you should see it immediately." Nodding to the clerk, Barguado took his seat.

A head-and-shoulders image of Jenetta Carver appeared on the council chamber's huge monitor as ministers reached for translation headphones.

"I am Admiral Jenetta Carver of the Galactic Alliance Space Command. You have violated our borders and perpetrated unprovoked attacks on our space stations, planets, and citizenry. Since all of these acts occurred without a declaration of war, the Galactic Alliance Council has branded you a rogue nation and Space Command has treated your acts as piracy.

"To date, we have destroyed six hundred fifty Uthlaro warships and their crews in Galactic Alliance space. I inform you now that the five hundred ten vessels left behind at your staging area will not be continuing their mission after making repairs. We returned to the location and concluded our business there.

"Since these incredible losses appear not to have convinced you to halt your attacks, I've formulated a new plan of action. The Galactic Alliance Council requires that a declared state of war exists before Space Command military forces enter the territory of another government with intent to do damage. Therefore, as of today and with the approval of the Galactic Alliance Council, I am formally notifying you that in response to your border incursions, attacks, and known objectives, an official state of war exists between the Galactic Alliance and the Uthlaro Dominion.

"Jenetta Carver, Admiral, Commander of the Second Fleet and Military Governor of Region Two, aboard the *Colorado*. Message complete."

"What did she say?" Minister Ellwano Murcuro asked aloud. "Does she mean she's coming here?"

"It sure sounded that way," the minister on his left said.

"Ridiculous," Minister Neddowo said. "It's all a ploy to have us recall the two hundred six ships headed to Quesann. She realizes their sneak attack on our fleet failed and she's desperate for us to cancel their mission."

"I would hardly call her attack a failure. In mere seconds she stopped five hundred ten ships. We've been unable to contact any of them since the ships with working envelope generators departed. We have to assume she did as she said, and they are lost to us."

"Well, she can't stop our fleet while it's traveling faster than light, so this is an attempt to get *us* to stop them."

"That doesn't make sense," Minister Valhallo said. "If all she wants is for them to stop, she can wait until they reach Quesann. They'll have to drop from light speed to commence their attack."

"She doesn't just want to stop them where they are, she wants to stop them from reaching Quesann on schedule. If she can delay them, she'll have more time to marshal her forces around the base."

"It sounded to me like she intends to come here," Prime Minster Taomolu Barguado said. "How are we going to stop her if she does? Except for a handful of old home-guard warships, our reserve ships were all sent to join the fleet."

"Relax," Minister Neddowo said. "If she was part of the force that struck our fleet recently, she can't be here for another four annuals. By then we will have launched two hundred more warships— all faster, stronger, and more heavily armed than all previous classes."

"And if she wasn't part of that attack?" Minister Valhallo asked.

"She said she couldn't cross our border until she had declared war. That means she's at least three annuals away. We'll simply speed up production and have those two hundred warships waiting for her when she arrives."

"Will two hundred be enough?"

"She won't catch our people napping again. When she approaches our planet, she'll be picked up on long-range sensors and they'll be waiting for her ships to arrive."

* * *

We've received a message from Admiral Carver," Admiral Moore said to the other members of the Admiralty Board." Turning to his clerk, he said, "Play the message."

The silence in the room was pervasive for some thirty seconds after the message and the attached bridge logs had played. It was finally broken by Admiral Hillaire, who said, "Five hundred ten ships! Amazing! She virtually wiped out their armada in one quick attack. I'm glad Admiral Carver is on our side. I sure wouldn't want to have to oppose her in battle."

"She's reckless," Admiral Hubera said. "She took too big a risk by leaving Quesann to search out the enemy fleet. She trusted the word of an intelligence officer who had recently been aligned with the Uthlaro. It could have been a trick to get the DS ships away from the base so the Uthlaro could attack."

"It was a gamble," Admiral Moore said, "but it paid off with major results. Now she only has to face two hundred six instead of seven hundred sixteen."

"I say it was a reckless act," Admiral Hubera said. "She's far too impulsive and bold."

"You feel she should have ignored the intelligence data from her contact in the Hudeerac Order?" Admiral Hillaire asked. "The same one who provided information about the Milori— information that proved so invaluable? You feel the wiser course would have been to wait until the seven hundred sixteen ships arrived at Quesann and surrounded the ninety-nine ships of the Second Fleet?"

"It would have been the prudent course."

"Admiral Carver weighed the options available to her," Admiral Moore said, "discussed the matter with her Intelligence Director, and made a decision that turned out to be correct. She took a calculated risk based on the information available. It was neither impulsive nor reckless. It's why Admiral Carver is out there doing the job instead of you, Donald. You've been a valuable member of this Board, but in matters concerning battle strategy, I will continue to defer to Admiral Carver."

"What about her decision to invade the Uthlaro Dominion instead of returning to defend Quesann?"

"We know where the Uthlaro fleet is," Admiral Bradlee said, "and how fast they can travel. Therefore, we know exactly how long it will take it to reach Quesann. Admiral Carver can enter the Uthlaro Dominion, complete her mission, and still be back at Quesann months before the Uthlaro fleet arrives. The intel from the Hudeerac Order, which has so far been proven accurate, indicates she shouldn't expect to encounter any Uthlaro battle groups during the mission. Most of them were destroyed at the staging area."

"I don't think there's any question that Admiral Carver made the right choice about attacking the Uthlaro fleet in the staging area," Admiral Platt said. "The results speak for themselves. I also don't think there's any question on the subject of carrying the fight into Uthlaro space. If all the fighting were done on our side of the border, there'd be less incentive for them to cease hostilities. I stand firmly behind Admiral's Carver decision to take the fight to the enemy."

"What will we do if she doesn't make it back to Quesann before the Uthlaro arrive?" Admiral Hubera asked. "The Second Fleet will be outnumbered two to one."

"If I know Admiral Carver," Admiral Hillaire said, "and I like to think I have begun to understand her a bit, she has something in mind for evening up the odds. She keeps her cards a little too close to the vest at times, but she always seems to have a solid hand."

Chapter Fourteen

~ January 12th, 2284 ~

Jenetta divided her command up into three groups and each group was then assigned responsibility for one of three different shipyards where the Uthlaro produced their warships. The yards were located over sixty light-years apart. In addition to laser weapon satellites, two ancient battleships reportedly guarded each yard. The SC ships would be able to disregard the satellites because they had no torpedo capability.

Upon reaching their destinations, each force stood by out of DeTect sensor range until the time set by Jenetta. The attacks would occur simultaneously. The two ancient battleships were taken out within seconds of the SC ships beginning their attack runs. Apparently their hulls were as lightweight as those of the Tsgardi warships because they ripped apart like tissue paper wherever a high-explosive torpedo struck. With the battleships destroyed, the scout-destroyers were free to press their attacks on the docks.

The small SC battle group attacked like a squadron of fighters, with each ship completing a pass before the first returned for its next attack. Since there was no defense to worry about, the SC ships could have just fired from stationary positions, but this form of attack made it less like shooting fish in a barrel. It made it a little more challenging and interesting for the helmsman and weapons specialists.

The battle, if you could call it that, lasted just minutes, with six or seven ships firing at the incomplete vessels parked in open or enclosed docks. When the SC ships left the yards, there wasn't a single vessel that could ever be made usable. They would have to scrap everything, including the docks, and start anew.

Jenetta's group left its assigned target area immediately after the attack. Their destination was the planet Uthlarigasset, the home world of the Uthlaro. The other groups would rendezvous with hers as soon as they could get there. It would take just four hours for the *Colorado* to reach its objective.

* * *

"Prime Minister," the Uthlaro face on the com said, "the shipyard at Plello has just been attacked. The message line indicated the call was originating from the Military High Command."

"Plello? By whom?"

"Unknown, sir. Six small ships appeared from nowhere, destroyed the guard ships, and then wiped out all the docks."

"Was everything destroyed?"

"Yes, sir. There's nothing left except broken hulls and destroyed docks. The yard manager states that nothing is salvageable."

Breaking the connection, Uthlaro Prime Minster Taomolu Barguado immediately buzzed his secretary. When she answered, he said, "Notify the Council of Ministers that there will be an emergency meeting in two hours."

"Yes, Prime Minister."

Two hours later, Barguado called the meeting to order. Only half the ministers had shown up so far, but the news was too urgent to hold.

"Space Command has just destroyed the shipyard at Plello," he said, and sat down.

"What?" Minister Ulalahu Valhallo said. "The Plello yards?"

"Yes," Barguado said. "According to my early information, the Plello yards have been left in complete ruins."

"Impossible," Neddowo said, jumping up. "You've been given faulty information.

"It came from Military High Command, not a news service."

"Carver said they had to declare war before entering our territory. They could not possibly have reached Plello yet."

"Well, someone did. Unless someone else takes responsibility, I'm going to assume Carver is responsible."

Neddowo sank slowly back into his chair as two more ministers entered the chamber and took their seats, turning to other ministers to ask what was going on. The clerk bent over and whispered something to Barguado, which caused him to blanch.

Valhallo noticed and asked," What is it, Prime Minister?"

In a quaking voice, Barguado said, "Carver is attempting to reach us."

"Play the message," Valhallo said.

"It's not a message— it's a live transmission."

"Impossible," Neddowo said. "She'd have to be within our solar system for an instantaneous transmission."

"Exactly correct, Minister Neddowo," Barguado said. "The transmission is originating from somewhere near Delqueeta."

"Impossible. We would have known if she was in-system. Our defensive net would have alerted us of her approach."

"Our net isn't responding. She must have disabled it."

"Impossible! It's a trick."

"Would you care to speak with the phantom then?"

"Put her on the monitor!" he screamed. As soon as Jenetta's image appeared, he screamed, "Carver, when I get my hands on you, you'll die a slow and painful death."

Jenetta grinned and calmly said, "My, such hostility."

Ministers were still scrambling to get their translation headsets on.

"I assume this is the Council of Ministers," Jenetta said, "the ruling body of the Uthlaro Dominion. I'm here to tell you that when you chose to attack the Galactic Alliance, you made a grievous error. By now you know your shipyard at Plello has been destroyed. I made quite a mess and I don't believe anything can be salvaged. By

236

tomorrow you'll learn that the yards at Waqutta and Zenolo have also been completely destroyed."

"You bitch!" Neddowo screamed, "You'll pay for this outrage!"

"No, I think not. You started this aggression, but I'm here to finish it. I haven't finished destroying your fleet yet, but I'll make you the same offer I made the Tsgardi. Surrender unconditionally and I'll spare your planet. Refuse, and those who survive will spend the next dozen years trying to rebuild your infrastructure. And every decade we'll return and destroy all your progress again."

"You can't do that!" Neddowo screamed.

"I can and will. I did it to the Milori, and that was enough of an example for the Tsgardi, Gondusans, and Hudeera to surrender. I know you were behind the whole plot from the beginning, and I'm almost hoping you refuse."

"If you fire even one weapon at this planet, you little bitch, we'll track you down and kill you!" Neddowo screamed.

"Does this screaming fool speak for the entire council?" Jenetta asked.

"No, he does not," Minister Valhallo said. "We speak as a body, but many members are not yet in attendance. Your attack caught us unaware. What are your terms?"

"Complete and unconditional surrender. You will immediately recall the two hundred six ships headed for Quesann. Except for a small caretaker and security force left at each location, you'll immediately remove all members of the military from every planet, moon, and space station outside your solar system. You will immediately cease production of warships—" Jenetta paused for a second. "I think we can dispense with that one; you have already ceased production of warships. But you cannot reinstitute production of warships at any time. Lastly, you will cede your territory to the Galactic Alliance for annexation."

"Never!" Neddowo screamed. He was frothing at the mouth now and had to be restrained by the ministers on either side of him.

"I will give you ninety-six GST standard hours to give me your *official* answer," Jenetta said. "That should give you time to verify the information about your shipyards and assemble all ministers for a vote. I will contact you then. Oh, and someone should get that fool a doctor. Carver out."

The monitor turned momentarily black and then displayed the official seal of the Council. The council members looked glumly at one another.

"I never dreamt it could come to this," Barguado said, breaking the silence.

Even Neddowo had ceased to rant and was now sitting quietly in his chair.

"We have to face the fact that Carver has beaten us," Minister Valhallo said. "We committed all our warships in an effort to impress her with our strength and she has turned the tables on us. If we refuse to capitulate, she'll destroy us. She'll do to us what she did to the fleet and to Milor."

"Not necessarily," Minister Neddowo said, calmer now that the transmission had ended.

"What do you mean? You heard her."

"We still have an impressive force in Region Two. She's trying to get us to recall it voluntarily. She must fear it, or she would simply destroy it if she could."

"How can that help us?" Minister Ellwano Murcuro asked. "She'll destroy us before she leaves here."

"We'll surrender," Neddowo said, "to avoid destruction and allow the fleet to destroy Carver when she finally gets back to Quesann. They'll have new incentive now that they know what hangs in the balance."

"But she demanded we recall the fleet," Barguado said.

"We tell her it's too late to recall them. We tell her that once they reached a certain point they will not listen because messages can be faked. We tell her that the fleet will assume that any attempt to recall them is a trick and ignore it."

The council chamber was silent again as the ministers deliberated.

"But what if the fleet is destroyed after we surrender unconditionally?" Minister Ulalahu Valhallo asked.

"Will we be any worse off than if we surrender unconditionally and recall the fleet? She'll force us to destroy all the returning warships."

"She won't buy it," Barguado said. "She's not a fool."

"She'll have no choice. We'll tell her that we surrender and are fully willing to comply in all other matters. She'll have to leave at some point. When our fleet destroys her ships at Quesann, we'll recant everything and continue our takeover of Region Two."

"But if our fleet is destroyed, we will have surrendered our territory to her."

"It appears she can destroy our planet and annex the territory whether we cooperate or not," Neddowo said. "This is not the end of this war— it is only the beginning. We'll simply move our shipbuilding operations to new, more secret locations and build a fleet larger and more powerful than anything the galaxy has ever seen. When we're strong enough, we'll retake our territory from the Galactic Alliance. It may take many years, but we're businessmen. We can be patient as we wait for a long-term investment to yield profits."

When Jenetta again called the Council Chambers, exactly four days later, the other ships had rejoined her group. Keith Kanes was sitting in her briefing room when she placed the call, but only her image would be transmitted. This time the Council Chambers were packed with the planet's ministers.

"Gentlemen, have you made a decision?" Jenetta asked.

"We have," Uthlaro Prime Minster Taomolu Barguado said as the official spokesperson. "We surrender unconditionally."

"A wise decision," Jenetta said. "On behalf of the Galactic Alliance Council I accept the surrender of the Uthlaro people and formally declare the annexation of the territory formerly known as Uthlaro Dominion space. You will *immediately* notify all planets, moons, and space stations via public transmissions on *all* major news programs and audio channels that the Uthlaro Dominion government has been officially dissolved, that this region of space is now part of the Galactic Alliance, and that all within it are subject to GA laws. All bases, space stations, and other property formerly owned by the Uthlaro Dominion government are now the legal property of the Galactic Alliance. You will establish and maintain caretaker staffs at each location to ensure that the bases are not sacked by scavengers before we arrive to take possession. You will not remove or destroy any equipment, furnishings, or records. Do you understand and agree to everything I have said?"

"We do," Barguado said.

"Then my business here is ended, for now. My forces will remain in the area until we verify you have made the required surrender announcements and that the people of this territory have acknowledged the same. And I would be remiss if I failed to mention that any further resistance by yourselves or anyone in this territory will be treated not as an act of war, but rather as an act of sedition. The penalties for sedition are, in most cases, far more serious than the penalties allowed for war prisoners under Galactic Alliance law. Once you've completed the tasks I've spelled out, the actions of this body will be directed solely to planetary matters. If anyone on your planet has any ideas of initiating an insurgency either from within or without the borders of this region, they should be aware that the planet as a whole will be dealt with most severely."

"Ah, Admiral, there is a problem."

"And what is the problem, Mr. Prime Minister."

"We cannot recall the fleet headed for Quesann."

"And why not?"

"Because they've passed the recall point. Once they reach that point, they won't acknowledge our signals because they could be faked by the enemy. They will continue on until they complete their mission or they're dead."

"You didn't mention that the other day when I told you their recall was a requirement."

"I didn't realize they had passed the recall point. I was told when I attempted to initiate the recall."

"That's a shame, Mr. Prime Minister. We have destroyed so many of your people, I'd hoped I wouldn't have to destroy more. I'm sure the families of those crew members would prefer to see them home again."

"We would recall them if we could, now that their mission has become futile."

"Yes, I'm sure. Very well, I'll simply deal with them when they arrive at Quesann."

"You?" Neddowo said. "How can you deal with them? They are already close to Quesann."

"Oh, they won't reach Quesann for more than a GST year. I shall be there to greet them."

"But Quesann is sixteen hundred light-years from here."

"Yes, that's about right."

"How can you possibly beat them to Quesann?"

"Gentlemen, for such astute businessmen I find it hard to believe that you started a war without even knowing your enemy's strengths. I assure you that I will be back at Quesann *long* before the remnants of your fleet arrive, and I will easily destroy those ships that refuse to peacefully turn back. Then I shall decide whether or not to return here and punish this new treachery. Be sure to carry out the other instructions I gave you or my return with a taskforce to lay waste to your planet is assured. Good day."

The Council seal replaced the image of Jenetta, leaving the ministers confused with her statement about not knowing the enemy's strength.

"What did she mean, Ambello?" Minister Valhallo asked. "What strengths was she talking about?"

"I'm sure I don't know."

"That appears obvious. This venture was your idea, and now we're ruined. You most of all."

"Me?"

"Of course. You guaranteed the venture would be a success or you would reimburse the treasury for the loss. Do you have enough to pay for this debacle?"

"You can't seriously expect me to pay for everything."

"I do. That was the agreement. Everyone here was a witness. At least you have one thing in your favor."

"What's that?"

"The Galactic Alliance forbids slavery, so after all your assets are sold off, you needn't fear being sold to recover the balance."

Neddowo stiffened and paled as he stared wide-eyed at his fellow council members. With the loss of his fortune, they no longer feared him. He could not remember ever feeling so powerless and vulnerable.

* * *

On board the *Colorado*, Keith Kanes looked at Jenetta and grinned. "Did you clear the annexation of the Uthlaro Dominion territory with the Galactic Alliance Council?"

"No, not yet, but I don't see what choice we have. It's the only way we can keep them in check."

"You used that argument with the Milori and the Tsgardi annexations."

"And it's even more true with the Uthlaro. I've seen fanaticism, but never anything like these beings. We were unable to capture a single one alive from among all of the ships we fought. They're not going to stop, just as Maxxiloth would never have stopped. The Tsgardi probably would have stopped, but their annexation was punishment for having enslaved the Flordaryn people for so long." Jenetta sighed. "In the end we might very well have to return and lay waste to this planet. It might be the only way to finally end the conflict."

"We probably could have gotten one of the Uthlaro crewmen alive if we had really wanted one."

"I wasn't willing to sacrifice a single one of my people just to get a live Uthlaro, especially after they murdered the rescue party from the *Nile*."

Keith nodded, then said, "Uh, you didn't believe the Prime Minister, did you?"

"About not being able to recall the fleet? No, of course not. They're still hoping their fleet will destroy us. I decided that rather than making an issue of that point now, I would allow them to openly surrender and publicly announce their acceptance of the annexation. If they continue to plot against our control, I still have the option of coming down hard on them."

"You don't seem too concerned about their fleet."

"Oh, but I am. I'm not concerned about the outcome of the battle. The information we got from the Hudeera enabled us to whittle their numbers down enough that I'm confident we'll defeat them now. But I'm very concerned for the Space Command lives that will be lost aboard our older ships that don't have the protection of the Dakinium."

"There always seems to be someone looking for a fight, but after the Uthlaro are finally put down, we should be able to rest for a while."

"I certainly hope so, Keith. Too many good people were lost when we fought the Milori, and I was hoping we'd never have to face another formidable foe in my lifetime."

"How are you going to handle your new territory? Region Two was already more than twice as large as Region One. With the Tsgardi and Uthlaro territories, it's almost four times as large."

Jenetta sucked in her breath and let it out quickly. "I haven't really worked that out yet," Jenetta said, grinning. "We hadn't even begun to get a handle on things before the THUG invasion started and I had to drop all my plans in order to fight the Tsgardi. One thing we've learned, however, is that the DS ships will be invaluable. With a few hundred, I could have had Region Two in shape in no time, at least enough to ensure it didn't sink into complete anarchy. I suppose I'll need a thousand now. The Admiralty Board is *not* going to be pleased with me. I can hear Hubera already."

* * *

"Good morning," Admiral Moore said as he opened the special meeting of the Admiralty Board in their meeting hall on Earth. From his place at the center of the horseshoe-shaped table, he could see that everyone was anxious to receive the news from Region Two, even Admiral Hubera.

"Let's begin by reviewing the message received from Admiral Carver overnight," Admiral Moore said after the preliminary processes of reading previous minutes and the like had been handled. He nodded to his clerk and the full-wall monitor illuminated with the image of Jenetta.

As the message ended, Admiral Hubera said, "Is she insane? We can't annex the Uthlaro Dominion. We don't have enough ships to staff Region One. Moreover, she just finished annexing the Tsgardi territory. What is she trying to do, annex the entire quadrant?" His comments brought chuckles from around the room. "I'm serious," Hubera said loudly. "This isn't a laughing matter."

"Donald, you heard her arguments as well as we did," Admiral Platt said. "Do you feel we should just leave their territory and wait for them to start preparing for war with us again? As it is, they've refused to even recall their fleet. They're still hoping it can unseat us in Region Two. This is the most formidable enemy we've ever fought, and we'll have to watch them very closely in the future."

"Alright, Evelyn, suppose you tell me just how we do that. We simply don't have the resources. As it is, we're giving Carver every single ship we're able to produce. How are we going to secure another territory the size of Region One?"

"I don't know yet, Donald. I suppose Admiral Carver's fleet will have to patrol both territories. Our primary

244

concern is that the Uthlaro not be able to rebuild their war machine."

"We'll have to find a way," Admiral Moore said. "Initially, Admiral Carver will be responsible for the new territory because she's the only one with the resources to do it. Eventually we'll have to redraw the regional borders to create three areas that are more equally sized. We'll also have to establish a new command structure to govern Region Three."

"But what of Carver?" Admiral Hubera asked. "She wasn't authorized to annex more territory. I think her title has gone to her head. She shouldn't even be the military governor of Region Two. She doesn't have the experience, and she needs someone to keep her in line. She has to stop annexing territories!"

"Are you volunteering for the job, Donald?" Admiral Hillaire taunted with a dead serious look on his face.

"You think I couldn't do it?"

"That's not an answer, but I'm willing to put my money where my mouth is. I nominate Donald for the post of Military Governor in Region Three."

Admiral Hubera blanched slightly as he groped for words and a way out. Finally he said, "How am I supposed to govern a territory without any ships?"

"I further propose," Admiral Hillaire said, "Admiral Hubera be given a number of ships equal to Admiral Carver's Fleet."

"And how do you propose I tame a territory the size of Region One with a hundred tiny ships? Admiral Hubera asked.

"Admiral Carver just defeated four interstellar powers with far fewer than that."

"Okay," Admiral Moore said, "let's get back to business. Arnold's nomination and proposal is permanently tabled because Admiral Hubera isn't qualified."

"Now wait a minute, Richard, I'm as qualified as Admiral Carver. I can do anything she can do."

"Donald, you're a valuable member of the service, but you're not a line officer. You've never commanded a ship, much less a ship in battle. You've never been a base commander because you're not a line officer. According to Space Command Regulations, you're not eligible to assume either the role of Military Governor or Fleet Commander."

"Oh, well, I suppose you're right, according to the book."

Admiral Hillaire didn't say a word but couldn't resist a smirk.

* * *

The small SC taskforce reached Quesann two months and four days after leaving the Uthlarigasset system. Jenetta smiled when she saw the picket line of new DS ships at the outer perimeter of the solar system. The new destroyers and cruisers were not radically different from the previous classes of ships, but their black Dakinium hull couldn't hide the fact that some modifications had been made. Jenetta looked forward to taking a tour of the new destroyers and cruisers at the earliest opportunity.

As her shuttle set down at the base's parade grounds, she could see the assembly waiting to welcome her. She would have preferred a quiet return using the shuttle pad within the palace grounds, but knew this was part of the job. Her small taskforce had, after all, destroyed hundreds of enemy ships and extracted an unconditional surrender from the Uthlaro, albeit a somewhat insincere one. She smiled as she stepped out of the shuttle and pretended to enjoy the band and cheering throngs.

The occasion called for more speeches and Jenetta gave as rousing a speech as she could, telling the crowd of the battle and the surrender of the Uthlaro. She didn't want to put a damper on the mood, but she felt she must remind this crowd of Space Command personnel that an enemy fleet who refused to acknowledge the surrender of their government was still proceeding towards Quesann. She again reminded everyone to use their duty hours to improve their knowledge and skills in preparation for the final battle. The latter part of her speech may have been a bit disconcerting, but you'd never know it from the enthusiasm of the crowd when she climbed into the driverless vehicle for the short trip to the governor's palace.

Knowing the approximate date when the enemy would arrive allowed the base to function normally while they waited, but everyone was counting down the days as time marched inexorably towards the showdown with the Uthlaro fleet.

Chapter Fifteen
~ May 23rd, 2284 ~

In May, twenty new scout-destroyers arrived, accompanied by three new DS Battleships of the new *Ares* class and two DS frigates of the new *Franklin* class. The DS Quartermaster ships were each making three runs a year now, but since the as yet uncompleted base was intended to be the central supply point for all of Region Two, it would need as much equipment, supplies, and ordnance as could be sent to it for years to come. All of the newly arriving ships had been filled with supplies from bulkhead to bulkhead for the fifty-two-day trip. Jenetta waited until all the ordnance and supplies had been transported down to the planet before shuttling up to visit an old friend aboard the *Ares*.

As Jenetta walked down the ramp from the open hatch of the shuttle, full honors were rendered. Captain Gavin stepped forward to greet her as she reached the bottom.

"Welcome aboard the *Ares*, Admiral."

"Thank you, Captain. Your new ship is a welcome addition to the Region Two fleet."

"Allow me to introduce my senior staff."

After the introductions were complete, Captain Gavin took Jenetta and her aide on a tour of the ship, ending up at the bridge.

"I believe you know my second officer," Captain Gavin said as the doors opened and they stepped inside. Since a ship's second officer is the watch officer on the third watch and should be sleeping at that hour, she was obviously waiting around for Jenetta's arrival. She immediately climbed down from the first officer's chair and came to attention with an 'Admiral on the bridge' announcement. Everyone not at a station came to attention.

"As you were," Jenetta said. "Welcome to Region Two, Commander Carver. I didn't know you had been reassigned."

"The posting came with my promotion, Admiral," Lt. Commander Eliza Carver said.

Captain Gavin was grinning like a satisfied customer in an orthodontist advertisement.

"I think I've been set up," Jenetta said.

"Just a small surprise, Admiral," Captain Gavin said. "We thought you'd be pleased."

"I am." Looking around the bridge, Jenetta said, "This is an unusual configuration. Why the rounded walls and domed overhead. Is there a special purpose?"

"There is indeed," Captain Gavin said. As he gestured to the tactical officer, the lights dimmed slightly and the walls and ceiling seemed to melt away. Space outside the ship could be seen in every direction she turned. It was like standing in an EVA suit on top of the ship despite the bridge being located in the center of the ship and separated from outside space by numerous decks, bulkheads, radiation shielding, and ship's armor. Only the consoles, chairs, bridge equipment, and floor remained fully visible.

"My God!" Jenetta said. "I hadn't heard about this. It's incredible."

"It's the latest advancement in SimWindow technology. The entire bridge can become transparent— even the deck, although that tends to disturb some individuals, so we've only used it infrequently."

"Really! I'd love to see that if there's no one on the bridge who would be unduly disturbed."

Captain Gavin looked around at the crewmembers on the bridge, then nodded at the tac officer. Instantly the floor melted away, leaving only a grid-work of thin lines that allowed a visual reference for the deck beneath their feet. It was like being in a clear bubble. She could actually look down and see the planet below. The other ships in orbit were all visible now.

"Amazing," Jenetta said, grinning. "I love it, but I can see where it would disturb some people. Even though I know there are more than a dozen decks beneath this one, I'm almost afraid to walk around for fear I'll slip through one of the grid openings and wind up outside the ship. This would take a bit of getting used to."

Captain Gavin smiled. Nodding at the tac officer, the floor solidified again, but the walls and overhead remained transparent.

"Are the new frigates like this?" Jenetta asked Captain Gavin.

"Yes, they have the same basic design on a smaller scale."

"Wonderful. Let's talk in your briefing room, unless you have other marvels of technology to show me?"

"Well, there is one small feature you should see now. If you would follow me, Admiral?"

Captain Gavin led the way out of the bridge and to a lift. Down one deck and five hundred meters towards the stern, a corridor guarded by two Marines required hand-print verification to open the transparent polycarbonate security doors. They passed two solid doors on the sidewalls as they proceeded down the secure corridor.

"The doors on either side are Admiral's suites, should any be staying aboard," Captain Gavin said. "Each contains a suite for an aide and another for a steward."

"You didn't bring me down her to see VIP quarters, did you?"

"No, ma'am. This is what I wanted to show you," he said as the doors at the end of the corridor opened."

The room was similar to the bridge.

"It's spacious for Auxiliary Command and Control," Jenetta said.

"AC&C is another deck down and forward of the bridge. This is the Flag bridge. It's similar to the Command bridge, but it has no helm, navigation, or engineering stations, and no fire-control stations. The tactical station is designed to accommodate just two tac officers. One can assess the current situation while another is plotting possible actions."

Jenetta looked around with a smile. "And it has the same transparent overhead, bulkhead, and deck capability?"

"Of course," Captain Gavin said, smiling.

"This represents a significant departure from previous ship designs. Warships haven't had a Flag bridge since wet navy days."

"The designers have acknowledged the changing conditions that make such a bridge feasible and desirable. I think the images of you standing on the bridge of the *Prometheus* hanging onto my command chair for dear life during the engagement with the first Milori invasion force had something to do with it. SHQ decided that an admiral commanding a taskforce should have a proper bridge of her own. Your refusal to displace either myself or my XO really had an effect."

"Neither Commander Ashraf nor myself could take your chairs. You were the two people responsible for fighting the enemy. We were only there as bystanders."

"Standers maybe, but hardly bystanders. But you won't have to stand in the future. As you can see," he said, gesturing toward six command-style chairs arranged in a slight arc that faced the full bulkhead monitor at the front, "this bridge provides six chairs for the Admiral and a staff of five advisors. The Admiral can be concentrating on the overall battle while the captain is on the main bridge concerning himself or herself mainly with the actions of the ship. Every new battleship will have a Flag bridge— at least until the class is changed in fifteen or twenty years. SHQ realizes it was a bit shortsighted not to make provision for admirals to command in space. You're still our only battle-experienced Flag officer."

"I hope the need never arises again, but I agree that we must be prepared. Is there anything else to show me?"

"No," he said, smiling, "I'm afraid everything else would seem anticlimactic now."

* * *

"Beverage, Admiral?" Captain Gavin asked as the briefing room doors closed behind them.

"Thank you, Larry. A mug of Colombian would hit the spot if you'll stop using my rank when addressing me behind closed doors."

"Of course, Jen," Captain Gavin said as he prepared two mugs of coffee and carried them to his desk before taking his seat. Jenetta was already seated.

"This briefing room is every bit as great as your office on the *Prometheus*, but I think I preferred the honey-oak wall covering over this medium walnut look."

"I liked the oak, but I also like this look. Perhaps I've just gotten used to it since I see it every day."

"Congratulations on getting the first ship in the new class, Larry. It's beautiful. And I'm sure it's as deadly as it appears."

"The designers returned to the drawing boards for the new weapons systems. Before the Battle at Vauzlee, one torpedo from every tube every fifteen seconds was more than adequate. Vauzlee, Higgins, Stewart, and two wars with the Milori showed us we needed a faster rate of fire. Torpedoes are stored and loaded in clusters of sixteen now. The time required to have another torpedo in position to fire has been reduced from fifteen seconds to two-point-three seconds for each torpedo in the cluster. It takes six-point-nine seconds to swap clusters, so the average time to fire is under two-point-six seconds. The ship has fifty-six tubes, so we can put eight hundred ninety-six torpedoes on target in under thirty-five seconds and be ready to begin firing another eight hundred ninety-six less than seven seconds after that. All loading is handled automatically, so we won't lose people if a torpedo room is struck during an engagement unless something happens that requires the presence of engineers. There will always be a torpedo ready when a tactical officer has locked onto a target and the number of available tubes means the tac officer can instantly select from high-explosive, bomb-pumped laser, nuclear, or WOLaR torpedoes.

"Better still, the new torpedoes don't fly a straight line to the target— they zigzag randomly, which makes it much more difficult for enemy gunners to kill them. Just when you think you'll get a lock, the torpedo changes direction—just enough to make you miss."

"That's great. Will guidance specialists still have a role?"

"The designers have improved the software considerably and the torpedo will still strike the target in the approximate area identified by the tactical officer at the time the torpedo is fired. If the ship is in the enemy database, the torpedo will target the weakest point within the target area, but having a guidance specialist assigned to each torpedo can improve the kill rate because he or she can alter the trajectory if another torpedo arrives at the intended target first. The specialist can then retarget another point or, during a battle, another ship."

"This ship is aptly named. *Ares*, the Greek God of War. I'm glad I don't have to go into battle against him."

"More tubes with a substantially higher rate of fire, more laser arrays, *and* Dakinium shielding. We can't go wrong. I'm sorry you weren't able to get the ship command promised to you."

"Admiral Moore did tell me at the time it would only happen if I could be freed up from whatever duty assignment I had when the ships were ready to launch. Given our current situation, I can't argue with the fact that I've been too involved to be freed up here. It's hard to believe the promise was made during a different war."

"Let's hope this war is the last one we'll know in our lifetimes."

"Amen. Did you arrange for Eliza's promotion?"

"I was staffing the ship, needed a good second officer, and she was on the Promotion Selection Board's list for Lt. Commander. I naturally grabbed her as quickly as I could before someone else did."

"Christa is on the list as well."

"I know, but Steve Powers wanted her for his new ship. And since he was already her commanding officer on the *Chiron*, she went with him."

"Steve got a new ship? That means that..."

"Yes, Christa is on the *Hephaestus*. She's probably asleep now since you didn't schedule a visit to any of the other newly arrived ships."

"I would have if I had realized Steve was here as well as you. As soon as I spotted your name on the *Ares* crew list, I stopped what I was doing and made arrangements to come up here."

Captain Gavin chuckled. "We'll have plenty of time for socializing. I don't imagine any of us will be going anywhere until after we deal with the Uthlaro."

"I like your optimism. I *hope* we'll be going somewhere after they arrive."

"We will. With Admiral Jenetta Carver in command, nobody doubts that. You have an unparalleled talent for tactics. If anyone needed more proof than what you've done before this latest war, they only need look at the record so far in this one. You've destroyed more than nine hundred ships in combat and lost just— what— seven people and no ships. All four of the belligerents have surrendered unconditionally and we only need mop up this last taskforce to end the fighting."

"We've been…"

"Don't say you've been lucky, Jen," Captain Gavin said, interrupting. "I know you like to think that, but it does you a tremendous disservice to say it. The people you've defeated know it wasn't just luck— at least those who survived the encounter with you. And even your detractors in Space Command have finally started to acknowledge it wasn't just luck."

"I have detractors in Space Command?" Jenetta said, feigning surprise.

Captain Gavin smiled. "Not all that many— just the ones who are jealous of your abilities, success, and popularity. Of course, that probably includes half the officer corps."

"I've never let it bother me."

"It hasn't hurt your career. Even the ones who are highly positioned haven't been able to touch you. Admiral Hubera, for instance."

"Well— I knew about Admiral Hubera. He was just as rude to me when I appeared at the Admiralty Board a couple of years back as when he was my instructor at the Academy. I was recounting some basic facts so everyone would understand my position, and he snapped at me that they already knew what I was saying and that I should get to the point."

"He sure wouldn't win any popularity contests with the people he's worked with over the years. He's probably the most vocal among the detractors. The rest of us are solidly behind you and tremendously grateful *you're* out here instead of an officer like Hubera."

"Thanks, Larry. I'm grateful *you're* here. The Uthlaro are definitely coming and we need our best commanders for that conflict. They don't have Dakinium, but their ships have three layers of tritanium and are well constructed. Worse, their warriors always fight to the death. They won't stop coming at us while a single warrior lives. The fighting so far has mostly been with small battle groups, and we've fought only with the DS ships, but the Uthlaro have massed for the final battle. Our DS ships are seriously outnumbered, so I'm forced to use older, non-DS ships. It's going to be a lot tougher and a lot bloodier."

"What's the line-up like?"

"With the arrival of your force, I have one hundred forty-one ships, seventy-four of which are non-DS. Sixty-two of those are M-Designate and twelve are Mars built. Most are destroyers, but we have two battleships and six cruisers. Our DS ships include fifty scout-destroyers, four destroyers, two frigates, two cruisers, and nine battleships."

"And you're expecting the Uthlaro when?"

"Around the beginning of March."

"Based on the activity at the yards when we left, they must be readying additional ships for your command."

"I'm expecting perhaps as many as twenty more scout-destroyers, but that should be it. The yard folks busted their backsides to get us all the large warships that could be completed before then at the expense of working on ships that they knew couldn't be ready in time. I'm grateful for their efforts and will be happy with whatever additional ships we can get. At this point, I'm not afraid the Uthlaro will overrun us. It's the potential cost in lives that bothers me."

"Have you worked out your plan?"

"Pretty much. We'll jump in with the DS ships first and do as much damage as we can. If things get too hot, I'll call in the reserves. But if we can do it with just the DS ships, I'll hold the others back."

"What are the odds?"

"We're expecting two hundred six Uthlaro warships, so if we get those additional twenty scout-destroyers we'll only be outnumbered by forty-five ships. Of course I'll try to convince the Uthlaro commanding officer to turn around and go home, but I seriously doubt that will happen. And once we engage, we'll have to crush the life out of them because there can be no other outcome."

* * *

"This is so incredible, sis," Christa said, as the three sisters toured the governor's palace after dinner. Cayla and Tayna padded along on either side of the trio. "I thought your quarters on Stewart were incredible when you were the commanding officer there. This place makes *them* look like a hovel."

"It is the Governor's *Palace*, Christa. I think there must be a law somewhere that says it has to put you in awe," Jenetta said, grinning.

"Do you think your palace on Gavistee is anything like this?" Eliza wondered aloud.

"I've learned that our palace was used for the basic template, but this place is quite a bit smaller."

"Smaller?" Eliza questioned.

"You have to remember that our palace on Obotymot was originally built for the king and queen when they visit there. Much of the Royal Court travels with them whenever they go anywhere, so they need adequate accommodations for hundreds of people. There are a hundred suites, and each suite has five bedrooms. The main bedroom is for the Royal and the others are for their attendants. Perhaps we can take some downtime after this war is over and visit there. I'd love to see the look on mom's face when she gets there."

"What's the current situation with the atmosphere?" Christa asked.

"Every report I receive states that it continues to improve with each passing year. The planet is warming again and the growing season is lengthening. Soil erosion has slowed considerably, but the loss of topsoil will be a problem without major fertilization efforts. The outlook for a complete resumption of crop production in the next decade is good."

"How far has the estate sunk into debt supporting your citizenry without any income from crop yields?" Eliza questioned.

"Not nearly as bad as I originally expected," Jenetta said. "Between the royalties from the books we wrote about Dakistee and the manufacturing royalties on my patents, we're in good shape. When things get rolling again, we could break even in a few years."

When they had returned to Jenetta's quarters and the corridor door was closed, Christa asked, "Has anyone ever raised any objections to the patents you stole?"

"I didn't steal anything, Christa. I discovered a few examples of consumer products that the Raiders were using on their stations but which were unfamiliar to me. I paid some people to reverse-engineer the products and prepare construction plans and specifications with my own money. I then paid for an exhaustive search of patent records in the galactic archives. Finding no encroachment on existing patents, I patented them and then found companies willing to manufacture and market the products for consumers. Every single penny from royalties went into the Obotymot Relief Fund we established. I didn't even reimburse myself for my expenditures. To my way of thinking, the Raiders are just reimbursing the citizens of Obotymot for the suffering inflicted on them when the Raiders hijacked relief shipments from Nordakia."

"I don't have a problem with it," Eliza said. "The Raiders missed a good bet by not patenting them first, and I'm happy they've been deprived of any benefit from them."

"I don't have a problem either," Christa said. "I'm glad to see the royalties going to help our people."

"How are things on the romance front?" Jenetta asked. "Have you heard anything from Adam lately, Christa?"

"Not in almost six months. I guess it's over. We had some good times together, but we could never seem to get past the issue of me not aging. It bothered him a lot more than he would admit. Since the *Hephaestus* launched, I've been spending a little off-duty time with a doctor aboard ship, but I'm still trying to determine if he's more interested in me or in our DNA."

"How about you, Eliza?" Jenetta asked.

"My love life is just as lackluster these days. And it was difficult leaving so many of my friends on the *Bellona*— but I couldn't wait to get out here where all the excitement is. And I love the new ship; it's incredible. I guess I'll have to make new friends. How about you and Hugh?"

"We still exchange vidMail a couple of times each week. It's been difficult not telling him what's going on out here, but he understands the need for security even with the special encryption codes I made for our correspondence. Any code can be broken, as we've proven often enough. So, much of what we talk about is inane stuff. He knows he'll never get out this way while he's on the *Bonn*. That ship, while ideal for most patrol activities back in Region One, is too old and too slow to be used out here. So he's applied for transfer to a scout-destroyer. It's possible he might make it out here in one of the next groups to be launched."

"That's great, Jen," Christa said.

"Yeah," Eliza said in agreement. "What's it been, like eight years since you've seen one another?"

"Eight and a half. It seems like twenty, though. Long distance romances are difficult, but at least he doesn't seem to have any hang-ups about me not aging, or any intense interest in my DNA that make his affections suspect."

"Speaking of DNA," Eliza said, "has anything ever been heard about Mikel Arneu? Did he die on Scruscotto when the Milori attacked Raider Ten?"

"I haven't heard anything," Jenetta said. "As far as I know, the site hasn't been excavated yet so we don't know how many died in the underground complex. I've been too involved out here— first with the Milori and then with the THUGs— to look into it. The mine that fronted for their operation was rich in platinum and palladium, so it stands to reason that someone will eventually dig it out. Perhaps then we'll find out if Arneu survived. If he did, it's a sure bet he's set up a lab somewhere to continue his work in age prolongation. He's obsessed with becoming immortal."

"Immortality seems so overrated," Christa said. "I can understand the desirability for a DNA process that allows a person to enjoy the strength and vitality of a young body throughout their life, but why would anyone want to live forever? It seems to take all the excitement away. If you know you'll live forever, there's no urgent need to explore and learn. You figure you'll absorb it anyway at some point. It seems you'd lapse into a kind of ennui about everything. We haven't suffered from those feelings because we don't know how long we'll live. We really only have Arneu's statement that we might live to be five thousand years old. The scientists admitted they didn't know— only that we'll live beyond the average hundred fifty years modern medicine gives us."

"There's also the fact that our profession is highly dangerous," Jenetta said. "We may not live long enough to die of old age."

"Yeah, we heard about the fighter you've reserved for your exclusive use," Eliza said, grinning, "and the treetop-level flights over islands and open sea at full speed. Everyone's worried you might kill yourself before the Uthlaro get here."

"You get just as much pleasure from speed as I do," Jenetta retorted, "but I've attained a position where I can explore such proclivities without *open* censure. It's one of the few perks of being the supreme military commander of Region Two."

Chapter Sixteen
~ June 17th, 2284 ~

The mantled figure ducked quickly into a darkened alleyway at the sound of voices approaching from around a street corner. Wearing a dark cloak that extended from head to toe, the figure melded easily into the deep shadows of the moonless night and remained unseen by two men who passed the alley entrance. As the sounds of footfalls receded into the distance, the furtive figure re-emerged and walked with undisguised haste through the narrow back streets of Old Boston on Earth. The buildings that lined the streets were dark at this hour except for an occasional ray of light that peeked from between window curtains.

With a final glance over its shoulder, the draped figure climbed several stone steps to a wooden door and gently knocked in a coded sequence. A narrow slot in the door slid open and a pair of evil eyes squinted out.

"Let me see your face," a gravelly voice said.

The thin figure pulled the cloak back slightly, just enough to expose facial features to the eyes in the slot. As the door opened enough to permit entry, the figure restored the cloak to its former position.

"Top of the stairs," the burly bodyguard grunted.

The covered form brushed past him and glided up the stairs without uttering a word. Upon reaching the upper floor, a slender hand snaked out from between the folds of cloth and twisted the handle of the first door on the right, then pushed gently.

An enormous cigar hung from the lips of the large man sitting behind a hopelessly scarred desk in an otherwise empty office. The small room was hot and stuffy, and reeked of cigar smoke. Wet with perspiration, the occupant's short black hair was matted down on his head. He was leaning comfortably back in his 'oh-gee' chair when she entered, his feet propped up on the desk. He dropped them to the floor with a loud thud.

"It's about damned time you got here," he said.

The figure pulled back the cowl to reveal a fifty-something woman. With shoulder-length brown hair, her average face would not have seemed out of place at a parent-teacher night or perhaps at a civic meeting where community betterment issues were being discussed.

"I tried to come during my last trip dirt-side, but I thought someone was following me."

"Who?"

"I don't know. I never spotted anyone for sure, but I couldn't shake the feeling. I didn't want to lead anyone here. I simply went shopping before returning to the shuttle."

"Do they suspect you?"

"I don't think so. I've heard that Intelligence agents follow different employees from the Jupiter Foundry Works at times— not because they're suspected of wrongdoing but simply on a random basis. I left the thing in a rental locker at the skyport rather than carry it back to Jupiter. I retrieved it tonight after I was sure no one was behind me."

The man looked at her intently for several seconds before asking calmly, "What have you got?"

"What you asked for, of course," the woman said with a shaky voice as she pulled her hand from her pocket and held out a long cotton sock with something weighing down the end.

The man accepted it and let the contents slide out onto his hand. The cylindrical chunk of composite material was about eight centimeters long and three centimeters in diameter. "This is it? This is all you could get?"

"You're holding the best kept secret in Space Command. They don't exactly hand out free samples and I couldn't just walk out with a large chunk under my arm. The entire manufacturing process is contained within a single, kilometer-long forge/foundry machine. The raw material arrives from— somewhere— in huge shipping containers that are handled exclusively by bots. The input end of the forge is in vacuum, so there's no chance of getting any raw material samples, and access to the forge on the two sides is limited to bots, senior technicians, and supervisory inspectors. On one side, large tanks of chemicals are replaced by bots when they're empty. The only markings on the tanks are color codes. On the other side, scrap from the cutting and shaping process is ejected for recycling. Bots handle that chore exclusively. Only supervisory inspectors with top clearance have full access to the two sides of the forge. Senior techs are allowed in when a supervisor or inspector is with each of them. Finished parts, already cut and shaped, come off the end of the line and are stacked and packed for shipment. That's where I work as a parts inspector. Every single milligram of material coming out of the forge must be accounted for and a dozen cameras watch our every move."

"So how did you get this?"

"It fell off a pile of scrap being carried to a recycle container by a bot in the limited-access side room just as a supervisor entered. It rolled, unseen by everyone but me, out the open door and wound up under a parts cart. I was just fortunate to be passing at the time. I waited until the shift was changing and retrieved it when no one was watching. Good thing they don't perform cavity searches. They rely on simply having all employees strip and discard their disposable overalls. We're then passed through showers before being allowed to enter the locker room, naked, where our regular clothes are stored."

The man looked at the woman and then down at the sample in his hand. A look of disgust shrouded his face.

"Don't worry, it's clean," the woman said with a scowl. "I washed it off after I took it out. Damn thing hurt like hell. I bled for a week afterwards."

"You're being well compensated."

"Speaking of which," the woman said, "when do I get what you promised?"

The man grimaced and said, "How did you get this through the screening machines at the skyport?"

"I told the inspector it gave me peace of mind when I walked the streets of Boston. If anybody attacked me, I swung it at them. He could see it wasn't dangerous in any other way. He even suggested I get myself a heavier piece of metal."

Gadobi grunted and said, "Wait here. We have to verify this is what you say it is before we discuss payment."

He stood and dropped the composite material into a side pocket before carefully knocking the glowing embers from the end of his cheroot. After patting the tip to ensure he had extinguished it, he slipped it into a vest pocket and left the room by a side door.

Not knowing how long the purported verification process would take, Dawn Palmer stepped around the desk and sat down in the room's only chair. There was no doubt in her mind the small ingot was genuine. She had been working at the orbiting Jupiter foundry since the first material had rolled off the line.

The manufacturing process required such tremendous energy that locating such operations next to a planet whose 'atmo' was predominantly hydrogen made perfect sense. Automated hydrogen collection ships with enormous intake scoops continuously dipped into the atmosphere and sucked in their fill. Tank farms surrounding the planet completed the gas separation processes and were always ready to deliver the cheap and abundant fuel to any of the millions of manufacturing concerns located around the planet. The only downside was that employees had to live at the plant. Being able to get dirt-side on Earth only once a month meant that each trip was welcomed with great enthusiasm.

Civilian employees of companies producing controlled products exclusively for Space Command were required to pass an intensive background investigation. Palmer never imagined she could betray the trust placed in her.

She'd always felt there wasn't enough money in the universe to 'turn' her— but they had found something that would.

Now in her fifties, her once youthful and attractive looks were beginning to fade. When notified she had been selected to receive a free weekend at a plush resort that specialized in beauty rejuvenation, she jumped at the opportunity. The two days at the spa were wonderful. It wasn't the pampering by resort personnel trained to engage in excessive cosseting— it was the rejuvenation processes that had made her look twenty years younger. Unfortunately, within a week of returning home, the wrinkles had reappeared and her skin again began to take on a sallow look.

Before her next trip dirt-side, she received a note from the company that had offered the free spa weekend. A representative invited her to come in and discuss a membership at a greatly reduced price.

Upon arriving on Earth, Palmer had anxiously hurried to the address she'd been provided. Rather than the exquisite office complex she'd seen on the company's computer site, she found a simple office in a small commercial building. The salesperson, Brandon Hines, according to the nameplate on his desk, was the only person in evidence in the office. He explained that most memberships were purchased electronically, so there was no need for fancy quarters or a large office staff. Through electronic manipulation of images taken during her visit to the spa, he showed her how a series of treatments could not only enhance her appearance but actually restore her youthful looks on a permanent basis. The promise of looking youthful for a lifetime was a hook she couldn't ignore. The salesperson even used the expression 'Fountain of Youth' repeatedly.

Dawn Palmer was ready to sign on the dotted line before the salesperson had even produced a contract. But when she learned the price, she pulled back.

"You can't be serious," she said.

"I'm completely serious," Hines said. "The youth restoration program is brand new, and until now, only a few women have received it. They mostly include the wealthiest women on the planet."

"Such as who?" Palmer asked.

"I can't name our customers without their permission, but there is one well-known person who received it and for whom the fact was made known to the public."

"And who is that?"

"Admiral Jenetta Carver."

"Carver? But her treatment was performed by Raiders without her permission."

"Yes, that's true. That's where we 'borrowed' the process," Hines said. "Our lead scientist was part of the team that did the original research here on Earth. When he learned the research company was a front for the Raider organization, he got scared. He feigned a debilitating illness that forced his retirement from the team. Fearing for his life if the Raiders discovered his ruse, he went into hiding until after the Raiders took all the research work off-world; however, he maintained contact with a couple of close associates and they kept him informed on where they were focusing their efforts because they needed help in his area of expertise. The other scientists got the help they needed and our guy learned enough to refine the procedure here on Earth. Now, if you have enough money you can bathe in our Fountain of Youth. We know you can't afford to participate monetarily, but your position at the Jupiter Foundry Works can buy your way into the program."

"No, I won't betray Space Command." Palmer wanted to get up and run, but the attraction of what she was being offered kept her rooted to the chair.

"I'm not asking you to betray anybody and I'm not asking for any secrets. I simply want a small scrap of the new material being made at the JFW."

"Why?"

"Delcorado Engineering owns The Gardens of Venus Spas. Have you heard of them?"

"They make weapons for the military, don't they?"

"Exactly right. The military is letting all their contracts expire now that they have this new 'so-called' indestructible material. Delcorado will have to shut down their plants and furlough tens of thousands of employees if they can't produce new weapons as rugged as those made by JFW. After Space Command selected JFW to produce the material for their ships, they awarded them dozens of other contracts to produce military weapons and related products. If Delcorado can get a small sample of the material, they can reverse-engineer it and compete with JFW on ruggedness and durability. You'll actually be doing a public service. As long as JFW is the only company with access to the material, there is no competition to keep the price down. Taxpayers are getting hosed without any say in the matter."

"I work for JFW. Aside from the security issues, if I do something to harm company earnings, I could lose my job."

"Once you look twenty-one again, like Jenetta Carver, you won't need that job. You'll be able to pick from thousands of employers who have a need for the most beautiful women on the planet. And you won't be stuck at Jupiter anymore. You can live on Earth full-time, instead of for just a few days each month."

"I'll— I'll have to think about it," Palmer heard herself saying.

"You do that." Hines slid a small piece of paper towards her. It contained only a phone number. "Call if you get what we want. If you deliver, you'll look twenty-one for the rest of your life. And your beauty will stop men in their tracks."

Palmer stood without saying another word and left the spa sales office. She walked trancelike as she returned to the hotel where she'd spend the next few days before returning to Jupiter. She couldn't stop imagining herself as young again and more beautiful than she'd ever dreamed possible.

* * *

Gadobi, after descending to the basement, unlocked a door and descended another two floors. He then began a trek through a tunnel that took him two city blocks. Upon passing through the final door of five, he emerged in a large lab. He passed several technicians monitoring equipment processes and approached the lead technician.

"Here it is," Gadobi said, holding out the cylindrical piece of material.

The tech stopped what he was doing and took it from Gadobi's hand. "It's light," he said. "I expected it to be heavier. You'd think it should be extremely dense to accomplish what it purportedly can do."

"Yeah. Whatever," Gadobi said, as he took the cheroot he had extinguished in the upstairs room and relit it. "Just test it."

"I've told you not to smoke in here," the tech said. "The smoke interferes with our testing processes."

"Too damn bad. Now test the freaking sample."

"Yeah, whatever," the tech said as he carried the sample to a large piece of equipment on a work table and lifted the cover. He clamped the material into a jig and closed the lid. At a monitor, he aligned the equipment using a double set of crosshairs and pushed the power switch. A laser beam shot out and struck the object where he had placed the crosshairs. Over the next five minutes he watched the monitor as the laser tried to punch its way through the sample. When it failed to make the slightest dent, he powered down the laser and lifted the cover. He placed a probe against the sample and shook his head. Then he reached out and removed it from the clamping assembly.

"Amazing," the tech said, "not even warm to the touch."

"Is that it then?" Gadobi asked.

"Not just yet, but it's looking real good."

The tech took the sample to another large piece of equipment and opened the two doors at the front. After clamping the material in place, he closed the doors and moved to the control pad. He watched through a dense black glass window as a plasma torch tried to cut through the sample. By now, the other techs in the room had come over to watch. After ten minutes, the tech shut the plasma torch down and removed the sample.

"Astounding! It's barely warm. I've never seen anything like this."

"Is that it then?" Gadobi asked.

"That's it. It's what we've been trying to get our hands on ever since we heard about it."

Gadobi walked to a phone and placed a call. The lead tech could only hear one side of the conversation.

"Gadobi here. We have it."

"Yes, it's been tested and certified as genuine by our people."

"What about the woman?" he asked after a brief pause.

"Okay," he said after another thirty seconds had elapsed, then hung up.

Gadobi placed another call immediately. When someone answered, he asked, "Anything going on outside?" After a couple of seconds he said, "Good. Keep your eyes open," then hung up. Dropping the stump of his cheroot to the floor and crushing it under his shoe to extinguish it, Gadobi said to the lead tech, "You know what to do." He then began his trek back to the house where Palmer was waiting.

* * *

"Are you satisfied it's real?" Palmer asked, coming up out of her reverie as she vacated the chair.

Gadobi, having just climbed three flights of stairs, was out of breath. He dropped heavily into his chair and pulled out a fresh cheroot. He lit up, took several puffs, and then leaned back in the chair.

Palmer waited for him to say something.

When Gadobi was breathing easier, he said, "Okay, it's seems to be the real thing."

"And my payment?" Palmer said anxiously.

Gadobi unlocked the desk and pulled out a boarding pass. "Here's your ticket to Earth Station 3. Someone will meet you there and give you a boarding pass for the flight out."

"A flight to where?" she asked as she accepted the small folder.

"To where you'll get what we agreed on— a passport to the Fountain of Youth and a new life."

"Where's that? I have to be back at work in three days."

"You won't be going back. The initial process takes weeks, and during that phase, you're unable to perform any work. The complete changes take years to complete."

"Years? How many years?"

"I'm told eight to ten years, but the major changes happen the first year. In any event, during the first few weeks of treatment you mostly sleep unless you're in prime condition to begin with."

"Why wasn't I told? I would have packed up my stuff and quit my job. All my personal possessions are at Jupiter. And people will wonder what happened to me. Someone will notify the police."

"Your appearance will change so much that no one will ever recognize you and you'll get a new ID. You'll also get other things, such as a new wardrobe that better suits your new body and custom jewelry that will suit your twenty-one-year-old appearance. It will all be yours when you've completed the initial phase."

Palmer's eyes glazed over slightly as she thought about having a designer wardrobe for the first time in her life and a jewelry case full of expensive jewelry. "Uh, okay," she managed to squeak out.

"You have your ticket and you're ready to begin your new life," Gadobi said. "You know the way out."

Palmer turned and left the room without looking back.

* * *

Palmer slid her credits card through the payment machine in the rear of the driverless cab and hurried into the skyport terminal to catch her flight. She almost made it to the departure gate before two large men appeared at her sides and took hold of her arms. One flashed a badge as they lifted her and pivoted to walk towards a sidewall where a third agent stood holding open the door to the security hallway. None of them said a word as she was half carried and half dragged to an interrogation room. She didn't fight them. The SCI badge and the size of the agents was enough to show her that resistance would be futile.

"I want a lawyer," she said nervously as they deposited her in a chair.

The interrogation room only had a table and two chairs.

"Do you believe you need one?" one of the agents asked as he took the seat across the table from her.

The other agent stood against the wall near the only door.

"I want a lawyer. I know my rights," Palmer said.

"Maybe there won't be a need—" the first agent said, "if you cooperate. I have a recording of a phone conversation. It was made a little over a half-hour ago. Tell me if anyone sounds familiar."

The agent slipped a data ring into a playback unit on the table in front of her and selected a file from the com display. It began playing through speakers mounted at the ceiling in all four corners of the room. Palmer expected to hear her own voice, but instead she heard the voices of two men. She instantly recognized Gadobi's raspy voice but the other was unfamiliar.

"...Gadobi here. We have it."

"Are you sure?" the second voice said. "Has it been certified?"

"Yes, it's been tested and certified as genuine by our people."

"Finally. This will get Arneu off my back. He reams me out daily because I haven't been able to get a sample of that damn material."

"What about the woman?"

"Follow the plan. Give her the ticket and send her on her way to the Fountain of Youth. As soon as she boards the ship at Earth Station 3, she'll be drugged and put into stasis. When she reaches the lab we'll process her as promised, then put her on a ship to the resort. When she finally wakes up, she'll look twenty-one again and have a body to die for."

Palmer smiled.

"Then we'll wipe her mind," the voice continued, "and put her to work for us." Palmer's smile withered as she heard an evil chuckle. The voice continued with, "No one will ever be able to track her down and interrogate her. And we have a never-ending need for beautiful, compliant whores we don't have to keep drugged. It's easier to make our own from the 'plain janes' that come to us willingly than kidnapping beautiful women the way we used to."

"Okay..." Palmer heard Gadobi say as the conversation ended.

"In case you didn't realize it, they were talking about you," the agent said.

"I don't know what you're talking about."

"Sure you do. If you cooperate, we'll put you into witness protection. We'll even let you go, if that's really what you want, and help you catch your ride."

Palmer looked at him suspiciously. "Why would you do that?"

"If we let you meet the ship, we're sure you'll never commit a crime in GA space again. Plus we won't have to feed, clothe, and keep you healthy for the rest of your life. The Raiders will do that for us."

"What do you mean, Raiders?"

"Who do you think you've been working for?"

Palmer was beginning to understand she had been duped. "Delcorado Engineering," she said. "They said they needed a sample of the material because Space Command is letting all their regular military contracts expire. They need the material to compete in a difficult market by making more durable weapons and support products."

"Delcorado Engineering has nothing to do with this outfit. And contracts for old products expire all the time as contracts for new products are signed. Delcorado is a prime contractor and important supplier of military supplies to Space Command. They're not losing any business or shutting any plants. In fact, the current situation in Region Two has tripled their business."

"But they said…"

"I'm sure they did. They got you to betray your government with promises of youth and beauty, and even made it seem patriotic by fabricating some lies."

"They said I'd be like Admiral Jenetta Carver, young and beautiful for almost my whole lifetime."

"And it appears they meant it. You'd look young and beautiful as you spent the rest of your life as a mindless sex slave. That was what they'd intended for the Admiral. Doesn't sound like a very good deal to me."

"They never mentioned the slavery part. Or the mindless part."

"I wouldn't expect them to mention that. Would you?"

"Um, no. How do I know you're not lying to me also?"

"You heard the phone call."

"That could be faked."

"You'll have to decide that for yourself. Now, do you cooperate, or do we help you make your flight?"

"Uh, I'll take the flight."

"Suit yourself. Pete, see she makes her flight. If she goes, fine. If she tries to miss it, take her to lockdown and I'll begin processing the charges for treason."

"Uh, wait," Palmer said, holding up her hand as the agent named Pete approached her. "I just wanted to see if you'd really let me go. I really do want to cooperate."

"Okay," the first agent said, holding up his hand towards Pete, who retreated silently back to his standing position by the wall. "Start at the beginning and tell us everything you can remember. Describe everyone you've had contact with and everything that was said, exactly as said, as best you can remember."

"Six months ago I was notified I had been selected to receive a free weekend at The Gardens of Venus Spa in Cuba. I hadn't entered any contest, so I was skeptical, but I was told I was automatically entered when I bought

273

some facial products at a store here in Boston. I'd heard it was a fantastic place and the weekend was 'all expenses paid,' so I…"

Chapter Seventeen
~ March 1st, 2285 ~

During the final months, scout-destroyers made weekly trips to check on the progress of the Uthlaro fleet. The Uthlaro were probably not even aware of the Space Command vessels as they flashed by at Light-9790 on the edge of sensor range, but the Space Command vessels charted the position of every ship, their speed, and course. During the time they were monitored, the readings rarely varied. They were far too spread out for a WOLaR torpedo to take out more than one ship. The Uthlaro had learned their lesson.

The projected date of the Uthlaro arrival had originally been based on the earliest possible arrival time after the ships still able to move under their own power left the RP that Jenetta had named the Graveyard. The actual arrival date was considerably later, and Jenetta speculated that the decimated fleet had been forced to stop somewhere to make repairs. The additional time had allowed Space Command to provide a far better array of warships than originally projected. As the Uthlaro fleet neared the base, the complement of Dakinium-sheathed ships stood at nine battleships, three cruisers, two frigates, five destroyers, and seventy scout-destroyers. Each arrival of a DS ship bolstered Jenetta's confidence they could minimize the death toll of Space Command personnel. The eighty-nine DS ships, when combined with the M-designate ships and the older Mars-built ships, swelled the Second Fleet to one hundred sixty-three.

Purely as a precaution, the underground bunkers were readied for use and all base personnel were assigned quarters in the underground chambers. They were required to study the layout to the point where they could find their way in darkened tunnels using only emergency lighting to find shafts that led to the surface. The food stores were checked and all equipment was certified to be working at one hundred percent. When the Uthlaro arrived in the vicinity, Jenetta would order all non-ship personnel down into the bunkers. She wasn't taking any unnecessary chances. Holo-domes on the surface would hide the base completely. From space, it would appear as a large grassy area. Special images had been prepared for the areas where the Milori had left partially completed buildings. If the Uthlaro managed to reach the planet, they would only see what had existed when the Milori ceased construction of a base here. Since roadways were already grass and buildings were always coated in special thermal protection materials, there would be no unusual heat signatures to betray building locations in an infrared scan.

With all the plans and preparations made, there was nothing to do except wait while conducting normal everyday business.

* * *

Strauss glanced slowly around the orotund table at his fellow council members as the group completed the 'old business' portion of the meeting. The powerful reach of these people, all members of the Lower Council, extended down to the lowlifes and riffraff that actually performed many of the nefarious deeds throughout the known galaxy.

Since the very first day the council began conducting meetings here, no one had ever been able to eavesdrop on conversations, celebrations, or tirades. Today would be no different. Sheathed in the best sound-deadening building materials available and protected by state-of-the-art electronic equipment, the room and building were as secure as the most protected government meeting centers in the galaxy. Just breaking through the security of the legitimate industrial conglomerate housing the spacious elliptical chamber was next to impossible. It would be easier to win a battle in unarmed combat with a Taurentlus-Thur Jumaka than to get into this building. Many corporate spies, unaware of the real business conducted here, had tried and died. Those taken alive were never heard from again as they spent the remainder of their years in slave labor camps in distant solar systems. If they had known the building was home to the Raider Lower Council, they would have immediately chosen other targets.

Chairman Arthur Strauss had nodded his approval following the long presentation by new Councilman Neil Soroman, then shifted his body slightly to get more comfortable in the executive chair at the head of the table.

"Earlier, you and I briefly discussed the important matter you wish to present to the Council, Ahil," Strauss said as he looked towards Councilman Ahil Fazid. "You have the floor."

"Yes, Arthur," Fazid replied as he stood up at his seat. "As everyone here knows, for some time we've spared no expense trying to obtain the manufacturing formula for a material being produced under license by one Space Command contractor. The Tsgardi mercenaries we hired to retrieve the cloning equipment on Mawcett were never able to gain access to the underground lab where the equipment was stored because the entrance door was made of this material, now known as Dakinium. During a month-long effort where they used every technology, weapon, and explosive in their possession, they weren't able to break into the lab. In fact, they did nothing more than bend the entrance door sufficiently to pass a microprobe through the crack.

"If I had known about the almost-indestructible material, I would have ordered them to forget about the cloning equipment and bring us a piece of Dakinium instead. However, only Space Command was able to get the material, and it is now being used to sheath all their new spacecraft. Their ships were powerful before— now they're almost unbeatable. If we ever wish to restore the smuggling operation to its former profitability, we must have Dakinium-sheathed ships that can withstand an attack by a Space Command warship and escape unscathed."

"Ahil," Councilwoman Erika Overgaard asked, "are you suggesting we attempt a takeover of Galactic Alliance space as former Council Chairman Gagarin attempted to do?"

"No," Fazid said. "That was sheer folly. Even if he had accomplished the takeover of Higgins, we couldn't have held it. Space Command would have marshaled its forces and driven us out. We never had a chance. All Gagarin succeeded in doing was wiping out a good part of our warship fleet. He also instilled a fierce determination by Space Command personnel to eradicate us once and for all. With one failed major operation after another, we barely survived those years. When the Milori Emperor decided to invade GA Space, it gave us a respite from Space Command's attention and we've been able to return to profitability in most of our operational areas. The loss of our Platinum and Palladium mining operation on Scruscotto was a setback, and I don't suppose we'll ever find out what compelled Maxxiloth to attack our base like that. We were doing everything possible to support his fight against Space Command."

"Psychotics make very bad business partners," Councilman Bentley Blosworth said. "They often act irrationally and waste valuable resources with their irresponsible behavior."

"Yes," Fazid said in agreement. "But back to our main topic. Mikel Arneu has succeeded in acquiring a piece of Dakinium."

"Wonderful," Councilman Frederick Kelleher said. "What did it cost us? I believe the appropriation was five billion credits."

"The final cost was under a hundred thousand, not counting the loss of the meeting place we were renting. When SCI burst in, a security alarm was triggered. The technicians working in the lab collapsed the tunnel to their location and escaped through the restaurant above. SCI only collared a bodyguard, who knew nothing about the operation or even that there was a company connection. He was only there as a doorman."

"But what use is it now?" Overgaard asked. "Space Command has defeated both the Tsgardi and the Uthlaro, and annexed their territory. We have no one to build those 'indestructible' ships."

"I've begun negotiations with the Uthlaro. It's true they surrendered and ceded their territory to the Galactic Alliance, but they are still hopeful their fleet can defeat Carver at Quesann. If it does, they'll deny their surrender and we can resume operations as before. We have a sample of the material now, but our scientists still have to reverse-engineer it and develop a manufacturing process to produce it. Space Command did it, so I'm confident we can also."

"Where is the sample now?" Blosworth asked.

"It's on its way to Raider Fourteen. Mikel Arneu is also headed for the base from Raider Nine. As soon as he arrives, he'll begin setting up a new lab. He says it'll be ready to begin operations as soon as the sample arrives. The bad news is that it will take almost three years for the ship carrying the sample to arrive. And it's being conveyed on our fastest ship."

"Three years?" Kelleher questioned.

"Raider Fourteen is in that area of space between the former outer border of the Galactic Alliance and the pre-war border of the Milori Empire. We'd hoped we finally built a base that would be safe from Space Command interference, but we again find ourselves in their space. However, it's part of Region Two and so remote it might be decades before they begin patrols there. Presently, there's not an SC base within a thousand light-years."

"This is definitely a long-term project," Strauss said, "but it will pay huge dividends in the future. I'm not proposing we take on Space Command in the future, but knowing our ships will be impervious to laser fire will not only assist our crews in evading capture but will help us sign crews who haven't trusted the Tsgardi ships in the past. Good work, Ahil. Keep us posted on any progress. Any other new business?"

* * *

"Morning, Jen," Admiral Kanes said as he entered her office. He walked to the beverage dispenser and prepared a cup of coffee before planting himself in a chair in front of her desk. Although he only wore a single star to her four, their working relationship had progressed to a point where military protocol only intruded when in the presence of others.

"Hi, Keith," she said. "What's so urgent you needed to see me right away?"

Kanes sighed. "I've received distressing news in the form of a briefing message from Admiral Bradlee. It seems the Raiders have acquired a sample of Dakinium from an employee at JFW."

Jen tilted her chair back and stared up at the ceiling, saying nothing for a minute. "Well, we knew we couldn't keep it from them forever. Do we know how large a sample?"

"The inspectors at JFW are charged with accounting for every milligram. When the tally came up light one night, the line was shut down and a full investigation began. From the weight, they knew it was fairly small. All completed parts were accounted for, so it had to be from the scrap. Nothing is removed from the site until the accounting process is completed each night, so they were able to perform a detailed analysis of the waste products and identify the missing piece. It's cylindrical in shape, seven-point-eight-eight centimeters long by three-point-one-four centimeters in diameter. The size allowed some-one to hide it in a body cavity, which is the only way someone could have snuck a piece out given the proced-ures they've been following. They've changed the opera-tion so that all tiny pieces are held in a special scrap pile and must be accounted for before a shift is allowed to leave the floor."

"A little late for that."

"It'll prevent such thefts in the future."

"Have we learned who the traitor is?"

"Yes, we have her. You'll never guess why she did it."

"Then you'd better just tell me," Jenetta said, smiling.

"She wanted to be like you."

"Me? By sharing our secrets with our enemies?"

"She didn't want to be a military leader; she wanted to be young and beautiful again. The Raiders convinced her that by getting them a piece of Dakinium, she would get her wish and also be performing a valuable public service."

"I'm waiting for the punch line."

"They told her Delcorado Engineering was behind the acquisition. Allegedly, they needed the sample to win new supply contracts. They convinced the woman that Delcorado was going to have to close all its plants if they could no longer compete. Tens of thousands would lose their jobs. Of course, it was all a lie. I think she was so blinded by her desire to be young again that she would have fallen for any line that sounded reasonable and allowed her to temporarily ignore her moral code."

"The Raider process doesn't restore youth-- it only changes one's appearance. Mikel Arneu still looked his age when the process was performed on him. I saw vids taken of him on Scruscotto before Raider Ten was destroyed. He looked the same as he did on Raider One. If a youth-restoration process existed, he would have been the first one in line after it was proven. I only look this way because I was essentially twenty-one when they performed the process on me."

"I suppose the real question is how much of an impact this will have on this war," Kanes said.

"None. I'm not sure they can reverse-engineer the process from a sample. Our people have said no. They claim they wouldn't have been able to do it without the computer files I recovered on Dakistee. However, the Raiders can hire the best and the brightest. They might find a way. Even if they do, it will take years before they can produce any ships that use it as a covering. Then there's the matter of the new drive system required to establish the double envelope. No, the theft won't affect the outcome of the upcoming battle, but we'll have to solidify our control of this region before the Raiders can get ships into production or they might be tempted to try carving a section off for themselves. I don't want to fight another war over this territory."

"Amen," Kanes said. "Two has been enough."

* * *

"I still don't understand why we're being sent to Region Two," Byers said. "We don't know nothing about the Milori, except they're ugly as all get out."

"You're talking about a fellow Galactic Alliance race," Nelligen said.

"That don't make them any prettier."

"They probably feel the same way about you."

"What? I don't have tentacles that shoot out and crush you to death."

"Some of the food you serve up is almost as dangerous."

"Me? You're the one that likes molten lava chili."

"They wouldn't eat your food anyway. If it ain't still wiggling, they won't eat it."

"That's disgusting."

"Don't you eat raw clams?"

"Well, yeah. But they don't wiggle."

"They're still alive when you eat them though."

"That's different."

"How?"

"Uh— it just is."

Vyx entered the quarters where Byers and Nelligen had been playing cards for several hours and said, "Brenda, Kathryn, and I are headed down to the mess hall. You guys want to go?"

"Yeah, I think I can tear myself away," Nelligen said. "My stomach started grumbling a while ago."

"Your stomach is always grumbling. And I don't blame it with what you eat. I'd grumble also."

"You're just jealous because if you eat anything hot, you spend all night running to the head."

"I just go to the head to get some quiet. I don't know how you sleep through all the burping and belching you do in your sleep."

"If you're coming, let's go," Vyx said, before turning and walking out of the room.

Byers and Nelligen tossed their cards to the table and hurried out to join the other three SCI agents who were already a dozen paces ahead.

From that point on, there would be only small talk until they were again in a secure area.

* * *

"We're heading for Region Two because that's where the action is," Vyx said later when they were back at their quarters. "Admiral Carver requested we be assigned to her command. Our mission has nothing to do with the Milori. We're to head into the former Uthlaro Dominion, which is now part of Region Two, and begin working our way into the criminal circles there. The *Scorpion* is Uthlaro-built, so that should give us an edge."

"I'll never figure out how they got the *Scorpion* into the hold of this ship," Byers said. "The hatches are one tenth the size. They must have taken it apart and put it back together."

Vyx grinned before saying, "This is the largest, single-hulled Quartermaster transport ever built in GA space. For really large loads, they can open the bottom part of the hull for a length of ten frame sections. After the load is stored and locked down, the hull is closed and sealed. Even so, it was so tight they were considering removing the side-mounted engine nacelles. Luckily, they didn't have to do that. Once we reach our destination, the *Scorpion* will be launched and we'll be on our way. If not for this ship, we would have spent a decade getting to our assigned area. I heard the yard at Mars is currently planning even larger transports. The front sections will swing out of the way and a battleship, two heavy cruisers, three frigates, or five destroyers can be loaded inside."

"Five destroyers?" Nelligen said, his face reflecting his awe. "Good Lord. Why?"

"The older ships in Space Command are perfectly adequate for patrol duties. The problem is getting them to where we need them, when we need them there. The new

283

ships, like this one, can travel at Light-9790, but the older ships are limited to Light-262. With the new transports, the warships can be ferried to where they're needed and dropped off. If an emergency arises in Region Two, they can move the fleet around as needed."

"Wow," Byers said. "Where are we being dropped off, by the way?"

"We're heading to Quesann first. If the battle with the Uthlaro fleet goes as hoped, this ship will pick up a warship escort for the trip into the former Uthlaro Dominion. I haven't been given the exact location yet. Admiral Kanes will brief me before we leave Quesann."

"And if the battle doesn't go as hoped?" Brenda asked.

"I never bet against Admiral Carver. And I sure wouldn't play poker with her. She always seems to have an ace up her sleeve."

Chapter Eighteen
~ March 10th, 2285 ~

During the final weeks, two scout-destroyers were assigned to shadow the Uthlaro fleet. For the most part, they remained just out of sensor range, but, hourly, one or the other would zip across the extreme corner of the Uthlaro sensor envelope to ensure nothing had changed. They weren't there long enough for the Uthlaro to detect a real presence, but it was enough for the scout-destroyer sensors to record the needed data.

"The Uthlaro are roughly one-half light-year away," Jenetta said, "and headed directly towards us. The *Euphrates* and the *Zambezi* are keeping a close eye on their progress." Only images of the battle group leaders filled the wall monitor in the conference room aboard the *Colorado*, but the captain and senior staff of every ship that would participate in the confrontation was in a conference room aboard their ship watching the vid link. Jenetta probably should have been on the Flag Bridge of the *Ares*, but she wanted one more time in the command chair of the small ship before she surrendered to the inevitable.

"They'll reach our position in roughly twelve hours if they maintain their current course and speed. The DS ships will confront the enemy first at our current location one light-year from the base. It's possible the Uthlaro will immediately try to blast through us, but I expect them to stop when confronted by our picket line of ships. If they do stop, I'll attempt to persuade them to return peacefully to their homes. I don't expect them to comply. When I give the signal, the groups behind us will advance according to their instructions. Our goal is to show them our strength in the hope they'll leave without engaging, but if they refuse to leave or if they try to blast through us, the DS ships will engage immediately. We should have several minutes to do as much damage as possible before they realize their laser weapons are useless. When that happens, they'll probably switch to torpedoes exclusively. With a two-to-one superiority in ship numbers and four-to-one superiority in the number of tubes, the torpedoes will be coming at us fast and furious. At that point, I'll order all warships to move up and join the melee. With luck, the Uthlaro will have forgotten about their laser arrays, thinking all SC ships are impervious to such weapons. If they choose to press their attack, they won't stop until they're dead— or we are. I'm sure you understand which option I prefer. If we must fight, I don't want anyone to let up while a single Uthlaro can pull a trigger. Pound them hard. Pulverize their ships. Blast them to space dust.

"Each group has their assigned position. Does anyone have any questions about their assigned location or role?"

Jenetta waited for a few seconds before saying, "I'll assume from your silence you understand the task ahead of us. Okay, let's take our positions and wait to see what the Uthlaro will do."

Jenetta tried to spend the hours until the confrontation by catching up on the mountain of reports in her computer queue, but her mind kept drifting back to the upcoming battle. She finally gave up and just sat in her briefing room going over every detail and possibility. She hoped she was prepared for any eventuality, but every warrior knows it's impossible to predict every action an enemy might take.

Ten minutes before the Uthlaro were expected to arrive at their positions, Jenetta returned to the bridge and sat in her bridge chair. Lt. Commander Gallagher, her first officer, took his seat to her left. Neither spoke a word. When the Uthlaro were five minutes away, Jenetta ordered the tactical officer to engage the AutoTect.

"The AutoTect, Admiral?"

"Certainly. We don't want them to run into us. We know they deactivate their ACS if they think the signal is an electronic debris device."

"Aye, Admiral. AutoTect is activated. They should be able to see us."

"Message from the *Zambezi*, Admiral," the com operator said. "The Uthlaro have dropped their speed from Light-375 to Light-187."

"It's going to take them an extra five minutes to get here," Jenetta said. "Oh well, we weren't going anywhere for a while anyway."

Ten minutes later, the Uthlaro fleet finally appeared. They dropped their envelopes and came to a relative stop some ten thousand kilometers from the picket line of DS ships, but the sensors on the *Colorado* made them visually appear as if they were a mere kilometer away.

"Com, hail the Uthlaro," Jenetta said. "Ask for the fleet leader."

"Admiral Krakosso is hailing you, Admiral."

"Really? Put him up on the front monitor."

A second later the image of an Uthlaro officer appeared on the monitor. He immediately began speaking, and the translated words emanated from speakers mounted at the sides of the monitor.

"Admiral Carver, I am Admiral Krakosso of the Uthlaro Dominion. I order you to immediately surrender. You will be given safe passage to the area you call Region One if you do not resist. If you resist, you will be destroyed. I need your answer immediately."

"Admiral Krakosso, welcome to Region Two. I'm afraid you don't represent the Uthlaro Dominion because the Dominion no longer exists. The Council of Ministers surrendered unconditionally sixteen GST Standard months ago, as I'm sure you've been advised. I'm afraid you've had a very long journey for nothing. The former territory of the Dominion was annexed by the Galactic Alliance at that time. Since you are now a citizen of the Galactic Alliance and I am the military governor of Region Two, I order you to return home to Uthlarigasset."

The Uthlaro officer stared dispassionately at Jenetta for a few seconds, then said, "I don't believe you. You're famous for your tricks."

"I expected you to dispute the accuracy of my words, so I have a copy of the surrender ready. Watch it for yourself." Jenetta nodded towards the com chief, who sent the video copy.

After watching it, Admiral Krakosso said, "That is a fake. The ministers would never surrender so easily. Your tricks won't work, Admiral. Are you going to leave peacefully, or must I destroy you?"

"Your ministers had no choice. After destroying the five hundred ten ships at your staging area, I went into the Dominion and destroyed the shipyards at Plello, Waqutta, and Zenolo. I was prepared to lay waste to Uthlarigasset if the Council of Ministers didn't surrender. Fortunately, I haven't had to do that— yet."

"What do you mean— yet?"

"Simply that once they had surrendered and the territory was annexed by the Galactic Alliance, only further resistance would require me to return there. I know they lied when they said they were unable to recall the fleet. They hope you'll destroy me so they can retract their surrender. You can't. The surrender is already a matter of public record throughout the former Uthlaro Dominion. All you'll do by engaging my forces is guarantee your home planet will be destroyed. I'm sure you realize we can't allow such obvious treachery and sedition to go unpunished. If you persist in this endeavor, I shall destroy you as easily as we destroyed your five hundred ten ships at the staging area, then return to your home planet and reduce it to ashes."

"You lie. You would not return to destroy my planet."

"I warned the ministers that further resistance would be dealt with harshly. This sure looks like further resistance to me. Do you still have family on Uthlarigasset? Would you like to take a few moments to send them a goodbye message and tell them it would be wise to leave the planet as soon as possible?"

"I have no need of messages. I shall see them when I return home."

Jenetta sighed. "You're going to force me to destroy you, aren't you, Admiral? I was hoping you'd see the futility of fighting, but I expected no less. Throughout this entire undeclared war, your warriors have all fought to the death, even knowing their death was both inevitable and meaningless. It's a shame for so many more of your people to die here today, but I've prepared my fleet in case you refused to yield."

"Surely you don't think that eighty-nine ships, most of which are too small to classify as warships, are going to stop my fleet of two hundred six battleships, cruisers, and destroyers?"

"Don't dismiss the small vessels you see facing you too quickly, Admiral. Just twenty of them destroyed most of the fleet at your staging area. Each is more than the equivalent of one of your battleships. But if you feel quantity is more important, then tell me what you think of this."

Jenetta held up one finger and the com chief tapped a point on his console.

"What is it you hope to prove by that gesture, Admiral?" Krakosso asked.

"Stand by, Admiral," Jenetta said.

Something unintelligible was heard over the com line, and Krakosso said, "At least the remainder of your fleet are full-size warships, Admiral. I'm told most look to be Milori in design. We see seventy-four ships, giving you a total of one hundred sixty-three. You are still vastly outnumbered, Admiral. Are you going to leave peace-fully?"

"You want more?" Jenetta held up two fingers, and the com operator tapped another button on his console.

Admiral Krakosso watched calmly and didn't flinch when someone on his bridge cried out loudly.

"I was fully expecting this, Admiral. I read, with great amusement, about the way you fooled the Milori into quitting the battlefield by having freighters pose as

289

warships. They thought you had many more warships than you really had and ran back to their own territory. That trick won't work again."

"The four hundred eighteen ships that just appeared on your sensors are real military vessels, Admiral. I don't have to bluff this time. The fleet opposing yours is composed of five hundred eighty-one warships. I don't want to destroy you, but we will do so if you force my hand. You will not survive this hour if you won't return home. We outnumber you almost three to one."

"I claim this territory for the Uthlaro Dominion!" Admiral Krakosso shouted. "And we will defend it to the death."

"Then you leave me no choice!" Jenetta said immediately before giving the signal to cut off the communication. "Com, signal Phase One. Helm, attack plan Delta-Niner. Engage!"

The *Colorado* surged ahead in unison with the other DS ships. Each helmsman had already plotted his course through the first layers of Uthlaro ships and was already working on the rest of his or her route when the gunners opened up with laser arrays and torpedoes. They had standing orders to fire as soon as they could get a lock, so no further instructions were required.

Space was suddenly filled with brilliant flashes of light as the DS ships passed through the front line of the Uthlaro ships, but the Uthlaro didn't reciprocate with their laser weapons. The dearth of laser fire from the enemy ships told Jenetta immediately that the Uthlaro were aware of the black ships' invulnerability to laser pulse fire. That information could only have come from their military command on Uthlarigasset, who would have learned of it when they examined the logs of the attacks on the shipyards. The Phalanx systems on the DS ships began to absorb more and more of the laser array resources as wave after wave of torpedoes came from the Uthlaro ships. Unlike the Tsgardi, who maintained their positions during the Space Command attacks, the Uthlaro started jockeying for positions of their own as the Space

Command vessels wove their tortuous routes through the enemy fleet.

Realizing the Uthlaro were putting all their effort into firing torpedoes, Jenetta said, "Phase Two." The command released all other ships from having to sit on the sidelines. The ships that had until then simply watched the fight from afar moved towards the battle and began pounding the enemy with everything they had. Admiral Krakosso watched in horror as wave upon wave of warships approached. The ships he had dismissed as a hoax began firing their laser weapons and torpedoes as soon as they came into range. Too late, he realized Admiral Carver hadn't been bluffing when she said her warship fleet was five hundred eighty-one strong. For the first time he began to fear for the safety of his family and friends back home. Perhaps one might consider it merciful that several torpedoes found their way to Admiral Krakosso's vessel at roughly the same instant and ended the long career of the Uthlaro Fleet's commander.

One might have expected a battle between seven hundred eighty-seven ships to have lasted for hours, but in fact it was over in less than fifteen minutes. The battle was just too one-sided and the Uthlaro never had a chance, as Jenetta had tried to tell them. Consistent with Jenetta's earlier instructions, the Uthlaro ships were reduced to space dust because warriors continued to fire until they drew their last breaths.

The carnage at the battle site paled in comparison to that of the staging area destruction, but it was horrific nevertheless. As soon as all ships had ceased firing, Jenetta called for damage assessments to be collected. She steeled herself for the worst, but they weren't as bad as they might have been. The overwhelming preponderance of ships pouring laser fire and torpedoes into the Uthlaro fleet had made all the difference. Many of the M-designate ships had suffered hull breaches from laser fire and several had been hit by torpedoes. The Phalanx system had once again proved its enormous value, but it wasn't yet infallible. At least not when thousands of torpedoes filled space around the ships. Additionally, there had been seven ship collisions during the fighting. Most had been between Uthlaro ships and Jenetta's forces as each maneuvered for fighting position, but one had been a minor brush between two ships in Jenetta's command.

After reviewing the damage lists, Jenetta said to the com operator, "Get me Supreme Lord Space Marshall Twillaaq." A moment later, the image of a Milori officer filled the front viewscreen. "Well done, Supreme Lord Space Marshall," Jenetta said.

"Thank you, Admiral Carver."

"How serious is the damage to your forces?"

"About half my ships suffered torpedo strikes, some minor, some major. We also had a dozen minor collisions or brushes with Uthlaro ships. Early estimates indicate total deaths will approach two thousand, with an additional seven thousand seriously injured."

"I'm sorry for your losses, Supreme Lord Space Marshall."

"Thank you, Admiral, and I for yours. How badly have you been damaged?"

"The preliminary death toll has been set at twenty-six, and serious injuries are estimated to be approximately one hundred twenty-four."

"My congratulations, Admiral. Those numbers are extremely light considering the ferocity of the battle we just fought."

"Thank you, Supreme Lord Space Marshall. Our weapons systems deserve much of the credit. Once your forces are officially recognized by Space Command Supreme Headquarters as the Region Two Territorial Guard, we can outfit your ships with our Phalanx system. It's too bad there wasn't time to do that before the Uthlaro arrived."

"I'm glad we were able to arrive here in time to help fight these invaders, Admiral. It was unfortunate that we had to leave two battleships and a cruiser at the yards because of systems problems that might have made them undependable in battle."

"As soon as my engineers finish handling our emergency repairs, they'll be available to assist you with your repairs. If you need anything else, just communicate your needs to my aide, Lt. Commander Ashraf."

"Thank you, Admiral."

"Thank *you*, Supreme Lord Space Marshall, for coming to assist us in this battle and for fighting so well against our common enemy."

"It has been our very great honor to fight alongside Admiral Jenetta Carver. Even while Maxxiloth was vilifying you, your name evoked awe and respect in the Milori military ranks. You were responsible for the greatest defeats the Milori forces have ever known, but every Milora in the new Territorial Guard is proud to serve under your command."

"Thank you Supreme Lord Space Marshall. I'm delighted to welcome you into the service of the Galactic Alliance."

* * *

It took several weeks to make repairs and drag the Uthlaro hulks back to Quesann. Jenetta had images of the broken ships tethered together for transport to the base sent to the Uthlaro Council of Ministers. With the destruction of the Uthlaro invasion fleet, it appeared that things would finally quiet down somewhat. The logs of all ships that had participated in the battle were forwarded to Space Command Supreme Headquarters. Jenetta sent along a lengthy message detailing the action. The War College would prepare a vid simulation of the battle that could be viewed and examined in minute detail. With the number of ships involved, it would take them some time to complete their full analysis. Keith Kanes stopped in to visit Jenetta at her huge office in the new Headquarters Building the day after the material had been sent off.

"Good morning, Keith. Make yourself a beverage and have a seat," Jenetta said.

As he sat down with his coffee, he said, "You weren't serious when you told Admiral Krakosso you were going to return to Uthlarigasset and destroy it if he attacked, were you?"

"No, of course not. I was trying to find something— anything— that would give him reason to turn around and go home. I thought the image of his home and family being destroyed might overcome that fierce dedication he felt for leaders who apparently couldn't care less whether he and his command lived or died."

"Good. I've completed my report to Admiral Bradlee and sent it off. I said that your statement regarding Uthlarigasset was only a psychological ploy."

"I sent my report to the Admiralty Board yesterday. I didn't mention the ploy at all. I would hope that they know I wasn't serious."

"I'd love to be sitting in the gallery when they listen to that."

Jenetta smiled. "I imagine there will be some gnashing of teeth when they watch it, *especially* from Admiral Hubera."

"He doesn't like you very much, does he?"

"No, he doesn't, and I really don't know why."

"I believe he feels that you rose too quickly through the ranks, while it took him most of his life to get his two stars. But you've been out here risking your life year after year fighting the Raiders, the Tsgardi, the Milori, the Hudeera, the Gondusans, and the Uthlaro, while he spent most of his service years sitting safely in classrooms scowling at frightened kids who were afraid he would flunk them out of the Academy. What does he expect?"

"I'm just glad he's not on my staff," Jenetta said, smiling.

"Because of his age, it's unlikely he'll ever make it out this far, but if you become the Admiral of the Fleet you may have to put up with him."

"Admiral of the Fleet? You're joking, right?"

"It's not so farfetched, Jen. Every four-star in Space Command is now in their nineties, except for you, and mandatory retirement age is one hundred. Admiral Moore is ninety-five. Once he retires, the available replacements will all be short-timers themselves. You're the most logical candidate. You've twice defeated invaders to our territory, and you've increased the size of Galactic Alliance space by about a factor of five. You're the most famous officer in Space Command history and you've never been touched by a hint of scandal. The Galactic Alliance Senate and Council love you, and the law-abiding citizens of our member worlds adore you. The Nordakians idolize you. The Raiders hate you, but that's an endorsement, not a disparagement. And now, amazingly, even the Milori love you."

"All I want is one of the new battleships the Admiralty Board promised me while I was still the base commander of Stewart."

"Wasn't that before you defeated the Milori?"

"Yes, but I'm going to hold them to the promise."

"Wasn't that while you were still at brevetted rank?"

"Yes."

"Then I don't know how they can possibly give you a ship, unless it's simply to add one to the fleet you command. You can't be its captain."

"I'm the Captain of the *Colorado*."

"But you can't keep a battleship sitting in orbit around Quesann, waiting until you have an excuse to go for a joyride. You shouldn't even keep a scout-destroyer tied up. Your job is here now, flying that desk."

Jenetta breathed in deeply and then exhaled. "I know. I've been hoping the Admiralty Board will find a replacement for me."

"A replacement for Jenetta Carver?" Admiral Kanes said, smiling. "That's a tall order."

"Oh, you and I both know that any good administrator can handle my job here. Admiral Poole did an excellent job while I was away."

"I'm sorry to point out the obvious, but your job here hasn't even begun, Jen. You've been the base commander of two new, major bases in the past, so you know the demands of the job continue to grow with each month for the first few years. Admiral Poole will have his own problems with this base and he'll try to rely on you as the senior officer in this new region, but you'll be busy administering the affairs of a territory four times the size of Region One; the task ahead of you is monumental. For example, what are you going to do about the slavery issue in the former Uthlaro territory? I understand that slavery has been legal there in twenty-three occupied star systems for centuries. You'll have to put an end to it now. Then there's the matter of cleaning up the former Tsgardi territory. That alone could be a full-time job for a few years. And lastly, the former Uthlaro Council of Ministers is not going to go gently into the night. They'll have to be closely monitored because they're going to use every resource available to buck our attempts to govern that space. No *mere* administrator will be able to handle this job for some time. Your job here isn't ending; it's just beginning."

"Are you trying to depress me, Keith? If so, you're succeeding."

Admiral Kanes smiled. "You know these facts as well as I do. I just don't want you to delude yourself that you're not needed here, desperately."

"I know. Damned depressing, isn't it?"

* * *

"I know you're all as anxious to see the message from Admiral Carver as I am," Admiral Moore said, "so we'll skip the reading of the previous minutes and jump right to that. Play the message, Brian."

A head-and-shoulders image of Jenetta Carver filled the full-wall monitor as Admiral Moore's aide began playing the message. The size made her seem larger than life—as if that was even necessary—and she began to speak. She gave a full account of the battle and then spoke about a variety of other topics. The Board watched the logs of the battle from the *Colorado*, but declined to watch any others at this time. The War College and Intelligence Section would be charged with reviewing them in detail and presenting any issues that needed the Board's attention.

When the messages were over, Admiral Hubera was the first to speak. "Territorial Guard? Now she's starting her own military. We must replace her as soon as possible."

"Oh, Donald, you're absolutely hopeless," Admiral Platt said. "It was you who complained the loudest that we didn't have any way to control these territories, and now that Admiral Carver has found a way to quickly get a handle on a good part of Region Two, you complain about it. I think her solution is ideal. The Milori may have been our enemies at one time, but now they've shown signs of their allegiance to the Galactic Alliance by fighting with us to defeat the Uthlaro."

"Of course they did. They didn't want the Uthlaro to gain power in their former territory because it might hinder their efforts to recover the territory for themselves later."

"If Admiral Carver is satisfied the Milori are sincere, then I support her," Admiral Hillaire said. "Her perspicacity has always been excellent. We've been agonizing over how to staff her territory and how to provide the ships she'll need, and now Admiral Carver has laid this partial solution at our feet. The Territorial Guard that Admiral Carver has created will have a fleet of over six hundred ships when all the Milori ships Admiral Carver attacked in the Milori shipyards are rebuilt..."

"My point exactly!" Admiral Hubera shouted, interrupting Admiral Hillaire. "They'll have rebuilt their ships under our very nose and even with our blessing. When they feel strong enough, they'll attack us and try to drive us out of Region Two."

"That's always a possibility," Admiral Bradlee said, "but Admiral Carver isn't naïve, and she'd never have set up this Territorial Guard if she thought there was the remotest possibility that would happen."

"Admiral Carver, Admiral Carver, Admiral Carver!" Admiral Hubera yelled. "I'm sick to death of hearing about Admiral Carver. You all talk about her as if she's some kind of god. She's just a young upstart who's been incredibly lucky. Why can't you see that? Are you all blind? Ask her yourself and she'll tell you she's been lucky. You keep handing her more and more power. You're creating a monst..." Admiral Hubera suddenly clutched his chest and fell back into his chair, his face as chalk-white as his hair.

Admiral Moore's clerk punched a button on her console and said, "Medical emergency in the Meeting Hall."

* * *

"Well, Ambello," Uthlaro Minister Ulalahu Valhallo said to Minister Neddowo as he gestured to the large monitor at the front of the Council Chambers, "are you quite satisfied? Carver has destroyed what was left of our fleet. There's the proof. We could have recalled them and at least had the beginnings of a new fleet with which to oppose her. Now we don't have a single ship. Not one decent ship we could use to protect our planet, not that we could really oppose Carver if she came back. Space Command is far too powerful. How could you not know about their indestructible hulls and incredible speed advances before you convinced us to undertake this venture?"

"It was just rumor— I thought it was mere propaganda. You all know how tricky she is and none of our agents could confirm anything. All our informants told us Space Command wasn't able to defend their new territory. The Raiders said they didn't even have enough ships to begin patrols during the next five years. It was the ideal time to conduct the venture."

"And now we're destroyed. You've brought complete ruin down upon us."

"We'll rebuild. I've already made arrangements to begin building new shipyards in the Galekku system. It's outside our former border in unclaimed space and has a dead sun with seven frozen, useless planets. Space Command has no reason to go there. The Raiders will provide protection for the base and we'll provide the technology, engineers, and workers."

"And who will provide the funding?"

"The Treasury, of course! This will be a government venture, but the Raiders have promised to buy all the ships we can provide as long as those ships have the advancements we've always restricted to our own military. The profit from the ships we'll build for them will pay for our own ships and the Raiders *have* to buy from us because the Tsgardi will no longer be producing warships for sale. The Gondusans and Hudeera won't build ships for anyone else because they're too afraid of the Galactic Alliance and the Ruwalchu don't want anything to do with anybody. The Aguspod would never sell any ships to the Raiders because they've been at war with the Raiders for more than a decade and the Clidepp are totally occupied with rebels trying to take over their government. Of course, the rebels would probably build ships for the Raiders if they gained control, but I wouldn't bet on their chances. The Kweedee Aggregate, like the Ruwalchu, isn't interested in trading with outside systems. We'll have an exclusive on the market in this part of the galaxy."

"How long will it take us to assemble a fleet capable of opposing Carver?" Prime Minister Barguado asked.

"This is a long-term venture, but it will provide a solid return on our investment. We can probably count on having a sufficient fleet in fifteen years. The Raiders have secured a sample of the hull material used to protect the Space Command ships. As soon as their engineers have recreated the manufacturing process, they'll communicate that information to us and we'll sheath all new ships with Dakinium. They've also promised to find out how Space Command attains their incredible speeds and will share that information with us so we can incorporate it into the new ships."

"So in fifteen years we'll have a new fleet as fast and indestructible as Space Command's?" Minister Ellwano Murcuro asked.

"I'd stake my fortune on it," Neddowo said.

"What fortune?" Valhallo asked. "We accepted your word that you turned over every credit to the treasury when we released you from the obligation to pay the balance."

"I misspoke," Neddowo said apologetically. "I've become so accustomed to using that phrase for so many years, it's become automatic."

Valhallo looked at Neddowo through narrowed eye-slits for a moment. "I hope that's the truth, Ambello."

"It is, but it won't always be so; I'll make another fortune. And I'll use every penny of it to destroy Carver if it's the last thing I ever do."

* * *

"I have the latest communication from our contact in the Uthlaro Dominion government," the Ruwalchu Security Officer reported to the assembled group of officers and government officials. All seats at the enormous table in the War Conference Center were occupied for this important session; lesser officers and officials lined the walls of the room. "Space Command has destroyed what was left of the Uthlaro fleet. Since their brave warriors always fight to their last breath, we don't expect any to have survived."

"And what of Space Command?" General Ardlessel asked. "Have they been weakened to a point where they no longer pose a threat to us?"

"The final message received from Admiral Krakosso, the commanding officer of the Uthlaro fleet, stated quite clearly that he was battling a Space Command fleet of five hundred eighty-one vessels. He reported that his ship's computer confirmed the count and ship class. All vessels were warships. He'd been told Carver had fewer than a hundred warships in her command."

"Five hundred eighty-one warships? What did they do— strip every ship from their Region One fleet?"

"As far as we can determine, their Region One fleet still consists of over three hundred first-line warships."

"Then where did this enormous Region Two fleet come from?"

"We don't yet have that information, sir."

"If they can suddenly produce five times the number of warships our intelligence service estimates," Ardlessel said to the people seated around the table, "then our data would seem to be faulty as well."

"How many of the Space Command vessels were destroyed in the battle?" the chair of the Space Services committee asked.

"Reports by their news services indicate Space Command lost no ships."

"How can that be? The Uthlaro claimed their ships were as powerful as the Space Command ships."

"Our contact reports that in a succession of battles, Space Command has destroyed all eight hundred seventy-six warships the Uthlaro possessed. He also states Space Command destroyed hundreds of new ships in various stages of completion when their shipyards were attacked. They have no evidence Space Command lost any vessels in the engagements. Our contact further reports that Space Command vessels appear to be impervious to laser damage."

"What?" General Ardlessel said loudly. "That's impossible."

"It would explain how the Space Command fleet escaped without damage in battle after battle with Uthlaro forces. Our contact sent security footage of the three shipyard attacks. It shows the Space Command warships being struck repeatedly by laser fire from protection satellites. They ignored the satellites as if they were inconsequential. Following the destruction of the shipyards, Admiral Carver, in her role as the senior military officer in Region Two, proceeded to Uthlarigasset where she threatened to lay waste to the home planet unless they surrendered unconditionally. As part of the surrender, they were forced to immediately cede all territory to the Galactic Alliance. The Uthlaro leadership had sent every available warship to confront her at her HQ base. A military person might consider the act foolish perhaps, but it's doubtful a few home system protection ships could have stopped Space Command. The planetary leadership, aware of what Carver had done to the Milori home world, capitulated.

"Following the surrender, Carver ordered the planetary leadership to announce the surrender and annexation in the news media. The entire territory learned of it long before the final battle."

"If their surrender took place before the final battle, why didn't they recall their ships?"

"Our contact says they did attempt to recall them, but Space Command ruthlessly tracked down the remnants of the fleet and destroyed them without giving them a chance to surrender."

"Unconscionable," General Ardlessel said. "You don't kill an enemy after they've surrendered. What kind of animals are these?"

"Obviously, they are the most dangerous and malevolent species we've yet encountered in space," the chair of the Space Services committee said. "We believed Maxxiloth to be a serious threat, although one which we could conquer, but Space Command destroyed him easily and annexed his empire. Now they've defeated the combined forces of the Tsgardi, Hudeera, Gondusans, and Uthlaro, and absorbed most of their territory. What I don't understand is why Space Command only took seventy-five percent of the Gondusan space but ninety-five percent of Hudeera space. Why didn't they simply absorb both nations?"

"You can be certain it wasn't because they feared to engage either nation in battle," the Ruwalchu Security Officer said. "Our Uthlaro contact intimated that the Gondusan and Hudeera governments grew frightened after Space Command destroyed the Tsgardi and threw themselves on the mercy of the Galactic Alliance. They immediately withdrew their token forces and offered up territory in the hope Space Command wouldn't wipe out their races. The area each possessed was insignificant, but the Gondusan were the shrewder. The Hudeera apparently offered everything except their home system in an effort to be spared annihilation. The Galactic Alliance must have agreed to the terms simply to be done with them because they could have swatted them aside like a bothersome insect."

"It's apparent," General Ardlessel said, "that the Galactic Alliance is pursuing a manifest destiny like that of Maxxiloth's great-grandfather, Conniloth, who believed it was his destiny to control the galaxy. The Galactic Alliance might have chosen their name for the same reason. They believe they should control the Galaxy. And now they're moving in this direction. We must be next on their list for annexation."

"Great Protector, they can't possibly believe we're going to allow that to happen," the chair of the Space Services committee said.

"They might believe they're invincible. We have to admit that no one has been able to stand for long before their onslaught. If their ships really are invulnerable, we may not be able to stop them."

"We must be ready with every ship we have to repel their invasion."

"Repelling their invasion might be a little difficult, sir," General Ardlessel said. "Your committee has reduced the appropriation for new ships and personnel every annual since you became the chair. After twenty annuals of force reductions, we don't have any spare ships or spare people to man them."

"You mean we've left ourselves open to attack?"

"As I've been telling you for annuals, it was only a matter of time before some interstellar superpower decided to conquer us. It looks like that day has finally arrived."

"But there's still time, right? I mean, they're not here yet."

"There may still be time, if the Galactic Alliance gets bogged down while exercising control over all the new territory they've conquered. Perhaps if we began a massive shipbuilding and recruiting effort immediately, we might have a chance of repelling them. Otherwise," General Ardlessel just shrugged his shoulders, "we'd better begin learning this language they call Amer.

~ finis ~

*** *Jenetta's exciting adventures continue in:* ***
Return to Dakistee

Appendix

This chart is offered to assist readers who may be unfamiliar with military rank and the reporting structure. Newly commissioned officers begin at either ensign or second lieutenant rank.

Space Command	Space Marine Corps
Admiral of the Fleet	
Admiral	General
Vice-Admiral	Lieutenant General
Rear Admiral - Upper	Major General
Rear Admiral - Lower	Brigadier General
Captain	Colonel
Commander	Lieutenant Colonel
Lieutenant Commander	Major
Lieutenant	Captain
Lieutenant(jg) "Junior Grade"	First Lieutenant
Ensign	Second Lieutenant

The commanding officer on a ship is always referred to as Captain, regardless of his or her official military rank. Even an Ensign could be a Captain of the Ship, although that would only occur as the result of an unusual situation or emergency where no senior officers survived.

On Space Command ships and bases, time is measured according to a twenty-four-hour clock, normally referred to as military time. For example, 8:42 PM would be referred to as 2042 hours. Chronometers are always set to agree with the date and time at Space Command Supreme Headquarters on Earth. This is known as GST, or Galactic System Time.

Admiralty Board:

Moore, Richard E.	Admiral of the Fleet
Platt, Evelyn S.	Admiral - Director of Fleet Operations
Bradlee, Roger T.	Admiral - Director of Intelligence (SCI)
Ressler, Shana E.	Admiral - Director of Budget & Accounting
Hillaire, Arnold H.	Admiral - Director of Academies
Burke, Raymond A.	Vice-Admiral - Director of GSC Base Management
Ahmed, Raihana L.	Vice-Admiral - Dir. of Quartermaster Supply
Woo, Lon C.	Vice-Admiral - Dir. of Scientific & Expeditionary Forces
Plimley, Loretta J.	Rear-Admiral, (U) - Dir. of Weapons R&D
Hubera, Donald M.	Rear-Admiral, (U) - Dir. of Academy Curricula

Ship Speed Terminology	*Speed*
Plus-1	1 kps
Sub-Light-1	1,000 kps
Light-1 (*c*) (speed of light in a vacuum)	299,792.458 kps
Light-150 or **150 c**	150 times the speed of light

Hyper-Space Factors	
IDS Communications Band	.0513 light years each minute (8.09 billion kps)
DeTect Range	4 billion kilometers

Strat Com Desig	Mission Description for Strategic Command Bases
1	Base - Location establishes it as a critical component of Space Command Operations - Serves as home-port to multiple warships that also serve in base's defense. All sections of Space Command maintain an active office at the base. Base Commander establishes all patrol routes and is authorized to override SHQ orders to ships within the sector(s) designated part of the base's operating territory. Recommended rank of Commanding Officer: **Rear Admiral (U)**
2	Base - Location establishes it as a crucial component of Space Command Operations - Serves as home-port to multiple warships that also serve in base's defense. All sections of Space Command maintain an active office at the base. Patrol routes established by SHQ. Recommended rank of Commanding Officer: **Rear Admiral (L)**
3	Base - Location establishes it as an important component of Space Command Operations - Serves as homeport to multiple warships that also serve in base's defense. Patrol routes established by SHQ. Recommended rank of Commanding Officer: **Captain**
4	Station - Location establishes it as an important terminal for Space Command personnel engaged in travel to/from postings, and for re-supply of vessels and outposts. Recommended rank of Commanding Officer: **Commander**
5	Outpost - Location makes it important for observation purposes and collection of information. Recommended rank of Commanding Officer: **Lt. Commander**

Sample Distances

Earth to Mars (Mean)	78 million kilometers
Nearest star to our Sun	4 light-years (Proxima Centauri)
Milky Way Galaxy diameter	100,000 light-years
Thickness of M'Way at Sun	2,000 light-years
Stars in Milky Way	200 billion (est.)
Nearest galaxy (Andromeda)	2 million light-years from M'Way
A light-year (in a vacuum)	9,460,730,472,580.8 kilometers
A light-second (in vacuum)	299,792.458 km
Grid Unit	1,000 Light Yrs² (1,000,000 Sq. LY)
Deca-Sector	100 Light Years² (10,000 Sq. LY)
Sector	10 Light Years² (100 Sq. LY)
Section	94,607,304,725 km^2
Sub-section	946,073,047 km^2

The two-dimensional representations that follow are offered to provide the reader with a feel for the spatial relationships between bases, systems, and celestial events referenced in the novels of this series. The mean distance from Earth to Higgins Space Command Base has been calculated as 90.1538 light-years. The millions of stars, planets, moons, and celestial phenomena in this small part of the galaxy would only confuse, and therefore have been omitted from the images.

Should the maps be unreadable, or should you desire additional imagery, .jpg and .pdf versions of all maps are available for free downloading at:

www.deprima.com/ancillary/agu.html

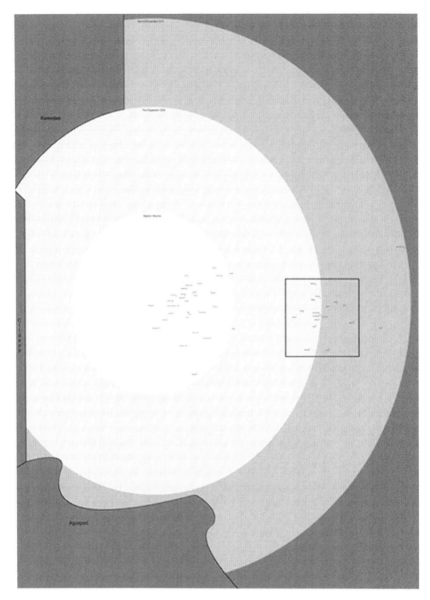

This first map shows Galactic Alliance space after the second
expansion. The white space at the center is the space originally
included when the GA charter was signed. The first outer circle
shows the space claimed at the first expansion in 2203. The
second circle shows the second expansion in 2273. The 'square'
delineates the immediate area around Stewart SCB, and shows
most of the planets referenced in Books 4, 5 and 6 of this series.

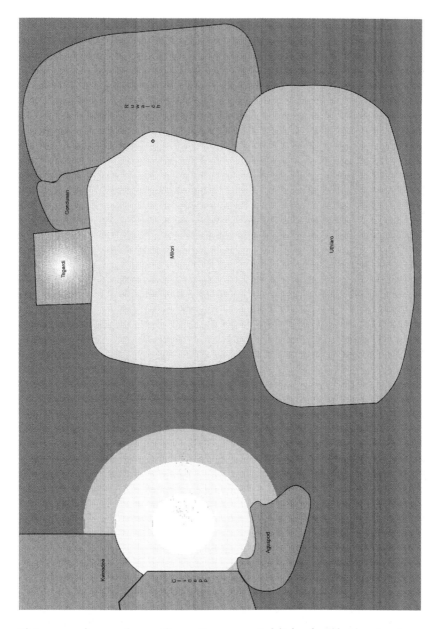

This second map shows the nations as established at the beginning
of book 5. The Milori Empire is the large, light-grey area nearest the
center of the image, while the Uthlaro Dominion is the larger, and
slightly darker area below that. The Tsgardi Kingdom is the more or
less square area above the Milori Empire, with the Gondusan nation
to the immediate right, and the Ruwalch Confederacy to the right of
that. The Hudeerac Order is the small circle near the right edge of
Milori space. This represents a time after the Milori have conquered
and absorbed most of the Hudeerac territory.

Made in the USA
Lexington, KY
24 August 2013